MW00561434

THE
WITCHSTONE

BOOKS BY HENRY H. NEFF

STANDALONE NOVELS
The Witchstone
Impyrium

THE TAPESTRY SERIES
The Hound of Rowan
The Second Siege
The Fiend and the Forge
The Maelstrom
The Red Winter

HENRY H. NEFF

THE
WITCHSTONE

BLACK
STONE
PUBLISHING

Printed in the United States of America

First edition: 2024
ISBN 979-8-212-01554-7
Fiction / Fantasy / Humorous

Version 1

Blackstone Publishing
31 Mistletoe Rd.
Ashland, OR 97520

www.BlackstonePublishing.com

For those who keep at it

Profit is sweet, even if it comes from deception.

—Sophocles

TABLE OF CONTENTS

CHAPTER I
LASZLO

Not a bad crew, Laszlo decided. Better than most of the grifters prowling New York's subways. He watched them do their thing as the F train trundled uptown. There were three, naturally: the Kid, the Shill, and the Watchman.

The Kid was twentyish, with a hint of beard and the surety of youth. The Shill was a middle-aged gal masquerading as an office drone. Laszlo admired her attention to detail: no wedding ring, a child's macaroni bracelet, sensible flats. Just another single mom working to make ends meet.

The Watchman's appearance was irrelevant. His only job was to signal if trouble approached. This one was comically inconspicuous: a wizened schlump of sixty in a pilling cardigan. Laszlo took a long pull of his milkshake and watched the gentleman pretend to peruse a magazine. Only a fellow crook would have spotted him.

The game was running smoothly. The latest marks were some Belgian tourists who had boarded at the last stop, three couples chattering in Dutch and toting shopping bags. The Kid had moved in immediately. Sliding into the nearest seat, he set a tray on his lap along with three small paper cups. The tourists looked over as the Kid displayed a red ball the size of a chickpea and placed it under the center cup. Shuffling the cups about, he challenged his audience to guess where the ball might be hiding. One of the Belgians, a florid-faced ox, muttered something to his wife that made her giggle. When he pointed at a cup, the Kid raised it to reveal the red ball. The tourists cheered. The Kid laid a twenty on the tray. Did they care to make it interesting?

The Belgians waved him off. They knew that once money was involved, the hustler would reveal his skill. The cups would become a blur, one's choice no better than a guess. No, thank you. They were tourists, not fools.

That was when the Shill made her entrance. She boarded at the next stop, pretending to file in with passengers who had been waiting on the platform; in fact, she had been watching from a neighboring car all along. Taking a seat by the tourists, she checked her watch and groaned. One of the Belgian women gave her an inquiring look.

"Running late," the Shill explained. "Daughter's sick."

The Belgian offered the commiserating smile of a fellow mother; she'd been there. The Kid whistled at the Shill.

"Baby sick? Win some cash; buy her something nice."

The Shill ignored him.

"Come on," the Kid urged. "Pick one."

The Shill's eyes flicked to the tray. She watched with a wary, noncommittal expression as the Kid shuffled the cups. When he'd finished, she uncurled her pinkie and pointed at one. Lo and behold, out rolled the little red ball.

The Kid grunted. "Sharp eyes," he said, and laid down the twenty. "Wanna spice it up?"

The Shill folded her arms. "Bug someone else."

"Tell you what," said the Kid. "You win, you keep the twenty. I win, you don't lose shit."

The Shill glanced at the Belgians and raised her eyebrows. Was the creep being serious?

The ox spoke up, his accent heavy. "Don't," he warned. "It's a trick."

The Shill agreed. She was a seasoned veteran of the subways. There was *always* a catch with these hustlers. Even so, her interest had been piqued. The Shill conveyed her indecision with a subtle quirk of the mouth. Laszlo almost applauded. Ten to one, she'd come to New York with dreams of Broadway.

The Shill looked inquiringly at the hustler. "I win, I keep the twenty?"

"Yes, ma'am," said the Kid. He grinned and waited for the green light.

The Shill gave it.

The cups moved faster this time, but not too fast. When the Kid arranged them in a line, the Shill made her choice. Out rolled the ball. The Belgians cheered as the Kid handed over the twenty.

The Shill flushed pink with pleasure. "Lucky guess."

The Kid shrugged. "Double or nothing?"

The fellow mother touched the Shill's arm. "Put that money in your pocket."

The Shill appeared ready to follow this sensible advice; then a girlish grin flashed across her careworn face. "But why?" she wondered aloud. "Even if I lose, I'm not really out anything."

The Shill risked the twenty she'd won. Once again, the cups were shuffled; once again she found the ball. Now she had two rumpled twenties in her possession. Everyone but the Kid was delighted. He moped but kept at it.

The game continued. The Shill didn't win every time. Once, she picked the wrong cup and the Belgian loudmouth groaned. It was obvious where the ball had been hiding!

Pigs get fat, hogs get slaughtered, thought Laszlo. Loudmouth was a hog. Every group had one.

The Shill had done well. By the time they reached Herald Square, she was a hundred dollars richer and visibly giddy with her good fortune. Gathering up her things, she bid the Belgians adieu, advised the Kid to find another line of work, and fairly skipped out of the car. An amused Laszlo watched her pretend to join the crowds milling toward the exits. Any moment, she'd dart into the next car to await another pigeon.

Chimes sounded. The doors clattered shut. Laszlo glanced at the Kid, who was packing up his tray with a sullen air.

Loudmouth chuckled. "Anything left?"

The Kid wiped his nose. "Mind your own business, man."

The Belgian produced a crisp hundred-dollar bill. His male companions hooted. "One more?" he asked.

The Kid shook his head. "Nah. I'm done."

A second hundred appeared. "You can make it back," Loudmouth goaded. "Come on."

The Kid managed to sound reluctant. "Yeah, okay."

Laszlo stifled a smile. The trap was set. Once again, the Kid hid the ball and slid the cups about. Loudmouth watched closely, eager to impress his mates. When the cups stopped, he jabbed a finger at the center one.

"There!"

Up came the cup. No ball. The Belgian's jaw dropped open.

"Where is it?" he demanded.

The Kid raised the cup on the right. The ball rolled out and made a wobbly circle before coming to rest. The Belgian reddened even further as his companions teased him. He thrust the hundred-dollar bill at the Kid.

"Again," he demanded.

The Kid was happy to oblige. Within two minutes, Loudmouth had lost five hundred dollars and was begging his appalled wife to lend him whatever cash she had in her purse.

Laszlo took a sip of his milkshake. The hustlers had had their fun. Now it was his turn.

The Kid glanced up as he strolled over. Laszlo flashed a hundred-dollar bill.

"I'll have a go."

The Kid gave him an appraising look. The newcomer was wearing an expensive suit, but one so wrinkled he might have slept in it. He wasn't old—no more than thirty—and was Hollywood handsome, despite his bloodshot blues. The Kid's gaze traveled up to Laszlo's hat. Scratching his ear, he shot the Watchman an irritated look: *How did you miss this guy?*

"You a cop?" he asked Laszlo pointedly.

"Nope."

"You gotta tell me if I ask you."

Laszlo yawned. "That's a myth. We playing or not?"

The Kid eyed the cash. He was a hog too. He just didn't know it.

The game began, and Laszlo promptly lost. He handed over the hundred and produced two more.

The Kid clapped enthusiastically. "Ladies and gentlemen, we have got ourselves a *player*! Where'd you get that hat? It's dope. You're like an old-timey detective."

Laszlo merely sipped his milkshake as the hustler started a new round.

The shell game was an age-old con whose origins dated back to Ancient Greece. Everyone and their mother knew it was a scam, and thus it only worked on marks who grossly overestimated their own abilities. Fortunately, 100 percent of men fell into this category. It had worked like a charm on Loudmouth. During the Shill's turn, Loudmouth had made it clear to everyone in earshot that he was a Clever Man. Clever Men weren't fooled by common tricks. They kept their eyes on the ball, and those eyes were *sharp*. They'd caught that twitch of the hustler's hand, the one that flicked the ball under cup number two. The hustler tried to pull a fast one, but the Clever Man was onto him. A Clever Man could not be fooled . . .

Needless to say, the Clever Man was wrong.

It never occurred to a Clever Man that he was *meant* to spot the feints. Doing so boosted his ego; it convinced him that the hustler's hands might be too quick for *some* eyes, but not *his* eyes. The Kid would then repeat the cycle with subtle variations. Once a Clever Man was convinced that he'd figured things out, the Kid would simply palm the ball and hide it elsewhere. The switch happened in a blink—so swift and smooth the mark had no idea anything was amiss. A Clever Man *never* picked cup number three.

Until now.

"That one," said Laszlo.

The Kid hesitated. Laszlo wondered if he would try some chicanery, but the hustler resisted temptation.

"Lucky guess," he muttered, and raised the cup to reveal the ball. "Let it ride?"

"Sure."

In the next round, the Kid upped his game to include a variety of offhand feints. When he'd finished, Laszlo pointed calmly at cup number two.

"That one."

Right again. Laszlo ignored the Kid's bewilderment and glanced out the window. The subway had entered his station. He held out a hand for his winnings.

"This is my stop."

A muscle twitched in the Kid's jaw. "And I took you for a *player*," he grumbled. "One more? Double or nothing?"

"Let's see the cash."

The Kid flashed some bills. Laszlo nodded, then winced as Loudmouth walloped his shoulder.

"Ha!" the Belgian barked. "You've got the little punk's number!"

The Kid rolled his eyes. "Yo. Did someone forget I'm playing with *his* money?"

Loudmouth merely crowded in for a better view. Other passengers edged over. The Kid's playful manner vanished. His eyes went cold and reptilian as he set up the game.

This time, he made no effort to mask his skill. The cups darted about like hummingbirds, too fast for the eye to follow. When they stopped, the Kid folded his arms and fixed his opponent with a defiant stare.

"Which one, chump?"

Laszlo tapped his chin. "Hmmm . . . I guess I'll go with that one."

He pointed at the center cup. A twinkle flashed in the Kid's eye. He chuckled as he raised it. "Sorry, man. You—"

A little red ball rolled out.

The car erupted. Laszlo ignored the cheers. He was having too much fun. "Something wrong?" he asked pleasantly.

The Kid said nothing. His confusion was understandable. The ball shouldn't have been under that cup; the ball should not have been under *any* of the cups. It was still in the Kid's hand, artfully tucked between thumb and forefinger. Either he was going certifiably insane, or his would-be pigeon had slipped a second ball into the game. Impossible. Houdini couldn't pull off a stunt like that. It wasn't human . . .

The Kid went rigid.

It. Wasn't. Human.

He craned his neck up at Laszlo. Their eyes met. A glimmer of understanding flashed between them, instant and electric. The Kid looked away.

"I've heard about you."

"I'm tickled. Pay up."

The Kid reached mechanically inside his jacket and came out clutching a roll of bills. He held up the money, presenting the cash like a holy offering.

Laszlo took only what he was owed. As the train stopped, he tossed back what remained and left an extra fifty on the tray to soften the blow. He gave a second fifty to Loudmouth's wife and a third to the bewildered Watchman before disembarking. As for the Shill, she received a tip of the hat as Laszlo strolled past her car.

Laszlo was still chuckling as he emerged from the subway stairs into the soft October air. Tossing his cup in a garbage can, he strolled toward Fifth Avenue. On days like this, he simply loved being a demon.

Within the hour, he would change his mind.

Laszlo's workplace was in Midtown, at what had once been a famously sinister address opposite a neo-Gothic church. Laszlo found the church's proximity hilarious and occasionally wondered what the rector would do if he learned who'd set up shop across the way. Poor fellow would probably have a stroke.

In grander days, the building's lobby had boasted undulating steel panels designed by a Japanese sculptor, but the place had been remodeled during the pandemic, and Laszlo no longer bothered going in that way. Instead, he entered via a loading dock, passing a group of construction workers on break. No one looked up as he breezed past. No one saw him slip through a door they had never noticed and never would.

Closing it behind him, Laszlo stepped aboard an old-fashioned elevator that, according to the Department of Buildings, did not exist.

Neither did its destination.

The elevator had but one button, and Laszlo pressed it. The car shuddered, then lurched into motion with a metallic screech. Laszlo grimaced as he descended through the floor. Someone really needed to oil the goddamn thing.

The journey down was painfully slow, so Laszlo passed the time by whistling Sinatra. When the car finally settled, he was nearly a thousand feet beneath Manhattan, amid the labyrinth of tunnels and waterways that composed the city's underworld.

The air was heavier at these depths, and sufficiently nippy that Laszlo usually wore a cashmere scarf. Torches shone in the darkness, guttering in an endless breeze that stank of sewage and seawater. They illuminated a columned archway whose inscription would have stumped all but a dozen long-dead scholars who had dared to peruse a forbidden grimoire. The language was older than Sumerian and could be translated as follows:

THE ANCIENT AND INFERNAL SOCIETY OF CURSE KEEPERS

EST. 5036 BC

⌒ OUR REACH ENDLESS, OUR GRASP ETERNAL ⌒

Below the archway stood a pair of tall glass doors smudged with handprints that ranged from Possibly Human to Definitely Not. Laszlo was about to push them open when a pair of faces not unlike hideous Greek masks bubbled up from the flanking columns.

"You're late," said one.

"Oh, fuck off," said Laszlo pleasantly.

"There's no need for vulgarities," the other face groused. "It's our duty to reprimand you."

"You're condemned souls," Laszlo reminded them. "Your only duty is to suffer eternal torment. Besides, what do you care when I show up? Does it honestly upset you when I'm late?"

"Yes," sniffed one of the souls. "It does."

"Then I guess I'm doing my job."

With a wink, Laszlo pushed through the doors and left the damned behind. As he crossed the threshold, his appearance changed—not his clothes but his person. The trim and tousled investment banker became a trim and tousled fiend with cobalt skin, moonstone eyes, and the needle-sharp teeth of a house cat.

The room he entered was not some sulfurous pit crammed with torture racks. Those places were long out of fashion. Like the rest of Hell, the Society had had to get with the times, and its American branch took the form of an office complete with cubicles, fluorescent lights, and water coolers. Here and there one might encounter a condemned soul jamming up a photocopier, but these were exceptions.

Normally, the office hummed with sin-seeking activity, but today it was conspicuously quiet. Laszlo chalked it up to lunchtime.

"Psst!"

He turned to find the nightmarish face of a goblin shark peeking out from the coatroom. Laszlo suppressed an impulse to flee.

"Hello, Clarence."

The shark-headed figure pressed a finger to his lips, or what passed for lips on that grotesque and distended snout. He beckoned for Laszlo to join him.

Laszlo obliged with an inward sigh. Clarence was always fretting about work, bemoaning his love life, or failing to rally a Friday happy hour. Today, however, he seemed more agitated than usual. As he entered the coatroom, Laszlo noted that his colleague's eyes were red and somewhat puffy. He braced himself for another therapy session.

"Clarence, have you been crying?"

The shark nodded and fumbled in his waistcoat for a handkerchief. As Clarence blew his snout, Laszlo could not help but admire his colleague's wristwatch, a vintage Breguet.

Refolding the handkerchief, Clarence leaned close. "We have an emergency," he whispered.

"What now?"

"We're being audited!"

Laszlo stifled a yawn. "Clarence, are you getting enough fiber?"

The shark paused. "I think so. I take a supplement."

"Take two. You need to relax, my guy. This isn't the first time the bigwigs have sent someone down here to poke around. You know the drill: they ask questions, we lie, they go their merry way."

"But those are just bean counters," said Clarence. "This time, they sent an *Overseer!*"

Laszlo blinked, then studied Clarence more closely. Could his nebbish colleague possibly be correct? Overseers were Class VIII demons and occupied some of the highest perches throughout the Hierarchy. Laszlo and Clarence were lowly Class IIIs—mere functionaries and specialists. They were lucky to have physical bodies, and even those were nothing great, most cobbled together from whatever happened to be at hand when a Class II was promoted. In Clarence's case, this had been a beached goblin shark and a rotting Highland sheep. The poor fellow spent a fortune on cologne.

Laszlo mastered his surprise. "Why would they send an Overseer?" he muttered to himself.

Clarence flapped his hands. "I don't know! All I know is that I'm going to be crucibled!"

"Pfft," said Laszlo. "You never call in sick, and you've got a sexy curse."

The shark head drooped. "Not anymore," said Clarence with a sniffle. "I mean, okay—I'll admit that being doomed to a life at sea used to be a pretty sweet curse. Ships were leaky and maps were terrible. Tormenting my Bearers was a snap. But times change, Laszlo, times change."

"What do you mean? The family's still cursed, aren't they?"

"Yeah," Clarence sighed, "but these days, the descendants just take cruise after luxury cruise. Their lives are one big party. Frankly, I envy them."

Laszlo raised an eyebrow. "Isn't there a clause prohibiting lavish ocean travel?"

Clarence started pacing. "No. You'd think there would be. Honestly, I don't even think they mind being cursed anymore. Whenever I drop in and try to scare them with tales of typhoons or cannibals, they howl with laughter. Have you ever been mocked in a buffet line?"

"No."

"It's mortifying. I got so flustered my disguise went haywire. Some kids cornered me on the leisure deck. One started screaming, 'A Pokémon! A Pokémon!' and insisted she'd captured me fair and square. I had to fling myself overboard."

The demon began to hyperventilate. Laszlo reached out a hand to steady him.

"You're a good Keeper, Clarence. I know that. You know that. Most importantly, *they* know that."

Clarence could only nod. Tears were welling up. Laszlo clasped the shark's moist and spongy hands between his own. He patted his colleague's wrist.

"Pull yourself together, amigo. When you leave this closet, I want that glorious snout held high. Just tell this Overseer the truth. It's not your fault cruise ships became a thing." Releasing Clarence, Laszlo clapped him on the shoulder and made his escape.

Once on the floor, there was no time for coffee, no flirting with that slinky new assistant in Accounting. Laszlo made a beeline for his office. He was one of the few Keepers who had one, and a bit of privacy was just the thing to get his thoughts in order.

Why had they sent an Overseer?

As Laszlo hurried along, he scanned the sea of cubicles for his assistant. When he reached her desk, the only thing he found was half a turkey club. That clinched it; everything had gone pear shaped. Ms. Spiegel never left her post.

Slipping into his office, Laszlo tossed his hat on the stand and collapsed in his chair. A message light flashed on his telephone. As he reached for it, something bumped against the window. Spinning about, Laszlo opened the blinds to reveal a gargantuan alligator with a rat in its jaws.

Laszlo thumped the window. The sewer gators were becoming a downright nuisance. Hundreds lurked throughout the deeper tunnels, pale as milk and blind as moles. Apparently, the brutes didn't need eyes to eat like kings. The one outside was the size of a Cadillac.

Laszlo rapped the glass again. "Get lost! I can't think with you thrashing around."

The alligator heaved its leathery bulk about to face the window. Laszlo repeated his message in blunter terms. Gulping down its lunch, the reptile gave him a reproachful look and waddled off into the darkness. Laszlo let the blinds drop just as Ms. Spiegel burst through the door.

"Where have you been? There's an Overseer in Thatcher's office!"

"I know," said Laszlo coolly. "By the way, that alligator's back and she's being sassy."

"Forget the gators. We have an *Overseer* on the premises."

"Heard you the first time. And I'm a little curious why you didn't give me a heads-up. I had to get the news from Clarence."

Ms. Spiegel went stony. "Check your phone."

Laszlo did so, only to find that the battery had died. "I see," he said. "Well, pull up a chair and we'll strategize."

His assistant rolled seven of her eyes. "*There's* an idea. I'm sure we can come up with something brilliant before your meeting."

"Meeting?" said Laszlo. "What time?"

"Ten minutes ago."

He consulted his new watch. "You're joking."

"I'm not. And where did you get that?"

Laszlo shoved the Breguet in his pocket. "Estate sale. Do you have my reports?"

"Real or doctored?"

"Doctored."

His assistant held up a leather folio. The two hurried to the supervisor's office, Laszlo on his feet and Ms. Spiegel on the snakelike coils that composed her lower body. As she undulated alongside, Laszlo pressed her for information. They spoke in whispers.

"Who's the Overseer?"

"Malignis Androvore."

"Never heard of him."

"He's new. Word is they jumped him up from Class VI. Must be a real go-getter."

Laszlo smirked. Go-getters. Overachievers. Whatever the label, they were all the same. Flattery was the key. Make them feel smart and superior, then hint at incompetence elsewhere, some juicy problem requiring their "expert" attention. Really, it was no different than the shell game. A little misdirection went a long way.

As they reached the supervisor's office, Ms. Spiegel handed Laszlo his reports. Her expression softened as she straightened his tie.

"Don't get cute. This Overseer means business. Scylla and Kozlowski already went in."

"And?"

Ms. Spiegel leaned close. "*They never came out!* Play it straight. Forget that 'a little misdirection goes a long way' crap. It always bites you in the keister."

Laszlo flushed a shade of indigo. What did Spiegel know about his keister? Anyway, she hadn't seen him work his magic on the subway. He patted the cash in his pocket and felt its reassuring crinkle. "Ms. Spiegel, I must humbly beg to differ."

With his report in hand, Laszlo spun about and strode up to Thatcher's door. She bade him enter, and he strolled in with his most dazzling smile.

A moment later, he almost fainted.

CHAPTER 2
THE OVERSEER

As far as demons went, Laszlo was a relative nipper; he had arrived during a demonic "baby boom" that took place during the Middle Ages. Still, eight hundred years was not an insignificant amount of time. Laszlo had witnessed the Fourth Crusade, the Renaissance, and the Industrial Revolution. But in all those centuries he had never seen another demon crucibled.

Until now.

The crucible stood in the corner, an industrial funnel supported by a sturdy tripod. The funnel's iron was bathed in heat shimmer, and its scorched and blackened spout extended into a Mason jar etched with glowing sigils. At present, the jar was empty.

The jars on the desk were not.

There were two of them, and each contained a bubbling goo. Now and again, one would defy gravity and ooze up the jar's sides as if trying to escape. Whenever it reached the sigils, however, the symbols pulsed a sinister red and the goo retreated. An appalled Laszlo leaned on the doorjamb for support. The spectacle was nauseating, yet he couldn't look away. He also couldn't help wondering which goo was Scylla and which was Kozlowski.

Thatcher's monotone snapped him out of it. "Of all the days to be late."

Standing beside the credenza, the toadish Class IV held a stack of files. A stranger was behind her desk, a powerfully built figure in scarlet robes whose leonine head was crowned with a mane of flickering white flames. Ms. Thatcher made a deferential gesture.

"Laszlo, it is my privilege to introduce His Fiendishness Sir Malignis Androvore. The Society now falls under his authority."

Laszlo touched a knuckle to his forehead. "Honored."

The Overseer fixed Thatcher with an acid stare.

She cleared her throat. "When meeting a demon of executive rank, it is customary to bow." The statement was delivered in Thatcher's habitual drone, but Laszlo knew her well enough to catch the alarm in those bulbous eyes: *Get down, you moron.*

Laszlo dropped to one knee. "Uh, sorry. We don't usually see anything above a Class IV. It's an honor to meet you, Your Fiendishness."

Androvore replied in a patrician baritone. "Lower."

"Excuse me?"

The Overseer made a downward gesture. Laszlo caught his drift and complied. This continued until Laszlo was lying face down with his arms limply at his sides, like a toddler holding a protest in the cereal aisle.

"That will do," the Overseer finally growled. "Get up."

Climbing to his feet, Laszlo brushed fibers from his pants while Androvore consulted a file.

"You are Curse Keeper Number 923," he said.

"I also go by 007."

"Was that meant to be amusing?"

Laszlo coughed. "Just trying to lighten the mood, Your Fiendishness. You see, I can't help noticing that *crucible* in the corner and those *jars* on the desk . . ."

In response, Androvore took one of the jars and cradled it in a hand the size of a catcher's mitt. The contents quivered.

"These demons were failures, 923," remarked the Overseer impassively. "Now that I'm running this division, I intend to find out who is use*ful* and who is use*less*." He set the jar down. "Why are you late?"

For a nanosecond, Laszlo considered telling the truth. Then instinct took over. Standing tall, he thrust out his chest. "I was engaging the Enemy."

The Overseer raised a flickering eyebrow. "Explain."

"Parochial school, sir. K through eight. I popped in to frighten the nuns. I realize this falls outside my duties, but I spotted an opportunity and felt compelled to step up."

"I see. You were being enterprising."

"That's the word, Your Fiendishness. The *mot juste*."

"And the nuns?" said Androvore. "How did they receive your efforts?"

Laszlo fixed his attention on a portrait of a Flemish cheesemonger, or what he assumed was a Flemish cheesemonger. When lying, he always found it helpful to focus on something in the background. It kept one's eyes from darting about and added a touch of earnestness. "Two nuns locked themselves in the chapel. The third was a tough old bird named Sister Frances. She threw an apple at me and recited the Lord's Prayer."

Androvore grunted. "Plucky."

"Yes, sir. Fortunately, I caught the apple and chucked it back, pegging her in the noggin before she could finish said prayer. I then chased her toward the cafeteria, babbling in tongues and leering in a menacing fashion."

The Overseer nodded approvingly. "How did things end?"

"Once I'd shown them who was boss, I left and hailed a cab. Unfortunately, the driver was new, and we ended up in Queens."

"Next time, take the subway."

Laszlo bowed. "There's an idea, Your Fiendishness." He glanced at Thatcher to see if she was buying any of it. The supervisor had taken a page from his own book and was staring into the middle distance, her expression one of contained nausea.

Androvore gestured at an armchair. "Make yourself comfortable, 923."

Laszlo was always happy to sit, even if it put him at eye level with liquefied colleagues. Up close, he noticed the goo in one of the jars had purplish undertones. Definitely Kozlowski.

"Would you like me to put them out of sight?" asked Androvore.

"Not necessary," said Laszlo. "But what happens now? Are you going to . . . *drink* them?"

The Overseer's lip curled. "Absorb these sluggards into my essence? No, they'll be tossed back in the Primordial Ooze."

"But their curses—"

"Will be reassigned," said the Overseer curtly. "I intend to put things in order, 923. Once upon a time, the Society was the Hierarchy's crown jewel." He swept his arm across an imaginary marquee. "Atlantis! The Black Plague! The Napoleonic Wars! COVID misinformation! Each the result of clever and enterprising curse management. Those Keepers spread misery on a grand and glorious scale. Which brings us to *your* curse . . ."

"Yes, Your Fiendishness?"

Androvore leaned back in his chair. "Tell me about it."

"Elevator version or Tolstoy?"

"Elevator."

Laszlo steepled his fingers. "Well, it's not exactly Atlantis, but it does have some shelf appeal. The spell goes back to the seventeenth century, when England dispatched a magistrate named Ambrose Drakeford to investigate rumors of witchcraft in the colonies. While traveling through the Catskills, this magistrate heard about a place the original Dutch settlers called the Heksenwoud."

"What does that mean?" grunted Androvore.

"Witchwood."

"Convenient."

"Indeed. Anyway, the locals told the magistrate about a woman who'd been living in the Heksenwoud for as long as anyone could remember. Drakeford went searching, caught her 'performing vile sorceries' in the forest, and had her burned at the stake."

Androvore stifled a yawn. "How medieval."

"Quite," said Laszlo. "But the witch didn't go quietly. While being flambéed, she invoked a curse on Drakeford and his descendants. Voilà. The Drakeford Curse was born."

The Overseer consulted the file. "I see that you aren't the original Keeper."

"No, sir. Some other guy had it—Basil or Borage, something with an herby vibe. Anyway, he went AWOL and I was ushered aboard."

Androvore jotted down a note. "And the curse's terms?"

"Nothing fancy. To break the curse, Drakeford's descendants have to complete the witch's spell."

"And if they don't?"

Laszlo paused for dramatic effect. "They turn into monsters."

"Literally or figuratively?"

"Real monsters, Your Fiendishness. The genuine article."

Androvore clucked his forked tongue. "Interesting. When does meta-morphosis begin?"

"Early adulthood. By all accounts, Drakeford kids look normal enough. By forty, you'd never guess they were human."

"Sounds like a hoot."

"Indeed, Your Fiendishness. I'm a lucky demon."

But Androvore wasn't listening. A furrow appeared on that massive brow as the Overseer drummed his fingers. "So how does the curse maintain itself?"

"Excuse me?"

"If they turn into monsters, why hasn't the family died out? What sort of half-wit marries a Drakeford?"

"Ah," said Laszlo. "That's the beauty of it. The curse contains a perpetuity clause that compels Drakefords to breed before they go full Swamp Thing. By the time they're twenty, most have a kid or two. The other parent's never a local, and they don't stick around. They must be under some sort of glamour that wears off once the curse has a new Bearer."

"Clever witch."

"Yes, sir."

The Overseer returned to his notes. "When was the last time you paid the family a visit?"

Laszlo scoured his memory. He vaguely recalled taking a bus one summer that had broken down and forced him to brave the mosquitoes in search of a cheeseburger. He'd walked for ten minutes before abandoning the cause and catching a lift with some hippies back to New York. Fun ride, he recalled, despite the dude who kept breaking out his guitar. Few things were worse than a songwriting hippie. At least there'd been weed.

He coughed. "It's been a few."

Androvore raised a flaming eyebrow. "Two years? Three?"

"Let's go with three."

"Why so seldom?"

Laszlo twiddled his thumbs. "The curse's terms kick in automatically. That witch was dynamite."

A frown appeared on the Overseer's face. He jotted something down. "I see. And when was the last time a Drakeford tried to break the curse?"

Laszlo's smile became a grimace. "The exact year?"

"If you can recall," replied the Overseer stiffly.

"Well, the date's a bit foggy, but it was when Henry Ford was selling those Model Ts. Damn things were everywhere. You couldn't cross the street without a Model T zooming past. Well, not really *zooming*, but puttering along at a decent clip. I guess what I'm trying to say is that I hated that fucking car."

Androvore turned to Thatcher. "Would you say 923 has difficulty maintaining focus?" She nodded. Opening a folder, the Overseer retrieved a chart and held it up. Laszlo swallowed. Data was never good.

"Do you know what this is?" inquired Androvore.

"I believe it's an MM&D graph, milord. It tracks mortal misery and despair."

"Correct. Notice anything unusual about the red and blue lines?"

Laszlo squinted. "The blue one's kind of wavy, and the red one's . . . I don't see a red one."

"Look at the bottom."

It took a moment to spy a thin strip of red hugging the horizontal axis. "There she is," said Laszlo approvingly. "Admirably straight."

"Admirably?" the Overseer growled. "The despair ratings for this curse are negligible, 923. Your Bearers have spent the last century in a state of moderate misery and negligible despair."

Laszlo wrinkled his nose. "And that's . . . *bad*?"

The Overseer tossed the chart aside. "It's pathetic. Clearly, your

Bearers have grown used to their misfortune. Any hope they possessed vanished ages ago. You see the problem, of course."

An emphatic nod. "I really do. But I'd love to hear it in your words."

Androvore narrowed his eyes. "Your Bearers have no hope. As you know, it is the act of *losing* hope that generates despair. One cannot lose what they do not possess, 923. Unless something changes, the curse's despair production will remain at a standstill."

Laszlo blinked. "And that's . . . also bad?"

"*Yes!*" the Overseer snapped. "What in the Seven Hells is wrong with you?"

"I might be coming down with something. It's nearly flu season."

"Demons don't get the flu."

"I'm so relieved."

Androvore's nose twitched. "Back to basics," he growled. "Misery and despair are vital resources, 923. Only souls are more valuable. Despair makes us *stronger* and makes the other side *weaker*. Its production is why this Society exists. Why else would we bother with curses?"

"To keep unemployment down?"

Androvore stared at Laszlo. At length, he sighed and massaged his muzzle.

"It's not complicated," he said wearily. "We build up people's hopes, then yank the rug out. We tempt mortals. We seduce them. We drive them to wicked acts. We do this over and over again. It's Demon 101."

"Yes, sir," said Laszlo, inwardly pleased with his ability to play dumb and grind down the opposition.

"Back to your curse," said Androvore. "What do you have to say about your ratings?"

"I'd say they're consistent."

"Consistently dreadful."

"That's a little harsh."

"They literally can't be any lower."

Laszlo held up his hands. "I'll admit there's room for improvement. But in my defense, I did harass those nuns. That has to count for something."

"Ah, yes," the Overseer said dryly. "Those feisty nuns." He turned to Thatcher. "Fetch my associates."

The supervisor avoided Laszlo's quizzical look as she left the office. Resisting the urge to fidget, he wiped his palms on his trousers and feigned an interest in the room's trappings. The books, the binders, that air vent in the corner . . .

Androvore chuckled. "Planning your escape?"

Laszlo pried his attention from the vent. "Why would I need to escape?"

The Overseer did not reply, for at that moment Thatcher returned with six strangers in tow. Laszlo eyed them warily as they assembled. It was a motley bunch: Class IIIs with bodies salvaged from various birds, weasels, and a mange-riddled jackal. Not one met Laszlo's gaze as they stood about with a shifty, somewhat hangdog air.

"Recognize them?" asked Androvore.

"Nope."

The Overseer snapped his fingers. The newcomers vanished in a ripple of dark magic. In their places stood six Belgian tourists.

Laszlo stifled an urge to vomit.

Don't panic, he told himself firmly. *Admit nothing.* That was always the best policy when caught in a lie. Gaslight galore. Make the other side think they were crazy.

"How about now?" inquired Androvore.

Laszlo blinked with polite befuddlement. "Sorry. Still not ringing a bell."

"Oh, come off it," Androvore snapped. "They've been tailing you for days. When you're not hustling humans, you're shoplifting, gambling, or sunbathing in the park."

Laszlo examined his fingernails. "Those are ugly charges. I assume you can prove them?"

The demoness who had played Loudmouth's "wife" held up an iPad and scrolled through photos of Laszlo in human form enjoying four-martini lunches, seducing his landlord's wife, and pawning a variety of stolen goods. When they reached a photo of Laszlo snoozing on a beach blanket while clutching a bag of Fritos, Androvore had seen enough.

"Well?" he said. "Do you have anything to say?"

Laszlo eyed the faux Belgians with contempt. "Only that it's a sad day in Hell when Class IIIs betray their own. I've been called my share of names, but at least no one can call me an informer."

The faux Belgians exchanged guilty looks.

"Yes, I'm sure we're all deeply impressed with your principles," said Androvore dryly. "Keeper 923, you are unworthy of your assignment. You have neglected your curse and proved yourself incompetent. Better demons than you have been crucibled for less. Do you wish to make a statement before I pronounce judgment?"

What passed for Laszlo's heart hammered in his chest. His eyes darted to the crucible's scorched iron and glowing runes. He'd heard the experience was excruciating; one's flesh melted to gravy, their essence forced through a virtual juicer. *No, thank you.* With a surge of panic, Laszlo played his last and most desperate card.

Leaning forward, he fixed Androvore with an acid stare, the one he reserved for maître d's and bill collectors. "I didn't want to do this," he said waspishly, "but do you have any idea who I am?"

The Overseer consulted his file. "If I'm not mistaken, you are Curse Keeper 923, an imbecilic fraud and sad embarrassment to the Society."

Laszlo waved a hand impatiently. "No," he said. "Not me. Forget *me.* Do you have any idea who my *father* is?"

For several seconds, the Overseer did not reply. Laszlo studied the massive lion's head with its flaming corona. An amused gleam flickered in Androvore's eyes.

"I'm well aware of who your father is."

Laszlo folded his arms as though the matter were settled. "Then you know I'm not one of your sorry globs ladled from the Ooze." He nodded dismissively at the other Class IIIs. "I was *sired*, good sir. I have a *pedigree.*"

"And this is relevant how?"

"I'm untouchable!" Laszlo retorted. "Mess with me, and *you'll* be the one bubbling in a jar."

The Overseer chewed his lip in apparent contemplation. "How distressing. But if that's true, perhaps you can explain this."

The demon slid a letter across the desk. Laszlo took it warily and scanned the typewritten message.

```
SIR MALIGNIS,
     RECEIVED YOUR REPORT. YOUR FINDINGS CONFIRM
MY OWN CONCERNS. DO AS YOU SEE FIT. ALL I ASK
IS THAT THE BOY BE GIVEN A WEEK TO PROVE HIS
WORTH. IF HE FAILS, SO BE IT.
```

Laszlo stared in horror at his father's all-too-familiar seal. Even worse, the signature was a hasty scrawl, as though the letter was just one more document in a tedious stack of paperwork. He attempted to look nonchalant as he slid the letter back across the desk. Androvore returned it to his file.

"So," said the Overseer, "shall we do each other a favor and get this out of the way?"

Laszlo thumbed a speck of dirt from his Guccis. "What about my week?" he asked in a chastened tone. "It says I have a week to prove myself. By the way, are we talking one Hell week or one Earth week?"

The answer mattered quite a bit. In Hell, a standard week was only six days long as opposed to seven. Lucifer had never been fond of Sunday.

"One *Hell* week," said the Overseer pointedly. "But what difference does it make? You've had centuries to prove yourself. You think another week will make any difference?"

"It might. What would I have to do?"

Androvore examined the claws that tipped his fingers. "I'm not an unreasonable demon. Let's see . . ." He pondered a moment. "All right, 923. If you can either obtain a mortal soul, maximize your MM&D ratings, or prevent a Curse-Breaking Event, I'll give you another chance."

Laszlo gaped. "B-but that's impossible," he stammered. "I'm only a Class III. I don't have the juice to pull this off in a year, much less a Hell week. I can't even teleport, for Satan's sake. I take the subway!"

"We're aware."

Laszlo clasped his hands in a supplicating gesture. "Lend me some powers," he pleaded. "Some Class V evocations. Or even some Class IVs! Give me a fighting chance!"

The Overseer closed the file. "A chance is precisely what you've been given. Be grateful. Keepers 901 and 877 didn't have Grand Dukes asking favors on their behalf. Of course, if you prefer to forfeit the opportunity, I can promise swift and seamless processing. Next week things might not go as smoothly. I'm a busy demon, and crucibles have been known to malfunction . . ."

"Is that a threat?"

Androvore shrugged. "Do we have a deal?"

A parchment materialized on the desk with the conditions spelled out in copperplate. A fountain pen appeared beside it, along with an hourglass the size of an egg timer. Its grains were exceedingly fine and gave off a sinister red glow. Rising from his chair, Laszlo took up the pen. He studied the document before him.

"Diabolical Contract," he observed admiringly. "Always wanted to make one of these."

Androvore smiled. "They're fun. Too bad it's a Class V power."

Laszlo tested the pen. The ink hissed as it touched the vellum. "I hear you get all kinds of perks at Class V," he said wistfully. "New abilities, a new body if you want one—"

"Even a new name," added the Overseer complacently. "You get to pick it yourself."

Laszlo glanced up sharply. "Wait. I'm sorry, but did I hear that right? You *chose* to be called 'Malignis Androvore'?"

"Indeed." His voice was a low purr.

"My Latin's rusty, but doesn't that mean something like 'Evil-Fire Man-Eater'?"

A pause. "Yes. What of it?"

Laszlo returned his attention to the contract, which he signed with a dramatic flourish. "Nothing, sir. It's a *fantastic* name. Not the least bit tacky or bourgeois."

A pall fell over the room. The Overseer had gone eerily still and was now contemplating Laszlo with an abstracted, almost predatory gaze. As he set down the pen, Laszlo wondered if he'd finally gone too far. Forget crucibled; he was going to be devoured on an IKEA desk blotter. An unsettling smile appeared on the Overseer's face. He rose from his chair.

Laszlo craned his neck. Goodness, Androvore was big. Was he nine feet tall? Ten? Whatever the number, the Knicks could have used him. Laszlo intended to make a quip along those lines but instead gave an inadvertent shudder as his testicles retracted into his abdomen. Their withdrawal, coupled with the bile rising in Laszlo's esophagus, erased any doubt that he had pushed his luck too far. Something cruel and unusual was about to happen. He just hoped it wouldn't involve his face.

Androvore now towered over everyone in the room, radiating an aura of such malevolence that no one could do anything but stare. Laszlo was pinned to his seat by the force of the demon's gaze. When the Overseer spoke, there was a throaty rawness to his voice, as though his patrician veneer had sloughed off like a discarded skin. Dr. Jekyll had left the premises; all that remained was Mr. Hyde.

Androvore stepped around the desk to loom over a now-petrified Laszlo. "Have you ever seen a demon crucibled?" he rasped softly.

Laszlo opened his mouth to answer, but nothing came out.

Androvore's grin widened to grotesque proportions. A drop of saliva burned a hole in Thatcher's beloved Turkish rug. "I thought not," he said. "Your tongue would not run so freely. Do you know what you require?"

Laszlo gave an infinitesimal shake of the head.

"A demonstration."

One of Androvore's arms shot forth and snatched up the Class III who'd played the part of Loudmouth. Clamping his hand about the lesser demon's throat, the Overseer lifted him clear off the floor, where he proceeded to wriggle like an eel fished from the Thames. One squeeze, and Loudmouth went limp. Had Androvore broken his neck? Apparently not, for the demon now managed to turn his head and gaze in stupefied horror at the crucible, whose funnel was rapidly heating up. Already, the iron had turned an incandescent orange, and nearby paneling was beginning to smoke.

Laszlo longed to close his eyes but feared that would simply give Androvore an excuse to stitch his lids open.

And so he watched what transpired over the next three minutes and forty-seven seconds. He watched as Androvore held Loudmouth over the funnel. He watched as Androvore released Loudmouth, and the demon hovered above the shimmering iron, held fast by some insidious force that pulled him inch by excruciating inch into the funnel, whose eager maw expanded to accommodate its victim.

It took the crucible two minutes to consume the demon's lower half. Loudmouth screamed throughout, with some of the shrieks rivaling those of a castrato. The sound was even worse than the spectacle. Eventually, even Androvore tired of Loudmouth's histrionics and twisted the demon's head off. The screaming was replaced by the soft crunch of the Overseer's consuming the head as easily as a Honeycrisp.

Revolting as this was, Laszlo still felt a stab of dental envy. Loudmouth's skull gave Androvore no trouble whatsoever—the Class VIII's jaws sank through bone like butter. Laszlo struggled with flank steak.

When the last of Loudmouth's body had disappeared, the crucible began humming grotesquely. Moments later, bluish-gray sludge issued from the funnel's spout. It came in sporadic trickles, then pulpy spurts as the demon's essence gushed into the Mason jar. When the final drops had been extracted, the crucible let out an indecent moan that recalled a cocktail waitress Laszlo had met at Mardi Gras.

At last, the awful machine went still and the iron cooled to a dull black.

No one spoke. No one dared move.

The only sound came from Androvore, as he savored the last of Loudmouth's brain stem.

After he had wiped his mouth and smiled, the Overseer plucked the Mason jar from its stand and held it to the light to appraise its contents. Whatever he saw must have been enticing, for he quaffed the essence in a single gulp.

Poor Loudmouth. Centuries of work just to end up as an energy drink.

Androvore shuddered as he absorbed Loudmouth's essence into his own. By consuming his own kind—a Class III wouldn't count for much, but the effect wasn't negligible—he was a smidgeon stronger than he had been a moment earlier. Such was the way with demons.

But where Hell was concerned, everything had its price. Thatcher shuffled to a file cabinet and fetched a long and intricate form in triplicate.

"What is that?" asked Androvore.

"Employee-Consumption Report," Thatcher replied in a nasal twang. "'Any demon who devours an employee's essence instead of re-turning it to the Ooze shall have the equivalent docked from their pay.'"

"Surely that doesn't apply to me. I'm an Overseer."

Here he had met his match, however; Thatcher was a creature of the bureaucracy and lived to enforce its endless rules. "You can take it up with the High Council."

"Perhaps I will," Androvore muttered. "After all, one of its mem-bers is expecting to hear from me." His gaze found Laszlo and held as he returned to the chair behind Thatcher's desk. "So, 923, do you have a clearer understanding of your predicament?"

Laszlo's voice was barely a croak. "Yes, sir. I believe I do."

"Good," said Androvore. He added his own signature to the con-tract before pressing his seal into the wax that bubbled up from the vellum. Setting the document aside, he turned the hourglass over and held it out to Laszlo.

"Six days," he whispered. "Six days, and you belong to me."

Taking the hourglass, Laszlo bowed stiffly and made what he hoped was a dignified exit despite the spot of pee that had blossomed on his trousers. Once outside, he broke into a white-knuckled sprint.

He arrived at his office to find Ms. Spiegel boxing up his things. "What are you doing?" Laszlo panted.

His assistant's tentacles stiffened in surprise. "You're not crucibled?"

"No," said Laszlo indignantly. "I'm still here, thank you very much. They're giving me time to turn things around."

"How much?"

"Six days."

Spiegel continued packing. Sidestepping her, Laszlo hurried to a safe beside a filing cabinet. Crouching, he spun the dials. There was a click, and he opened the door to reveal an ebony case with a handle carved from something's femur. Its appearance was not unlike an ancient and uncommonly morbid backgammon set. Laszlo took hold of it.

Ms. Spiegel looked up. "That's not supposed to leave the office."

"Desperate times," said Laszlo. Tugging the case free, he stood and snatched his trilby off the coat stand. As he turned to make his exit, he found a goblin shark hovering in the doorway.

"Hi, Laszlo. Have you seen my watch? I must have misplaced it, and Esther in Accounting thought—"

Clarence dove for cover as Laszlo came rocketing out the door. Interns scattered as the blue-skinned demon made a mad dash for the elevator, the briefcase cradled in his arm like a football. Amid the chaos and general outcry, a familiar voice rose above the throng. It belonged to Ms. Spiegel.

"Consider this my notice!"

CHAPTER 3
THE SIN-EATER

It was beginning to drizzle when Maggie Drakeford spied a car creeping down the road. Both the driver and his passenger looked anxious as they gazed about at the sagging trees and storefronts. Such expressions were not unusual among those who stumbled upon Schemerdaal, New York. People came to the Catskills for charming lodges and antiques. What was this godforsaken backwater?

The driver caught sight of Maggie and gave a tentative wave. She returned it with a civil nod as they eased the car to a stop beside her. The window came down. Maggie pointed ahead.

"Nine miles," she said.

The driver blinked. "Excuse me?"

"It's nine miles to the next village, or you can turn around and go back to the highway."

The man smiled, exhibiting a kind of dental perfection unknown in Schemerdaal. He wore a tweedy blazer that fairly screamed *professor*.

"How do you know we're lost?" he asked.

"Lucky guess."

The passenger leaned across her . . . boyfriend? Husband? Maggie didn't see a ring. "Where are we?" she asked. "My phone's not getting a signal."

"You're in Schemerdaal," Maggie replied. "Population one hundred ninety-three—scratch that. One hundred ninety-two." The words tumbled out absently. Her attention had returned to a cottage across the road, set back among the pines. It had a still, gloomy air, not helped by the windows covered in black fabric.

Maggie checked its front door. Still shut tight. Rubbing the chill from her arms, she wished her client would hurry up. The sky was darkening, and she'd left her umbrella back in the truck. And that umbrella wasn't all she'd left behind. Maggie cursed herself for a fool. She hated when her mother was right.

Professor said something. Maggie glanced back at him.

"What?"

"A gas station?" he repeated. "We're almost empty, and I'd rather not get stuck out here. No offense," he added quickly.

The man could have called Schemerdaal a radioactive shitheap without offending Maggie Drakeford. She conveyed this with a shrug. "There's a pump at Earl's, but they'll be closed. Most everything's closed today."

The girlfriend leaned across and spoke in a hushed voice. "Is this an *Amish community*?"

"No," said Maggie. "The Amish are quaint."

The woman's smile vanished. "Then what's with the—" She gestured at Maggie's outfit: the petticoat and apron, the homespun waistcoat and shift.

Maggie touched the linen coif atop her braids. "My work clothes."

"Colonial reenactments?" inquired Professor.

"Something like that."

"Did the colonists wear Chuck Taylors?"

Maggie considered the sneakers poking from beneath her skirt. Aside from her brother, they were possibly her favorite things in the world, a prized discovery at the Salvation Army in Kingston. "No," she allowed. "They're a creative liberty."

"I approve," said Professor. "Much more stylish."

Maggie almost snorted. Style was the last goddamn thing she cared about.

Movement across the way. The cottage door had opened, and an ominous silhouette filled the doorway. It beckoned to Maggie.

She spat out her gum. "Gotta go," she said to the couple. "Nice talking to you."

Maggie did not look back as she crossed the road. If she did, she might have been tempted to wonder where the two lived and how they'd met, if they were happy together, what subject Professor might teach. No use in that. The car idled on the roadside, its occupants no doubt puzzled by her abrupt departure. Maggie was halfway to the Schuyler home when she heard them turn around and putter back the way they had come.

Out of Schemerdaal. Out of her life.

Maggie focused on her surroundings. On the weeds and gravel, the smells of rain and resin, the sound of water rushing over stone. The Schuylers' porch was just ahead. Rotted floorboards sagged under Maggie's weight. Their groan brought her father's warning to mind.

Get in.

Get out.

Go home.

She glanced up at the figure blocking the doorway. Reverend Farrow was an imposing man, tall and ascetic with a lean El Greco face. Even before she'd assumed her duties, Maggie had been afraid of him. In his suit and clerical collar, the Reverend did not seem so much a man as a monument: a marble carving with pale eyes, thin lips, and an air of reserved hostility. Standing before him, Maggie bowed her head and waited for the catechism to begin.

The Reverend spoke as though at his pulpit. "This is a house of mourning," he intoned. "Who would enter here?"

"Something low," replied Maggie dully. "Something vile, something hungry."

A bony finger jabbed her forehead. "The mark of Cain is upon thee, stranger, red as blood to my pious eye. Art thou wicked?"

"Wicked as a Samhain witch, a sly and cunning Jezebel."

The clergyman crossed himself. "And why would I admit a wolf amongst my flock?"

Maggie raised her head to meet that disapproving gaze. "The sins of the dead call to me. On these I'll feast, as is my right, and leave a soul unblemished."

The Reverend sniffed as though weighing the proposition, then stood aside to admit her.

She swept past and padded down a muddy carpet runner to the dining room. Dozens of grim-faced adults packed its shuttered confines. They stood in dense rows against the walls, three and four deep, a motionless assembly that stank of sweat and old wool. To a person, their attention was focused on Maggie.

Maggie's attention was on the corpse.

Mr. Abraham Schuyler lay upon the table, illuminated by a pair of beeswax candles. The deceased wore the gray suit he'd been married in, along with a tie purchased in Kaaterskill. In life, Mr. Schuyler had been dreadful—fond of tailing and harassing a younger Maggie in his Chevy. In death, he cut a more dignified figure: clean shaven, his sparse white hair combed back from a bluish-gray forehead. Candlelight glinted from the pennies resting on his eyelids. Upon his chest sat a small loaf of coarse brown bread sprinkled liberally with salt.

Maggie sat at the table's only chair and pocketed the envelope placed there. Looking about, she scanned the stoic faces lining the walls. She could recite every name present and even those of their forebears chiseled on the gravestones in Schemerdaal's churchyard: Schuylers and Ruyters, Groots and Fishkills, Leeuwens and Smits, Farrows and Mulders. Centuries ago, their ancestors settled this tangled corner of the wilderness, raised their clapboard church, and scrabbled a living from the mountain. Their descendants had never left.

They're prisoners too, thought Maggie. The notion almost moved her to sympathy. Then her gaze fell upon the stones clutched in their hands.

Get in.

Get out.

Go home.

Maggie took the bread from Mr. Schuyler's chest. Raising it high, she spoke in a clear voice that did not waver.

"I give easement and rest now to thee, dearly departed. Wander not down the lanes, or on the moors or meadows. And for thy peace, I take thy sins upon myself and barter my mortal soul. Amen."

Tearing a piece off the loaf, Maggie swallowed it with a sip of sour red wine from the glass set before her. She ate methodically, chewing with exaggerated motions so everyone could see that Abraham Schuyler's sins had been thoroughly consumed. When she'd finished, Maggie folded her napkin and pushed back from the table. As she rose, a chair leg squeaked on the floorboards.

Long seconds passed while Maggie stood motionless. Head bowed, eyes averted, her calves tense as a sprinter's.

A cry shattered the quiet. "Begone, devil!"

Maggie bolted. Shouts and curses erupted behind her, accompanied by footsteps in pursuit. A stone whizzed past her head, cracking a picture frame.

She flew out the front door, veering left toward a creek that ran alongside the house. Some of the village children were waiting in ambush. They sprang out from behind a mound of old tires, howling like savages as they cast their missiles. A stone nicked Maggie's ear, drawing blood. She never stopped running.

Crack! Crack!

More stones whistled past, chipping bark off nearby trees. Maggie bounded nimbly across the icy creek, her sneakered feet picking out the surest path. Once across, she wove through the trees, her attention fixed upon the wooded slope ahead. When she reached its base, she dashed straight up the steep terrain as swift and steady as a mountain goat.

Her pursuers fell by the wayside. No one in Schemerdaal could run as far or fast as Maggie Drakeford, and they knew it.

When she reached the summit, Maggie leaned against a boulder and wiped blood from her ear. She stayed put a moment, panting as she gazed down at the mist-veiled village. Once she'd caught her breath, she continued down the back slope, shuffling and sliding over the scree, bending her path toward a pullout where she'd left Gladys.

Gladys was a truck, an ancient Ford the Drakeford family had kept running for seventy years. A horse trailer of the same vintage was hitched to her bumper. A battered hulk with a reinforced frame and tar-papered windows, a battleship on wheels, it held none of Gladys's charm.

As Maggie reached it, there was a triumphant shout behind her.

She turned as a pair of young men emerged from a stand of fir trees. At first glance, the Ruyter brothers could be mistaken for twins, with matching mops of white-blond tangles, pale pebble eyes, and freckled beaks perched above meaty lips. At twenty-two, Willem was a year older and stouter. But Abel seemed to Maggie the crueler one. Her gaze traveled to the stone in his hand. It was larger than a chicken egg.

As always, Maggie refused to show fear. Fear suggested weakness, and weakness might drive them into a frenzy. Instead, she spat and eyed the two with cool disdain. "Fun's over. You missed your chance at the Schuylers'."

Abel raised his stone. "Says who, bitch?"

"Says me." Maggie unpinned the coif from her hair and folded it neatly into quarters before placing it in her pocket. "This game's played in the village. Throw a stone down there, and I'll run like a good girl. Throw a stone up here, and I'll break your fucking arm."

The brothers exchanged uncertain glances before Willem stumbled on the obvious. "There's two of us."

"Then I break two arms."

The grim certainty of Maggie's statement caught the Ruyters off guard. They had only ever encountered her in the village: Meek Maggie, Freak Maggie, one of those miserable Drakefords who lived in the Witchwood. Village Maggie was quick to scurry when anyone looked at her sideways. The young woman before them was not sheepish, shy, or cowed. This Maggie was a stranger.

The wind picked up, shaking the trees as rain began to fall. Maggie watched the brothers closely. The Ruyters were bigger, but they were village soft and Maggie was mountain strong.

Her mind went back to the towheaded cherubs she'd met ten years earlier.

Maggie remembered the event because it was the first time she'd visited the village by herself. She had begged her parents to let her fetch the mail on the used bike they had fixed up for her birthday. When they finally caved, Maggie had set out alone, coasting down the trail, practically giddy with her newfound freedom.

When she reached Schemerdaal, Maggie had spotted the Ruyter boys sitting outside their father's grocery. They looked to be roughly her age, and when they waved to her, Maggie stopped her bike to say hello. She'd barely lowered the kickstand when their mother rushed out of the store, swinging a broom like a battle-ax and shrieking at the "Drakeford whore" to get away from her boys. Terrified, Maggie had pedaled off, her face burning with a shame she was too young to understand. When she got home, she lied and told her parents there had been no mail. They did not question her. Her father merely nodded and went out to the porch, where he sat and gazed at the vegetable patch. He did not come inside until nightfall.

That was then.

Those little cherubs from the store were gone now, replaced by a pair of smirking goons. Ten years older, ten years bigger, and brimming with the bile of their ancestors.

And just like that, Abel threw his stone.

Maggie ducked. The stone just missed her, striking the trailer with a crack like a gunshot. Willem let his stone fly. It struck Maggie hard in the left forearm, tearing her sleeve and the flesh beneath. The brothers laughed and cast about for more ammunition.

Maggie was on them in an instant. Punching, gouging, even biting when a chance presented itself. The ferocity of her onslaught stunned the Ruyters. Having knocked Abel down, Maggie dug her knee into his back while twisting Willem's arm in a direction it did not want to go. He grunted in pain and swung his other fist. It thudded into Maggie, knocking her off Abel, who scrambled to his feet and tried to land a kick. Maggie twisted aside and yanked his feet out from under him. He landed hard on his backside and promptly had his nose smashed by Maggie's fist.

Abel recoiled, covering his face as blood streamed between his fingers.

Maggie turned just as Willem drove a shoulder into her and tackled her into the underbrush. His weight pressed down, but Maggie was able to roll onto her side and throw an elbow that clipped his cheekbone.

To her dismay, Willem didn't seem to notice. His eyes had gone strangely vacant, their pupils dilated to the extreme. A grubby hand fumbled at Maggie's shirt and tried to grab her breast.

"Get off me!"

She swung her elbow again. It landed flush but had no apparent effect. Maggie threw another. And another. Willem's eye had swollen grotesquely, but he didn't even appear to notice. He was on something. He had to be. Oxy was no stranger to Schemerdaal.

It was then that Maggie noticed a buzzing in her ears, like some kind of bee or mosquito. She shook her head to drive it off, but the buzzing only intensified.

A twig snapped to her left. Turning, Maggie saw that Abel had regained his feet and was staggering toward them. Beneath the blood, he wore the same terrifyingly blank expression as his brother. He fumbled absently at his belt, trying to pull it free of his jeans.

Maggie's efforts grew frenzied.

Get up, she told herself. *Get up!*

A resounding *BOOM!* brought everything to a halt.

All three whipped their heads about. The trailer was rocking from side to side.

BOOM!

The second impact was even greater and sent a shiver through the entire frame. To Maggie's dismay, the trailer began to topple. With a furious shove, she heaved Willem off her and ran to it. She threw her body against its side. Something heavy within was lumbering like a maddened bear.

Maggie smacked the trailer with her palm and hissed into one of its air holes. "Stop! Stop before you hurt yourself!"

The reply was hoarse and guttural, unintelligible over the wind. The trailer groaned as its occupant shifted its weight. Rust shivered off the frame as it crashed back onto solid footing. Exhaling slowly, Maggie turned to see the Ruyters staring at her. Their clothes were smeared with dirt, and Maggie registered with satisfaction that she'd broken Abel's nose and Willem's left eye was swollen shut. Shock appeared to have snapped them out of their trancelike state. Willem pointed a shaky finger at the trailer.

"T-there's a monster in there," he stammered. "I heard it!"

Maggie scowled. "Go home."

Abel wiped blood from his chin. "You attacked us! You *bit* me! When I tell people a Drakeford *bit* me—"

Maggie stepped forward. "You tell them. Tell the whole village! If anyone has a problem, they know where to find us."

The Ruyters slunk away. Maggie watched their dwindling forms make their way down the mountain. She glanced up at the clouds sagging and scraping along the ridgeline. With any luck, the storm would be a doozy.

As if in answer, lightning split the sky, followed by a crack of thunder that sent Maggie racing for Gladys. Climbing into the cab, she pulled the door shut and lay across the seat and hugged her chest as she took in the truck's comforting scent of cracked leather and tobacco. There was no sound or movement from the trailer. It had gone so still the storm might have been a lullaby. Focusing on the rain, Maggie tried to scrub the Ruyters from her mind. The blank look on their faces, that mindless pawing at her body . . .

Fuck those assholes.

Sitting up, she brushed away a strand of hair and eased into the driver's seat, where she turned the key and waited for Gladys to stir. The truck obliged, albeit reluctantly. Pressing down the clutch, Maggie shifted into first and eased out of the turnout.

Maggie was careful to take it slow. Some of her caution was due to the storm. Most was due to Gladys. While she usually answered the bell, Gladys was old and cranky and needed every one of her horses to haul the trailer uphill. Maggie hunched forward as they trundled along, her hands positioned at ten and two. The cut on her ear was stinging something fierce, as was the gash in her arm, but she tucked the pain away into a corner of her mind, just the way her dad had taught her.

Half a mile later, the road ended at a wall of trees so tall and massive they were like something from a fairy tale. Ash and oak, fir and beech, hornbeam and maple. The trees were so huge and spaced so closely together that they formed an almost impenetrable hedge that circled the summit like a jagged crown.

There was but one chink in this barricade: a narrow opening some ten feet tall. Beside it was a weathered sign nailed firmly to a post.

WARNING

PRIVATE PROPERTY
NO TRESPASSING
INTRUDERS WILL BE ~~SHOT~~ *EATEN*

The last word was in red spray paint, a bit of vandalism that had begun well before Maggie's time and was renewed by local teens whenever beer or boredom got the best of them. The Drakefords never bothered fixing it. For one, the family no longer valued its public reputation. For another, the warning might well have been true.

Every man, woman, and child born to this corner of the Catskills knew that entering the Witchwood was forbidden. To do so invited a terrible fate. For proof, one need only look at the Drakefords themselves. Long ago, their ancestor had dared to venture beyond that hedge. His descendants were still paying the price. No one from Schemerdaal—no matter how bold, drunk, or stupid—would set a toe beyond that sign.

For Maggie, however, the sign held no particular terror. For her it was a welcome mat, a reminder that she was home and safe from those who wished her harm. Steering Gladys through the gap, she plunged ahead without a second's hesitation.

Had Maggie known what really lived in the Witchwood, she might have reconsidered.

CHAPTER 4
THE DRAKEFORDS

Once past the hedge, it was another half mile to the farmhouse. The track wound past creeks and streams, dark waterfalls, and knuckled hills crowned with rowan.

As she drove, Maggie mused absently on iodine, stitches, and the flurry of questions that she knew awaited her. What would the Ruyters tell their family? What would Maggie tell hers? The farmhouse was ahead now, a dark structure with a gambrel roof flanked by a barn and several vegetable patches. A kerosene lamp burned in the front window.

Living miles from any grid, the Drakefords did not have electricity or public utilities. Years ago, the family had salvaged a coal-fired generator, but it stopped working within a week and had never been replaced. The Witchwood had no love for modern things. These days, the only technology the Drakefords utilized was a battery-powered radio, and even that only operated when the wind was in the west.

Maggie pulled up by the barn. She hadn't even set the brake when a flashlight from the porch cut through the rain. The beam hovered on her face before sweeping along the trailer's side. It stopped where Abel's stone had dented the sheet metal.

Oh, perfect, she thought. Grabbing the umbrella, she opened the door and hopped down from the cab. A voice called out but was lost in the thunder. Maggie turned to the porch.

"What?" she called back. "I can't hear you."

Her mother made an impatient gesture and went back in the house.

If you're in such a hurry, you could help, Maggie thought irritably. She grimaced at the pain in her arm, then hurried to fetch a wheelbarrow, which she steered to the back of the trailer. As she opened the doors, Maggie braced herself for the smell that came wafting out, a nauseating miasma of chemicals and spoiled meat.

"We're home," said Maggie cheerfully.

Something shifted in the far corner, thrusting piles of damp straw aside as it dragged itself toward the opening. Its progress was slow and accompanied by ragged breathing. Maggie refused to look away as her passenger emerged into the gray light. Her gaze traveled slowly over misshapen forms and the tragic hints of what they used to be. A twisted spine, a fused wedge of jointless fingers, the glint of a solitary eye. Her passenger was wearing a work shirt, altered in June but already ill fitting. Crouching, Maggie took firm hold under her father's arms and planted a foot against the trailer's bumper. With a grunt, she heaved him free.

He fell into the wheelbarrow with a boneless slap, like an octopus spilling onto a trawler's deck.

Maggie winced at the sound. "Did that hurt?"

Bill Drakeford writhed about in the wheelbarrow, the rain drawing trickles of steam from his feverish skin. He tried to answer, but speech had become difficult and the effort caused him agitation. The few words he managed were pitifully garbled; all Maggie could make out was "control."

"Shoot," she said. "I lost control too. Let's get moving, or we'll be late for tea."

A spasm rippled through him. Laughter. Her father had always had a sense of humor. The restless struggling ceased, and Bill Drakeford lay still in the wheelbarrow, resigned to letting his daughter run the show. Maggie gazed down at the ruined face turned up to hers. His lips were gone, and his facial muscles had grown so taut that even a neutral expression resembled a death's-head grin. But that solitary eye, even with its cataract, could still convey a range of emotions. In its depths, Maggie perceived boundless trust.

She tried to muster a smile, but it flickered and died away.

A year ago, her father could climb into his wheelchair. He could hold a conversation and handle the chess pieces when he played with her brother, Lump. Hell, he even cheered whenever the radio announced that the Yankees had lost. For some reason, Maggie's father simply loathed the Yankees. She suspected it was the pinstripes.

Those days seemed a lifetime ago.

Her father's bones had softened. He struggled to hold himself upright, much less brush his teeth or advance a pawn. Soon, he wouldn't look remotely human. And while the physical decline was heartbreaking, it was the mental aspect that kept Maggie up nights. From what she could tell, her dad's mind remained largely unaffected. Bill Drakeford *knew* what was happening to him. That was the cruelest stroke of all.

But Maggie couldn't dwell on that now. Just getting Dad into the house was a chore in itself. The key was to hit the ramp with enough oomph for the momentum to carry the wheelbarrow up onto the porch. Maggie managed it on the second try and then transferred her father into the wheelchair by the door. Once he was settled, she maneuvered him inside.

The room they entered was long and low ceilinged, with exposed beams and a soot-blackened mantel. The walls were largely bare: no photographs, no mirrors, nothing but a few childhood drawings. A kettle was heating in the hearth near a trestle table, where Maggie's brother, George—whom she had called Lump from the day he was born—was studying a battered atlas. Firelight reflected on his glasses, giving him the look of a studious beetle. He shot Maggie an anxious glance.

Mom's angry, he mouthed.

Even as he said this, their mother emerged from the pantry. Elizabeth Campbell Drakeford took in Maggie's disheveled state before shifting her gaze to her husband. Only now did Maggie notice there was blood on his shirt. Coming forward, Mrs. Drakeford motioned her aside.

"But I can help," Maggie said.

"You've done plenty," said her mother tersely. "Quiz George on geography."

A dejected Maggie watched as her dad was wheeled to the back of the house. When the bathroom door shut, Maggie came and sat by Lump, who leaned into her affectionately.

"You're a mess," he observed.

Maggie took the atlas. "I'm aware. What's the capital of Hungary?"

"Budapest. So what happened?"

"In Budapest?"

Lump gestured at Maggie as though her person were an active crime scene. "At the Schuylers'."

Maggie maintained a casual air. "The usual, until I got jumped near Gladys. What's the longest river in Europe?"

"The Volga, followed by the Danube. Who jumped you?"

"The Ruyter brothers."

Lump made a face like he'd tasted sour milk. "Those two are pigs. Not piglets. Hogs. Even their store smells. You're lucky you're okay."

Maggie gazed at the fire. "They're the lucky ones. Where's Mount Etna?"

"Sicily. What do you mean, they're the lucky ones?"

"Meaning I've never been so angry in my life. They got off worse than you did when you 'discovered' my diary."

The "discovery" in question had occurred five years ago, when Maggie was fourteen and dared to write down her private thoughts. After she found a giggling Lump flipping through its pages, she vowed to never make that mistake again. She'd swatted his behind so hard her own palm had stung for an hour.

Lump's china-blue eyes blinked in astonishment. "Worse than me? You're joking."

Maggie showed him her raw knuckles. "Not a word," she warned. "I know it was stupid."

At eleven, Lump had mastered the art of understatement. "Awesome."

Maggie turned the page and surveyed a map. According to their outdated atlas, Yugoslavia still existed. "Definitely *not* awesome," she corrected. "Those idiots will tell their family, and their parents will complain to Reverend Farrow."

"Maybe not," said Lump in his thoughtful way. "They'd have to admit they got whupped by a girl. They'll probably just say they fought each other."

Maggie's heart wished this were true. Her head knew better. "Something else happened," she muttered. "Something worse. With Dad . . ."

Lump raised his eyebrows just as their mother called from the bathroom: "Next patient."

"Tell you later," Maggie said, and walked briskly down the hall to where her mother stood in the bathroom doorway. Maggie slunk past her like a guilty hound and took a seat on the edge of the claw-foot tub.

Pulling up a stool, her mother inspected the cut on Maggie's ear. In the meantime, Maggie inspected her mother.

Elizabeth Drakeford somehow managed to make her secondhand clothes look elegant. Her life had veered off its track when she was just out of high school and had gotten pregnant with Maggie. "By mountain trash," her prominent family had said after she had decided to have the baby instead of attending Dartmouth. They had disowned her.

Maggie had never met her Campbell grandparents. They lived in a ritzy Connecticut town and did not send birthday cards. The only other thing Maggie knew was that her mother had intended to major in history and perhaps become a teacher.

Maggie could attest that her mother was a first-rate teacher, but she might have made an even better doctor. Her movements were deft and assured, no hesitation or squeamishness. Just a brisk assessment of what to do and how best to do it. Turning to the sink, Mrs. Drakeford reached for the brown bottle that Lump called "liquid evil."

Maggie did not flinch as her mother dabbed her ear. But that didn't mean the iodine didn't sting. Every touch felt like a hornet's jab.

After cleaning the wound, her mother applied antibiotic ointment. Maggie sat quietly as she worked, admiring her mother's graceful neck and the clean composition of her features. Good bones. When Maggie was younger, she'd wanted desperately to look like her. She'd even aped her mother's mannerisms and tried to phrase things just as she did. But it was a losing proposition. Her mother had been born Elizabeth *Campbell*. Not a drop of Drakeford blood in her veins. Campbell birthrights included auburn hair, hazel eyes, and the privilege of remaining human.

Maggie wasn't so fortunate. She was fast and strong, clever and capable, but her hair was a mousy brown, her eyes a steely blue. Maggie would never look like her mother. And her days as a human were numbered.

Mrs. Drakeford set aside the cloth. "What are you thinking about?"

"Nothing," Maggie lied.

Once upon a time, she might have opened up. Little Maggie used to tell her mother everything. The two would gab away as they worked in the garden or hung up washing to dry. They would pick thistles and Indian pipe as they strolled in what they called their Hundred Acre Wood. Mrs. Drakeford was Kanga and Maggie was Roo and tiny George became Piglet, once he tumbled on the scene.

That ended when Maggie was ten.

The Reverend Farrow had informed the Drakefords that Maggie was to take her father's place as the village sin-eater. The congregation wanted to replace her father. They had been willing to overlook his appearance, so long as he remained meek and dutiful. This he had done, but the man's afflictions had reached a point where people wondered if his appearance was a sign that he had absorbed too much sin. What if his future services were ineffectual? Would mortal souls be put at risk?

The community's patience had run out. It was time for Maggie to assume the Drakeford mantle.

Her mother had been horrified. She volunteered to take her daughter's place, but Reverend Farrow would not budge: tradition demanded that the sin-eater be of Drakeford blood. After a month had passed, the Reverend threatened to contact the authorities and request a search of the Drakeford property. There had been so many odd disappearances over the years; perhaps it was time someone looked into them . . .

That did it. Maggie became Schemerdaal's new sin-eater.

The Drakefords' relationship with the village returned to its usual antipathy—but something in Elizabeth Drakeford changed. Something had died.

As she grew older, Maggie wondered if some instinct or defense mechanism had caused her mother to withdraw. She couldn't say, but whatever the reason, the outcome was clear. Any maternal feelings and affection that remained were reserved for Lump and Lump alone.

"So," said Mrs. Drakeford, "I've heard your father's version. Let's hear yours."

Maggie shrugged. "There's not much to say. The Ruyters jumped me by the truck. We fought."

Her mother's response was measured. Everything she did was measured.

"You *fought*," she repeated. "And did it occur to you this was not a wise thing to do?"

Maggie's cheeks flushed. "They threw stones." *And that wasn't all,* she added inwardly.

"I'd imagine many people threw stones at you today. Did you fight them too?"

"That was in the village. The Ruyters have no business on the mountain."

"Maybe not. But you could have ignored them. You could have gotten in the truck and come home. Those boys wouldn't have gone past the sign."

Maggie resolved then and there never to speak about Willem groping her in the dirt, the vacant hunger in his and Abel's expressions. There was no point. Her mother would still find a way to make it all her fault. If Maggie hadn't lingered, nothing would have happened.

"But of course, you didn't drive away," her mother continued. "That would have been too sensible. Instead, you allowed them to provoke you. You gave the village an excuse to make our lives even harder, and endangered your father in the process. Do you recall me saying that taking him was a bad idea?"

"I do," said Maggie hotly. "And I recall him *begging* to come. Dad hasn't left this place for over a year. Forgive me for thinking of *him* and what *he* might like for a change."

"I see. And were you thinking of your father when you decided to brawl with two boys?"

"They're not *boys*, Mom. They're grown-ass men who assaulted me. Calling them 'boys' makes it sound like this happened on a playground."

Her mother looked her in the eye. "Answer my question. Were you thinking of your father when you decided to fight?"

Maggie hesitated. Strictly speaking, she hadn't. She'd been so furious at the Ruyters that she hadn't done much thinking at all.

"Is it true your father threw himself against the trailer?" her mother pressed. "Is it true he almost tipped it over?"

Maggie squirmed beneath that unblinking gaze. "Yes."

"I see. Maybe next time you'll do me the courtesy of heeding my advice. Now, let me see your arm."

"I'll do it," said Maggie.

"Don't be ridiculous. You can't sew your own elbow."

Before Maggie could protest, her mother had rolled up her left sleeve. When she saw what lay beneath, the color drained from her face.

The gash was ugly and would certainly require stitches, but that was not what horrified Maggie's mother. It was the patch of skin just below it, a leathery red blotch some two inches across. At first glance it resembled a birthmark, but a closer look revealed that the skin was crawling with small, semitranslucent feelers that undulated like sea anemones. The sight of their mindless movement was revolting.

Maggie sat perfectly still while her mother stared at the mark in silence.

"When did it appear?" she said at last.

Maggie looked away. There was no point reliving the details: the discovery of a pinkish spot earlier that month, the jolt of pain when she pressed it, the sprouting of those repulsive growths as the spot darkened and solidified before her eyes. Maggie had fled the house and run deep into the Witchwood, where she'd vomited again and again and screamed into the silence until her throat was raw. Her mother didn't need to know that. Her mother didn't want to.

When Maggie finally replied to the question, her voice sounded detached and almost alien. "Two weeks ago."

"And when were you planning to tell me?"

A shrug. "I don't know. Guess I've been working up to it."

"I see. Does George know?"

Maggie gave a tiny shake of her head. A moment later, she registered that her mother's hand had closed about her own.

"We knew this day was coming," said Elizabeth Drakeford softly. "We'll manage. Give me a few days to break the news to your brother. This will be hard on him."

Maggie almost laughed. *Hard on Lump? What about me?*

She sat in stoic silence while her wound was tended to. When the job was finished, her mother rose from the stool and packed up the first aid materials. Maggie remained where she was, her mind preoccupied by what had just transpired. Her mother's voice snapped her from the daze.

"What?" said Maggie.

"I'm going to ask you something, and I'd like an honest answer."

"Shoot."

"When I was tending to your father, he became agitated. He said again and again that he 'lost control.' He's terrified he could have hurt someone." She paused. "Possibly even you."

A sickly sensation pooled in Maggie's stomach. "He's just upset," she said quickly. "He wasn't himself."

Her mother nodded. "That's precisely what scared him, Maggie; he wasn't himself. Your father and I have been talking, and he thinks it might be time he moved out to the barn."

Maggie stared up in disbelief. "Move out? But that's crazy. He'd never hurt me—he'd never hurt any of us!"

"I want to believe that," said her mother, "but he isn't so certain. You see, he's been having nightmares lately. He won't discuss them with me, but they upset him terribly. I think . . . I think he's worried they could come true."

Maggie set her jaw. "Never," she said firmly. "He could *never*."

Her mother's tone softened. "A dog with rabies doesn't want to bite its family, Maggie. It can't help itself. So I'm going to ask my question. Did your father lose control? Did he frighten you?"

Long seconds passed. Maggie could not bring herself to reply.

Her mother nodded. "I thought as much. Clean up and put the Schuyler money in the jar. It's come just in time—we're running low on kerosene. Fetch some more firewood, and I'll get started on dinner."

"Sure," said Maggie. "But there's one more thing."

Her mother paused in the doorway.

"There was this professor in the village," Maggie continued. "At least, he looked like one. He and his girlfriend were lost, and when I gave them directions, I couldn't help but think—"

Elizabeth Drakeford pursed her lips. "We've been over this."

"It wouldn't have to be full time," Maggie hurried on. "I could take classes at Vassar or RPI, wait tables, maybe even rent an apartment and—"

"And leave your village duties to George?" her mother interrupted. She never mentioned sin-eating by name. Not when a euphemism was handy.

"Of course not," said Maggie. "If someone died, I'd come right home. I'd never make Lump take that up. How could you even *suggest*—"

"Now is not the time."

"But why?" Maggie was tense with frustration. "Whenever I bring it up, you shut down the conversation and say 'Now is not the time.' That's not an answer."

"You want an answer?" said her mother. "Look at your arm."

"I'm nineteen. I have a right to live my life—or whatever's left of it. It's not my job to raise Lump."

"George is your brother."

"Exactly. My brother. He's not my child, and he isn't a baby. He doesn't need constant care."

"But your father *does*," Mrs. Drakeford reminded her. "Which is why I need you here and not indulging some pointless fantasy. Honestly, Maggie, I don't have the energy to argue about this. Please get some firewood. I have other things to do."

She left Maggie sitting on the edge of the tub, studying her bandaged arm in exasperated silence. Reaching in her pocket, she took out the envelope from the Schuylers. Three folded twenties were inside. Maggie double-checked to see if she'd missed something. No such luck. The widow Schuyler had left her forty dollars short.

"Well, that's just *perfect*." Tossing the envelope aside, she rose and splashed water on her face before examining her shift. The fabric was badly torn along one seam. Across the front, Willem's muddy handprints stood out like angry bruises. The mere sight of them made Maggie want to scream and set her clothes on fire.

She didn't do either of those things. Instead, she stood and gazed meditatively at the water in the basin. When she'd mastered her emotions, she went to her bedroom and changed into a sweatshirt and jeans.

Lump looked up from the atlas as Maggie walked to the front door.

"Back to my quiz?" he asked hopefully.

"Later," said Maggie. She pulled on a pair of work boots.

Lump sighed dramatically. "But what will we do when we tour Europe? We'll be lost! Wayward! Ignorant!"

Opening the door, Maggie shot her brother a glance. "Yeah, that's not happening."

"Europe?"

"Anything."

Lump returned to his beloved maps.

Outside, the storm had pushed on, leaving the air velvet soft. Leaning against a post, Maggie surveyed the distant ring of trees that encircled her home. In the twilight, it looked almost beautiful, a fairy kingdom tucked away behind an enchanted veil.

The illusion vanished as the wind picked up. It came from the east, a section of the forest that Maggie avoided whenever possible. Even in the winter, its scent was sweet with an undercurrent of rot, like gardenias growing from a corpse.

Her grandfather was buried in that part of the forest, along with twelve other generations of Drakefords. Sixty-one graves arranged around a hill and the hellish monument that marked the center of Witchwood. On clear days, one could make out some of the graves in the sunlight that filtered through the canopy, but Maggie hadn't gone there since last January, when something had whispered to her from beneath a headstone.

Maggie walked down to fetch wood from the pile they kept in the barn. The building smelled of damp and was barren except for some colorless drifts of old hay in the empty stalls. The Witchwood did not agree with domesticated animals. For centuries, any livestock the Drakefords managed to acquire had inevitably lost their minds. Within a week they'd go from crying out in mindless panic to braining themselves against the doors of their enclosures.

The barn had twelve stalls, but only three were ever used. These were located at the far end and reinforced with metal plating and iron bars. Having grabbed an armful of logs, Maggie peered into the nearest.

A black pit had been dug straight down into the hard-packed earth. Eight feet across and twice as deep. A rusted bucket and rope lay by the edge, along with a rocking chair, some busted lanterns, and a stack of old paperbacks that had largely disintegrated. Maggie's gaze wandered over the scene with mounting disgust. She could not bear the idea of her father in such a place.

"Never," she muttered, and marched away with her bundle.

Dinner was a quiet affair. Her father remained in his bedroom, too spent to join them. Maggie, Lump, and their mother ate by candlelight, sopping up carrot stew with homemade bread. Twice Lump tried to lighten up the mood by quizzing them on world history, only to receive a pair of weary stares. He appeared to be gauging whether more trivia would be advisable when something made them all jump.

There was a knock at the door.

No one moved. The three simply stared at one another in astonished silence.

They had not had a visitor in a decade, not since Reverend Farrow demanded a fresh sin-eater.

A knock meant someone was on the porch. And if someone was on the porch, that meant they'd ventured past the sign at the Witchwood's boundary. Impossible. No one would dare. A branch must have fallen, or perhaps a bird had flown into the door . . .

But there it was again. Louder, sharper, insistent.

Who in hell could it be?

An answer flashed in Maggie's mind: *the Ruyters.*

Her mother appeared to have reached the same conclusion. Getting up from the table, she snatched the shotgun off its pegs over the fireplace and loaded two shells into the receiver.

"Who's there?" she called, her voice tense and alert.

The knocking took on a frantic quality.

Mrs. Drakeford brought the shotgun up to her shoulder as she inched toward the door. "Thom Ruyter, you've got exactly three seconds to get your flabby ass off our property."

"Please open up," said a man's voice.

The voice outside sure didn't sound like Thom Ruyter. It was too cultured, too urbane. Hell, no one in Schemerdaal talked like that.

"Who is that?" called Mrs. Drakeford. "If you're from the census, I already mailed that in."

"Oh, for fuck's sake—I'm *not* from the census!"

A perplexed Elizabeth Drakeford glanced at her children before sliding back the dead bolt. As the door opened, Maggie leaned forward to glimpse a strikingly handsome man on the porch.

He wore a dark suit and an old-fashioned brimmed hat and might have struck an elegant figure if not for his stance, which was oddly hunched and pigeon toed. Maggie glanced at the objects he was holding. One was a black briefcase; the other a half-eaten burrito.

Mrs. Drakeford could barely find her voice. "Who are you?"

The stranger raised the burrito by way of greeting. "I'm Laszlo— and I need your toilet."

CHAPTER 5
A ONETIME OFFER

Mrs. Drakeford rested the shotgun on her forearm. "Didn't you see the sign?"

"Pff," said the visitor. "Signs are for *outsiders*. I'm an *insider*. Hell, I'm practically family and I'm here to help."

"He's insane," muttered Mrs. Drakeford, before addressing him directly. "You don't know the first thing about us."

"Oh, really?" Tapping his chin, the man looked her over in what Maggie thought was a very forward manner. "You're not a Drakeford by birth, or you'd look like something that slithered out of a crypt. But I'd wager Hubby isn't so lucky. Let me guess: he resembles a human omelet and is tucked someplace out of sight. Am I getting warm?"

Mrs. Drakeford gasped in surprise and rage. "How—"

"Listen, lady. If you don't point me to a toilet, you're going to have a second curse splattered all over this porch."

"There's a privy! Out back by the birch trees."

"How quaint," he said. "Back in a few." Clutching his briefcase, the man hurried out of sight.

Mrs. Drakeford closed the door and turned to her children. "Am I dreaming, or did that really just happen?"

"Really happened," Lump affirmed.

Elizabeth Drakeford hesitated, then bolted the door and rejoined them at the table. She did not return the shotgun to its pegs but laid it across her lap and gazed dazedly at the fire. Maggie had never seen her mother so unmoored.

"Should we wake up Dad?" she asked.

Her mother blinked. "What? God, no. I don't know how he'd react to a visitor."

"Do you think he's from the government?" said George.

"No."

Maggie reflected on the glimpse she'd gotten. "What about FBI? That hat's kind of FBI-ish."

Her mother shook her head. "Definitely not."

"How can you be certain?"

"The shoes."

Maggie had not noticed the gentleman's shoes, but she was now curious about what kind of footwear precluded a career in federal law enforcement.

She was about to inquire further when her mother raised a hand. "I need to think, Maggie."

The three sat in silence until there was a playful drumming on the door.

"I'm baaack," called a familiar voice.

When no one answered, their visitor tried the doorknob. "Weren't you listening?" he said impatiently. "I'm here to help!"

At length, Mrs. Drakeford rose and went to the door. "You can't help us," she said. "No one can."

The reply fairly dripped with sarcasm. "Well, I had no idea I was dealing with bona fide curse gurus. I'll just be on my way, then. Give my best to the frittata."

Lump swiveled toward Maggie. *What's a frittata?* he mouthed.

She held a finger to her lips.

"I didn't say I was a guru," said Mrs. Drakeford shakily. "It's just—"

The man groaned. "This isn't a time-share, lady. Curses can be broken."

"Not this curse."

"*Every* curse. That's part of the deal. Listen, I'm going to spare you details of what I did to your outhouse, but it might have been a war crime. The least I can do is help break the spell that's turning loved ones into breakfast entrées."

Mrs. Drakeford stiffened. "That's not funny. Bill's in pain!"

"Which is why you should hear me out," said the man reasonably. "Listen, I trekked all the way out here with a very special onetime offer. But the offer expires and the clock's ticking."

Biting her lip, the woman turned to Maggie and Lump. "What do you think?"

Maggie held up her bandaged arm. "Do we have anything to lose?" she asked pointedly.

Lump shrugged. "I'm with Maggie."

With a slow exhale, Mrs. Drakeford opened the door. Outside, their caller was now leaning against a post, examining his nails.

Mrs. Drakeford eyed him dubiously. "You're not a reporter?"

The man's grin reminded Maggie of a playful fox. "A reporter? Jesus, I'd rather work retail. No. I'm in the curse business, and I've come with a proposal that benefits all concerned. Play your cards right, and you could be torment-free this very week. I assume that would be agreeable?"

"Of course," said Mrs. Drakeford. "I'm sorry—did you say your name was Larry?"

The smile vanished. "Laszlo."

"Sorry. And your last name?"

He bridled. "What's wrong with Laszlo?"

"Nothing. Do you have a business card?"

The man laughed. "What, are you going to google me? You don't even have indoor plumbing. Besides, this is better than any card." He held up his briefcase. "Behold!"

Maggie's mother peered at it. "Is that backgammon?"

Laszlo looked affronted. "No, it is most certainly *not* backgammon. Madam, I give you the Drakeford Curse file. Original invocation. Terms. Conditions. You name it, it'll be in here."

The more Maggie listened to this Laszlo, the more she found herself disliking him. He was too flashy, too familiar. Everything he said had a smug and patronizing quality, as though he were doing them an enormous favor just by gracing them with his presence. When he was invited inside, Maggie glimpsed his shoes.

Definitely not FBI.

At least Laszlo had manners enough to remove his hat. He used it to fan himself as he gazed about the farmhouse and praised its "rustic appeal" before launching into a breezy anecdote about how he'd nursed a hangover one Sunday by watching HGTV and the couple (Laszlo didn't know why they were married; he thought she could do better) had renovated a place in Dutchess County. Had the Drakefords ever considered updating the backsplash? A new backsplash could work miracles. Just a tiny pop of color—something bold and zingy—could really spruce up these old shitboxes . . .

Mrs. Drakeford told Maggie and Lump to introduce themselves. When they did so, their visitor abandoned his rambling and made a courtly bow.

"Margaret and George," he purred. "How regal."

"Call me Lump."

"Yet possessing the common touch," added Laszlo smoothly. Those dazzling eyes turned to Maggie. She had never seen such a pure cornflower blue. The irises almost looked fake, like something touched up in a fashion spread. "And you?" he asked. "Any endearing nicknames I should know about?"

"Just Maggie."

Their visitor smiled but also appeared to size Maggie up. He turned his attention back to her brother, who was practically spellbound. "Would you like some advice, young man?"

Lump stood taller. "Yes, sir."

Laszlo adopted a stage whisper. "Never buy the last burrito! Remember that."

"I will, sir."

"Good boy."

The guy actually mussed Lump's hair. Maggie assumed her brother had enough sense to recoil, but instead he displayed a look of imbecilic rapture. Maggie was disappointed. At eleven, she'd been miles sharper when it came to reading people. Then again, she'd had to be.

No, this Laszlo was too slick and oily. Maggie studied him closely, looking for wires or hidden cameras. Spies and reporters always had that sort of thing on them.

Laszlo caught her staring. "I see someone's ready to get down to business."

Without further ado, he sat at the head of the table and set his briefcase upon its stained and knotted planks. Now that Maggie saw it up close, she found it disturbing. The object was clearly very old, with a delicate, almost dainty handle of ivory or bone. The sides were a black and dully lustrous material, intricately carved with bizarre figures and symbols. Maggie had no idea what the symbols meant, but the central image was chillingly familiar.

She'd seen its silhouette countless times, a bizarre outcrop that towered over her ancestors' graves in that sickly section of woods east of the farmhouse.

In local parlance, it was known as the Witchstone.

Maggie gestured at the case. "Where did you get this? Who told you what the Witchstone looks like?"

"No one," said Laszlo. "I've never even heard of this 'Witchstone' before. Forgive me, Maggie, but I'm sensing some skepticism. Rest assured that both this case and my proposal are authentic."

"And what is this proposal?" said Mrs. Drakeford.

"As I said, I'm in the curse business," Laszlo replied. "My firm doesn't cast the spells, but we manage them once they're up and running. We're an old outfit—downright ancient—but you won't read about us in the *Wall Street Journal*. We prefer to keep a low profile."

"Are you magicians?" asked Lump excitedly.

Laszlo flashed an easy smile. "If you like. Magic is part of the trade."

Mrs. Drakeford looked uneasy. "Does this firm have a name?"

"Of course," said Laszlo. "Officially we're 'the Ancient and Infernal

Society of Curse Keepers,' but that's a mouthful. Most just call us the Society. Call us whatever you like. What matters is that we exist, and I'm your humble Curse Keeper."

The three Drakefords stared at him.

"Our *what*?" said Maggie.

"Your Curse Keeper," Laszlo repeated. "Case Number B217, a.k.a. the Drakeford Curse, is assigned to yours truly. And while it's been my honor to look after it, I'm afraid the firm's clearing out stale inventory. Your curse has been marked for termination."

"Termination?" said Mrs. Drakeford. "Does that mean the curse is broken?"

"No," said Laszlo. "Quite the opposite. Termination means you have six days before I'm reassigned. Once that happens, your curse will no longer have an official Keeper, and you'll be stuck with it forever."

"But you said all spells could be broken."

"I said all *curses* could be broken," Laszlo countered. "Without a Keeper to certify that all the terms and conditions have been met, a curse isn't technically a curse anymore. It's just a nasty spell that can— and will—last forever."

"But that isn't fair," said Maggie. "It's not our fault you're being re- assigned."

Laszlo spread his hands. "I'm in your camp. But I don't make the rules. Just this morning, my boss said, 'Laszlo, those Drakefords haven't tried to break that curse in ages. They're happy the way things are, and I can't waste your talents on a dead-end case. You've got six days to wrap up this Drakeford business before I give it the old heave-ho.' Well, as soon as I heard that, I came straight here. The least I can do is give you a fighting chance."

"What's in it for you?" said Mrs. Drakeford.

Laszlo blinked. "Excuse me?"

She had recovered from the initial shock at receiving a visitor. Her manner had become more direct and businesslike, more like the person Maggie dealt with on a daily basis.

"You said your proposal benefits *both* parties," she said. "What do *you* get out of it?"

"Ah," said Laszlo, unfazed. "Excellent question. Here's how it works: your family gets a broken spell, and I get credit for ushering the curse through its life cycle, which means a nifty bonus and promotion. So when I say it's a win-win, that's exactly what I mean."

Maggie rested her elbows on the table. "Then why haven't you helped us before?"

"Sorry," said Laszlo. "Did I wander onto a witness stand?" He chuckled lamely before continuing. "Well, to answer your query, Margaret—"

"Maggie."

"Okay, Maggie. The answer's straightforward enough. I'm a busy guy, and your curse isn't the only one I manage. Ever hear of the Reykjavík Rat-Boy or the Topeka Terror?" She shook her head. Lump was fascinated. "Well, they're very prominent," said Laszlo. "And those are just a few of the curses in my portfolio. I can't hold everyone's hand, and frankly, it was never my job to break the Drakeford Curse. That's *your* job. It's not my fault you've been slacking."

"Slacking?" Maggie exclaimed. "I didn't even know this was something that *could* be broken! I thought it was a disease we inherited. This is the first I've ever heard of a curse, much less someone who manages it. What does a Curse Keeper even do?"

She glared at their visitor, her eyes blazing in challenge. How dare this jackass waltz in here and suggest they'd been negligent! Had this Laszlo *ever seen* her father? Did he honestly believe Maggie wouldn't be doing everything humanly possible if she thought it could help? As her outrage soared, their visitor merely yawned. She had never seen such a complacent and dismissive gesture. It was like a cat waking from a midday nap.

"Listen," he said. "We can point fingers all night. I may be handsome, witty, and modest, but I'm not perfect. If it makes you feel better, I'll admit I could have been more—what's the word?—*proactive* with my communications. Happy?"

"No."

The man glanced at his fancy watch and drummed his fingers. "We've only got six days, but if you want to spend the time being *snippy*, that's up to you." He looked to Mrs. Drakeford. "You know, maybe it's better if I leave . . ."

As he pushed back from the table, Maggie made no attempt to stop him. This Laszlo was a fraud and a liar. Lump might not see it, but it was obvious. The guy probably worked for one of the tabloids whose headlines advertised alien abductions and miracle diets. His name probably wasn't even Laszlo. It was probably Steve or Lance. She could definitely see him being a Lance.

Clutching his case, he walked slowly toward the door. Maggie stifled a laugh. She hadn't seen such a hammy performance since Bonnie Groot sobbed through her husband's funeral.

Mrs. Drakeford rose from her chair. "Please don't go, Laszlo. Maggie didn't mean to offend you. She just has a habit of being rather direct."

"Wonder where I got that from," muttered Maggie.

Her mother shot her a warning glance before hurrying over to intercept him. "We'd love to hear more about this offer you mentioned. Please sit down, Laszlo. We're so grateful you've come all this way. Can I make you some tea?"

Laszlo smiled appreciatively. "That would be lovely. Unless you have anything stronger."

"What did you have in mind?"

"Tequila?"

"Ha!" Maggie snorted. "Some professional!"

"Maggie," Mrs. Drakeford snapped. "That's enough. Apologize."

"I won't! The guy's a fraud, and he's been lying since he got here. A 'Curse Keeper'? Don't make me laugh. It's ridiculous!"

Maggie felt Lump poking her shoulder, but she barreled on. "So who tipped you off about us?" she pressed Laszlo. "The Ruyters? That's how you know our history, isn't it? You heard a few stories and drove up here to trick us into giving you a scoop for some sleazy tabloid. So tell me, O Curse Keeper . . . *am I getting warm?*"

The final line was delivered in what Maggie thought was a pretty decent impression of Laszlo's earlier line about her dad resembling an omelet. Leaning back, she folded her arms and waited for a response. She did not expect it to come from behind her.

"Who . . . ?" said a barely intelligible voice.

Maggie turned. Her father was in the hallway, hunched low in his wheelchair. His solitary eye shone from the shadows, round and pale as the moon. It was fixed on Laszlo.

"Who . . . ?" he repeated, followed by something guttural Maggie could not understand. He rattled the wheelchair in agitation. "*Who!*"

Bill Drakeford pushed himself forward. Springing up, Maggie intercepted the chair and took firm hold of its arms. "He's just a salesman, Dad. He's leaving."

Her father's arms might have been malformed, but their strength was superhuman. The ensuing scene was absurd, like a rabbit trying to hold back a rhino. Maggie slid backward over the floorboards.

"Let . . . go," her father wheezed.

Maggie's mother and Lump hurried over to help. Laszlo held up a tentative hand.

"Mr. Drakeford," he said. "Bill? *Billy?* Please calm yourself . . ."

But Mr. Drakeford had no wish to calm down. Despite his family's efforts, the wheelchair advanced steadily like a tank through mud. Laszlo backed against the door.

And then Maggie's father let out a gasp. That hideous strength ebbed like an outrushing tide. As she felt his body go limp, Maggie relaxed her grip and let go.

Her father did not move. Bill Drakeford sat panting in the wheelchair, his glaucous eye fixed not on Laszlo but on the ebony case their visitor held up like a shield. His manner was oddly quiet, even awed. When he spoke, his voice was choked thick with emotion. For the first time in months, Maggie could make out every word.

"Are you the Curse Keeper?"

CHAPTER 6
TERMS AND CONDITIONS

Dad Thing was even more revolting than Laszlo had imagined: a twisted mountain of muscle and sinew adorned with a single eye, a nose like melted candle wax, and the rictus of a two-week-old corpse. And there he was, bulling forward in his wheelchair, his family clinging to him like starfish trying to halt a barge. Laszlo found his back pressed flat against the door, his pulse dancing the rhumba. Dad Thing's gaze alternated between him and the briefcase.

"Are we . . . quite calm?" Laszlo inquired.

Dad Thing's reply came in hoarse wheezes. "You . . . Keeper?"

"The Curse Keeper?" said Laszlo. "Why, yes, I am." He shot Maggie an indignant glance.

The girl ignored him. "Dad, why didn't you ever tell us about this man?"

Dad Thing gazed up at his daughter. "Didn't believe . . ." he rasped. "No Keeper for years . . ." That hideous eye swiveled back to Laszlo. "*Why?*"

Dabbing his forehead with his pocket square, Laszlo tried to rekindle his mojo. "Why am I here? Simple. I'm here to bring this travesty to a close. My boss wants your curse off the books, Mr. Drakeford, and if you'll forgive me, it looks like you've had enough of it yourself. I was about to offer my services when the young lady accused me of being a fraud."

Raising his chin, Laszlo did his best to look like a martyr. The girl muttered something he did not catch. Laszlo was going to enjoy watching her devolve into a monster.

"If *Margaret* would permit me to continue," he said drolly, "I'd be happy to explain."

Mrs. Drakeford righted a toppled chair. "By all means. Please sit down."

Once again, Laszlo sat like a pasha at the head of the table. When the others joined him, he set the ebony case before him and cleared his throat.

"As I was saying, this is the official Drakeford Curse folio. It's got all the goodies we're going to use to break the spell by next Thursday. Normally, I wouldn't give out hints, but desperate times require desperate measures. I read that somewhere."

"Hippocrates?" said Mrs. Drakeford.

"Fortune cookie. Anyhoo, what I'm saying is I can't break the curse for you. I can give winks and nudges. Hell, I'll give you the recipe. But you'll have to do the work."

Mrs. Drakeford looked anxiously at her husband. "What would we have to do?"

Laszlo unfastened the case's clasps. "Let's have a look, shall we?" As he opened it, the Drakeford boy—Dump or Stump or whatever his name was—made a face.

"Eww," he said. "It smells disgusting."

"It's a curse," said Laszlo. "It's supposed to reek."

Reaching within, he removed three scrolls and fanned them out on the table like a card dealer. The nearest was tied with a red ribbon labeled *Incantatio*. Taking it up, Laszlo passed it beneath his nose like a Cohiba cigar.

"Original spell," he purred. "I'm getting notes of blood, sulfur, and a dash of citrus." He fluttered the scroll at Maggie. "Care for a whiff?"

"I'll pass. What does it say?"

Unrolling the parchment, Laszlo glanced at the spell and immediately did a double take. *Is it all like this?* He scanned the dense script with rising panic. So many vowels. No language should have that many vowels. It was indecent. Why couldn't the witch have gone with a classic like Latin or Greek?

"Is there a problem?" said Mrs. Drakeford.

"No," said Laszlo. "It's just . . . well, do any of you happen to speak High Dutch?"

Seven eyes stared at him.

Laszlo rolled the scroll back up. "No biggie. Who needs all that 'double, double toil and trouble' nonsense? Pretentious tripe, I say. These witches all think they're poets."

"But could the spell contain information we need?" wondered Mrs. Drakeford.

"I doubt it," said Laszlo. "But don't worry. I've got a guy who lives for this stuff. Rare breed. Pure nerd. Besides, all we need at the moment is this baby."

He waved the second scroll, which had *Materia* inscribed on its ribbon. "This is more like it," he said, perusing its contents. "Good old English, plain as . . ."

Once again, the demon trailed off into preoccupied silence.

"Are you okay?" asked Lump.

Laszlo shot the boy a glance. "Of course," he muttered. "Everything's peachy. Just a big ol' delicious peach . . ."

"But you look ill."

"Do I? There's a first. No, it's just that this list is a bit more *involved* than I remember."

As he spoke, Laszlo caught Maggie watching him closely. He didn't care for those steely blue eyes. Too shrewd by half. Just as he was about to request a glass of water, the girl snatched the scroll from his fingers.

"Hey," said Laszlo. "Hand that over."

"It's the *Drakeford* Curse," she retorted. "We have a right to see it for ourselves."

"Maggie," said Mrs. Drakeford warningly. Laszlo didn't know why the mom even bothered. It was clear the daughter had already left the nest—if not in body, then in mind. Any day now she'd be living on ramen, bouncing rent checks, and stealing her neighbor's Wi-Fi.

Sure enough, Maggie ignored her mother and was already reading. "It's a list of what we need," she said eagerly. "'Something loved, something hated, something found . . .'" She scrunched up her face. "'Blood of saints'?"

Laszlo rolled his eyes. Humans didn't know anything. "Holy relic," he translated.

"'Wealth of nations' . . ."

"Crown jewels."

"'Spark of creation'?"

"Magic item," he yawned.

Maggie looked round the table, visibly dismayed. "Crown jewels? A magic item? Where are we supposed to get this stuff?"

Laszlo snatched back the scroll. "Let *me* worry about that. And it wouldn't hurt if you showed a little respect. I am a demon, after all."

The boy sat up with interest and adjusted his glasses. "A demon! You're joking."

"I'm not."

Maggie sneered. "A *demon*? Please. If you're a demon, prove it."

Laszlo paid back the sneer with interest. "Listen, Katniss, I don't have to 'prove' anything. What are we, on a playground? Take it from me—you're looking at a bona fide demon. Class III, thank you very much."

The boy was now appraising him with unsettling intensity. Laszlo felt as though he were an exotic species of butterfly. "How many classes of demon are there?" Lump asked eagerly. "Is Class III a high rank?"

"Not important," said Laszlo quickly. "What *is* important is breaking the curse that's turning your dad into a sloppy joe." He held the scroll up for all to see. "Now, I'll admit this isn't your everyday shopping list, but I'm not your everyday shopper. I can show you where to get this stuff. You just need to gather it up and follow the witch's recipe."

"And where is the recipe?" said Maggie. "As far as I can tell, that's just a list."

Clucking his tongue, Laszlo scanned the scroll more closely. He had to admit that the girl was right. It didn't contain anything resembling instructions. He took up the third and final document, the scroll labeled *Cruciati*. No good. That one just spelled out the curse's punishments.

Laszlo set it down. Three things vexed him at the moment. The first was this sharp and troublesome Maggie. The second was her creepy-ass brother, who looked ready to pin him to a corkboard. The third was himself. Laszlo really should have examined the case's contents before dropping in on these hicks. Now he'd have to improvise. Fortunately, improvisation was his specialty.

Just as he was about to speak, however, Laszlo caught the mother eyeing him. "What?" he asked.

"Are you really a demon?"

"Yes. Is that a problem?"

"It might be."

Leaning back, Laszlo knit his fingers together. "Is this when you tell me you've got something against demons?"

"Don't most people?"

"Not the smart ones," said Laszlo. "Not the ones who understand that we're just independent thinkers who didn't like being ordered around. Really, demons are no different than the Pilgrims, and you celebrate those stiffs every Thanksgiving. Where's *my* holiday?"

Lump raised his hand. "Does Halloween count?"

Laszlo ignored the twerp and kept his attention on the mom. If Mrs. Drakeford found his argument persuasive, her face did not show it.

"How do we know we can trust you?" she asked.

Laszlo shrugged. "You don't. But believe me, I'm not here out of charity. Breaking the curse gets me some goodies, but it's nothing compared to your haul. Wouldn't you like your husband back, Mrs. Drakeford? Wouldn't you sleep better knowing your sassy daughter and strapping son have been spared the hideous doom that awaits them? I'm giving you that chance. Are you going to throw it away because I happen to be a *demon*? Forgive me, but that sounds a bit discriminatory."

Was she buying it? Laszlo couldn't tell. The woman could have joined the poker circuit. At length, she sighed.

"Okay," she said. "Assuming we can get everything on that list, what are we supposed to do with it? I mean, what was this witch trying to accomplish anyway?"

Laszlo rubbed his hands together. "Solution oriented. I like it. Well, seeing as the instructions aren't in the file, I'm going to guess they're on this 'Witchstone' thing. Is there any writing on it? Any mysterious inscriptions?"

"We stay away from the Witchstone," said Maggie. "That part of the wood doesn't feel right."

Laszlo nodded knowingly. "That's common with Curse Objects. In the city we call such feelings 'the willies.'"

Mrs. Drakeford pursed her lips. "These aren't *the willies*, Mr. Laszlo. There's something wrong with that stone. Something evil."

A voice spoke up, the words distorted by a swollen tongue. "They . . . call to me."

All eyes turned to Mr. Drakeford. Throughout their discussion, he had been sitting quietly with his hands folded in his lap. Now, those hands were twisting the hem of his shirt.

"Who calls to you, Bill?" asked his wife.

The man struggled to form the words. "Drakefords . . . dreams!"

Laszlo waved off the drama. "Standard stuff," he said. "Death doesn't end a curse, my speech-challenged amigo. If mortals could weasel out of a curse just by *dying*, everyone would head to the nearest cliff."

Maggie Drakeford had gone pale. For a moment, her bristling toughness was gone. She looked younger, more vulnerable, as if some inner spark had been extinguished. *Good*, thought Laszlo. Maybe now she'd show some proper respect.

The girl turned to her father. "So they're suffering? Grandpa and Uncle Dave and all the rest? After all that suffering, they're *still* not at peace?"

Time to apply some pressure, thought Laszlo. "Peace?" he laughed. "Oh, there's no chance of that. Like I said, PMT—a.k.a. postmortem torment—comes standard with curses, even basic models. And you should see some of the fancier spells. Why, there's a curse in my office where—"

Maggie smacked her fist against the table. "We need to end this."

And the flame rekindles, observed Laszlo wryly. His first instinct was to be annoyed; Maggie had interrupted one of his favorite anecdotes, a gruesome tale with a kick-ass twist. Was there anything worse than a plucky human? Probably not. Then again, maybe that pluck could be put to good use. This girl wanted to be a hero. Hell, she *longed* to be a hero in some secret corner of her heart. Well, far be it from Laszlo to deny a young lady her dreams . . .

The demon thumped the table in kind. "Amen! That, ladies and gentlemen, is *precisely* the kind of spunk that's going to free this family. Let's go have a peek at that Witchstone. I've got an awful good feeling about this."

CHAPTER 7

CHERNOBYL

Only three of them made the trip.

The area near the Witchstone was too swampy for a wheelchair, so Dad Thing and the boy stayed behind while Laszlo and the gals set out with lanterns and flashlights. Mom also brought the shotgun, which made Laszlo a wee bit uncomfortable. A shotgun might not hurt a greater demon, but it worked just fine on Class IIIs like Laszlo. He knew firsthand from a robbery he'd committed in the Hamptons back in the Gilded Age.

Laszlo recalled the event with a trace of nostalgia. Yes, he'd fallen two stories into a rosebush. And no, it didn't bolster one's self-esteem to flail about and shriek in front of a US senator and fifty of his favorite donors. But on the whole, it had been a magical evening, from the soprano to the stars to the bubbly. Sure, Laszlo had been obliged to flee and caught some bird shot in the ass, but no one had threatened to *crucible* him. No Overseers had loaded him up with impossible demands or were counting the minutes until he could be rendered into gloop. And with official permission, no less!

Laszlo still couldn't believe his father had given Androvore his blessing.

He tapped the hourglass in the inside pocket of his jacket. Nothing seemed to affect it. Flipping it upside down, turning cartwheels, minor cantrips, nada. Almost nine thousand grains, and not one was beholden to gravity. It wouldn't matter if Laszlo launched the fucking thing into outer space. Every minute, a grain would tumble dutifully into the collecting bulb. When the last one was gone, his time was up.

Laszlo reviewed his plan. In retrospect, maybe he should have forged some docs that made breaking the curse look like a snap. Then again, that might have backfired. The Drakefords were a shrewder bunch than he'd expected, and might have balked if the solution appeared too easy.

At any rate, that ship had sailed: Maggie had seen the list. And what a list it was. He needed to speak with Dimitri as soon as possible. If anyone knew how to acquire the rare and exotic, it was Dimitri.

A voice intruded on his thoughts. The girl herself was walking beside him. Her lantern illuminated her from below, giving her face the appearance of an evil, or at least disapproving, jackrabbit. Laszlo smiled down at her. What would that face look like when he ground its dreams beneath his heel?

"Come again?" he said.

"Who's Dimitri?"

"Who?"

"Dimitri," said Maggie. "You keep muttering his name."

"No one," said Laszlo. "A friend." He craned his neck at the surroundings. "So where is this Witchstone thing? This field's practically a swamp. It's ruining my shoes."

Maggie glanced down at his Guccis. "Pity."

"Not much farther," said Mrs. Drakeford. "A little past that stream."

Laszlo peered some hundred yards ahead, where moonlight rippled on a ribbon of water. Beyond was a dark wood, its depths impenetrable even to Laszlo's eyes, which were attuned to a broader spectrum of light than a human's.

And then he felt it.

The jolt was so strong and unexpected it stopped Laszlo cold. Startled, he glanced at the others to see if they had sensed what he had. The Drakefords looked at him with puzzled expressions.

"Mosquito," he said, and smacked his neck.

But this was no insect. Laszlo's entire body was tingling. His instincts were whispering to him now, urging him to turn around and scamper back the way he'd come.

The idea was tempting, until he recalled those falsetto screams as Loudmouth was melted down in a superheated funnel. He had no choice but to proceed.

With every step, however, it felt like wading into an ocean, into waves of intensifying force. His skin no longer tingled, but throbbed like the dull ache from a sunburn. Whatever was in those woods didn't just feel magical.

It felt radioactive.

It felt *dangerous*.

The sensation was unsettling, but it also made Laszlo curious. And Curiosity (Laszlo pictured her as a buxom redhead) was something he'd never been able to resist. Over the centuries, Curiosity had broken both his heart and his bones. She'd left him humiliated, bankrupt, even clapped in irons. And yet, despite countless betrayals, Laszlo continued to love her with a deep and abiding passion. Curiosity kept life interesting, no small thing when one was immortal. No matter how many times she burned him, he would always take her call.

And she was calling now.

What the hell is in those woods? Laszlo hadn't felt power like this since his father's last investiture. By the time he reached the stream, every nerve was on fire. Normally, running water wasn't high on Laszlo's list of favorite things. As was the case for most magical beings, the stuff left him feeling unsteady and disoriented. Now its effects barely registered. Laszlo's curiosity was so thoroughly piqued that he didn't even care that his Guccis were caked in mud. Something unusual—nay, *unique*—was ahead, and Laszlo desperately wished to see it.

Moonlight vanished as they ventured in among the trees. Yellow light from their lanterns danced on tree trunks and undergrowth. The terrain underfoot was uneven and hummocky with centuries of accumulated leaf fall. The Drakefords each clamped a hand over their noses. A moment later, Laszlo understood why. A miasma seeped up from the soil, a clinging sweetness mingled with the smell of death and rot. He reached for his handkerchief.

More streams lay ahead. A network of them laced the wood, gurgling softly as they ran in dark rivulets. Some could be traversed with an ambitious hop. Others required old-school clambering, a skill at which Maggie Drakeford excelled. While Laszlo gasped and grunted, she bounded over banks like an overachieving fawn. He was tempted to trip her.

The latest bank was the steepest yet. Laszlo had nearly reached the top when the root he'd grasped pulled free of the soil. He lunged for a stone slab above, clinging to its slimy base and kicking wildly for a foothold. Lanterns bobbed toward him. Mrs. Drakeford extended a hand, pulling him up until he was on solid footing. With a grunt of gratitude, Laszlo leaned against the slab to catch his breath. Its surface was pitted and scored with crude chisel marks.

EMILY DRAKEFORD
1781–1827

Turning about, Laszlo saw similar stones jutting from the soil like broken teeth. There were dozens of them arranged in concentric rings around a nightmarish monument that sat atop a hill dotted with dead trees and tangled undergrowth. Laszlo stared at it in stunned and speechless awe.

He had had no idea the Witchstone would be so huge.

It towered above the nearest graves like an eruption from the underworld, a mass of black stone some thirty or forty feet tall. Laszlo's gaze wandered over its tortured shapes and cresting spires. He could not say if the contours were natural or the product of some artistic fancy. All he knew was that to look upon the Witchstone struck a chord of dread he had never experienced before.

Was it a sculpture? A shrine? As he climbed the hill, Laszlo took a winding path to get a better sense of the whole. From one angle, the Witchstone resembled a skeletal hand; from others, a set of alien bagpipes or some prehistoric sea creature dredged up from the ocean floor. The object utterly baffled him. What *was* this thing?

"Well?" said Mrs. Drakeford expectantly.

Laszlo cleared his throat. "Not exactly a Bernini."

"But what *is* it?" said Maggie eagerly. "What was that witch doing?"

Good question. Laszlo borrowed a flashlight from Mrs. Drakeford and continued circling. The pale beam jittered over twisted forms and planes. Laszlo did not like this Witchstone one bit; it was every flavor of wrong. He took several pictures with his phone. There was no writing or any symbols he could see, but the lower section, which had a more architectural flavor, was overgrown by creepers. He turned to Maggie.

"Be a good assistant and clear those away."

"Are you going to help?"

Laszlo ignored her and continued his perusal. Maggie began to argue, but her mother merely got started. Maggie eventually joined her, and the pair made short work of the vines, which they piled in a stinking mound off to one side. The smell and surroundings took Laszlo back to his grave-robbing days, a brief dalliance involving lots of mess and several transactions at a local medical college. Repositioning his handkerchief, the demon used his flashlight to revisit sections the Drakefords had uncovered. The surface was coated in lichen and grime, but there didn't seem to be—

Hold on.

Laszlo stepped to one edge of the cleared portion and tugged at the nearest vines. They pulled free with little resistance, revealing a series of letters or symbols. Unfortunately, the inscriptions were so worn away Laszlo couldn't read them. Not that he was much of a linguist.

"Over here," he called. "Clear away these creepers."

As the Drakefords ripped and pulled, Laszlo swept his flashlight over the surrounding wood. The atmosphere was changing. The air had become tinged with a different sort of energy than the raw power pulsing from the Witchstone. More emotional, more human. There was a watchfulness in it. And malice.

"Hurry up," he said, and snapped another series of pictures.

More vines fell away, revealing a crude bowl or basin several feet across. Laszlo shuddered at the sight of it. From his vantage, the thing looked like a primitive mouth carved into the stone. He took another photo.

"What is that?" said Mrs. Drakeford, gazing uneasily at it.

Laszlo shrugged.

"Aren't *you* supposed to know?" said Maggie.

"Listen," said Laszlo. "I handle lots of curses. I can't be expected to memorize every scrap of minutiae. Get closer, so I can fit you in the frame."

"Why?" said Maggie.

"Scale." She obliged, and he snapped the photo. As he did, an anguished cry sounded nearby. Laszlo nearly jumped out of his shoes.

"What was that?" he hissed. "A fox?"

Maggie and her mother had gone perfectly still, a pair of spooked does. The cry sounded again, from a different location. Laszlo spun about, trying to pinpoint the source.

There was a third cry to his right. And now another just behind him. Trickles of cold mist issued from the forest floor. The Drakefords backed away from the Witchstone. So did Laszlo, who promptly tripped over the grave behind him. As he lay sprawled in the dirt, a spectral scream—hoarse and earsplitting—issued from the headstone.

"*Ghosts!*" Laszlo shouted to no one in particular. "We're surrounded by ghosts!"

Scrambling to his feet, he did what any sensible demon would do when confronted by the supernatural.

He fled.

Despite his love of leisure and cigarettes, Laszlo had always been a decent runner. It was half a mile from the Witchstone to the Drakeford residence, yet the demon covered it in less than three minutes. Once there, he found the Drakeford men—or rather, Dad Thing and Future Thing—on the porch, anxiously watching the woods.

Laszlo waved before succumbing to a fit of coughing.

"Where are they?" asked the boy. "Where's my mom and Maggie?"

"Right . . . behind . . . me," wheezed Laszlo.

"Are they okay?" pressed the boy. "We heard noises."

Laszlo spat out a wad of phlegm. "They're fine. Everyone's fine! There were some spectral screams and whatnot, but that's standard stuff. Perfectly normal. Hold on—I have to make a call."

The boy said something else, but Laszlo ignored him and tried his therapist.

Dr. Nussbaum had warned him about pestering her at home, but this was a goddamn emergency. Nobody had told him that the Drakeford Curse involved hostile ghosts! Pressing the phone to his ear, Laszlo waited impatiently for it to ring. When it did not, he glanced at the screen. *No service.*

"Oh, for fuck's sake."

"I tried to tell you," Lump said. "Cell phones don't work up here."

"No," Laszlo muttered. "Of course not. Why would they? It's only the twenty-first century."

"Sorry."

Laszlo simmered a moment before glancing over. "Uh, just out of curiosity. What *is* the Witchstone?"

Before the kid could answer, a voice sounded behind Laszlo. "Aren't *you* supposed to know that?"

He turned just as Maggie and her mother emerged from the darkness. Once again, Mrs. Drakeford was hefting the shotgun. This time, it was pointed in his direction.

"Well, well," she said. "I guess you were telling the truth."

"Listen," said Laszlo. "Sorry for freaking out, but I kind of have a thing with ghosts. I was in Tibet once, and—"

Maggie shot him a disgusted look and gestured briefly at Laszlo's face.

The demon quickly covered it with his hand. "What's wrong? A booger? Jesus, do I have boog—"

"Your disguise slipped, jackass."

What? Laszlo used his phone's camera as a mirror. Sure enough, when he peered into the screen, he found a disheveled blue-skinned fiend peering back at him.

"Well, that's awkward," he admitted, and reverted to his human guise. "But hey, at least you know I'm not a reporter." He laughed weakly.

Mrs. Drakeford took dead aim. "No," she said. "You're a demon."

Laszlo held up his hands. "Calm down, will you? If you let me explain—"

A click as the woman cocked the shotgun's hammer. "Enough with the BS," she snapped. "*Who are you and why are you here?*"

Laszlo tried not to stare down the gun's barrel. "As I said, my name's Laszlo, and I'm your Curse Keeper. Every word of that is true. I may have stretched things a little with *why* I'm here." He scrambled to put a convincing spin on the situation, which meant seasoning his story with the incomplete truth. "You see, I've got a new boss—a bona fide prick—and the guy has it out for me. Long story short, I've got six days to put your curse to bed, or I'm going to be crucibled."

"Crucibled?" said Lump. "What's that?"

"I'll be melted down," Laszlo explained. "Destroyed. Annihilated. So really, we're on the same team. We've got until Thursday to break the curse. If we don't, you'll be monsters and I'll be toast. More of a Slurpee, actually."

"How do we know you're telling the truth?" asked Mrs. Drakeford.

Laszlo removed Androvore's hourglass from his jacket and held it up. "See this? When the sand runs out, I'm kaput, and so's your chance at breaking the spell. Like it or not, we need each other."

Maggie spoke up. "But what good *are* you?" she asked coldly. "You don't seem to know anything about this curse. You don't even know what the Witchstone *is*!"

"But I know who to ask," Laszlo countered. "And I know where to find the things. Do *you* know where to find relics and royal jewels?"

Maggie opened her mouth and promptly closed it again.

"Didn't think so," said Laszlo. "Look, we got off on the wrong foot. That's my bad, and I apologize. I get that you're pissed, but that doesn't change the situation. Can I make a suggestion?"

Mrs. Drakeford did not return his grin. "Do."

"Let's sleep on it. I'll grab a room in the village and come back bright and early. In the meantime, talk things over and decide if you want to take your only shot at cracking this."

"And if we say no?" said Mrs. Drakeford.

Laszlo spread his hands. "I've got a head start on the boss's goons."

Maggie Drakeford pointed at the ebony case. "And the file stays with us."

Laszlo set the case down. "All yours."

The family went inside and held a brief conference, in which it was decided that Laszlo's proposal was acceptable. Mrs. Drakeford delivered the verdict from the porch. She gazed down at Laszlo, the shotgun resting casually on the railing.

"Come back at seven," she said. "Don't be late."

"Yes, ma'am."

Snapping off a salute, Laszlo turned and set off for the hedge. As the night swallowed him, a grin spread across his film-star features. The Drakefords could play hard to get, but they'd be joining the fun whether they liked it or not. Late? Not a chance in hell. Laszlo had no intention of being late.

In fact, he'd be several hours early.

CHAPTER 8
DEAD LETTERS

Once the demon left, the Drakefords again gathered around the table. Laszlo's briefcase sat in the center like a ticking time bomb.

Maggie wanted to open it at once and scour the contents, but haste was apparently not on the agenda. Her mother had returned to her measured self. She made tea and draped a blanket over Maggie's father, who sat in his wheelchair gazing at the dying fire.

As usual, it was Lump who broke the silence. "Did anyone think they'd meet a demon today?"

No one answered him.

"Well, I didn't," he continued. "Sort of creepy, I guess, especially when his disguise slipped. But also kind of neat."

"George," said Mrs. Drakeford, "there is nothing *neat* about meeting a demon."

"But he's trying to help us."

"Really? I get the sense he's trying to help himself."

Maggie saw her opportunity. "But it comes to the same thing, doesn't it?" she said. "We *all* need the curse broken."

"You said yourself he doesn't know anything about the Witchstone," her mother replied. "And you saw his reaction to the spirits. Demon or not, he was terrified."

"I did see," said Maggie. "Which is why I think he's telling the truth. Laszlo didn't *want* to come here. He doesn't care about this curse, or any one of us. If he did, we'd have heard from him before."

"Exactly," said Mrs. Drakeford. "Which is why I know we can't trust him. Maggie, I'm sorry, but you haven't seen anything of the real world."

"Well, it's not for lack of trying," Maggie snapped. Two years earlier, she'd borrowed Gladys to "run errands" and secretly taken the SATs at a high school in Kingston. When her scores arrived in the mail, Maggie thought her mother would be proud. Instead, she'd received a lecture about the difference between being honest and being forthright.

Her mother caught the drift at once. Pursing her lips, she stirred her tea. "What I meant is that the world is full of hustlers like this Laszlo. Let me deal with him."

"Let *you*?" said Maggie. "Sorry, but are you kidding?"

"No, I'm not. Is there a problem with that?"

"Yes," said Maggie. "A big one. It's insane for the one person here who *isn't* cursed to be making decisions for those who are. Forgive my language, but it's batshit crazy."

Lump looked stunned, and Maggie felt a twinge of guilt. She hadn't intended to raise her voice, much less cuss with her brother present.

Their mother had gone very still.

"You don't think I'm cursed?" she said quietly. "You don't think this affects me too?" She gestured at the briefcase on the table.

Maggie exhaled. "It's not the same thing," she said wearily. "I'm sorry, Mom, but it isn't."

"Well, you're right about that," said Elizabeth Drakeford. "I can only be a spectator to my family's suffering. I can stitch wounds, but I can't take away your pain. I can't even share it—Reverend Farrow won't let me. My experience may not be the same, Maggie, but don't pretend for one second that this curse doesn't take a toll on me. I'm practically a slave to it."

It was the word *slave* that triggered fresh indignation. Maggie glared across the table, wondering how such a smart person could be so stupid. She supposed it came from always needing to be right.

Her mother caught her look and folded her arms, braced for battle. "You don't agree?"

Maggie nearly laughed. "You're *not* a slave, Mom! Can't you see that? You don't have to be here. You can leave this place whenever you want. Nothing will follow you. Nothing's in your blood. Anytime you feel like it, you can mosey on back to Connecticut. You can forget all about us and—"

"Enough."

Her mother had not raised her voice a single decibel, but Maggie felt as though she'd been slapped. She sat in silence, fingernails digging into her palms, ashamed of how, even at nineteen, her mother could make her feel like a child. The next time she spoke, it was in a more deliberate tone. "All I'm trying to say is that you have choices we don't have."

"Yes," replied her mother. "I could have gone—but I *chose* to stay." She paused. "You don't have to like that, Maggie, but I ask you to respect it. Do we understand each other?"

Another pause. "Yes."

An awkward silence ensued. Lump looked from one to the other. "So what are we going to do?" he asked.

Mrs. Drakeford took a steadying breath. "We'll start by examining that case. Maggie, please hand it over."

Maggie did so and watched complacently as her mother struggled with the clasps. No matter what she did, Elizabeth Drakeford's fingers slipped off the metal as if they'd been coated with the slickest substance imaginable. Three times. Four. She simply couldn't get a grip. On the fifth attempt, she tried using a dish towel. It made no difference.

"Just a thought," said Maggie. "But maybe the case only opens for people who are *cursed.*"

Her mother gave a warning glance but conceded defeat. "All right," she said. "You try."

Maggie was only too happy. Taking the bony handle, she set the case on her lap and took firm hold of the clasps. Or tried to. Maggie had no more success than her mother. Neither did Lump.

"That's so weird," he said, rubbing his forefinger and thumb together. "It's like there's an invisible layer of oil."

Maggie grunted. "Maybe Laszlo's the only one who can open it."

"You're probably right," said Mrs. Drakeford, "which is all the more reason not to trust him."

"Why?" said Lump.

"Because he either knew we wouldn't be able to open it and didn't tell us, or he didn't know himself," replied their mother. "He's either sneaky or ignorant. Possibly both."

Maggie drummed her fingers on the table. "Then why do you think he came here?"

Mrs. Drakeford sipped her tea. "I don't know, Maggie, but I don't like it. This Laszlo says he's the curse's Keeper, but I'm finding that hard to believe. He's nothing like the other one."

Maggie ceased her drumming and looked up sharply. "*What other one?*"

Maggie would later wonder whether this was the moment her life truly changed course. Not the morning she noticed a mark on her forearm. Not even when Laszlo knocked at their door. It was *this* moment— that fleeting instant when Maggie registered the look of alarm and self-reproach on her mother's face.

For the first time in living memory, Elizabeth Drakeford had made a blunder.

Maggie kept her cool. "What other one?" she inquired evenly. "Another Curse Keeper?"

Instead of replying, Mrs. Drakeford looked long and searchingly at Maggie's father. Bill Drakeford shifted in his seat and returned his wife's gaze before giving an almost imperceptible nod.

She turned to Lump. "George, please go to your room." Lump issued his standard protests, but this time his mother wouldn't play along. "It's not up for debate."

"But why?" he asked. Unlike Maggie, Lump usually received answers to his questions.

"Because some things are inappropriate for the ears of an eleven-year-old boy. Please, George. I don't have the energy to argue."

Lump grumbled about "ageism" but relented nevertheless and

retreated to his tiny bedroom shoehorned beneath the eaves. Maggie knew he'd double back and try to hide on the landing, but their mother was wise to his tricks and sent him packing when he attempted it. Ultimately, he had no choice but to sit in his room with a battered copy of *The Swiss Family Robinson*.

When she was certain Lump was out of earshot, Mrs. Drakeford went to the back of the farmhouse and down some steps to the root cellar. She soon returned with a discolored cedar chest that she set heavily on the table. She did not look at Maggie as she spoke.

"Understand that we never wanted to mislead you. We wanted to protect you."

"From what?"

Her mother turned to her. "Hope can be a beautiful thing, Maggie. But it can also be dangerous. Hope took David's life."

Maggie blinked. David Drakeford had been her father's younger brother. Maggie had no memories of her uncle. He'd been killed shortly after she'd been born. "Uncle Dave? You said he died in a car accident."

"We lied," said her mother simply. "We wanted to spare you a sadder truth. Your uncle David committed suicide, Maggie. We didn't want you and George to know."

Maggie digested this slowly. "Why are you telling me now?"

Her mother tapped the chest. "It's the reason we've kept this secret."

Maggie's gaze alternated between her parents. "I still don't understand. What does that have to do with Uncle Dave?"

The reply was almost toneless.

"David hanged himself the very day he found it."

An eerie chill settled over Maggie. The moment she had seen Laszlo's case, it had seemed like an elegant menace, a scalpel or stiletto. The cedar chest had simply been a chest; her mother's statement had cast it in a more sinister light. Now, it registered like a carcass turned over with a spade, a sodden, dead thing. Maggie suddenly felt nauseated.

"What's in there?" she asked softly.

Her mother gazed down at the chest. "History," she replied. "Laszlo has his account of the Drakeford Curse. We have ours. Journals, news-paper clippings, even letters from the original Curse Keeper. Everything that's survived, anyway. Some of the documents are damaged. I'm afraid others may have been lost or destroyed."

Maggie stared at her parents, her emotions a turbulent mix of in-dignation and excitement. "Why would you keep this a secret?"

Her mother's tone was gentle. "You'll understand when you've seen it for yourself. If we made a mistake, Maggie, it was made with love."

With this, she wheeled her husband away, and Maggie was left alone to examine the chest's contents in private.

Maggie changed seats so her back was to the fire. Its warmth was a comfort.

What had this thing done to Uncle Dave? What had he found inside? It occurred to Maggie that he'd only been eighteen when he died; a whole year younger than she was. The longer she stared at the chest, the more insidious it appeared. It might have been Pandora's box, with all the world's evils locked behind its latch.

Like Pandora, Maggie could not resist the temptation.

The latch was rusted but gave after several determined pulls. As Maggie swung the lid open, she inhaled a dank vegetable smell, as though the chest had been moldering under old turnips and cabbage. Inside, she found none of Pandora's plagues or scorpions but bundles of papers in waxed covers, along with a packet of thin red envelopes tied together with twine. Some of the documents had been singed and looked so delicate that Maggie feared they would disintegrate at her touch. She set them carefully on the table before removing a variety of items stowed on wooden trays.

Maggie laid them out like museum pieces: a necklace of braided hair; a scrimshaw schooner; a crude wooden doll; a tarnished teaspoon; a human jawbone with seven teeth; the remnants of a poem stitched into a piece of linen; a daguerreotype of a dead toddler dressed in a suit and propped between his living siblings; a Spanish piece of eight, some-what nibbled at the edges.

Where to begin?

Maggie started with the letters, which were arranged chronologically in a packet of waxed canvas that bore evidence of smoke damage. The topmost was written in an antiquated script on yellowed vellum.

13 January 1666
Schemerdaal, His Royal Majesty's
Province of New York

Two months have passed since I rid the "Heksenwoud" of its witch. Never was there a more deserving candidate for the stake. Not even Hopkins or Stearne catalogued such maleficium.

The witch's crimes involved a stone near her dwelling, a monstrous formation alien to the region. I witnessed her performing rites before it, dark idolatries that drew fiendish spectators. My judgment was swift. The witch burned the next day. No trial was necessary—there was nothing her forked tongue could say that would have swayed me. I swore an oath to purge His Majesty's lands of witchcraft and papists. I have honored my vows.

And yet I am afraid.

I heard the witch muttering from the pyre even as the flames reached her flesh. Not once did the woman cry out. Not once did she look away. Never will I forget the satisfaction in her eyes when her invocations were complete.

I fear a Doom has been set upon me.

This is not superstition; a demon has told me this. It calls itself Bazilius. The fiend appeared in my dreams the very night she burned, a horned creature not unlike a jackal in aspect, but one that shuffled like a beggar and clutched a case of ebony and bone. It tells me that I, Ambrose Drakeford, am now the Bearer of a Curse and this foul creature is to be my "Keeper." My fate is chained to the Heksenwoud and the unholy object at its center. The witch's task has fallen to me. The price of failure is high.

A sickness boils in my blood. Even as I write, I feel it raging. Bazilius says the only remedy is to complete the witch's spell. A

Devil's Bargain if ever there was one. Ambrose Drakeford may
save himself or shield others from some evil design.

A simple choice were I the sole consideration. Alas, I am
not. Bazilius informs me—with no small delight—that the curse
extends to all of my line. It shall propagate among my descendants
so long as the witch's work remains unfinished. The idea of Henry
or Edward—or Heaven forbid little Charlotte—enduring such
torments is more than I can bear.

And so I find myself the witch's unwilling pupil. I have
gathered together what I could of her possessions and these, along
with the Keeper's counsel, have laid a course before me . . . AJD

9 May 1688

It is ten years since Father died. A son should mourn but I
cannot muster much feeling or sympathy. Father is to blame
for all that is happening. He is the reason I had to leave my
post at Harvard while Edward goes abroad in search of means
to break this enchantment: God speed Edward—he is our only
hope, for he is still fit to appear in public. I pray that Father's
instructions have merit. Meanwhile, I remain a prisoner in this
miserable house, scribbling in the dark, my body riddled by buboes.
Martha is bearing up nobly and the baby is all we could wish for.
Bazilius had the temerity to offer his "congratulations" after her
birth. I threw his letter in the fire but the wretched paper would
not burn. I shall not risk offending him again for the Keeper
frightens me. There are nights I fancy he is present, watching us,
basking in our misery. As for Tess, the girl is whole and healthy
and very much a Drakeford in her rosy bearing. Of course, I
dwell on what awaits her. It was unforgivable to bring a child into
this world and subject another to my fate. I am plagued with
regrets and yet burn with unspeakable urges, a monstrous desire to
sow my seed and expand my brood. Martha must have been mad

to marry me. Or perhaps she was bewitched. To look at myself, I fear she must have been. Already she talks of returning to her people in Boston. The baby is crying downstairs. Martha is in the fields with Lizzie, the only servant with the courage to remain. I will comfort Tess myself. God knows how much longer she'll suffer the sight of me . . . HJD

13 December 1729

I am changing. Not the boils that afflicted Father and Aunt Charlotte. This is deeper. Stranger. My dreams are all of blood. Rivers of gore winding through the Heksenwoud. I feel a yearning for masculine company . . . I will not say more. My arm no longer functions as once it did. The left hand has become misshapen, clawlike. Crippled yet possessing great strength. Alice Schuyler saw it poking from my shawl and gave a shriek. The urge to throttle her was overpowering. Dear Lord, I am frightened. I must press the Keeper for explanations. Perhaps Bazilius can explain why I have been chosen for such singular torments . . . Theresa D.

26 April 1758

Yesterday, I took a life. My first, I think. I was in the wood when he came upon me. A fur trapper. My appearance startled him and he brought up his rifle. In two bounds I was upon him. The horse tried to escape but I ran it down, poor creature. I have gorged for hours and yet still I am famished. The hunger is torturous. Mountains of flesh are not enough . . .

John returned last week with a necklace he purchased from a harpooner. He says it belonged to a chieftain, a king of some island in the Great South Sea. John believes it might work. He's also heard tell of magic buried near Salem and intends to journey there next month. John is so pleased by his success that I cannot bring myself to confess my crimes. It would break him. As for the trapper, I have buried what remains near the Witchstone. It is the Witchstone that has done this to me. The Stone must keep my secrets. —Thomas

19 July 1767

What we feared has come to pass. Thom killed one of the villagers today, a Farrow fetching a lamb what strayed upon the mountain. The boy is gone. Paul and I buried him. Thom is weeping inside the barn. It's been years since I saw my uncle without his wrappings. The sight has upset me. No one could call it human. Indeed, I struggle to believe he ever was so. The things growing from his back. Like coffin worms. I shall have nightmares. Thom is fifty and I but twenty-three, yet I wonder how many gentle years remain to me. That poor man. And that poor Farrow. Precious little of him went into the ground. What the villagers will do, I cannot guess. Our men are preparing for violence. —Willa D.

26 September 1818

Locked Mother in the barn this afternoon. Needed to be done. Her mind's unsteady and she's shown a cunning of late that makes me uneasy. Had to trick her down and pull the rope up quick. No easy thing with my arm still mending from Ben Ruyter's wake. Damn the villagers. I don't care what the church fathers say—we aren't the evil in these mountains. God wants sinners, he'll find plenty in Schemerdaal. Bad news from Caroline. Bazilius says the Indian belt's no good—no magic in it. We'll have to start over. I'm trying to stay brave for the others but my faith is wearing thin. What if Ambrose was wrong? What if that witch's spell is nothing but a humbug, a big joke to make the devils laugh down in Hell. Wouldn't surprise me. I don't trust that Keeper. —Isaiah D.

There were dozens of these entries. Individually, each provided a disturbing snapshot. Collectively, they painted a picture so bleak that Maggie struggled to keep reading. Nevertheless, it was impossible not to notice certain patterns.

At first, centuries ago, the Drakefords actively tried to break the curse before their symptoms became debilitating. They journeyed on horseback across the country or fanned out on merchant ships and whalers. Their travels took them to the far corners of the world.

Borneo. Van Diemen's Land. India. Norway. Peru.

Some died abroad. Others returned home with bits of bone or vessels of rumored magic, all in service to the witch's demands. None of it worked. Bazilius told them so. One by one, these Drakefords fell sick and saw their humanity drain away. One by one, outsiders who fathered or gave birth to new Curse Bearers abandoned the family and returned to wherever they'd been lured from: Boston, Providence, Philadelphia, Albany . . . But their offspring remained, chained by their Drakeford blood to the Witchstone.

The entries thinned after the Civil War. In 1868, one Philip Drakeford, age twenty-nine, apparently went mad and burned down several buildings on the property, along with most of the family records. Among the items destroyed were Ambrose Drakeford's original instructions regarding the witch's spell and how to break it.

Maggie double-checked the surviving documents for any hints or clues that might have escaped her attention. She found none.

As for the original Curse Keeper's letters, these shed little light. Each was written in a clerical script and conveyed an identical message:

On behalf of the Ancient & Infernal Society, allow me to extend my congratulations regarding the arrival of Ambrose Drakeford's blood descendant. The childe has been entered into our books and shall bear the Drakeford Curse, per the invoker's instructions.

Our Reach Endless, Our Grasp Eternal,

Bazilius, Keeper N°. 786

The last entry was dated January 23, 1919, and had been written by an individual who, judging by the penmanship, was in an advanced state of decline. The little Maggie could make out read as follows:

> *Go away. Must . . . Please Down, down . . . Send me down!!! Dreams . . . Cannot stay . . . Please . . . I love you . . . I love . . . God—please. Away. Don't want to . . . LOVE*

Maggie stared at the paper for some time before filing it with the others. Taking up the jawbone, she turned the object over in her hands and examined the fine filigree of cracks along the gumline. Why had anyone acquired, much less kept, such a grisly object? Did they believe it was magical? Had the jaw belonged to a holy man who'd used it to utter sacred words once upon a time?

Next, she examined the daguerreotype. Maggie studied the dead child's unseeing eyes. It was a heartbreaking image, the boy no older than four. She remembered Lump at that sleepy dormouse age: perpetually tousled, his fingers soft as dough when they closed around her hand. Maggie couldn't imagine losing him. She wondered about the child in the picture—a relative of hers, some distant uncle, perhaps. Maybe he'd been the son of Philip, the Drakeford who'd lost his mind and set everything ablaze.

The fire had been dead for some time when Maggie noticed her mother leaning against a post, watching her with a contemplative expression.

"Have you read it all?"

Maggie nodded.

"Mind if I sit?"

Maggie did not mind.

Her mother sat in the chair across from her and gently took the daguerreotype from Maggie's grasp. She glanced briefly at the image before setting it out of sight behind the chest.

"You have questions."

"I do."

"Well. I'll answer what I can."

Maggie struggled to find the proper words. Ultimately, she could only manage one. "*Why?*"

"Why did I hide this from you?"

Maggie tried to keep her voice steady. "Why did you *stay?*"

Elizabeth Drakeford did not answer immediately. Instead, she straightened and arranged the various objects on the table like items in a window display.

"Because I have children," she replied at last. "Because your father needs me. I've never been one to shirk my responsibilities, Maggie. It's not my nature to leave."

"Yeah, but do you ever wish you could?"

Maggie's mother sighed and, for a moment, looked ten years older. "You know, I'm going to plead the Fifth on that. Moms get to do that once in a while. One day you'll understand."

With a scornful laugh, Maggie poked her bandaged arm and felt the flesh burn at her touch. "I'll never pass this on to someone else. Never. Honestly, I don't understand why you stayed, much less had a second kid."

Elizabeth Drakeford said nothing.

Maggie searched her face. "Do you ever regret having us?"

Emotions cycled in her mother's eyes. Then the corners of her mouth turned down.

Maggie felt a stab of guilt. Her question wasn't really a question at all; it was an attack. "It doesn't matter," she finally said. "We're here."

"You are," said her mother. "And so is this." She gestured at the cedar chest. "Did we make a mistake in showing it to you?"

"No," said Maggie, and she meant it. "I want to know the truth, even if it's scary or hopeless."

Mrs. Drakeford waved a hand at the table's morbid display. "Well, here it is. The truth. Right here in the open. What do you think?"

Maggie considered the collection. "I think it's incomplete."

Her mother nodded. "I've combed through this chest countless times, looking for something—anything—that might be helpful. But there isn't, Maggie. Not really. There's enough to start a person down a path, but not enough to get anywhere. If there ever were instructions or some 'secret recipe' to breaking the curse, it's been lost."

"But Laszlo—"

"Doesn't know," her mother put in. "You've no idea how excited I got when he said he was the Curse Keeper. Finally, we might get some answers! But this Laszlo . . ." She shook her head. "'Disappointing' would be an understatement. At least Bazilius was on top of things."

Maggie eyed the stack of red envelopes. "What happened to him?"

"No idea. Bazilius stopped writing after Edith Drakeford was born in 1918."

"Weird," said Maggie. She hesitated a moment, uncertain whether to share what was troubling her. "Did you notice that the curse is getting worse?"

Her mother looked alarmed. "What do you mean?"

"The first Bearers just got sick. Henry Drakeford. Edward. They got sores or leprosy or something. It was only later that Drakefords turned into . . ." Maggie paused, unable to bring herself to say the word: *monsters*. "And it's happening younger," she added, and consulted the earlier entries. "Henry was teaching at Harvard before he exhibited any signs. He must have been in his twenties. Maybe his thirties." Maggie held up her afflicted arm. "I'm nineteen."

"It's a good question," said Elizabeth Drakeford. "Maybe Laszlo will know why." She glanced at the clock on the mantel. It was already past midnight. "Some sleep would do us good. Are you finished with all this?"

"For now."

The two women returned the items to the chest. Maggie placed the jawbone back on its tray.

"So Uncle Dave read these letters and decided to . . . check out?"

"Your father found him in the barn," said her mother softly. "He had no idea that Dave even knew about the chest. Your father tried to keep it hidden, you see. The guilt almost destroyed him. They had different mothers—your father's left a week after he was born—but David was always the baby. The darling. Your dad loved him to pieces." Maggie's mother shook her head bitterly. "As if Bill needed more on his plate."

Maggie gazed down at the letters. "Well, I've seen them now. Are you worried . . . ?"

The question hung in the air, awkward and incomplete. Mrs. Drakeford finished packing the chest before fixing her daughter with a penetrating stare. "Am I worried that *you* might 'check out'? No, Maggie. I'm not. That just isn't your way."

"Too strong?"

A ghost of a smile. "Too stubborn."

CHAPTER 9
RUNAWAY

Maggie had no intention of sleeping. Instead, she huddled in the darkness of her room, chin upon knees, waiting for the night to deepen.

She knew the sounds of the farmhouse by heart—the creak of its floorboards, the scratch of branches on the roof when the wind stirred outside. Lump was snoring softly in the next room, his wheezes familiar and comforting. Maggie considered looking in but could not risk waking him. If she did, he'd want to know everything about the chest, its contents, her plans . . . No, she couldn't say a proper goodbye. There was too much to do and not enough time to do it.

Even as a little girl, Maggie had always had faith in her instincts. She could sense when to speed up a ceremony and get out; she knew at a glance which mourners meant her serious harm. Her insights came from instinct, and Maggie's instincts told her that Laszlo was a fraud. Slick and glib, an easy and cheerful liar. Of this, she had no doubt.

But Laszlo *was* the Drakefords' Curse Keeper. And this might be their only chance.

The family's records—incomplete as they were—had strengthened her resolve. Once upon a time, Drakefords had embarked on quests to break the witch's spell. Yes, they'd failed. Yes, they'd eventually fallen to the curse's predations. But they'd tried, hadn't they? It was all a person could do.

It was all a person *must* do.

Maggie laid her things out by candlelight. It wasn't much. The demon said they only had six days, and Maggie doubted she'd be attending any galas. Some underwear and tees, an extra bra, woolly socks, a warm sweater, and a blanket she rolled up tight. Toiletries were minimal: hairbrush, hair ties, emergency tampons, toothbrush, toothpaste, a stick of deodorant, and some lip balm. Last but not least, she added a flashlight, two Agatha Christies, and a multi-tool she'd received on her fourteenth birthday.

She checked her wallet. Thirty bucks and a driver's license whose photo showed a young woman who didn't like to linger on government premises. No bank or credit cards. Her mind went to the jar on the kitchen sideboard. She wouldn't take it all—of course not—but she couldn't set out with thirty dollars to her name.

Downstairs, moonlight streamed through the kitchen window. It felt to Maggie like a spotlight following a thief as she padded to the money jar. She eased up the lid and found a handful of crumpled bills. Maggie lifted out two twenties and a five. She couldn't bring herself to take more. If seventy-five wouldn't cut it, neither would a hundred. If things got pricey, that demon could foot the bill. Heinous or not, his shoes looked expensive.

Back upstairs, Maggie checked her bedside clock. 1:37. Her mother was usually up by five; she needed to be long gone by then.

She scrawled a quick note—*A gal's gotta do what a gal's gotta do. Love you*—and slipped it under Lump's door. The house was eerily quiet. Hoisting her pack and the curse folio, Maggie slipped downstairs and out the front door, closing it behind her as silent as a wraith.

Her footsteps were brisk as she set out beneath the autumn moon. It would take half an hour to reach the village. Laszlo would be staying at Schemerdaal's only lodgings, a tiny motel attached to Earl's. It wouldn't be hard to track him down. The dump only had two rooms.

As she reached the path that led to the hedge opening, Maggie found that she was shivering. Her arms prickled with anticipation as she progressed deeper into the darkness among the trees. Was she really doing this? Indeed, she was. Once Maggie passed beyond the trees, she would be out of the Witchwood and in the Great Beyond: a woman seeking answers, seeking a cure, seeking hope.

She had officially assumed the mantle of her ancestors, and she would succeed where they had failed.

And what would happen when she did break the curse? Would her father return to the man she remembered? Would life return to normal? Maggie found the very notion absurd. Normal? She'd never lived a normal day, much less a normal life. It sounded wonderfully exotic.

She crossed the last footbridge. A sliver of moonlight peeked through the trees like an opening between stage curtains. It was the Witchwood's boundary.

Stepping forward, she gazed at the world beyond the Drakeford kingdom. The night was still, the mountain quiet as a tomb. No owls or insects. Nothing padding in the underbrush seeking an evening meal. Just a sweeping view of the slumbering Catskills.

And beyond? Maggie honestly had no idea. In her nineteen years, she'd never ventured more than forty miles from home.

Steeling herself, she continued past the sign to the pebbled track that wound down the mountain. She'd almost reached the first bend when she heard a sound that stopped her cold.

A truck was coming up the road. Its engine was low and throaty, and Maggie immediately thought of the Ruyters' old Dodge. Ducking behind a hawthorn bush, she kept still.

A pair of headlights rounded the bend, and the vehicle motored slowly toward the *No Trespassing* sign. It was not a truck, she realized with relief, but an old sedan. Big and pale, with something odd attached to the roof. Maggie sucked her teeth. Were those police lights?

The car rolled past her and stopped ten yards from the sign. It idled for several seconds before the driver cut the engine. With its headlights illuminating the trees, Maggie got a better view and exhaled. It was not a police cruiser but a taxicab whose driver's door swung open. A cigarette butt came flying out, followed by the driver himself. Maggie recognized the trim figure at once.

Laszlo.

She watched in bewildered silence as the demon stretched, inhaled the night air, and absently scratched his crotch. Then he strolled to the back of the taxi, popped the trunk, and proceeded to jettison a variety of items, including an ice scraper, a gallon of wiper fluid, beer cans, and armfuls of old newspapers and bits of junk. Maggie supposed demons didn't care about littering.

Laszlo paused to flip through a magazine he had discovered. He went straight to the centerfold and gave a low whistle before tossing the magazine in the driver's seat. Returning to the trunk, the demon shook out a ratty blanket and draped it over the interior.

Maggie abandoned her hiding spot, creeping closer as Laszlo brought out two industrial-size laundry bags. Whistling, he held them up to the moonlight and, evidently satisfied, slung the bags over his shoulder and made for the hedge opening.

A silent Maggie followed him some twenty feet into the woods before tapping him on the shoulder.

Laszlo yelped and dove into a juniper bush. There was some thrashing about, and his face emerged into the beam of Maggie's flashlight.

"Jesus!" he hissed. "What's wrong with you? You could have given me a heart attack!"

"Do demons have hearts?" asked Maggie coldly. "What are you doing?"

Laszlo clambered out of the bush, smacking leaves from his suit. "Of course we do—our own version, anyway. But that's not the point. The point is what are *you* doing, and why are you sneaking up on me?"

"I'm asking the questions," said Maggie. She nodded to the laundry bags. "What are those for?"

The demon slipped them behind his back. "Nothing. Nothing at all."

"Holy shit," said Maggie. "You were going to kidnap us. You were going to stuff us in sacks!"

"I was not. And I resent the imputation."

"Well, you can put those away," said Maggie. "Because, as it turns out, *I'm* kidnapping *you*."

"Come again?"

"You heard me," said Maggie. "I'm abducting you, and you're going to help me break the curse. End of story."

For once, Laszlo seemed at a loss for words. He sniffed and looked away from her as some animal scurried through the underbrush.

"Are you just going to stand there?" said Maggie. "You said every minute counts."

The demon's hand moved reactively to his inside jacket pocket, where Maggie knew he kept that hourglass. He clucked his tongue. "True."

"Then what are we waiting for?"

Laszlo glanced in the direction of the Drakeford house. "What about the little guy?"

Maggie was appalled. "Lump? He's eleven."

The demon scoffed. "The worst thing they ever did in this country was enact child labor laws. Kids can be useful." Maggie snorted. "Listen, trust me on this. For one, they don't ask so many questions. And those little fingers are ideal for picking locks and unjamming heavy machinery. There was this kid I saw once in Yorkshire. They called him the Worm, and—"

Maggie cut him off. "Absolutely not. Besides, Lump would only slow us down."

"Yeah," said Laszlo. "But he's also a Drakeford. It might not hurt to have a backup . . ."

"In case of what?" said Maggie.

"Unforeseeable circumstances, Your Highness. Death. Dismemberment. That kind of thing."

"Nothing's going to happen to me," said Maggie. She spoke with steely confidence, but she wasn't sure if she was trying to convince Laszlo or herself. "Anyway, we're wasting time. Come on."

Laszlo followed her back to the car.

"Is that a real taxi?" asked Maggie.

"Indeed."

"Where'd you get it?"

"Borrowed it from a dear friend," the demon replied. He held up the keys. "Shall I drive, or does my kidnapper prefer to tie me up?"

"That depends," said Maggie. "Where were you planning to take me?"

"The city. Remember that Dimitri fellow I mentioned? He's the man we've gotta see."

Maggie cocked his head. "Is he really a man?"

"Last I checked."

"I mean, is he *human*?"

"Figure of speech. Give me your pack."

Maggie eyed the taxi's trunk and the blanket lining as Laszlo took her backpack. "So you were going to stuff the two of us in there?"

The demon tossed her backpack in along with the laundry bags before slamming it shut. "You might prefer it," he said. "It's cleaner."

As Maggie opened the back door, she saw he might be speaking the truth. She climbed inside, grimacing at the duct-taped vinyl and mysterious stains.

"Sit up front," Laszlo said from the driver's seat. "I'm not a chauffeur."

Maggie shook her head. She preferred having a bulletproof partition between them. "I'm perfectly fine back here, thanks."

"Have it your way."

Laszlo turned the key. The engine gave a growl as it roared to life, causing the door locks to rattle. Flicking on the headlights, he reversed to the turn.

Maggie didn't look back as they puttered down the mountain. What would be the point? She'd made her choice. The only way was forward.

CHAPTER 10
SIR FLAPJACK

Laszlo was nearly giddy with his good fortune. Not only had he been spared the headache of kidnapping an unwilling Curse Bearer, but Maggie had left a note indicating she'd set out of her own volition. Leaving the brother behind was too bad; Laszlo could tell he was the eager-to-please sort and might have been useful leverage over the sister. Still, he wasn't going to gripe. Thus far, things had been a breeze.

Even the drive to Manhattan had been smooth. No weather, no traffic, and no yapping from the back seat. At first, the girl wouldn't shut up—What was the city like? Was everything as dirty as this cab? Did Dimitri know they were coming?—but Laszlo quickly found a talk radio station. Within minutes, Maggie was slumped against the door like a hobo dozing in a boxcar. Laszlo missed the days when hoboes ruled the railways. They always knew the best jokes.

When they reached the Bowery, Laszlo parked next to a fire hydrant and texted the cab's owner. If Serge was quick, he'd beat the tow trucks. If not . . . well, that wasn't Laszlo's problem. Demons didn't waste time hunting for legal parking spots.

Outside, hints of daylight streaked the sky, outlining the high-rises along the East River. Not much activity yet, nothing but joggers and garbage trucks and a few *Les Mis* types shuffling about in search of recyclables. Laszlo wondered if Mommy and Daddy Drakeford were awake. Would Mrs. Drakeford contact the police? Laszlo doubted it. What was she going to say? That her adult daughter had run off with a demon? She'd be laughed out of the station.

Sorry, Mom. You'll have to wait this one out. Fear and guilt are going to eat you alive. By the time we're back, you'll be ready to do anything . . .

A voice sounded behind him. "Why are you smiling?"

Laszlo glanced in the mirror to find Maggie rubbing sleep from her eyes. He shrugged.

"Daydream," he said airily. "Let's get something to eat, shall we? I'm starving."

As she stood in the street, Maggie yawned and stretched, pivoting on one heel to take in the city. "It's quieter than I expected."

"Give it an hour." Laszlo went to fetch her backpack. He opened the trunk and promptly slammed it shut. Maggie looked over.

"What's wrong?"

Laszlo glanced at her, then at the trunk, then back to her. How had this happened? *When* did it happen? His mind went back to the animal that scurried past them in the Witchwood. Had it been moving in the direction of the car? Upon reflection, Laszlo thought it had. The demon chuckled. That sneaky little shit . . .

"What is it?" said Maggie. "What's wrong."

Laszlo silently thanked the cosmos. Things really were lining up in his favor. "Look for yourself." He popped the trunk a second time and stood back to let Maggie have an unobstructed view. Peering in, she discovered that it contained not one backpack but two.

It also contained a boy.

Lump lay there blinking at them like a sleepy mole. His blond hair was matted into a bird's nest, and his glasses were askew, along with his grin. Laszlo considered the plump, cherubic face. The kid really was a roly-poly sort of thing. Those freckled cheeks even bore traces of baby fat; nothing like the hardcase sister. As Laszlo reflected on their differences, the boy ventured an uncertain wave.

"Hey," he said.

It took Maggie several seconds to find her voice. "Lump, I swear to God!—what the fuck are you doing in there?"

The boy shot her a reproachful look. "You shouldn't talk like that."

"I shouldn't be doing a lot of things."

"I know," said Lump cheerfully. "And I've come to help!"

Laszlo scanned the street in both directions. "Let's continue this conversation someplace else. Kids in trunks tend to draw attention."

Lump clambered out, brushing debris off his pants and gawping at the city. "Wow. The view's much better out here."

Maggie snapped him back to attention. "How did you know I was leaving? I was quiet."

"Not *that* quiet. Anyway, when I saw you going through that chest, I knew what you were planning to do."

"And how did you see that? Mom sent you to your room."

Her brother snorted. "Yeah, so I waited fifteen minutes and snuck back out. You never even looked up. Your nose was in those letters."

"Congrats. You're a ninja." Lump gave a slight bow. Maggie turned to Laszlo. "We need to take him home."

"I won't go," said Lump. "You need me!"

"We don't," said Maggie pointedly. "You're a kid, and this might be dangerous. Mom and Dad need you more."

"They can spare me for a few days. Anyway, the curse can only be broken by *Drakefords*. Laszlo can't do it for us, and who knows what you'll have to do to get jewels and magic relics. You'll need help, and there's only one other person who can give it."

Maggie merely stared at him.

"Um, that person's me," Lump clarified. "*Moi*. That means 'me' in French."

"I know what *moi* means, and there's no way you're coming with us."

"I am."

"You're eleven," said Maggie.

"Yes," he said, "which kind of stinks, because if I was older, I'd be bigger and more helpful. But I can't wait for that. We have less than a week, Maggie. This is my only shot to help you and Dad. And me too, I guess. You can't take that chance away from me. It isn't yours to take."

It was a good speech, thought Laszlo. The boy had also managed to convey an endearing blend of fear and pride, tempered with a longing for his sister's approval. Would approval be forthcoming? Laszlo couldn't tell. Maggie had inherited her mother's sphinxlike countenance. She could have been on the verge of hugging her brother or kicking his ass.

At length, she merely turned to Laszlo. "Lump needs to go home."

The demon consulted his watch. "Let's see. Heading back to Shitsville will cost us eight or nine hours. And that's assuming your parents don't sic the cops on us. Best case, we lose a day."

"Then we lose a day," said Maggie. "I'm not taking him along. It's too dangerous."

Laszlo sighed and nodded to a passing jogger who was eyeing them. "You saw the shopping list, Your Highness. Time isn't on our side."

"Maybe he can take a bus," said Maggie. "Where's the nearest station?"

Laszlo laughed. "Port Authority? I thought you wanted to keep the kid safe."

Closing her eyes, she swore softly. "Mom would never forgive me."

"I'll tell her it was all my idea," said Lump. "I'll swear it wasn't your fault!"

"Like that'll matter."

Laszlo intervened. The sooner he could get them moving, the harder it would be for Maggie to ditch her brother. Lump was annoying, but he was leverage, and a handy plan B should things with the girl go south.

"Listen," he said. "If we're going to argue, let's argue over something warm and fattening. Lump, I'll bet you could use a bite after bouncing around a trunk all night. How about breakfast?"

The boy practically saluted. "Yes, sir."

"Jesus," said Maggie. "You don't need to 'sir' him, Lump. He's a *demon*."

Laszlo nudged Lump onto the sidewalk. "Ignore her. You're a gentleman and a scholar. And Maggie—well, she's something else."

Maggie did not salute.

As the three walked along, Laszlo wasn't certain he'd ever seen two people more out of place. The Drakefords couldn't go ten feet without Lump stopping to gawk at the buildings or the mounds of trash bags piled by steaming grates. The noises, the smells, the three Chinese fellas sharing a cigarette outside a dry cleaner—it was all mind blowing to good ol' Lump. Maggie did her share of rubbernecking too, but only when she thought Laszlo wasn't looking.

Being so near Chinatown, Laszlo craved dim sum, but the only place open at this hour was a diner. Going in, he steered the Drakefords to a booth upholstered in peeling vinyl. As was his custom, Laszlo took the seat facing the door. A waitress dropped three menus on the table.

"Something to drink?" she said.

"Coffee," said Laszlo. "Extra cream."

Lump looked inquiringly at him. "Can I order a Coke? I've always wanted to."

"Go nuts."

The boy beamed. "One Coke, please."

The waitress turned to Maggie. "And you, hon?"

"Just water, thanks."

As she left to get the drinks, Maggie leaned forward. "Before we decide about Lump, I'd like to know the master plan. As in, what is it?"

Laszlo settled back against the vinyl. "The plan, Your Highness, is to break your curse. But seeing as it's a tad cryptic, we're going to visit my pal Dimitri and see what he can make of it."

"And where do we find him?"

"A few blocks away," said Laszlo. "He owns a pawnshop on Broome Street."

Lump looked to both of them. "What's a pawnshop?"

"It's a seedy place where sketchy people sell junk," Maggie replied.

Laszlo rolled his eyes. "So judgmental. Anyway, that's where we're going. Dimitri's been in the game a long time. And if he can't help us, he'll know someone who can."

The waitress brought the drinks, and they placed their orders. Pancakes for Lump and Maggie; a platter of eggs, bacon, toast, and home fries for Laszlo. Taking the creamers, the demon proceeded to peel and dump them one after another into his coffee.

Lump sipped his Coke, swishing it about like a wine aficionado. "Incredible," he declared.

Maggie stayed rigidly on topic. "What if Dimitri can't help us? What then?"

"One thing at a time," said Laszlo. "And let's get a few things straight."

"Such as?"

"You're not running this show, Your Highness. I am. You don't know jack about curses or magic or the places we can find the stuff we need. This isn't a committee. I'm in charge. Can you be a good little human and take orders, or am I going to have a mutiny every five minutes?"

Maggie's expression became flat and stoic. Lump remained occupied with his soda.

Laszlo leaned back as the waitress set his breakfast before him. "Well?"

"What kind of orders are we talking about?" Maggie asked.

The demon shook up the hot sauce. "That depends. What can you do? Are you actually good at anything?"

Maggie shrugged. "Running. Fighting. I'm pretty observant, I guess."

"Oh, really? How many customers were here when we came in?"

"Eight," said Maggie instantly. "Three at the counter. Four in booths. And that masked guy at the table by the hostess station."

Laszlo grunted. "Lucky guess. How 'bout you, Lump? Any hidden talents?"

The boy looked up from cutting his pancakes with the precision of a jeweler. "Yes," he said. "I'm a hero."

Laszlo nearly spat out his coffee. "A *hero*! With a name like Lump? Do tell."

"Well, I'm not a hero yet," said the boy modestly. "But I'm confident I will be."

He'll be dead by Tuesday, thought Laszlo. "Uh, that's fantastic. Any particular reason you think you'll end up a hero? Any skills or traits I should know about?"

"Well, I know lots of things," Lump reflected. "I've memorized the encyclopedia through the letter *O*, I'm already doing trigonometry, and I've read *The Lord of the Rings* eleven times, including *The Silmarillion*."

"Super," said Laszlo. "If we come across anything in Elvish, you can translate."

The boy bowed, then proceeded to rattle off some flowy, poetic-sounding gibberish.

Laszlo grimaced. "What the heck was that?"

"Elvish," replied Lump proudly. "In the Sindarin dialect, it means *I'm here to save you*."

Laszlo revised his death forecast to Monday.

"So what kind of things will we have to do?" said Maggie. "I still don't think Lump should come with us. How dangerous will it be?"

The demon twiddled his thumbs. "Well, I can't say for certain, but I'd imagine there will be some running. Maybe a little fighting. But probably more in the way of *stealing*."

Lump's face fell. "Stealing?"

"Sure," said Laszlo. "Unless you've got a secret treasure hoard, there's going to be some theft involved. Magic, jewels, and relics? People don't give that shit away."

Lump returned to his pancakes. "Stealing doesn't sound very heroic."

"Don't kid yourself," said Laszlo. "All heroes steal. The Argonauts didn't 'borrow' the Golden Fleece. Jack the Giant Killer was really just Jack the Beanstalk Burglar. Hell, Perseus stole Medusa's head."

"Eww," said Lump.

"And then there's Oedipus. He stole his mom—"

Maggie glared at Laszlo.

"The point is," he concluded, "show me a hero, and I'll show you a thief."

"And *we* have to do it," said Maggie. "I mean, you can't just grab the stuff for us?"

"Do I look like a thief?" said Laszlo.

"Very much so."

The demon wolfed down a strip of bacon. As a being who didn't worry about cholesterol, he made a point of eating it whenever possible.

"Listen. Even if I had a few skills along those lines, I can't just hand you the goodies. Curse Bearers have to do the work."

The waitress brought Lump another Coke.

"So," said Laszlo. "Now that we've gotten that out of the way, will you solemnly swear to be good Drakefords and follow orders?"

Lump answered at once. "Absolutely."

Maggie shot him a look. "I haven't even decided if you're coming."

"Oh, I'm coming," he said, between sips of Coke. "I mean, I'm already here!"

Maggie sighed. Her eyes flicked to Laszlo. "You have to swear something too."

The demon was all ears. "Lay it on me."

She studied the tabletop as though its Formica held her fortune. "You have to swear that you'll *help* us," she said. "That you won't run away like you did at the Witchstone. We need to know you'll stick with us through thick and thin."

"Like a champion!" cried Lump.

"A *champion?*" said Laszlo. "Well, that'll be a first. Fine. Anything else?"

"Yes," said Maggie. "If anything happens to me, you have to take my brother home."

The solemnity of the request appeared to catch Lump off guard. Putting down his Coke, he gave his sister a searching look. "But nothing's going to happen," he said solemnly. "We'll be okay."

Maggie kept her attention fixed on Laszlo. He nearly made a quip, but something in her gaze brought him up short. At length, he simply nodded. "I think I can do that."

"Nope. Not good enough. You have to swear."

"Okay, I swear."

"Maybe you could swear on a Bible?" Lump suggested. Laszlo stared at him. The boy promptly reddened. "Sorry. I guess that's not your favorite book. Well, at least swear on this."

Lump pushed a laminated menu across the table. Laszlo took it and raised his right hand. "In the name of Gus's East Side Diner, I solemnly swear to assist Maggie and George Drakeford on their quest, to be their champion, and to return George Drakeford—a.k.a. Lump—safely home, should an unfortunate event befall his sister." Laszlo set down the menu. "Will that do?"

"Perfect," said Lump. "Now all we need are names."

"We have names," said Maggie flatly.

"I mean quest names. Like we're knights!"

Laszlo desperately needed a cigarette. "Okay. I dub thee Sir Flapjack. And for Maggie—"

"I'll pass."

Sir Flapjack was less than pleased with his new title, but just as he began to protest, Laszlo's phone buzzed. Glancing at the number, Laszlo held up a hand for silence before answering. "You got my text," he said.

A man's soft, eastern-European-accented voice replied. "It is early, Laszlo."

"I know, but I'm in a bind. I need your expertise."

A pause. "Expertise is expensive."

"I'm aware."

The caller sniffed. "When?"

"Now."

"Is it really so urgent?"

Laszlo touched the hourglass nestled in his jacket pocket. "Yep."

"Very well."

Turning away from the Drakefords, Laszlo lowered his voice. "One more thing. I've got some humans with me."

"I do not buy humans."

"They're not for sale. They're with me. A girl and her brother."

"Did you abduct them?"

"No. What kind of person do you think I am?"

A small laugh. "I think you are Laszlo."

Laszlo cupped his hand over the phone. "I didn't kidnap anyone," he whispered indignantly. "If there's a victim here, it's me!"

"How so?"

"I'm stuck with two humans, and one of them speaks Elvish."

"How interesting. Authentic Elvish or Tolkien?"

Laszlo groaned. "Not you too."

A chuckle. "The gate will be unlocked."

Laszlo put his phone away and signaled the waitress. As she brought the check, he placed a crisp fifty on the table. She glanced at it, then returned her attention to Laszlo. "Anything else?"

"Is the pie any good?"

The waitress turned to assess the glass case near the register. "They're okay."

Laszlo shook his head and handed her the check along with the money. She returned with fifteen dollars' change, and Laszlo gave her back ten as a tip. The waitress thanked him and started busing their table as they gathered up their things and headed out.

They'd gone half a block when Maggie shot Laszlo a sideways glance. "You robbed them."

He scoffed. "What are you babbling about?"

"That waitress brought you change for a fifty, but you switched the bill for a twenty when she turned to look at the pie."

Laszlo raised an eyebrow. "Well, well," he said. "You really *are* observant."

"Three meals for five bucks?" said Maggie. "You should be ashamed."

"Fifteen," Laszlo corrected. "You're forgetting my generous gratuity."

"It's still stealing."

"Oh, come on," said Laszlo. "She's happy. We're happy. No harm done."

"Until they close out the register," said Maggie, and stopped to look at him severely. "No more stealing, unless it's for the curse."

Laszlo sighed and elected to humor her. "As you wish, Your Highness. Now, get your proverbial shit together. You're about to meet your second demon."

CHAPTER II
DIMITRI

Their destination was only three blocks away, but Maggie was already feeling spent. It was not the walk or the added stress of Lump but the constant barrage to her senses. Manhattan was awake now, the morning commute in full swing. All around them were people of every size, shape, and color. People walking, people on bikes, people in cars inching along like snails. The honking of horns, the drilling of jackhammers, the blare of sirens . . . all of it boiling over as she held Lump's hand and navigated the oncoming waves of pedestrians. The two were jostled like pinballs by people who did not scowl or snap but simply plowed ahead. Maggie found this oddly insulting, as if the two Drakefords were a pair of rats scurrying underfoot. Nuisances, yes, but not nuisances worth bothering about.

What would her mother do when she discovered they'd gone? Maggie leaving was one thing, but Lump? She chose to banish the subject from her mind. She couldn't think about home right now. It was hard enough to keep up with Laszlo.

At present, all she could see was his hat, which bobbed ahead as he glided against traffic with irritating grace. He turned onto Broome Street, where he doffed said hat to a woman in yoga pants who was walking an absurdly tiny dog. The woman smiled and actually stopped to follow Laszlo's progress down the street.

Maggie swept past her. "He's a demon."

The woman's look of confusion provided a small measure of satisfaction. These New Yorkers weren't superpeople, Maggie decided. They might seem fancier and more worldly, but they were just as ridiculous as the jackasses in Schemerdaal. Case in point: yoga pants. You might as well walk around naked.

Just ahead, they found Laszlo waiting for them in front of a dingy little building shoehorned between a fire station and a Vietnamese café. Unlike many of its neighbors on Broome Street, its facade wasn't remotely charming but was an apparent relic from an earlier and grittier era. Lump came to an abrupt halt as Laszlo raised the security grille.

"We're going in there?" said Lump.

"Yes," said Laszlo. "Is there a problem?"

Lump eyed the chipping paint and shuttered windows. "It looks scary."

Laszlo yanked the door open. "I didn't say it was the Ritz. C'mon, Sir Flapjack. Our quest continues."

Their quest continued into a dim and dusty space some twenty feet deep crammed with bookshelves and glassed cabinets displaying old coins, a trumpet, a World War I gas mask, and a variety of vintage dolls. The displays ended at a counter exhibiting watches and tool sets. A pair of heavy black curtains behind the counter blocked any view of the back of the shop.

There was a mildewy tang to the air, a smell of age mingled with something chemical. Maggie and Lump took it in, appalled. The pair flinched as a model train close to the ceiling gave a sudden toot and started circling the room on an elevated track.

As it vanished into a tunnel, a voice called out from beyond the curtain, a soft rasp with a strong accent. "Laszlo?"

"Righty-ho. Can we come through?"

"Yes, yes," said the voice. "I've lifted the charm."

Laszlo shot Maggie and Lump a look as if to say, *See? Nothing to worry about* and raised the counter like a miniature drawbridge. The Drakefords ducked under with their backpacks.

As Maggie trailed the demon through the velvety curtains, she felt a pop in her ears. Not painful but surprising. Behind her, Lump gave a squeak. Apparently, he'd felt it too.

The space beyond the curtains was considerably larger than Maggie had expected. Unlike the shop front, the interior was lushly appointed with exotic plants and colorful carpets and ornate lamps that cast a golden glow on the room's dark paneling. Tall bookcases lined the walls, flanking a central aisle of tables that displayed all manner of fantastical objects. At the far end was an enormous desk where an older man sat bathed in the glow of a banker's lamp. He beckoned them forward with a kindly gesture that put Maggie somewhat at ease. Whatever this Dimitri was, he didn't look like a monster.

As they filed between the crowded tables, Maggie could not help glancing at the yellowed tomes bound in leather; ceramic pots teeming with scrolls, crusted beakers, and used alchemical equipment; the articulated skeleton of some bizarre, six-limbed creature. Lump squeezed Maggie's hand, directing her attention toward a fish tank where glowing eels gamboled in mesmerizing patterns.

Their host rose to greet them as they approached. Dimitri was not much taller than Maggie, with spindly arms and a belly that strained the buttons of his shirt. That shirt was tucked into a pair of high-waisted trousers held up by a sturdy belt. The man's speckled head was hairless but for bristling side whiskers. To Maggie's mind, Dimitri looked like a retired sea captain crossed with an accountant. His being a demon seemed impossible. Then again, she had once taken Laszlo for a reporter.

Dimitri's eyes twinkled at the Drakefords. "Who do we have here?"

"I'm Maggie Drakeford, sir, and this is my brother, George."

Their host inclined his head. "And I am Dimitri. It is an honor to make your acquaintance."

Maggie reddened. People never spoke to her so courteously. She wasn't certain how to respond and found herself offering an awkward curtsy. To her horror, Lump gave a complicated bow.

Dimitri beamed. "They have manners. Whatever are they doing with you, Laszlo?"

"Don't let her fool you," said Laszlo. "Maggie's got quite the mouth, but we're trying to help each other out of a jam."

"What kind of jam?"

"Their family's cursed."

Dimitri blinked in apparent confusion. "And what do human curses have to do with you?"

Laszlo held up the ebony case. "I'm their Curse Keeper."

The old man chuckled and wagged a finger. "None of your jokes, now."

"No joke," said Laszlo. "They're cursed. I'm their Keeper. We've got till Thursday to break the spell, or they'll turn into monsters and—more to the point—I'll be crucibled."

Dimitri's smile faded. He eased back down in his chair and considered his visitors anew. Maggie felt like she was being x-rayed by an old but immensely thorough machine. It did not escape her that his eyes returned more than once to her bandaged arm. At length, Dimitri pressed a button beneath his desk. A sleepy voice crackled from a speaker and growled something in a guttural language. Their host replied in kind and added what sounded like a rebuke. The voice grumbled back and disconnected. Dimitri gestured for his guests to be seated in the chairs across from his desk.

"I think," he said, "we should begin at the beginning."

Maggie and Lump sat by as Laszlo brought Dimitri up to speed. The pawnbroker did not interrupt. Ten minutes into Laszlo's account, a section of paneling swung inward, and a bowlegged creature with a doglike face, three eyes, and a newsboy cap emerged pushing a cart laden with a silver tea service and a plate of gingersnaps. The creature gawked at the humans before, at Dimitri's urging, making a hasty bow. Having delivered the tea, it scampered back the way it had come.

As their host poured the tea, Maggie saw the panel open again. Three eyes glinted from the darkness. Dimitri turned and flung a teaspoon at the wall. The panel closed.

"I apologize," said Dimitri as he served Maggie her tea. "I would let Nyshki go, but I fear he'd come to a bad end."

"If you needed help, you could have given me a job," said Laszlo. "If you recall, I did once offer my services."

Dimitri looked amused. "I remember. Yet now I learn you are already employed. For shame, Laszlo. To keep such secrets from me."

"You never asked."

"I'm asking now. What do you want? And do not lie to Dimitri."

"He can't help lying," Maggie put in. "He just swindled our waitress."

"And gave her a generous gratuity," said Laszlo indignantly.

Dimitri smiled at the Drakefords. "I will tell you a secret about your Curse Keeper."

Maggie and Lump leaned forward.

"Your Keeper hails from a noble house," said Dimitri. "He is highborn and not without certain gifts. He is also a scoundrel. A wastrel. A lover of base pleasures—"

"Hey!" said Laszlo.

Dimitri held up a finger. "But he has a good heart. Laszlo does not admit this, of course. He likes to pretend he is as ruthless as the rest of his family. But some of us know better."

Laszlo rolled his eyes. "If I'm so great, why didn't you give me a job?"

"Because you're a thief."

"I was broke. Desperate."

"And I should hire a desperate thief?"

"Please. I wouldn't have stolen from *you*."

Dimitri tutted. "Are we forgetting the Monet incident?"

"Anyone can make a mistake."

"Yes," said Dimitri. "And you have made yours. So I ask again. What do you want?"

Fidgeting with his teacup, Laszlo shot the Drakefords a sheepish glance. "Maybe we should talk alone."

"No," Maggie burst out. "It's *our* curse. Whatever Laszlo says, I want to hear it too."

Laszlo glared at her. "Fine," he snapped. "Here goes. Here's the big reveal: I don't know where to start. Happy? I'm a Curse Keeper who doesn't know how to break his own curse."

"Well, I sure wish you'd said that before I kidnapped you."

The demon waved her off. "Oh, get over yourself. *I* kidnapped *you*."

"Perhaps," said Dimitri delicately, "it would be best if I see the materials for myself."

Laszlo scowled at Maggie, then thrust the curse file at Dimitri. The pawnbroker handled the ebony case with practiced care, turning it this way and that, and studied the carvings through a jeweler's loupe. At length, he set it down and sipped his tea.

"It appears to be authentic."

"Yeah, we knew that," Laszlo groused.

Dimitri laced his fingers across his broad belly. "Then you know that an active curse folio can only be accessed by its official Keeper."

Maggie glared at Laszlo.

"He did open it at our house," Lump volunteered.

"Wonderful," said Dimitri. "Perhaps he will be so good as to do so again."

"Oh, all these little tests," Laszlo grumbled. The demon set his tea on Dimitri's desk and flicked open the case's clasps. "Voilà! Official Keeper on the premises."

Dimitri cleaned his hands from a bottle of some kind of solution. "So it would appear. I confess I still have difficulty believing it."

"And why, pray tell, is that?"

The pawnbroker dried his hands on a handkerchief. "Because Curse Keeping is a serious business. It is not a job for coxcombs and dilettantes."

"I'm not a comb, Dimitri."

Maggie shook her head. Laszlo really was an idiot.

Dimitri inspected one of the scrolls through his lens. He gave a grunt that might have meant anything. "This will take time," he muttered. "Show the humans the choo choo. Humans like choo choos."

To Maggie's relief, Laszlo had no more interest in showing them the "choo choo" than she had in seeing it. Instead, they perused the shop's far more intriguing merchandise. Lump made a beeline for the weapons, while Maggie examined a variety of books and objects. Most of the books were in unfamiliar languages, but there were some English titles, such as *Advanced Lycanthropy*, *Weather Spells of the Caribbean*, and *Concealment in the Digital Age*. The last sparked Maggie's interest, until she looked inside and found a recipe involving pulped octopus brains. No, thank you.

She moved on to a table crowded with cauldrons. One had a blue flame burning beneath it, a flame with no source that Maggie could see. Lifting the lid, she peered down into a bubbling, rust-colored liquid in which a dozen fist-size objects bobbed, simmered, and . . . *pulsed*?

One of the things collided gently with its neighbor and shifted to reveal the stems of severed arteries. Even as she watched, the heart pulsed of its own accord and liquid dribbled out. Bile rushed into Maggie's mouth. She tried to replace the lid, which clattered off and fell to the floor. She bent hurriedly to retrieve it, but another hand snatched it away.

Maggie found herself face to face with a short, pimply teenager wearing a cap, an apron, and a grotesquely lopsided grin. Where had he come from? She watched in stunned disgust as the boy peered into the pot, gave the hearts a stir, and tasted the broth with a finger. He nodded with satisfaction before gesturing for Maggie to try some. Maggie backed away.

With a shrug, the boy replaced the lid, headed toward the front of the shop, and slipped through the velvet curtains. Moments later came the rattling of the security grille being raised.

Presumably the shop was opening for business.

The boy returned to find Maggie still in a state of stunned disbelief. Looking her up and down, he leaned forward on the balls of his feet, his nostrils quivering.

Maggie grimaced. "What the—are you *sniffing* me?"

The lopsided grin returned. This time, it had a leering quality. Maggie was about to tell the kid to fuck off when he suddenly picked his nose and ate the proceeds.

She made a noise of disgust.

Dimitri looked up from his desk. "Nyshki! How many times must I tell you not to do that!"

The youth slunk away to water some palms. Now Maggie recognized that bowlegged waddle and the little cap sitting atop that greasy red hair. This was actually the three-eyed creature who'd brought them tea! She went over to tell Laszlo.

"That kid is actually that dog thing, and there's a cauldron over there with living hearts."

"This ain't Walmart," said Laszlo, who continued to inspect a number of corked tubes arranged in a baker's rack. He held one up to a nearby sconce.

"What are you doing?"

The demon gave the tube a little shake and peered at it. "Trying to find a good one."

Maggie stood on tiptoe. "What are they?"

"Bits of old spells. Occasionally you find one with some oomph."

Maggie thought of the books she'd just seen. If nothing else, magic struck her as very scholarly and organized. "Shouldn't you check what kind of spell it is?"

Laszlo rolled his eyes. "Gee, there's a thought. Unfortunately, Your Highness, to do that you'd have to break the seal. And once you break the seal, the magic escapes. For all we know, you could be turned into a newt."

"Well, why aren't they labeled?" asked Maggie. "That seems sloppy."

"Not even Dimitri knows what they are," said Laszlo, returning the tube to its rack. "Spell Trappers catch wisps of stray magic and bottle 'em up. Most are useless, but you never know."

Maggie eyed the rows of tubes. "Are they dangerous?"

"I sure as hell hope so."

"Well, maybe I'll buy one," she said, taking out her wallet. "A little magic might come in useful. How much are they?"

"Thousand bucks a pop."

Maggie put her wallet away.

She meandered over to Lump, who had his face pressed against the tank of luminescent eels. He spoke with quiet ecstasy.

"Aren't they amazing?"

Maggie nodded. "I like their colors." But soon her attention drifted to a table of what looked like bird cages draped with paisley scarves. She raised a corner of the nearest, expecting some kind of exotica.

Instead, she found herself eye to eye with a scrawny humanoid no more than a foot tall. With its wrinkled face and greasy suit, it looked like a wizened maître d', but its skin had greenish undertones, and the tiny hands gripping the cage's bars were tipped with thorny black talons. Tiny playing cards littered the cage floor.

"Buy me," it said in an incongruous baritone.

Maggie recoiled. "What?" she gasped. "No—I would never!"

The creature looked indignant. "Why not? I can cook, clean, slice a throat, and devour the evidence. I even do windows."

"That sounds wonderful. But I'm not in the market."

The creature grumbled and sat down to resume its game of solitaire. Maggie let the covering drop and turned to Lump. "Did you hear that?"

Her brother was still mesmerized by the eels. "What? . . . No. Oh, I wish I could work in a shop like this," he said wistfully. "They wouldn't even have to pay me."

"You'd have to work with Nyshki, the nose-picking whatever-he-is."

"That's okay. I don't mind a little nose picking."

Maggie grimaced and turned away in time to see another peculiar spectacle.

A customer had entered the shop—a matronly woman in a fur-trimmed coat holding a fancy handbag, out of which poked the head of a toy poodle. Nyshki was showing her an assortment of antique chimes and gongs. Given what Maggie had already witnessed, none of this was particularly outlandish. What caught her attention, however, was the mirror leaning against a nearby pillar.

The mirror's surface was clouded with age, but it showed Nyshki in his true doglike form. And not just Nyshki. While the customer's body remained the same, her head was now that of an imperious catfish. Her barbels twitched as she stroked her pet, which was not a poodle but something reptilian with a pronounced underbite.

Another demon? How many lived in this crazy city? Maggie almost burst out laughing. Twenty-four hours ago, a demon was something that couldn't possibly be real. Now she had met several, and not one was the fiery monstrosity she'd imagined such creatures to be. This was oddly comforting, even sort of fantastic. She wondered if the demoness lived in a high-rise with an elevator and doorman, and whether the doorman had any idea that the lady in the penthouse resembled a catfish.

Probably not, Maggie decided. Then again, maybe the doorman was a demon too. Maybe there were entire apartment complexes whose occupants were nothing but demons. Her thoughts turned to the mirror itself. Did mirrors reveal a demon's true nature? That couldn't be the case for all mirrors; Maggie was certain she'd seen Laszlo's reflection in the taxi's rearview and the mirror behind the diner's counter. In both cases, he had looked perfectly human.

What was so special about *this* mirror? Did Dimitri have a different form, and if so, would the mirror reveal it to her? If Maggie repositioned herself, she just might be able to find out.

But when she looked for Dimitri, she discovered the pawnbroker had moved. He was no longer at his desk but in a snug little office just off the main floor. The door was open, and she could see him seated inside, his face illuminated by the glow of a computer screen as he examined the curse documents. The demon's brow was furrowed, his kindly face set in a troubled frown.

As if sensing her gaze, Dimitri looked up. Their eyes met, and he gestured for Maggie to fetch Lump and Laszlo. She did so, and the three squeezed into the office, which was crowded with boxes and old filing cabinets. There was only one other chair aside from Dimitri's. Of course, Laszlo promptly claimed it.

"So what's up?" he asked pleasantly. "Is Nerd Power going to save the day?"

Dimitri looked to Maggie. "Close the door, my dear."

As she did, she felt a knot forming in her stomach. Whatever Dimitri discovered had shaken him.

She turned back to find the pawnbroker stroking his side whiskers as though pondering how best to begin. "I have never seen such a thing before," he said quietly. "It is most unusual."

"What?" said Maggie. "What haven't you seen?"

Dimitri fixed her with a grim look before tapping the ebony case before him. "Your curse has been tampered with."

CHAPTER 12
ECHOES

Laszlo resisted the urge to scream. Complications were the last things he needed.

"What do you mean?" he said. "How can someone tamper with a curse?"

Dimitri spread his hands. "The documentation for this curse is incomplete. I have sold such objects before, Laszlo. Authentic curse folios fetch high prices. But only if they are intact. This folio is not."

Laszlo scanned the array of documents. "What's missing?"

"The last rites."

"What are those?" asked Maggie.

"Every curse has four components," Dimitri explained. "The *incantatio*, the *materia*, the *ritus*, and the *cruciati*. In English, they are the invocation, the materials needed to break the curse, the rites to perform, and the Bearers' torments. This case contains three of the necessary documents, but the ritus is absent. Do you know why this would be?"

Laszlo slumped on the folding chair and chewed his lip, well aware that Maggie was glowering at him. What had he possibly done to deserve this? "No idea," he said. "Last night was the first time I ever opened the goddamn thing."

"Then how did you learn of the curse's particulars?" asked Dimitri.

Laszlo consulted his memory. "There was an orientation when the Society brought me on board. Some handshakes, some cocktails, the usual bonhomie bullshit. The boss gave me a rundown of the curse and showed me my digs—corner office with a secretary, thank you very much. Since then, they've pretty much left me alone."

"How long ago was this?"

Laszlo blew out his cheeks. "Why is everyone so interested in dates? I don't know. Harding was president. Fantastic eyebrows."

Dimitri gave an inscrutable grunt. He was always grunting and looking you over with mild disapproval, like you had soup on your tie. It drove Laszlo nuts.

"So you never met your predecessor?"

"Nope. The old-timers say Basil or Bebop—whatever his name was—just stopped showing up to work. He's either dead, or he went AWOL."

The next grunt was accompanied by some rubbing of the temples. Dimitri was such a ham.

"Laszlo," he said wearily. "The ritus is missing. This we know. We also know that only the official Keeper can access an active curse's folio. If you are being truthful—and I know you are, because Laszlo cannot fool Dimitri—then it must have been your predecessor who opened the case when the ritus was removed. Now you say this demon disappeared under mysterious circumstances. And who does the Society choose to replace him? A notorious playboy who undoubtedly naps in that corner office, leaves his work to his assistant, and wastes his salary indulging countless vices. Does this not strike you as peculiar?"

"When you put it that way, it does seem a little odd."

Dimitri resumed the vigorous temple massage.

"Look, I'm not an idiot," admitted Laszlo. "I know I didn't exactly *deserve* the job, but I assumed Dad pulled a few strings. What's wrong with a little nepotism?"

"A great deal," Dimitri grumbled. "But tell me, has your father pulled strings before? From what you have told me of him, it does not seem in character."

Laszlo shifted uncomfortably. The truth was that his father never did anything for him except clear his debts when they ballooned to levels that might sully the family name. The last time Laszlo slunk home in need of funds, his father gave him the money along with a warning not to come scrounging for more. Laszlo had taken the cash, along with a case of golden spoons that were going to be used at a feast in Lucifer's honor. He promptly fenced the spoons and got himself a Maybach that was repossessed six months later.

His father never mentioned the theft, but Laszlo couldn't help but wonder if it lay behind his response to Androvore. The message still chilled him: *Do as you see fit . . . If he fails, so be it . . .*

"You're right," Laszlo conceded. "It's not his way."

"Well," said Dimitri, "without the ritus, I could not possibly guess what ceremony must be performed. Even if I could, the materia for this curse are not so easy to procure. Centuries ago, relics and royal jewels were more plentiful. So many kings and kingdoms! There were even three popes. Today?" He made a gesture of helpless sympathy. "Can you tell me anything about this Witchstone? Surely, the children must know something."

He looked expectantly at the Drakefords.

"It's in the woods near our house," said Maggie. "We don't go there unless we have to. Our ancestors are buried around it, and it's a pretty gloomy place."

Laszlo swiveled. "*Gloomy?* The spirits were *screaming*, Dimitri. I practically soiled myself. You know I have a thing about ghosts."

"I do."

Laszlo continued rambling as though it were three o'clock every other Tuesday and he was sprawled on Dr. Nussbaum's couch. "It was awful, Dimitri. There I was, surrounded by rustic ghosts. Meanwhile there's this big-ass bowl carved into the Witchstone like some sacrificial altar. It was so creepy—you really should have seen it." He sat up abruptly. "Wait. You *can* see it!"

Phone in hand, Laszlo swiped past several texts and went to Photos, found what he was looking for, and thrust the device at Dimitri. The pawnbroker squinted uncertainly at the images before transferring them to his computer. Seconds later, they appeared on the monitor, considerably larger but still rather dark and grainy.

"The light wasn't great," said Laszlo.

"There are ways around that," said Dimitri. He ran the picture through a program that displayed multiple versions of an image. These were markedly crisper. Some resembled negatives or displayed colors that could not be seen in the original. Dimitri tapped the screen.

"Who is the lady?"

"That's our mother," said Lump.

"Elegant face," said Dimitri. "Lovely cheekbones."

"Forget the mom," said Laszlo impatiently. "What about the Witchstone? What do you make of the inscriptions? I couldn't read them in the dark."

An amused glint shone in Dimitri's eye. He raised an eyebrow. "Can you read them now?"

"What is this, a pop quiz?" snapped Laszlo. "That's why I have *you*!"

Dimitri chuckled and zoomed in on a section where the vines had been removed. Even when it was magnified, he had to scoot so close that his bulbous nose nearly touched the screen. Laszlo watched the pawnbroker's lips moving silently as he deciphered the cryptic words.

A moment later, Dimitri rocketed back from the screen, his chair striking a file cabinet and knocking over a fern, which fell to the floor, its pot shattering into a dozen pieces.

The pawnbroker's face had taken on a sickly sheen. His eyes remained fixed on the image.

"Jesus, what's wrong?" said Laszlo.

Dimitri turned to Maggie. "Where did this stone come from?" he demanded.

"I-I don't know," she sputtered. "It's always been there."

The demon glanced back at the monitor. "No," he said. "I do not think so."

Laszlo's pulse quickened. In their long acquaintance, he had never seen Dimitri so ruffled. "What's wrong? What is that thing?"

Dimitri glanced at the Drakefords. "We should not discuss this matter in front of them."

Laszlo hooked a thumb at the door. "Hit the road, humans."

"I'm not going anywhere," said Maggie. "Whatever's wrong, I want to know."

Lump echoed this sentiment, but his hands were trembling.

Dimitri gave the Drakefords a frank look. "My suspicions may frighten you."

Squeezing past Laszlo, Maggie thrust out her left arm and ripped off a bandage. Near the crook of her elbow, Laszlo saw a line of fresh stitches. Below these was something far more disturbing; an oval patch not unlike that stormy splotch on Jupiter. Its surface swam with subtle, grotesque movement.

Everyone stared at it.

"I'm turning into a monster," said Maggie quietly. "Every day, this spot gets a little bigger, a little more alive. I don't have a parasite; I'm *becoming* the parasite. Nothing you say can possibly scare me more than that."

Lump shouldered past Laszlo for a better look at his sister's arm. The kid looked pale as a corpse. His voice was barely a croak. "When did this happen?"

Maggie stroked his shoulder. "A few weeks ago."

Her brother sounded on the verge of tears. "Does it hurt?"

"Not so much," she said gently. "Not yet, anyway. I'm sorry you had to learn this way, Lump. I'd meant to tell you when it was just the two of us. But Dimitri needs to see this. He needs to know the situation. There's no point sugarcoating anything—we don't have time."

Dimitri peered closely at Maggie's mark, and to Laszlo's surprise, it looked as though he too might start crying. The pawnbroker sniffed irritably and brushed any nascent tears away. "Why did they come?" he muttered to himself. "I should not be involved."

"But you *are* involved," said Maggie. "You know so much more about these things than Laszlo. I wish *you* were our Curse Keeper."

Laszlo found these comments rather rude and hurtful and said as much, but no one paid him any mind. Instead, Dimitri rebandaged Maggie's arm. "I wish I was too," he said gently. "The young should not pay for the sins of the old."

"How touching," Laszlo sneered. "But your busted fern and I have some questions. What got you so twitchy? You practically did a backflip."

Dimitri glanced down at the bits of soil and broken pottery. "I apologize," he said. "My reaction was undignified."

"Fuck 'dignified.' What *is* that thing?"

The pawnbroker turned back to the image on the screen. When he spoke, the words came reluctantly. "Have you ever heard of the Lost Magi?"

"What, the frankincense-and-myrrh guys?"

Dimitri shook his head. "No. The Magi were an order of sorcerers that lived in Alexandria long before your time. Before *my* time, even. There were seven, and it was said they became so powerful their very existence was a threat to demonkind. Naturally, this would not stand. Putting aside their feuds, the Lords of Hell united to hunt the Magi down. Five were destroyed outright. The other two vanished."

"What happened to them?" said Laszlo. "Where did they go?"

Dimitri chuckled. "That is the mystery. No one knows what became of the Lost Magi. There are rumors, of course: the sorcerers destroyed themselves, they fled to another dimension, they were welcomed into Heaven . . ." Dimitri made a dismissive gesture. "So many theories—it was worse than Elvis. Most are absurd, but several had a ring of truth. Or at least of possibility. One came from a beggar who claimed his ancestors served the Magi. He insisted that the Lost Magi had *never* left—that they were hiding in plain sight, preserved in stone like flies in amber. When Alexandria was destroyed, these stones sank into the city's harbor. And there the Lost Magi remain, submerged within their sanctuaries, awaiting the day their disciples might revive them."

Laszlo stared at the demon across from him. "And you believe this?"

Dimitri raised a stern finger. "I did not say I believe it. I said it had the ring of possibility. If you wish to know more of the Magi, you should consult the Signora Bellascura in Rome. She is the true expert."

"A signora, eh? Is she hot?"

"She is five thousand years old."

"I'll take that as a no."

Maggie spoke up. "When did this rumor start?"

Dimitri considered. "A thousand years ago. Perhaps more."

"If that's true, wouldn't the harbor have been searched by now?" said Maggie.

Laszlo snapped his fingers. "Bingo! Dimitri, I felt this thing from a hundred yards away. That stone's like Chernobyl. There's no way anyone could have missed it."

"So it is powerful," Dimitri said, confirming his instinct.

Laszlo laughed. "'Powerful' is an understatement, and that only proves my point. No one could have overlooked this thing. Especially if it was just sitting in a harbor."

"A fair point," said Dimitri. "But is it not possible that the stone was enchanted to be undetectable by the Magi's enemies? And if it was submerged, is it possible these concealments may have weakened over time? Water and magic do not mix, Laszlo. You know this. What if the Lords abandoned the hunt before the stones could be detected? What if, many centuries later, disciples of the Magi salvaged one of these 'Holy Grails' from the harbor—what then? The disciples must revive the Magus within, but it will not be easy; the enchantments are powerful. Protective spells take time to unravel. Where to undertake such painstaking work? Not Egypt; too many demons. Europe and Asia are little better. No, the disciples must hide their master somewhere safe, somewhere enemies would never think to look. And then it dawns upon them . . . the New World!"

Laszlo broke out in applause. "Hot damn. You should write fiction, Dimitri. Something pulpy and commercial. Maybe a bodice ripper."

Dimitri did not look amused. "I dearly wish this was fiction. My belly says otherwise."

"Come on," Laszlo chided. "Don't you think you might be reaching a teensy-tiny bit?"

The other demon jabbed a finger at the image on his screen. "*That* does not come from the Catskills. Obsidian is not native to this region, Laszlo, but it is common near Alexandria. The stone's inscriptions are ancient

Greek and archaic Latin, the very languages one might find in a Roman city with Macedonian roots. Archaic Latin went out of use in 75 BC, so we can assume the inscriptions were made earlier. As for the Greek, it is the Alexandrian dialect, which was not adopted until the fourth century BC.

"Put this together, and we have a powerful artifact whose inscriptions suggest Alexandrian origins during the very era the Lost Magi vanished. And let us not overlook that someone deemed this 'Witchstone' so important they transported it across an ocean and dragged it up a mountain. You tell me, Laszlo. Is this a coincidence?"

Laszlo whistled. "This goes way beyond nerd. You're a damn scholar."

"I prefer 'pawnbroker.'"

Lump looked to Dimitri. "So you're saying we live next to an Egyptian sorcerer who's been locked in a stone cocoon for thousands of years?"

Dimitri nodded heavily. "Yes, my boy. Your family's curse makes me all the more certain."

"Why is that?" said Maggie.

The pawnbroker knit his fingers together. "It is clear that this 'witch'—or whatever she was—dedicated her life to the stone. She considered her work with it to be of vital importance, even sacred. How do we know? Simple. Before she died, she bartered her very soul to ensure that work would continue."

"That's a real thing?" said Maggie shakily. "People can really do that?"

"Oh, yes," said Dimitri. "A mortal soul is always the price of invoking a curse, and this woman paid it willingly. If she could not complete her task, she would compel her accuser to finish it for her. The curse gave him little choice. The longer he delayed, the greater his suffering. Should he fail, the curse would pass to his descendants." Dimitri gestured sadly at Maggie's arm. "And that, alas, brings us to the present."

Laszlo gawked at Dimitri. "You're better than that Belgian detective—what's his name?"

"Poirot," said Dimitri.

"That's it," said Laszlo. "Listen, this is all super interesting, but there's still one problem. Even if we find all the materia, we still don't know how to use it."

"Yes," said Dimitri testily. "And perhaps, instead of making witty comments, you should be asking why the ritus is missing. Perhaps your predecessor looked into the stone's origins. Perhaps those inquiries cost him his life. Perhaps he removed the ritus to prevent the return of a powerful enemy."

Laszlo clucked his tongue. "You think he jumped on a grenade."

Dimitri threw up his hands. "I don't know! I am merely voicing possibilities. And now I am finished. I run a quiet shop, and that's precisely the way I like it. This Witchstone . . . these missing rites . . . These are dark echoes, Laszlo. They frighten me. How could you bring such things to my doorstep?"

"Hello? I didn't know what I was bringing. That's *why* I brought it."

"Well, you should not have!" Dimitri barked. "And now, if you will excuse me, I am going to delete these images, pot a fern, and have a drink. I intend to forget you were ever here."

Laszlo considered. "That'll take a lot of booze."

"Don't be ridiculous," said Dimitri. From a drawer, the demon removed a tin that contained a number of red capsules. "Mind scrubbers," he said. "Each pill removes an hour's worth of memories. Three should do it, I think."

He counted them out into his palm.

"Seems a little extreme," said Laszlo.

"Such practices are common in my trade. Do you think you are the first to come here with secrets I did not wish to know? Ha! Be grateful. Some would pay a fortune to learn about this Witchstone."

"Aw, you'd never sell me out," said Laszlo. "We have history."

Dimitri poured himself a brandy. "Everything has limits. Now go, before I change my mind."

"Wait," said Laszlo. "We still need to acquire the materia. If we don't have the components, it won't matter if we're missing the rites to break the curse. Any idea where we can track down a relic or some royal jewels? What about a magic item? Something more legit than spelltubes but not super well protected?"

Laszlo gave a little cry as Dimitri tossed the capsules back and chased them down with a shot of brandy. How could he help them if he was about to forget everything they'd discussed?

Setting down the glass, the pawnbroker thumped his chest. "Do not worry," he said. "The capsules will not take effect for several minutes. I may know of some magic nearby. Nyshki's clan lives in Central Park. You know Ramble Cave?"

Laszlo nodded. "Sure. That spot they walled off by the lake."

"Correct. Nyshki has no love for his people. He told me they brought a treasure from the old country—a magic porridge pot. He wanted me to steal it for him, but that was just spite. God knows I feed him well enough. I leave the pot's theft to you."

Already, Laszlo's mind was racing. "This cave," he mused. "The entrance will be hidden. We'll need the key . . ."

Dimitri nodded. "There is a man nearby who sells hot dogs from a cart. You cannot miss him—he's there every day. An ugly little fellow. He is the lookout and will have a key to the clan's lair. If you are clever, perhaps he will also reveal the entrance."

"Anything else?" said Laszlo.

"Yes. Do *not* eat his hot dogs."

Laszlo was tempted to ask why but thought better of it.

Rocking up from his chair, Dimitri came around to clasp the Drakefords' hands. "My dears, I bid you farewell. I hope we meet again. I will not remember you, but you will remember Dimitri, and that is something to build on."

Turning to Laszlo, the demon embraced him. "Goodbye, my friend. Be good. And if you cannot be good, don't be too bad." With this, Dimitri gave Laszlo a probing look that made him squirm. He could always tell when Laszlo wasn't being wholly forthcoming. The pawnbroker undoubtedly suspected something shady was in the works, but it wasn't the nature of a demon to interfere, not even as soft a touch as Dimitri. All he could do was appeal to Laszlo's better nature, which he did with a parting pat on the shoulder. "Look after them, eh?"

"Yeah, yeah," said Laszlo. "Those pills kicking in yet?"

"Oh, yes. My head is getting very—what is the word—*tingly*. Very tingly."

"So you won't remember any of this?" Dimitri shook his head. "In that case"—and Laszlo brought out a handful of spelltubes and a jar of faerie essence he'd stashed in his pockets—"I need to borrow these."

The pawnbroker's brow furrowed. "I do not lend disposables."

Laszlo herded Maggie and Lump to the door. "Put 'em on my tab, Big D. Try not to forget!"

Dimitri cursed and Laszlo cackled as he ushered the Drakefords out.

By now, the shop was considerably more crowded. Maggie and Lump hurried along, clutching their backpacks and trying not to bump customers who were bidding on a group of indentured imps Nyshki led out from their cages. Heads turned. The customers looked rather startled to see Maggie and Lump. They gave the humans a wide berth.

Laszlo was still cackling when the three stumbled out onto Broome Street.

"*Finally!*" he crowed. "I finally got him! Oh, Dimitri, you poor sap."

Maggie shouldered her pack. "I can't believe you'd steal from a friend."

Laszlo snickered. "I know, I know. I'm the worst. *Blah blah blah*. But we need this stuff. Speaking of which . . ." He handed the Drakefords two spelltubes each. "For emergencies only. Just pull the cork and let it fly."

Lump looked puzzled. "We throw the cork?"

"The tube, Einstein. The tube. Or you can just smash it."

The boy mouthed a silent *oh*. Hefting the curse case, Laszlo started for the subway station at Spring Street. The Drakefords fell in beside him.

"But what happens when we throw the tube?" asked Lump.

The three crossed Mott Street. "No idea," said Laszlo. "That's the fun."

The boy peered with greater interest at the vials. "Could they explode?"

"Possibly," said Laszlo. "Make sure it explodes on the other guys."

"What other guys?" asked Maggie.

Laszlo looped an arm around her. "Those kobolds we're gonna rob!"

CHAPTER 13
A WALK IN THE PARK

Maggie had questions. Dozens, in fact, but she held her fire as Laszlo took them zigging down streets and zagging up avenues. The crush of people still astounded, but she no longer felt like shutting her eyes and plugging her ears. She was adjusting. Besides, her mind was whirling with new information.

How she wished Dimitri were their Keeper! If he were managing things, they wouldn't be in such a mess. He would have realized the ritus was missing ages ago and gotten to the bottom of it. Dimitri was not only knowledgeable but also courteous and kind. Maggie wondered if he was the exception or if demons had been painted with too broad a brush.

Laszlo came up short in every category but height and arrogance. She watched him as he strolled along, carefree, eyes alert and mischievous, mouth set in a permanent smirk. His human form might have been handsome—no point pretending otherwise—but she knew it was all a mirage. Everything about him was a mirage. Hollow and flashy, false to the core. Dimitri was more like Gladys: old and battered, perhaps, but solid.

Laszlo glanced over. "I know what you're thinking."

Maggie coughed. Could demons read minds?

"You need to pee," he went on complacently. "You haven't tinkled since we hit the road. Your bladder's about to explode, but you're too shy to pipe up. Am I right, or am I right?"

"Bull's-eye."

"Well, you're in luck. That place on the corner has a decent crapper. Clean, well ventilated, and they don't use that cheapo single ply."

"Great."

Laszlo held a twenty between his fingers. "Take Flapjack and get me a chocolate shake, while you're at it. I've gotta make some calls."

"It's *Sir* Flapjack," Lump reminded him. The demon shrugged, already absorbed in his phone.

Maggie took the money and ushered Lump across the street when there was a gap in the traffic. The destination was a shop with the name *Mulberry Sweets* scripted on the awning. As they approached, Maggie caught their reflection in a window. For a moment, she registered the pair as strangers—a scruffy young woman and a kid in ratty clothes carrying backpacks. Maggie sighed inwardly. She and Lump didn't look like bumpkins; they looked homeless.

A bell jingled as she pushed the door open. Maggie gazed about and fell instantly in love. The shop was small and utterly charming with its round marble tables, glass jars brimming with sweets, and the warm scent of cinnamon in the air. A middle-aged woman with a brown bob and pink apron was arranging pastries in a counter display. She looked up as they entered and smiled.

"Can I help you?"

Maggie wiped her palms on her jeans. Why was she so nervous? "Hi. Can we use your bathroom? I promise we'll buy something," she added.

The woman laughed. "No worries. It's just around that corner."

"Thank you," said Maggie, and hurried past the tables with Lump in tow. When she opened the bathroom door, he darted in ahead of her.

"Emergency!" he squeaked, and pulled it shut behind him.

Maggie remembered all the Cokes he'd guzzled that morning. He must have been dying.

Instead of waiting at the door, she went back out front. The shopkeeper smiled sympathetically.

"Little man got the jump on you?"

"Yes, he did. Can I order a chocolate milkshake?"

"You most certainly can. What size?"

Maggie peered at a hand-lettered chalkboard. "Medium, I guess. Our friend didn't say what size he wanted."

The woman nodded and went to a cooler where a dozen different ice creams were displayed in stainless steel pans. "Where's home?"

Maggie reddened. "That obvious, huh?"

The woman scooped chocolate into a metal cup. "That you're from out of town? Oh, that's no biggie. Half this city's from someplace else."

Maggie inspected the caramels. "We live upstate. Tiny village. You wouldn't know it."

The woman laughed. "I'm from Wyoming. You wouldn't know my town, either."

Maggie looked at her with interest. "And you came all the way here?"

"The day I turned eighteen. Wanted to see what all the fuss was about."

"And?"

"Still here. My name's Susie, by the way."

"Maggie. Nice to meet you."

"Likewise," said Susie. She brought the metal cup to a blender and flipped a switch, and the machine began to whir. Lump returned from the bathroom looking visibly relieved.

"Stay put," Maggie told him. "I ordered Laszlo's milkshake."

Leaving her backpack with Lump, Maggie slipped into the bathroom and locked the door. She sat and peed and reflected on how nice it would be to have a real bathroom instead of an outhouse. When she finished, she flushed the toilet and washed her hands, mindful to wipe up the sink. The owner was so damn nice Maggie wanted to leave the bathroom spotless.

She returned to find Lump chewing a rope of licorice. "Where'd you get that?" They didn't have enough money to waste on candy.

"It's my fault," said Susie. "The kid was practically drooling, so I let him have one."

"Oh," said Maggie. "Well, I hope he thanked you."

"He did. My guy Lump's a perfect gentleman."

"I really am," Lump agreed.

Susie had already poured the milkshake into a pink cup. Maggie hurried over to pay. "How much do we owe you?"

"Nine bucks."

Maggie's eyes nearly popped out of her head. "For a *milkshake*?"

Susie laughed. "Welcome to New York. I'll knock off a buck for the conversation."

Maggie handed over Laszlo's twenty, and Susie gave her change, along with a little pink card that she punched.

"Nine more and you get a freebie."

Maggie glanced at it. "That's nice, but we're only here a few days."

"Well, pop back in and say hey before you go. Us country gals gotta stick together. See ya later, Lump!"

Lump raised his licorice in solidarity.

The Drakefords left Mulberry Sweets feeling considerably better than when they'd arrived. Outside, they found Laszlo pacing irritably on the sidewalk, engaged in what appeared to be a heated conversation. When he saw them, he muttered something into the phone and hung up.

"What took you so long?" he said.

"You're the one who told us to use the bathroom," Maggie reminded him. "Here's your milkshake, by the way, and your change. You're welcome."

Laszlo pocketed the money and hefted the milkshake before eyeing it suspiciously. "What size is this?"

"Medium."

The demon's face curdled. "*Medium?* Oh, for fuck's sake. Here's a life lesson, Maggie: Mediums are for indecisive pussies. Go big or go home."

"You didn't say what size you wanted," she retorted. "I had to guess."

"Well, next time guess *extra large*. This body requires a steady supply of sugar, salt, and lipids."

"Are you diabetic?" asked Lump.

Taking the boy's licorice, the demon bit off a sizable chunk. "Could be. Thanks for your concern, Lump. At least someone cares about my health."

Maggie snatched the licorice and returned it to her brother. "Next time you want a milkshake, you can get it your own damn self. Who were you talking to just now?"

The demon looked amused. "Hoo-hoo! Well, aren't you the nosy parker."

"I'm not nosy," said Maggie untruthfully. "But I have a right to know if you told anyone what we learned at Dimitri's. That stuff about the Witchstone sounded like a big deal."

Laszlo glanced around. "It *is* a big deal. Which is why I'll kindly ask you to shut your piehole."

"Then who were you talking to?"

But the demon did not provide an answer. Maggie pressed the issue all the way to Spring Street, but Laszlo wouldn't budge. When they reached the subway entrance, the Curse Keeper headed down the steps without a backward glance.

The Drakefords hesitated. As they stared down into the unknown, people flowed past in colorful shoals. Lump was clutching Maggie's hand so tightly that her fingers began to ache. So much about New York was unsettling, but at least there were familiar sights—sky, clouds, the occasional tree. But the subway? Pavement vibrated beneath their feet, followed by an updraft of warm and pungent air. It was like entering the lair of some beast or guardian of the underworld.

A voice crackled from below. "Mission Control to Drakefords. Come in, Drakefords . . ."

Maggie and Lump exchanged a look before heading down the steps. At the bottom, they stepped out into a large, dimly lit space with low ceilings and lines of people shuffling through metal turnstiles. Maggie looked about for Laszlo and found the demon leaning casually against a ticket machine. He started clapping.

"Bravo! My bumpkins made it all the way down to the big bad subway." Glancing at a nearby pillar, he gave a start. "Is that *graffiti?* Heavens. We'd best retreat!"

"Oh, shut up," Maggie snapped. "Let's see you fix a transmission."

Grinning, Laszlo sauntered over. "Touché, Lady Rube. Touché."

He led them to the turnstile, where he swiped a plastic card through a reader. Maggie went first, followed by Lump, and then Laszlo.

Once through, they found themselves on a platform with people awaiting the next train. There were hundreds, all in sweaters and jackets and staring at phones or simply gazing off into space as though the subway offered a welcome reprieve from the hectic pace above. Maggie decided that people watching in New York was a lot more interesting than back home. In Schemerdaal, everyone looked the same, talked the same, even thought the same. Scanning the platform, Maggie couldn't find two faces that were alike. And all of them strangers—

All except one.

Maggie did a double take. Thirty feet away stood the matronly woman from Dimitri's shop. The one whose catfishy form she'd spied in the mirror. And there she was, clutching her fancy handbag with the tiny "poodle" peeking through the zipper. Maggie elbowed Laszlo.

"What's up?" he said.

She spoke in an undertone. "How many of *your kind* live here?"

He shrugged. "A couple hundred, maybe. Why the hell are you whispering?"

"Because one's right over there," said Maggie from the corner of her mouth. "By the guy playing the violin. That lady with the fancy hat. She was in Dimitri's shop."

Laszlo glanced over. "The old bat with the pooch? You sure?"

"Yes! Nyshki was showing her chimes, and I saw her reflection in this mirror that showed what she really looks like. That lady looks like a catfish, and that cute little dog is *not* a cute little dog."

Lump tugged at Maggie's sleeve. "What's going on?"

Laszlo motioned for silence. When he spoke, Maggie caught a note of tension. "Follow me down the platform," he said curtly. "Don't look back."

The Drakefords did as they were told. When they'd gone a hundred feet or so, they stopped and took up position much as they had before.

Laszlo gazed stonily ahead. "Your shoe's untied," he said.

Maggie glanced down at her Chuck Taylors. "No, they're not."

"*Au contraire*, Your Highness. Retie them and check on our friend while you're at it."

"But—"

"Today, please."

Confused and irritated, Maggie dropped to one knee and fiddled with her sneaker. As she retied the laces, she darted a glance up the platform. To her relief, Madam Catfish remained planted by the violinist, a rotund figure in a fancy hat and coat waiting for the uptown 6.

"Hasn't moved," said Maggie when she stood back up.

Laszlo merely nodded as though she'd told him the weather.

"Why are we being so sneaky?" said Lump. "Is someone following us?"

Again, Laszlo didn't respond. Instead, he watched the train, which was now barreling into the station with a god-awful screech. When it stopped, they squeezed on after several passengers disembarked. The train was absurdly crowded, and Maggie soon discovered that people wearing camping packs were not very popular on subways. There were grimaces and grumbles, side-eyes and impassive death stares.

Fortunately, Maggie was immune to such things—one of the few perks of being a sin-eater. That said, there was no hope of shedding the pack when she could barely keep her face out of her neighbor's armpit. Poor Lump had practically disappeared into the bosom of a woman who was completely oblivious to his mortified presence. As for Laszlo, he appeared perfectly at ease, his expression one of urbane detachment. Maggie wished something would drip on him.

The train clattered along. Passengers bustled on and off until the stop at Grand Central, where a slew of riders disembarked and they could finally claim some seats. Maggie took Lump's pack and placed both on her lap so he could sit in relative comfort. Laszlo continued to stand. Every so often, he glanced casually about the car. Maggie assumed he was scanning for Madam Catfish. But Madam Catfish was nowhere to be seen.

At Fifty-First Street, Maggie did notice someone, however: a young man who had boarded the train and was standing some ten feet past Laszlo. She tried to look him over without being too obvious. He was perhaps five or ten years older than she was and, with his dark jeans and stylish blazer, struck her as someone who worked in a creative field. At least that was how all the creative types looked in the magazines at the Kingston Library. Like almost everyone else on the subway, the man was busy texting, until he suddenly stopped and looked over at Maggie. She smiled awkwardly, mortified that she'd been caught staring.

But he returned her smile, and it was then that Maggie became aware of a tingling at the base of her skull. The sensation soon became a pleasant buzzing, like the hum of bees inside an active hive. Within ten seconds, the bees had reached such a fervor they drowned out the subway's clamor. Lump pointed something out to Maggie, but she ignored him, just as she ignored the stinging pain beneath her bandage. All that mattered was that she keep this young man's attention, that she talk to him, that they connect.

The car gave a sudden lurch, knocking several passengers off balance as the subway ground to an unexpected halt. One of these passengers was the young creative, who had been staring so intently at Maggie that he'd let go of the handrail. Jolted off his feet, he broke eye contact and crashed backward into a woman, knocking the shopping bag from her hand. She yelled at him in Spanish, and the man seemed to come to his senses, apologizing profusely as he regained his footing.

When the train pulled into the Sixty-Eighth Street station, the man shot Maggie a confused look and hurried out of the car the instant its doors opened.

An explosion of searing, disappointed rage flashed in Maggie's mind, as hot and jagged as a thunderbolt. It vanished just as quickly, leaving behind an incandescent afterglow. Exhaling, Maggie put a hand to her forehead; it was burning. *Where in hell did that come from?*

She glanced over at Lump, relieved to find him busy reading the advertisements that ran along the car. As for Laszlo, the demon continued to look bored and aloof: a condescending cat enduring the company of mice. Folding her hands in her lap, Maggie sat very still as the bees subsided into discontented silence.

When they pulled into the Seventy-Seventh Street station, Laszlo had them gather up their things, which Maggie—still deeply unsettled— was more than happy to do. Off the train, up some stairs, and out they popped, blinking like moles in the daylight.

The Drakefords followed Laszlo past a hospital and down a one-way street that led toward Central Park. This neighborhood was quieter and less hectic than downtown.

When they entered the park, Maggie gazed about, inwardly amazed. It was as if someone had dropped the entire Witchwood smack in the middle of Manhattan. Not as wild and overgrown, perhaps, but just as verdant. She caught up as Laszlo led them down a path where joggers passed at regular intervals.

"Listen up," he said. "Our objective's simple: steal the pot and check a magic item off our list. Kobolds aren't exactly geniuses, but we'll still need to be quick and clever."

Lump asked a question Maggie had been wondering herself. "Um. What exactly is a kobold?"

Laszlo looked at Lump as if he were daft. "Who the hell hasn't heard of kobolds?"

"I haven't," said Maggie.

"Teutonic hobgoblins," Laszlo explained impatiently. "Homely little shits that lurk in caves and mine shafts. For Christ's sake, Nyshki was a kobold!"

"The dog with three eyes?" said Lump.

"That's right."

Lump looked relieved. In his native state, Nyshki had been roughly the size of a kindergartner. "So they're not dangerous?"

Laszlo laughed. "Thieving's more their game. Then again, they'll happily slit a throat if chance offers."

Lump turned the color of oatmeal.

"So what do we need to do?" said Maggie pointedly. "I mean, I assume you won't be helping because of some obscure Curse Keeper rule."

"Well, I can't actually *steal* the pot for you," Laszlo agreed, "but I won't let the little Fidos slice you to ribbons. Anyway, it won't come to that. There's a trick for dealing with kobolds . . ."

Laszlo shared his tip as they ventured deeper among the trees. The city gradually receded until the skyscrapers seemed like sentries or watchtowers looking out upon a foreign land. They were surrounded by emerald grass and majestic trees with sunlight filtering through their bright autumn leaves. They passed a class of high school students, girls dressed in identical sweaters and skirts standing by a fountain, where their teacher was pointing out the statue of an angel. Laszlo flipped off the angel before going to buy lunch from a food cart.

Maggie continued watching the girls. She wondered what it would have been like to attend a fancy school, to have had classmates and a uniform and go on field trips. All the books she'd read made high school seem like the greatest time in a person's life.

There was a tug on her sleeve.

"What do you think of Laszlo's plan?" said Lump.

Maggie glanced at the demon, who was now gabbing with the vendor. "No idea. It's not like I've ever done anything like this before. Hopefully his little trick works. Then again, I've also been thinking maybe it's better if you stay behind."

Lump's face fell. "Are you kidding? I want to help. And if there's trouble, I'll just use magic." Maggie's brother held up one of the spelltubes Laszlo had given them.

She peered at the twinkling mist within. "We don't even know what they do."

"Hey!"

They turned to see Laszlo hurrying toward them with an armful of drinks and sandwiches. "Put that shit away," he hissed. "You can't wave spells around a public park."

Snatching the tube from Lump, he off-loaded the food and drinks into their arms. While the siblings divvied up the sandwiches, Laszlo held the spelltube up to the sunlight.

"Hmm," he mused. "This one looks kind of oomphy. I'd better hold on to it."

"But it's mine," protested Lump.

Laszlo handed him a different tube. "This baby's more your speed."

Lump held the new tube up to the light, as Laszlo had done. This one did not swirl or twinkle. On the contrary, its contents had condensed on the bottom and gave off a brownish hue. To Maggie's eye, the spell looked like a bottled fart.

He thrust it back at Laszlo. "I don't want this one."

"Too late. No reswaps or take-backsies."

Lump sulked all the way to the Ramble, a wooded area apparently popular with bird-watchers. The paths here were narrower; Laszlo led them to one that skirted the rocky shoreline of a lake. Claiming a bench near a stone archway, they ate their lunch and watched a man sell hot dogs from a colorful cart with an umbrella. He reminded Maggie of Rumpelstiltskin, crooked and fidgety with bright eyes set in a wrinkled face. That face, she observed, was quick to smile when someone approached and even quicker to scowl if they passed without buying anything.

"So that's a kobold?" she murmured.

Laszlo licked hot sauce from his fingers. "Yup. Don't let the human guise fool you. He's a nasty piece of business. And the hot dogs? Ten to one, they're squirrel meat."

Maggie grimaced and abandoned the rest of her sandwich. "When do we make our move?"

With this, Laszlo grinned and knocked Maggie's drink with the back of his hand. The bottle fell on its side, spilling iced tea all over her pants. Maggie shot to her feet and glared at him.

"Oops," he deadpanned. "See if Captain Kobold has some napkins. Keep him busy, but don't buy anything." He held out a ten-dollar bill. Maggie took it and marched over to the vendor. Catching sight of her jeans, the old man offered several napkins.

"Thank you," said Maggie, blotting her jeans. "Do you have another of these?" she asked, and held up the bottle of peach iced tea.

The man spoke with a German accent. "No. But I have lemonade. The girl likes lemonade?"

Maggie quite enjoyed a tart lemonade, but she'd be dead and buried before she tried the concoction he now brandished at her. For one, the bottle had no label. For another, its contents were a cloudy chartreuse.

"No, thank you," she said. "Um, what kinds of chips do you have?"

The old man sniffed and squinted at an assortment of foil bags clipped to a string above him. "Chips, chips . . . Let us see. There are round yellow chips. And orange triangle chips. And pretzels. And a—"

"Ooh!" Maggie exclaimed. "Is that candy?"

The man glanced down at an array of chocolate bars. "Er, yes. This one has chocolate and *Erdnüsse*—er, peanuts. This has toffee. This has . . ."

Laszlo strolled casually behind the cart on his way to a garbage can. He tossed their trash, then turned and gestured for Maggie to wrap things up.

"You know," she said, "on second thought, I'm okay. Thanks, though."

The vendor's smile vanished. "You not buy anything?" he grumbled. "After I give you napkins? Off with you! Go away, you disgusting girl. You filthy little *Flittchen* . . ."

Laszlo sauntered over. "Excuse me. What did you just say to my niece?"

The man turned and blinked up at him. "Eh? Nothing. I said nothing!"

Maggie folded her arms. "That's a lie. He called me a name because I didn't buy anything."

Laszlo turned a haughty eye on the vendor. "Is that so? Well, I think the police might like to hear about this. Stay put. We'll be back."

Looking every inch the affronted gentleman, Laszlo called Lump to join them and led the Drakefords swiftly up the path. When they'd gone around the bend, Laszlo had them wait several moments before doubling back to the trails near the archway. Once there, Laszlo led them down a flight of narrow steps carved into the rock itself.

At the bottom, they found the old man standing before a stone wall, muttering angrily in German while turning out his pockets. Coins and crumpled tissues fell to the ground, along with a variety of dead rodents. Laszlo nudged a stiff gray squirrel with his shoe. "Hmph. I knew it."

The old man whirled to find Laszlo dangling a large, old-fashioned key before his eyes.

"Looking for this, *mein Freund*?"

CHAPTER 14
RAMBLE ON

The hot dog vendor was certainly feisty. The instant Laszlo grabbed him, there was a lot of spitting and cursing, but ultimately the demon managed to flip the old man onto his back and sit on his chest. The kobold writhed and wriggled, but his efforts were in vain. Laszlo tossed Maggie a roll of electrical tape.

"Where did you get this from?" she asked. "Were you going to use this to kidnap us?"

"No comment. Tape his yapper shut, will you?"

Maggie went to work. Within a minute, she'd silenced that remarkably foul mouth and secured the kobold's wrists and ankles. When she'd finished, their captive lay immobilized in the leaves, where he glared at them in mute outrage. Maggie had a flash of self-doubt: What if they'd made a terrible mistake? What if this nasty old man was just a nasty old man?

A moment later, her misgivings vanished.

Piebald patches blossomed on his skin while his jaw began to protrude, straining the tape. Then came the most startling development: a third eye appeared, pushing up like a bloodshot marble between those bristling brows. In less than thirty seconds, the vendor transformed into a hideous humanoid with clawed fingers and a decidedly canine face.

Laszlo checked the bindings before turning to Lump, who had

backed away against the stairs. "Come over here. I want you to try that trick I taught you."

The boy adamantly shook his head. A whimper escaped.

"Listen," said Laszlo. "If you can't do it to a kobold that's tied up, how are you going to do it once we're inside?" He gestured toward the graffitied wall.

Lump shot Maggie a pleading glance.

She shrugged. "You're the one who wanted to come. If you wanted to be coddled, you could have stayed home with Mom."

Maggie knew her words stung, but she refused to feel guilty. Soft wouldn't get them what they needed. Soft would get them killed.

Prying himself away from the steps, Lump inched over to their glaring captive. Steeling himself, he stood over the kobold and stared fixedly at the bulging marble of its third eye. Nothing happened for several seconds; then Maggie noticed the pupil had begun to contract.

"Good," said Laszlo. "You're locked on. He's resisting, but just keep your focus."

The kobold's pupil continued to thin until it was no wider than a hair's breadth. Then it reversed course, dilating rapidly until the entire iris was as black and glossy as a drop of ink. The creature began twitching like a dog having a nightmare. Laszlo poked it in the ribs, but it did not react.

"Didn't I tell you?" he said. "Kobolds are cream puffs if you know what you're doing. At this point, we could dress him up like Little Bo-Peep."

"I'll pass," said Maggie. "How long will he stay like that?"

"Couple of minutes. If you break eye contact, they'll snap out of it eventually, but they're still pretty foggy."

Maggie glanced at the stone wall. "How many will be in there?"

The demon shrugged. "Twenty or thirty, probably."

Lump made an anxious peep. "I-I don't think I can hypnotize thirty kobolds."

Laszlo kicked some leaves over their captive. "You won't have to. Kobolds are nocturnal. We just need to tiptoe in, find the pot, and tiptoe out."

Maggie stashed their packs and came over to inspect the wall. "I don't see a keyhole. What's the use of a key if we don't know where it goes?"

At this, Laszlo displayed a bag of cheese puffs. The Drakefords watched in puzzled silence as the demon proceeded to crush the bag between his hands, grinding the contents until they were thoroughly pulverized.

Lump looked devastated. "I was planning to eat those."

Ignoring him, Laszlo opened the bag and poured some fine orange powder into his palm. Crouching near the wall, the demon blew sharply on the powder so that it formed a swirling cloud. When it dissipated, that section of the wall had a fine dusting of artificial cheese—except for a camouflaged slot that had escaped Maggie's eye.

She whistled. "Clever."

"Old trick," said Laszlo. He inserted the iron key. "Ready?"

Maggie squeezed Lump's hand. "Be brave, and remember that this is for Dad." Her brother responded with a watery but determined smile.

Laszlo looked from one to the other. "Okay: Once we're in, it's up to you. No talking. Spelltubes for emergencies only."

"Got it," said Maggie.

As the moment approached, she found herself looking forward to the challenge.

What had happened on the subway—especially that surge of anger when the man had gone—left her with muscles that were tense and coiled with energy, eager for release. It felt not unlike the flood of adrenaline that accompanied a sin-eating. Perhaps her decade of dodging stones had been to prepare her for this moment.

Was she frightened? Of course. But Maggie Drakeford was no stranger to fear. Almost from her first breath, it had been a constant companion in her life, but one she had learned to cope with long ago.

Was it wrong to steal from the kobolds? Maggie didn't know or care. Her need was greater.

There was a click as Laszlo turned the key.

A stone slab the size of a garden gate swung inward. As it did, foul air seeped out, a nauseating blend of old garbage and wet dog. Lump promptly covered his nose. Kneeling, Maggie poked her head inside.

Ahead was a cluttered tunnel illuminated by strands of blinking Christmas lights. When her eyes adjusted, Maggie caught her breath. Something was looking directly at her from the far end. A face, huge and pallid with a dark-red smile.

Maggie stared at the nightmarish face. Waited for it to move. It was several moments before she realized that the flickering lights gave an illusion of movement. The face was simply a picture, a framed poster propped on a mound of trash.

With a slow exhale, she crept forward. The others followed.

Inside, the ceiling was high enough to accommodate a crouch, rather than a crawl. Maggie peered about. Every inch of the walls and ceiling was plastered with junk: street signs and flyers, sports banners and old license plates, assembled like a haphazard art installation. As they quietly proceeded, Maggie tried not to stare at the picture looming at the end.

The tunnel curved left at the poster and soon opened into a cavern strung with more holiday lights and piled high with metal scrap, disassembled phone booths, and broken arcade games. Maggie could not tell if the kobolds actually used any of this stuff or if they simply had a magpie's impulse to line their nest with shiny things.

She flinched as a hand closed about her wrist. Maggie turned to find Laszlo gazing down at her. In the darkness, his eyes were faintly luminescent, like a pair of glowing blue embers. He nodded to a shadowy area beyond the phone booths. Squinting, Maggie made out niches that had been cut into the wall. An arm dangled out of one, thin and speckled with matted fur. Its clawed hand gave a convulsive twitch.

Laszlo put a finger to his lips: *Quiet.*

No shit, thought Maggie. Looking past the demon, she saw Lump staring at the alcoves with an expression of mute, almost stupefied terror. Maggie waved to get his attention.

You okay? she mouthed.

Lump blinked. He gave an unconvincing thumbs-up and adjusted his glasses. Maggie's spirits sank. Her brother wasn't ready for this. He was too young and too soft. The second they'd discovered him in the trunk, they should have driven him straight home.

She pointed back toward the entrance: *Wait outside.* Lump shook his head. There was nothing to be done unless Maggie wanted to physically haul him out. Then again, Lump might be inclined to argue, and if they made too much noise—well, there went any hope of a swift, uneventful theft.

Turning back, Maggie refocused on the task.

Get in.

Get out.

Go home.

Across the cavern was another tunnel that extended perhaps thirty feet before branching off in two directions. The left-hand passage was dark and sloped downhill. Its air was damp, and Maggie wondered if it led beneath the lake. The right-hand passage was broader and reasonably flat, with barrels and crates stacked along one side. It extended some forty feet before curving off to the right, where the rock gleamed from some light source. It had the flickering quality of firelight, and fire might mean a kitchen. And where there was a kitchen, there might well be a magic porridge pot . . .

Stealing down the passage, Maggie glanced back; there was Lump, trailing them like a spooked gosling. To Maggie's dismay, she spied a spelltube clutched tightly in his fist.

That kid's going to blow himself up.

Just as Maggie hissed at him to put it away, there was a barking cough from up ahead. Whipping around, she saw a shadow projected on the passage where it curved away.

The shadow was coming toward them.

Maggie turned back to see if their Curse Keeper had any guidance, but the demon was nowhere to be found. His absence was so startling that Maggie actually reached back and groped at the darkness. Her hand passed through empty air.

Laszlo had vanished.

There was no time to wonder, for the shadow's caster now rounded the bend and came to a halt no more than twenty feet away. Maggie went absolutely still.

It was a kobold no more than three feet tall, wearing a flowered apron. The sight was so unexpectedly ludicrous that Maggie almost smiled. Then she caught sight of its canine teeth and that blank, chillingly feral expression as the creature peered down the passage.

Don't move, she told herself. *Don't breathe.*

The kobold coughed again, then nibbled at its underarm. It was thrown off balance, tottering sideways before falling to one knee. There was an irritated snarl.

It's drunk! she realized.

Maggie motioned for her brother to hide among the crates. She joined him, wedging herself between a pair of stale-smelling beer kegs. Almost immediately, she found she was crouching in a puddle that smelled far more like urine than Budweiser. There was no time to find another spot, so she held her nose and waited. With luck, the pungency would mask their own scent.

Maggie listened closely as the creature shuffled down the passage. It came slowly, muttering to itself in a singsong rhythm.

> *Backe, backe Kuchen,*
> *der Bäcker hat gerufen.*
> *Wer will guten Kuchen backen,*
> *der muss haben sieben Sachen.*
> *Eier und Schmalz,*
> *Zucker und Salz . . .*

The kobold swayed past with nary a glance in Maggie's direction. When it reached Lump's hiding place, however, it halted. A jittery blue light was dancing on the kobold's puzzled face.

Maggie grimaced. Had Lump uncorked the spelltube?

Peering round the stack of crates, the kobold bared its teeth. "*Ein menschliches Kind!*" it growled. "*Was machst du hier?*"

Maggie heard her brother's terrified voice. "S-sorry, I don't speak

German, but we really need your porridge pot." She gritted her teeth.

The kobold cocked its head. "*Den Haferbrei-Topf?*"

"If that means 'porridge pot,' then yes. Can we borrow it, please?"

The kobold was not prepared for such an earnest request. The creature stared at Lump in dumbfounded silence before bursting into laughter. "You make joke?" it said in English.

"It's not a joke, sir. We really need that pot."

As Lump replied, Maggie saw the kobold wobble. Its posture slackened, and Maggie realized what her brother was doing.

Yes! Hypnotize it! Come on . . .

But the kobold suddenly shook its head as though clearing water from its ears. Reaching into the apron's pocket, it brought forth a boning knife.

"*Betrüger!*"

As it reached for Lump, Maggie sprang from her hiding place and grabbed a sack off a nearby crate. The kobold turned just as she swung it. Twenty pounds of imported jasmine rice smashed into the grotesque muzzle.

The kobold dropped as if poleaxed. Scrambling out from his hiding spot, Lump gawked at the senseless creature before looking up at Maggie. "That was amazing."

Maggie checked the passageway. No sign of others. "Let's tie him up."

The two worked quickly, using wire and string that they tore from nearby packaging. Within two minutes, the unconscious kobold was bound, gagged, and stowed behind a crate of sardines.

"Where's Laszlo?" Lump whispered.

"No idea," said Maggie, arranging the crates. "Ran away, probably. He does a lot of that. Anyway, we can't worry about him now. And put that thing away before it explodes."

Lump glanced down at the spelltube, whose blue radiance shone on the surrounding walls. He tucked the vial away. "I just wanted to be ready. I didn't know it would light up."

Maggie peered over the sardines at the kobold. "Come on. I don't how long he'll be out."

They continued down the passageway, rounding the bend, which opened upon a large cavern, some sixty feet across, with a firepit at its center. Maggie looked left and right for any sign of kobolds. All she found, however, were wooden tables and benches, stained butcher blocks, and washing tubs piled with broken dishes. Overhead, hundreds of dead squirrels, rats, and pigeons dangled from clotheslines.

Lump gave a whimper of disgust.

No porridge pot. Amid the clutter, Maggie spied a glass cabinet atop an old refrigerator.

"Let's start there," she whispered. "It's the only thing in here that isn't trashed."

The two scurried like mice across the cavern. Maggie grabbed a stool and climbed onto the refrigerator to search the cabinet. All she found inside were enameled beer steins.

"What does a porridge pot look like?" whispered Lump from below.

Maggie shut the cabinet. "I don't know. Like a pot. It'll be old, so ignore anything modern."

An urbane voice spoke up from behind them. "Could this be it?"

The Drakefords whirled to see Laszlo holding a coffee mug with *Sassy Mama* inscribed upon it in sparkly pink.

Maggie tried to contain her fury. "*Where have you been?*"

"Here and there," he replied, before raising the mug to her. "Nice swing back in the passage. Smooth as DiMaggio."

Maggie climbed down from the stool. "Go away. You're useless."

"Useless? *Au contraire.* I was doing a bit of reconnaissance. That's how I know there are twenty-two kobolds snoozing just off this cavern, and another eight down the passage we didn't take. Only one was astir, and he's now unconscious, thanks to you. Our path is free and clear."

"But where's the porridge pot?" whispered Lump. "This place is like a junkyard."

"Well," said Laszlo, "I can't just *tell* you where it is. That would be cheating. But if I wanted to find a magic porridge pot, I'd be on the lookout for some seventeenth-century handiwork. And if I had to make a further guess, I'd say it's probably made of copper, crusted over with gruel, and sitting someplace warm."

The Drakefords turned in unison toward the firepit.

There, half-buried among the smoking logs and embers, was a copper pot with a dented lid and a handle so it could be suspended over a fire. Maggie forgave Laszlo at once. The demon might be a coward, but he wasn't entirely useless. Climbing down from the refrigerator, she hurried over to the firepit.

"Wait," Laszlo whispered. "Make sure it's the real thing."

"How?"

"Gee, I don't know. Maybe tell it to make some porridge."

Maggie sighed. She had walked right into that. Crouching, she waved her hand over the pot like it was Aladdin's lamp. "Um, make some porridge," she whispered, before adding a hasty "please." For all she knew, magic pots were touchy.

Nothing happened.

Laszlo sucked his teeth in irritation. "The pot only understands German, you dimwit."

Maggie swallowed a retort. "Yeah? Well, what's German for 'porridge'?"

Lump came and crouched by her. He studied the pot closely. "That kobold called it *Haferbrei-Topf*," he muttered. "I wonder if—"

The pot began rattling as though something mildly seismic was taking place within. Seconds later, hot porridge came bubbling down its sides like lava streaming down a volcano. The mush hissed as it struck the coals, sending up curls of oatmeal-scented steam.

"Great," said Laszlo. "Grab it, and let's go!"

The handle was scalding hot, so Maggie pulled her sleeve down over her hand to grip it. While the pot wasn't heavy, it continued to make porridge. Maggie carried it over to Laszlo, leaving a trail of steaming mush behind her.

"How do we tell it to stop?"

The demon shrugged. "How am I supposed to know?"

"What's German for 'stop'?" asked Lump.

Laszlo pointed a stern finger at the pot. "*Halt.*"

The command didn't work. If anything, the porridge was gushing out even faster. Gallons of the stuff was now pooling on the floor. Maggie stared at the spreading mess.

"We can't take it like this."

"No choice," said Laszlo. "I'll call Dimitri once we're outside. Nyshki will know what to say. Come on."

He strode off toward the tunnel by which they'd entered. Maggie followed, holding the pot at arm's length. They hadn't gone ten steps when they heard a startled cry followed by a bone-jarring crash. Turning, Maggie saw Lump sprawled on the slippery floor, surrounded by broken dishes. Their eyes met.

"I-I'm sorry," he stammered. "The porridge—"

Before Maggie could respond, a terrible clanging sounded throughout the caverns, like someone banging a hammer against a washtub. Laszlo hurried ahead to the archway and peered out into the passage.

He quickly withdrew and turned back to the astonished Drakefords. "We have company."

CHAPTER 15
ALPHA

Maggie looked frantically about. "Is there another exit?"

"Not that I saw," said Laszlo. "We need a barricade."

She carefully set down the gurgling pot and ran with Laszlo to one of the wooden dining tables. Together, they tipped the massive thing onto its side and tried sliding it across the floor. It moved all of six inches.

"No good," Maggie gasped. "It's way too heavy."

Running footsteps came down the passage from which they'd entered. From the other came a chorus of doglike yips and yowls. Maggie scanned every wall and corner. There was nowhere to run, no time to hide. They would have to surrender. Or fight. Laszlo herded the Drakefords from the archway.

"Put your backs against something," he said. "I'll bluff our way out."

Snatching up the porridge pot, Maggie ordered Lump to climb atop one of the refrigerators. He scaled the nearest, and Maggie took up position with a sturdy rolling pin she found on a butcher block. As for Laszlo, he strolled over to the firepit, where he stood casually contemplating the coals.

Kobolds poured in from both tunnels. Short kobolds, fat kobolds, kobolds with mange, kobolds in nightshirts. Some brandished hammers and knives; others carried more unorthodox weapons like plungers and brooms. They filled the room, barking angrily in rapid German. Several advanced upon the Drakefords, but most formed a yipping circle around the elegant figure warming himself by the firepit.

Laszlo surveyed the horde with disdain. As for the kobolds, they did not know what to make of this calm and aloof intruder. Their yammering died away until there was only the occasional yip. When one kobold poked Laszlo with a golf putter, the demon turned and dealt it a vicious backhand whose sound made Maggie jump. The creature staggered back, then toppled onto its behind. A stillness settled over the room. The only sound was the gurgling porridge that continued oozing from the pot at Maggie's feet.

"I'll make this brief," said Laszlo, in a voice dripping with condescension. "This is a robbery. My companions need your porridge pot, and you're going to let them have it. Play nice, and we'll be on our merry way. Make trouble, and I'll turn you into kibble."

A kobold in ill-fitting boxer briefs stepped forward. "No human gives us orders!"

"Who said I was human?"

As he spoke, Laszlo's skin deepened to cobalt and his eyes began to glow. A chubby kobold pointed in alarm.

"*Es ist ein Dämon!*"

Laszlo grinned, revealing a row of catlike teeth. "Correct, *mein Schatz*. I'm a demon. And seeing as I'm a demon and you're a bunch of tacky, flea-bitten schnauzers, you're going to stand down before I lose my patience. Do we understand one another?"

A barrel-chested kobold stepped forward. "*Was ist dein Rang?*"

"Excuse me?" said Laszlo.

"Your rank," the kobold repeated in English. "Your *Dämonen* rank!"

The question appeared to catch Laszlo off guard. "Well, that's really not your concern, is it? All that matters is that I'm very powerful and not to be meddled with."

Other kobolds began to speak up.

"He's lying!"

"This *Dämon* has no power!"

"They cannot even control the pot!"

At this last proclamation, all eyes turned toward Maggie, who was up to her ankles in warm porridge. The kobolds howled with laughter, and the crush around Laszlo began to tighten.

"*Back!*" shouted the demon. Raising his fist, he brandished a spell-tube whose contents sparkled ominously in the firelight. The kobolds eyed it warily. "This vial contains the very Fires of Hell. One more step and you'll be turned to ash!"

"Bah," spat a kobold. "The *Dämon* is bluffing. Seize him!"

"I warned you!"

Laszlo smashed the tube on the cavern floor. The glass shattered into a hundred pieces, releasing a wobbling bubble the size of a basketball, filled with a twinkling gas. The kobolds backed away, heads craning as it floated slowly upward. When it grazed the ceiling, there was a gentle pop, and the bubble expelled a single red spark. All watched with rapt attention as the spark spiraled down in a lazy descent to the ground, where it vanished with a hiss so weak it might have been an apology.

Maggie closed her eyes. *We're dead.*

Things escalated quickly.

The kobolds instantly swarmed Laszlo. Maggie heard the Keeper shrieking for help, but there was nothing she could do—three kobolds now surrounded her, and one was wielding a pitchfork. He jabbed it at Maggie while the others tried to grab hold of her arms. Fortunately, they slipped in the porridge, and she managed to seize the pitchfork's handle and wrench it away. That kobold swore at her and was promptly brained by her rolling pin. Maggie thumped him again for good measure, then set to whacking the others.

As other kobolds charged forward, Lump alerted Maggie like an attentive tail gunner.

"One on your left!"

"Two on your right!"

The never-ending porridge turned out to be her salvation. In order to reach Maggie, the kobolds had to cross its warm, slippery moat.

If they moved too quickly, they lost their footing. Too slow, and they met the rolling pin.

Thud. Thud. Thud. Maggie grunted each time hard maple struck matted fur. Already, seven of the creatures were on their backs in various states of consciousness.

But the kobolds kept coming. Maggie was slowly backed against the refrigerator. They stepped over their fallen brethren, baring murderous teeth. Her breath came in painful gasps. She went for the nearest kobold, but it cracked her knuckles with a police baton. The rolling pin slipped from her grasp and sank into the porridge.

Leathery hands locked about her wrists. Others seized her by the ankles. They were dragging her across the floor.

Amid the wild snarling and cursing, she heard a frightened voice cry out.

"Stop!"

The kobolds hesitated. The shout had come from Lump. Swiveling her head, Maggie saw her brother huddled atop the refrigerator. Firelight reflected from his glasses. In his hand, he clutched the spelltube.

"Let her go!" he cried. "Let her go, or I'll use this!" Lump showed them the glowing vial.

Kobolds doubled over with laughter. The ones who had seized Maggie continued dragging her toward the firepit.

The others began to mock and jeer at Lump. "Show us!" they howled. "Show us your power, boy! Let us see another spark!"

The instant Lump removed the cork, countless vine-like whips erupted from the tube, flashing forth into the morass to seize kobolds by the neck. Dead birds and rodents rained from the cavern ceiling as the creatures were whipped to and fro like rag dolls. Each received a savage thrashing before being slammed against one of the walls.

And there they remained, pinned in place by glowing blue tendrils that all led back to the vial in Lump's small hand.

"Ha!" the boy cried with glee.

An astonished Maggie struggled to her feet. "How are you *doing* that?"

Lump shot her a delighted look. "No idea!"

From behind Maggie came a dry cough. "If you're not too busy, I could use a hand."

Maggie turned to see smoke issuing from a rolled-up carpet beside the firepit. Laszlo's chagrined face was in the center, framed by a mane of knotted fringe.

She whistled. "What I wouldn't give for a camera."

"That's cute. But seeing as you don't have one, and seeing as I'm about to go up like the Hindenburg, maybe you could just . . . unroll me."

Maggie obliged, and Laszlo got to his feet, brushing dust from his suit. The demon glared at the kobolds pinned to the cavern walls. "This suit is Italian, you cretins."

The kobolds did not apologize.

He turned to Lump. "Can you keep up . . . whatever it is you're doing?"

Maggie's brother nodded. "I think so."

"Good. And for the record, that's *my* spell you're using."

"But we swapped. You gave me this one."

"*Still mine!*" Laszlo roared, before turning to Maggie. "Grab the pot, and let's go."

She gestured helplessly at the never-ending fountain of oatmeal.

"Right." He turned to the nearest kobold, a small and reedy-looking specimen pinned to the wall some ten feet above them. "How do we make it stop?"

The kobold licked its lips, its eyes seeking out several white-muzzled kobolds pinned about the cavern. Maggie assumed they were the clan's elders. The older ones shook their heads and gave harsh, guttural replies.

"What did they say?" asked Laszlo.

The young kobold looked almost sheepish. "I may only tell the Alpha."

"Alpha? Who's Alpha?"

The kobold looked past him to Lump. "The clan honors Alpha, Master of the Blue Fire. We beg forgiveness and wish only to serve." The creature bowed its head as deeply as its snare would allow.

Lump flushed a rosy pink. "Oh. Well, that's very nice of you. Apology accepted."

The kobold looked up eagerly. "May we bring you squirrels?"

"Um . . . no," said Lump. "But maybe you could tell the pot to stop making porridge."

The kobold grinned. "Just say '*Ich bin so satt.*' 'I am full.'"

There was a hissing, not unlike steam escaping a locomotive. It trailed away, and the pot gave a weary sigh. Porridge ceased oozing from its top.

"What else can we do?" asked the kobold.

"Plenty," Laszlo cut in. "We'll start with soap, hot water, and some abject apologies."

All of these were forthcoming, he was told, but only if the Alpha requested them. As it became clear that the kobolds truly regarded Lump as their rightful master, the boy recorked the tube, and the tendrils dissolved into oily smoke. Forty kobolds dropped to the cavern floor, some landing in cold porridge, all rubbing their necks and gazing at Lump with awe.

One cautiously approached Maggie. "Sister of the Alpha, what can we bring you?"

Maggie stared at the creature. *Sister of the Alpha?* She'd KO'd seven kobolds with a rolling pin. All Lump did was remove a cork. She didn't want to be petty, but it was a little exasperating. Then again, the last thing they needed was for the kobolds to realize Lump was just an ordinary kid who'd hit the jackpot with a random scrap of magic.

Maggie requested a towel.

The creature rushed off to do her bidding, returning with a box of fluffy bath sheets that were undoubtedly stolen. Maggie wiped porridge from her shoes and jeans while Laszlo ordered a pair of kobolds to polish his Guccis.

"I want them gleaming," he ordered. "While you're at it, you wouldn't happen to know where we could find a holy relic or royal jewels, would you?"

The kobolds looked up from their buffing. "Jewels?"

"*Royal* jewels," Laszlo repeated. "Rings. Scepters. That kind of thing. I realize flea collars and chew toys are more your thing, but it can't hurt to ask."

One kobold glanced at his neighbor. "*Herzogshut?*"

The other nodded. "*Jawohl. Herzogshut.*"

Another kobold glanced up from his mopping. "*Herzogshut?*"

"*Herzogshut,*" the others confirmed.

Laszlo looked from one to the next. "What the hell's a Herzogshut?"

But the kobolds would divulge nothing until the Alpha asked them. Once Lump did, they revealed there was another clan of kobolds back in Europe, known in English as the Shin-Barkers, who claimed to have stolen a crown long ago. The crown was called the Herzogshut, and the insufferable Shin-Barkers never failed to boast of it at clan gatherings. Lesser kobolds might scrounge for trinkets and squirrels; the mighty Shin-Barkers had stolen the ducal hat of Liechtenstein!

Laszlo chewed his lip. "Liechtenstein . . . sounds like a bratwurst."

"But it's not a bratwurst," corrected Lump. "It's a German-speaking microstate."

"A what?"

"A German-speaking microstate. A sovereign principality located in the Alps. It was formed in 1719 by a decree from the Holy Roman emperor, Charles VI."

Laszlo's jaw fell open. "It's a *country?*"

"Yes, but a very tiny one," said Lump. "Only forty thousand people live there."

The demon stared at him, his expression a blend of respect and disgust. "How the hell do you know this?"

To the kobolds, the answer was perfectly obvious. The clan broke into a chant. "*Alpha! Alpha! Alpha!*"

Maggie shouted over the din. "Lump studies atlases," she explained to Laszlo. "For fun."

The demon sighed. "When did I become a nerd magnet? So does this place have a royal family?"

"Of course," said Lump. "It's ruled by the Prince of Liechtenstein."

At this, Laszlo rubbed his hands together. "Sweet hallelujah!" he exclaimed, before telling the chanting kobolds to can it. When they obliged, he turned to one of the elders. "Where do we find these Shin-Barkers?"

The kobold almost looked embarrassed for him. "In Liechtenstein, *Herr Dämon.*"

"Yes, yes, I gathered that," Laszlo said sarcastically. "I mean where, *specifically?* Your 'Alpha' needs to go there."

A crude map was drawn on the back of a flyer advertising guitar lessons. Laszlo studied it, pressed for additional details, and checked the time on his phone. When he saw the screen was cracked, he cursed and showed it to the kobolds.

"You owe me a phone," he said. "And not one of those knockoffs. Something hefty and deluxe. Maggie, grab that porridge thing. We're outta here."

Leaving was easier said than done. The clan begged their Alpha to stay and take his rightful place as leader. Lump was magnanimous but firm in his refusal. Duty called, he declared, but he would certainly visit if and when opportunity presented. In the meantime, the kobolds must stop selling squirrels to an unsuspecting public.

As they made their departure, Maggie pointed out the two kobolds they'd already bound and gagged. The clan did not begrudge it.

Once they were back in the park, Laszlo made several phone calls. Maggie and Lump followed as he meandered around the lake, cursing and cajoling whoever was on the other end.

"What do you think he's doing?" wondered Lump.

Maggie gazed west, to where the sky was a gradient of blues and orange. "Buying plane tickets, I think. I heard him say something about 'first class.'"

Lump jumped about excitedly. "Are we really going to Europe?"

"Maybe," said Maggie. "But I don't see how. We don't have passports."

Lump ceased jumping. "How long does it take to get one?"

"Months," said Maggie. "And you need lots of documents. Birth certificates and stuff."

"But we don't have those."

"True," said Maggie. "But I get the sense Laszlo has ways around that. Anyway, we'll worry about it later. Thanks to you, we have an enchanted porridge pot. Nice work back there. You were kind of awesome."

Lump grinned and kicked a stone. "I pulled a cork. Big whoop."

Maggie pulled him into a hug. "Well, it worked. That's all that matters."

On the path up ahead, Laszlo beckoned for them to catch up as he backpedaled, his ear still pressed to the phone. Maggie and Lump followed him out of the park and onto an avenue by a sprawling museum.

He quickly hailed a taxi and climbed in. He barked at the Drakefords to hurry up. "Come on, come on. We've got a flight to catch."

"Which airport?" said the cabbie, as Maggie slammed the door.

Laszlo covered his phone with his hand. "JFK."

The cabbie nodded and honked at a sedan to let him merge into traffic. The other driver refused. An argument ensued.

Maggie couldn't imagine driving in Manhattan. She turned to Laszlo. "Just so you know, we don't have passports."

"Don't worry about it," he muttered, and resumed his hushed conversation. "Yeah, yeah, okay. Lower deck. White van . . ."

Maggie pursed her lips. Had he heard her? "But Laszlo—"

The demon ignored her. Even worse, he had the gall to actually put his hand in her face to shut her up. Maggie turned to look out the window. Their driver was now hammering on the horn like a lunatic.

She looked past the chaos to Central Park. In there, things remained remarkably peaceful—people biked and jogged and basked in the autumn sun, blissfully unaware that a clan of folk monsters lived beneath them. A clan whose magic pot was safely nestled in Maggie's backpack.

A grin spread across her face as she watched a woman pushing a baby stroller. They had really done it! What was more, they had a lead on the next item they needed. For the first time in memory, Maggie Drakeford allowed herself a glimmer of hope.

But even as hope reared its head, a figure caught Maggie's eye. The person stood by the nearest lamppost, her stillness eerily conspicuous. There was no mistaking the lady's hat or coat, or the toy poodle peering from her bag. Her eyes locked on Maggie's just as the cab finally pulled away.

Maggie felt a sudden impulse to wave goodbye.

Madam Catfish merely smiled.

CHAPTER 16
OUTBOUND

Laszlo had always liked airports. Well, not *airports*, per se, but air travel. Back in the day, people dressed up before flying the friendly skies. Suits and skinny ties, stylish dresses, stiff drinks, and stiffer shoes. Flying was glamorous. Today, you were lucky if your neighbor wasn't wearing a tank top and neck pillow. Laszlo had only been at JFK for twenty minutes, and already he'd counted more than thirty of those abominations, each one attached to a mouth-breathing galoot.

The demon sighed. Fashion standards might have regressed, but there was no denying that modern airports had better shops and amenities. He was sitting in one of those shops now, on a bench near the entrance, as a saleswoman helped Lump select a new outfit. It was hard enough having two humans as travel companions, much less humans wearing shitty clothes spattered with porridge.

Maggie had made her selections quickly. But not the brother; Lump wanted to "explore the options." The boy now stood before a three-way mirror, admiring his new look and bursting into giggles. Laszlo had to admit it was cute, but at this rate they'd be here for an hour. Not that it really mattered. Their flight didn't depart until nine at night.

"So what are we going to do?" said a voice to his right.

Laszlo did a double take. Maggie now wore a black sweater, jeans, clean white sneakers, and a travel blazer, the ensemble tied together with a matching scarf. Laszlo wasn't appraising a new outfit so much as a new person. She almost looked chic.

"Come again?" he said.

Maggie joined him on the bench and began stuffing her old clothes into a plastic bag, then packed the bag and her new backup clothing into a carry-on. New luggage had been their second purchase at JFK International. The first had been passports acquired from a nondescript van in the airport's parking garage.

"So," said Maggie. "What are we going to do about 'Madam Catfish'?"

Laszlo returned to people watching. "I've got someone making inquiries."

"Dimitri?"

"Nope. Dimitri took those little red pills. He's forgotten all about our visit."

"So who's looking into Madam Catfish?"

Laszlo winked at a pair of passing flight attendants. "My guy Clarence."

"Is he any good?"

"The best."

"So what's Clarence doing?" she asked archly. "Searching under 'catfish' in some kind of demonic phone book?"

"Let me worry about it. Has anyone ever told you you're a nag?"

"Has anyone ever told you you're incompetent?"

Laszlo laughed. "That's rich. Yesterday, you were farting around the Catskills without a goddamn clue. Today you've got new clothes, a passport, a red-hot lead, and a plane ticket to Europe. Hell, you've even got a magic porridge pot. And who made this happen? Me. I won't even mention my heroics with the kobolds."

"Lump took care of the kobolds. You shrieked for mercy."

"That was diplomacy," Laszlo said with a sniff. "Anyway, who gave Lump that spelltube? Who lifted the key from Hot Dog Man? Who found the keyhole and porridge pot? Face it, Your Highness, I'm the MVP of this squad. Without me, you'd be fixing butter churns back in Stinkerball."

"Schemerdaal."

"Whatever." Laszlo braced for another volley, but none came. Instead, Maggie merely sat quietly beside him and fiddled with her sleeve.

"You're right," she finally said. "Without your help, we wouldn't be here, and we wouldn't be any closer to breaking the curse. I was wrong to say you're incompetent. Thank you."

Laszlo swallowed the retort he had at the ready and checked his phone instead. "You're welcome," he said, and tried his best not to smirk. Slowly but surely, he was winning Maggie over. It wasn't her nature to trust, but trust would come and hope would follow. Androvore had underestimated him.

His father had too.

"Any word from Clarence?" Maggie asked.

"No," said Laszlo, "but that doesn't mean much. Clarence isn't exactly speedy."

"But you said he was the best."

"Yeah. The best at taking orders."

Maggie blew out her cheeks. "So what is he actually doing?"

"Reconnaissance. Snooping around the office, and so forth. If the boss hired Madam Catfish, there'll be a paper trail. Expense forms, that sort of stuff."

Maggie blinked in surprise. "Hell has paperwork?"

"Hell *is* paperwork."

Leaning closer, Maggie spoke in an undertone. "But what if your boss *didn't* hire Madam Catfish? What if she's working for someone else?"

Laszlo scoffed. "Don't be paranoid. Who else would she be working for?"

"I don't know. Maybe it has something to do with the Witchstone and those wizards."

"Magi."

"Whatever. Don't you think it's possible?"

"Doubtful," said Laszlo. "According to you, Catfish Lady was already in Dimitri's shop before we learned about the missing ritus and those Egyptian wizards."

"Magi."

"Whatever."

"But that's precisely my point," said Maggie. "If she was already in the shop, why would she start following us, unless she overheard something?"

Laszlo shook his head. "She stayed on our trail, so she's a pro. And if she's a pro, somebody hired her before we set foot in Dimitri's. The only person who would have done that goes by the name Malignis Androvore."

"And that's your boss?" A nod. Maggie whistled. "That's quite a name."

"No kidding." Laszlo stood as Lump hurried toward them, his face aglow with excitement.

"How do I look?" he asked eagerly.

Laszlo sized the kid up: new kicks, socks, jeans, sweater, and one of those jackets with too many pockets. "Like three hundred bucks."

As it happened, it was more like four hundred when you factored in the extra shirts, sweatpants, and underwear. Between the passports, luggage, plane tickets, and shopping spree, Laszlo was out almost ten grand. And that didn't include Lump's rapidly escalating soda addiction. Cursing silently, he paid the saleswoman.

"Kids," he said. "Rude and needy, but at least they're expensive . . ."

It was a pretty good quip, in Laszlo's opinion—pithy, clever, and he'd made it up on the spot. The woman merely handed him a receipt. Laszlo pegged her for a vegan. Maybe a Pisces.

When he returned to the Drakefords, Lump was showing Maggie his jacket.

"It has a secret hood," he said, unzipping the collar. "And plenty of pockets for my weapons and spells."

"Easy, Merlin," said Laszlo. "Nobody's waving any spells around an airport. It was no picnic getting those tubes through security."

"I've been meaning to ask," said Maggie. "Where did you hide them?"

Laszlo gave her a frank stare. "Do you really want to know?"

There was a silence.

After a moment, he headed out into the terminal swinging a bag that held the Drakeford Curse folio. Maggie and Lump followed, pulling their carry-ons, one of which contained the porridge pot—a "gift for some friends" they were visiting in Switzerland.

They'd nearly reached their gate when Laszlo's phone started to vibrate. Glancing down, he saw an unfamiliar number and waved the Drakefords on ahead.

Clarence's voice sent a knife into his ear. "*Laszlo!*"

"It's me. Stop shouting."

"*I can't stop shouting! I'm frightened!*"

Laszlo stepped out of the traffic flow. "Calm down. Where are you?"

"*A salon!*"

Leaning against a vending machine, Laszlo massaged his eyes. "Clarence, tell me you're just borrowing their phone."

"*Manicures relax me!*"

"Okay. Just calm—"

"*Don't tell me to calm down! My bestie's in danger!*"

Bestie? It took a moment to realize who Clarence was talking about. When Laszlo did, he was mortified. No information, no matter how valuable, could possibly be worth such a burden. He had to force himself to not hang up.

"Clarence, pull yourself together. What's got you so upset?"

Laszlo listened with rising impatience as Clarence started counting aloud to calm himself. By the time he reached ten, screechy hysteria had subsided to moist and breathy sniffles.

"You're being followed," Clarence whispered.

"I know," said Laszlo. "Androvore's goons."

"Yes! This morning, I snuck into Thatcher's office and saw something on the credenza. You know, the one with that fake orchid she pretends to water."

"I know it," said Laszlo grimly. "What did you see?"

"A manila folder with 'Laszlo' written on the tab. I figured it probably had something to do with you."

"Brilliant. What next?"

"I was about to open it when Thatcher came in. She looked me up and down and did that blinky thing with her nictitating membranes. I said, 'Hi!' and she said, 'What the heck are you doing in my office?' Only she used the f-word . . ."

Laszlo winced. Was Thatcher onto him? "Well, what did you say?"

"I panicked! I said we'd been working together for ninety-seven years, and it was time we got to know each other socially."

"You didn't."

"*I did!*"

"*Shh!*" Laszlo hissed. "Get a grip, for Chrissakes. So what did she say?"

Clarence's voice became muffled. "Do you happen to have those warm wax booties?"

"*What?*"

"Sorry. I was speaking to the manicurist. Her name's Sylvia. She's a godsend."

Laszlo banged his head against the vending machine. "Clarence, not to make this all about me, but can we get to the part where I'm in danger?"

"Right. Well, Thatcher said something about not having eaten lunch yet. I took the hint and said, 'Why don't we try that place in Times Square?' You know, the one with all the neon and gigantic onions? Well, she just transformed into her human disguise, went over to the other credenza—the one with the kitten pics—and grabbed her purse!"

Laszlo found himself motioning for Clarence to continue. "So you went to lunch . . ."

"We sure did. When the hostess sat us in a booth, I started to get all clammy. You know how I get all clammy when I'm anxious."

Oh, he knew. "I do."

"Well, I was so darn fidgety I ordered a cosmo to steady the ol' nerves. Thatcher ordered one too, along with three atomic onions, glazed salmon, and some potato skins without the chives, because she's never been a fan."

Laszlo ground his teeth. "And . . . ?"

"We *talked*, Laszlo! Oh, we talked for hours and hours!"

"And . . . ?"

"I've never felt so alive! So comfortable with another—"

Laszlo spoke in measured tones. "Clarence, I am going to murder you. I am going to reach through this phone, wrap my hands around that spongy neck, and—"

"Okay, okay! Sorry. Anyway, we were three cosmos deep when I said, 'Did Laszlo get fired or something?' and Thatcher says, 'Ha! He wishes,' and I say, 'Why do you say that?' and she says, 'He's as good as crucibled,' and I say, 'Really?' and she says, 'Yeah,' and I say, 'Why?' and she says, 'Androvore has it out for him,' and I say—"

"Skip the play-by-play!"

"Androvore hates you," said Clarence simply. "But he hates your dad even more. He's got a crew on your tail, and they've got orders to report on everything you do. Meanwhile, he's looking into your curse and how you got the job when Bazilius went AWOL. He thinks it's suspicious."

So do I, thought Laszlo. Aloud, he replied, "Clarence, did Thatcher mention anything about any people or places we might have visited in the city?"

Clarence sounded hurt. "You hit the town and didn't invite me?"

"I'm kind of busy."

"Well, she didn't say anything. But who's this 'we'?"

"I'm with my Curse Bearers. Long story, but I'm about to hop on a red-eye for Europe. We're picking up some things they need to break the spell."

Clarence's voice dropped to a horrified whisper. "You're *helping* your Bearers break their curse? That's taboo, Laszlo! That's—"

"—not what I'm doing. I know the rules, Clarence. I'm not helping the Drakefords *break* their curse; I'm helping them *think* they are."

"But why would you do that?"

Laszlo examined his fingernails. "Isn't it obvious? I'm building up their hopes so I can yank the proverbial rug out from under them. Voilà! Instant misery and despair."

A reverent gasp. "Oh, my stars, it's brilliant, Laszlo! Brilliant! But so *evil* . . ."

Laszlo admired his reflection in the vending machine. "You're kind, Clarence, but it's nothing extraordinary. It's our duty to tempt mortals, to drive them to wicked acts. One might say it's Demon 101."

"You should be running this place."

"Agreed," said Laszlo. "But at present, I have to save my ass. So what's the story with Androvore's people? Are they just spying, or is sabotage on the menu?"

"Sabotage—and worse!" yelped Clarence. "Thatcher says he's sparing no expense."

Laszlo was oddly flattered. "Well, I've seen his goons up close. They're nothing special. One against five is no picnic, but I've faced longer odds."

"*Six*," Clarence hissed. "There are six goons!"

Laszlo pictured the "tourists" Androvore had summoned into Thatcher's office. "Nope. There were six, but he crucibled one right in front of me. You wouldn't believe the stench."

"Androvore hired another," Clarence whispered. "A specialist. Some kind of bounty hunter or assassin. Thatcher was really miffed about it."

Laszlo grinned. "Good old Thatcher. Always knew she had my back."

"No, it's because the assassin's super expensive," said Clarence. "It put a dent in the holiday budget."

The smile vanished. "I see. Did, um, Thatcher happen to mention the assassin's name or what they look like? Any chance they resemble a catfish?"

"No idea. But Thatcher said they're a real killer."

"I think that's the idea."

Laszlo heard audible hand flapping. "That's not what I meant!" squealed Clarence. "She said once this assassin is on the job, *no one* gets away! And that's why I got so upset." There was a pause as the goblin shark tried and failed to maintain his composure. "*My dearest friend's going to die! He's going to die in hideous, painful ways. And I still can't find my watch!*"

Moving the phone from his ear, Laszlo checked the time on his

Breguet. "Clarence, stop crying," he said. "I gotta run. If you hear any-thing—and I mean *anything*—about what Androvore's doing, pass it along right away. Are you seeing Thatcher again?"

The goblin shark practically sang with delight. "*A double matinee on Saturday!*"

"Good. Keep digging, and keep me posted."

"*Be care—*"

Laszlo killed the phone and ducked into a Hudson News, where he made several purchases. All this talk of hope had given him an idea.

Minutes later, he found the Drakefords camped at the gate looking groggy while an attendant announced that the flight to Zurich would be boarding momentarily.

Laszlo poked Maggie in the shoulder. "Sleep on the plane. I need you to write something." He held up some prestamped postcards and pens. "Just a quick note to Mom and Dad telling them you're fine and we're crushing this thing."

Lump yawned and took one of the postcards. Maggie raised an eye-brow, but Laszlo headed off her questions.

"You want 'em to know you're safe, don't you? That we're kicking ass?"

Maggie reached for the other postcard. "I suppose."

Laszlo eyed Lump's rapidly scribbling pen. "Easy, Shakespeare. You can tell 'em the rest when you get home."

By the time the siblings were done, the flight was boarding.

Laszlo pressed the postcards upon an elderly couple whose flight had just arrived from Toronto. Canadians were notoriously trusting and de-pendable. Laszlo knew they'd mail them the minute they reached their hotel. With luck, they would reach the Drakefords in a few days. Laszlo congratulated himself. Not every demon could inflate mortal hopes in two places at once.

"Passenger Schmidt," said a voice over the loudspeaker. "Passenger L. Schmidt, please see the ticketing agent."

It took Laszlo a second to realize that he was the one being paged. That was always the danger with false identities; you forgot who you were. He hurried up to the gate counter with an inquiring look.

"Laszlo Schmidt?" said the agent.

"Yes," he said. "Is there a problem?"

The woman smiled. "Not at all. Your seat upgrade has been approved."

Laszlo exhaled. "Oh, thank God. To think I almost had to fly economy."

She glanced down at her computer screen. "I see you're traveling with a Margaret and George Schmidt?"

"Yep. My niece and nephew."

"Would you like to upgrade them as well? The flight isn't very full."

Laszlo glanced back at the Drakefords. "No," he said. "First class would just be wasted on them. Speaking of which, I trust the booze is all complimentary?"

As the agent printed out a new boarding pass, Laszlo reflected complacently that things were really starting to take shape. He'd acquired one of the more challenging materia, was on his way to another, and had a spy in place at the office. Clarence was exhausting, but if he could charm the goods out of Thatcher, it was worth every tedious, shrieked anecdote. Not only was Thatcher privy to Androvore's schemes—she might also know more about the Drakeford Curse and what had happened to its original Keeper.

Fifty to one said Bazilius was dead. Then again, you couldn't be certain unless you saw the body, and even then, it was wise to check the pulse. Laszlo knew this all too well. Over the centuries, he'd pulled that stunt with dozens of creditors. No, he couldn't say if Bazilius was alive or dead. But Laszlo was certain he smelled a rat.

"Excuse me," said a breathless voice behind him. "Are you finished?"

Laszlo turned to see a man and woman, early fifties, unremarkable but for their flushed and flustered state. Apparently, they'd just made a dash through the terminal.

Laszlo took his new boarding pass. "All yours."

Brushing past the pair, he rejoined the Drakefords and told them to join the line. Laszlo hung back a moment. Opening his briefcase, he removed a magazine, along with a spelltube he'd slipped in his pocket once they'd passed security.

He glanced at the couple speaking with the ticket agent. People running to catch a flight were common enough in airports. Hundreds had sprinted past Laszlo over the decades, pleading with time to be on their side.

Until now, not one of them had given off a hint of brimstone.

These newcomers were fellow demons.

CHAPTER 17
PHIL

Maggie had never been on an airplane. The novelty softened her indignation that their Curse Keeper was luxuriating in first class while she and Lump were seated in the last row by the lavatories. Laszlo had spun some tale about how there was only one upgrade available, but it was pure bullshit. The flight was half-empty.

Lump didn't mind a thing. To him, the 787 was a wonderland, a flying amusement park where everything from overhead compartments to seat belts was a revelation. Within five minutes, he'd tested all the buttons, giggled silently at the vomit bag, and assigned names to every character in the safety diagrams. Maggie envied his enthusiasm. It was a superpower, as was his ability to fall asleep the instant he got tired or bored.

This second power kicked in as the plane reached cruising altitude. For the past two hours, Lump had been curled against the window, snoring softly while a ginger ale languished on his tray table.

Maggie did not share her brother's gifts. She slumped in her aisle seat, exhausted yet unable to rest, silently praying that the drone of the airplane's engines would lull her to dreamland. It was a futile prayer. Whenever her eyelids drooped, thoughts of her parents intruded, and the ensuing guilt chased away any shred of sleep.

Would their mother ever forgive her? If Maggie had gone alone, maybe. With Lump there, it was out of the question. George was her darling, her baby, the only other member of the household who—for now—remained whole and unblemished. And curse-touched Maggie had lured him away into danger. It wouldn't matter that he'd been a stowaway. The instant Maggie let him tag along instead of taking him straight home, she'd become Laszlo's accomplice.

Now firmly awake, Maggie focused on the screen in front of her. It was tuned to a program about Greenland sharks. In clipped British tones, a narrator informed her that they were most unusual creatures: huge, slow moving, and deeply mysterious, with life spans measured in centuries rather than decades. But it was not their longevity that held Maggie in thrall.

It was their parasites.

She squirmed whenever they came into view—wormlike organisms that affixed themselves to the shark's eyeball. Once attached, they made a meal of their host's cornea and slowly blinded it. Maggie's heart went out to the sharks. The poor things must have known something was wrong, but there was nothing they could do. They couldn't dislodge or pluck off the parasite. All they could do was swim sluggishly through the icy depths and await the moment when everything went dark.

Maggie touched the bandaged arm beneath her new sweater. She could relate all too well.

"Excuse me?" She looked up to see a lady in the aisle, waiting for the bathroom: middle aged, with graying blond hair, a beige sweater tied preppy fashion around her shoulders.

The woman held out a package of airline cookies. "Would you like these? My husband's not a fan of gingersnaps."

A baffled Maggie took the package. "I'm sure my brother will eat them. Thanks."

"Are you two traveling alone?"

"No. Our uncle's in first class."

The woman smiled uncertainly. "And he left you all the way back here?"

"He's kind of . . . unique."

A man exited the lavatory and squeezed past the woman. "Well, we're in row eight. If you need anything, just come find us. My name's Kathy."

"Thanks, Kathy. That's nice of you."

The woman smiled and went in. The *Occupied* sign went on. Maggie set the cookies on Lump's tray and switched her screen to the channel tracking the flight's progress. Nothing but blue ocean surrounded that blinking icon. They still had hours to go.

Closing her eyes, Maggie tried to work things out in her head.

If they got their hands on this Herzo-whatever, they still had to acquire a holy relic. Even if they pulled *that* off, they'd only have a few days to gather the more ordinary items and figure out how to use them all. Time and again, Maggie returned to the same two questions:

Why was the ritus missing?

Could they break the curse without it?

Maggie didn't have any answers, but she knew they had zero chance of success if they didn't at least try. Taking a deep breath, she let the air out slowly. *One step at a time. Take it one step—*

Just as Maggie was beginning to relax, pain exploded in her skull.

It struck like a thunderbolt, a flash of searing intensity that dwarfed anything she had ever experienced.

Maggie's spine stiffened, and she writhed back, her hands seizing the armrests and her body shaking so violently she might have been strapped to an electric chair.

The pain became unbearable—a white-hot agony that radiated from her right eye socket. Her mind went to the Greenland shark, but instead of a worm, she could have sworn a long metal screw was being driven into her brain. The sensation was remarkably vivid: the twisting pressure of a sharp point tunneling through her eyeball until it severed the optic nerve.

Maggie's spine and muscles tensed to the snapping point. She wanted to scream—*needed* to scream—but her tongue had cleaved to the roof of her mouth. She could only jerk and writhe, enduring the unimaginable as the phantom bolt was forced ever deeper.

The torment stopped almost as suddenly as it had begun.

It was like someone had flipped a switch; the agony simply washed away like rain sliding off a windshield. Gasping for breath, Maggie brought a shaky hand up to her right eye. Her fingers wandered over the area, their touch soft and tentative. There was no metal screwhead, nothing beyond a faint tickling just beneath the eyelid.

She was mopping her forehead with a napkin when a wave of nausea sent her darting into the bathroom.

Yanking the door shut, Maggie slammed the lock into place and promptly threw up.

There was her dinner: an overpriced chicken wrap, fruit cup, and Pellegrino.

She held her hair back, shuddering as an aftershock of pure bile splashed into the bowl. Wiping her mouth, she glanced about the bathroom, taking in the fluorescent light, the tiny sink, the mingled reek of urine and air freshener. She rose slowly, her knees wobbling as the plane passed through some turbulence. Steadying herself against the sink, Maggie splashed water on her cheeks and looked in the mirror.

A different Maggie looked back at her.

Her right eye had undergone some sort of surreal mutation. All she could do was lean closer to the mirror and note the changes.

The first was that her iris, formerly an unremarkable blue, was now generously flecked with gold. That was strange enough. Stranger still, her right pupil was no longer round and black but vertical, like a cat's, and ringed with an angry nimbus of broken capillaries.

The effect wasn't merely strange; it was inhuman.

This isn't happening. Wake up, Maggie! Wake up—you're dreaming!

As if in response, she felt a throbbing in her left forearm. It wasn't exactly painful, but the skin under her bandage felt warm and tight. She yanked off her sweater, unbuttoned her shirt cuff, removed the bandage. A moment later, she let out an inadvertent shriek.

Her curse mark was changing before her eyes. Even as she watched, its scarlet borders were growing hazy and fibrous. With a purposeful surge, they spread outward, expanding like ink on wet paper. Within sixty seconds, the patch had claimed half of Maggie's forearm.

Then the edges solidified once more, and the skin hardened into something like cracked and scaly leather. Cilia began to appear, sprouting between the scales like translucent swamp reeds.

She muttered under her breath to God, or whoever was out there, but the powers that be weren't listening. Just as the cilia were blossoming, a boil appeared in the pale crook of her elbow.

Maggie watched in horror as it began to grow. She could *feel* it. Something inside was straining against the skin. When it had reached the size of a chickpea, the boil popped and released a stream of bubbling pus. Maggie retched, but there was nothing left.

Snatching up some tissues, she wiped the discharge away and peered at the tiny crater the boil had left behind.

A worm poked from the hole.

A scream escaped Maggie's lips—just a fragment—before she bit her lip hard enough to draw blood. She was about to scream again when there was a knock at the door.

"Hello?" said a man's voice. "Is someone in there?"

Thank God for door locks. "Yes!"

A pause. "Is everything . . . okay?"

"Perfect, thanks!"

Turning back to her arm, she watched with sickly wonder as the worm continued to inch forth. Its body was pinkish gray, with a questing tip that seemed to scent the air. Nauseated as she was, her mind was detached, operating on its own. What if the worm wasn't some sort of parasite? What if it was part of Maggie herself?

She had to find out.

Her actions became almost clinical. She took the ballpoint pen from her pants pocket, bent over the tiny sink, and probed the darkened flesh. The worm recoiled as the pen came near it, then withdrew entirely as Maggie poked the edges of the hole. She took a deep breath and pushed the pen's tip inside it. A dot of blood rose to the surface and dribbled down the pen. Maggie pressed again. More blood, thick as syrup.

She kept going until the sink was spattered with crimson blossoms. Yes, it ached, but compared to the recent pain in her eye, it barely registered. Maggie was so focused on prodding the flesh and following the subtle undulations that it was as if she had slipped into a dream. Pressing harder, she felt the worm retreat farther and take refuge near her elbow.

Maggie's face darkened. "You can run," she muttered, "but you can't hide."

Gritting her teeth, she thrust the pen into the hole. There was a flash of pain, but she overrode the impulse to stop. Instead, she forced it deeper and deeper still until there was barely anything left to grip. Sickly yellow pus dripped out in an oily sludge, pooling in the sink with a rancid smell that made her gag.

Maggie began to hyperventilate.

The breaths came quick and shallow, yet she wasn't able to stop working. Levering the pen up like a crowbar, she felt the tip grate against bone. Sweat dripped off her chin, but Maggie only pushed harder until the skin gave way and tore in a jagged gash an inch wide.

Adrenaline drowned out the pain.

Gasping for breath, she dropped the pen in the sink and began to tear at the gash with her fingers, forcing the ragged edges aside. Blood streamed out.

Maggie hit the faucet with her elbow. The water stung, but as it washed the blood away, she could see muscle, sinew, and what appeared to be something sprouting from a patch of bone. *Oh God*— The worm wasn't an invading parasite; it was part of her.

And it wasn't alone.

Flushing the wound, she spotted smaller specimens anchored to the bone like shoots growing from a branch. Clutching the sink, she retched again.

Another knock at the door, sharper than before.

An impatient voice spoke up. "Hello?"

Maggie wiped bile and saliva from her chin. "Occupied."

"Yes," said the man testily. "It's been 'occupied' for fifteen minutes . . ."

Maggie was growing dizzy. Despite the fan, the sight and smell were too much. She struggled to catch her breath.

More knocking. "Miss—"

Maggie smacked the door with her elbow. "*Go away!*"

The knocking abruptly ceased.

Gasping, she leaned her head against the mirror. Now she'd done it. The asshole had probably gone to fetch a flight attendant. What would Maggie say? How would she explain her eye, or anything about her arm?

What if the airline called the police? Worse still, what if they called a doctor and her secret was discovered? If nothing else, she needed to stanch the bleeding until they landed. No one must know what was happening.

She snatched a handful of toilet paper and pressed it firmly against her forearm. Blood soaked right through, but when Maggie took the sodden paper away, she saw to her shock that the skin was already healing. Threadlike filaments had emerged from the edges and bridged the gap, hooking into healthy skin and closing the wound more neatly than any suture.

A stunned Maggie daubed at the remaining drops of blood. All that remained was the original crater. And after a moment, the worm poked out as if nothing had happened.

Another knock.

"Still occupied!" said Maggie, and tossed the bloody paper in the toilet.

"This is the flight attendant," said a female voice. "Is everything all right?"

Maggie splashed more water on her arm. The worm retracted like a tape measure. "Yes, I'm fine." She paused. "Listen, I'm really sorry, but I need a few more minutes."

The woman's tone became maternal. "Honey, do you need some help? Can I get anyone?"

Maggie shut her eyes. Why couldn't they just leave her alone? Was this the only bathroom on the entire plane? *Piss someplace else!*

"Um, my brother's asleep and our uncle's in first class. There's no need to disturb—"

Instant perkiness. "Is your uncle the fella who looks like Paul Newman?"

Maggie had no idea what the woman was talking about. "Um . . . maybe?"

"I'll be right back."

"Really, I'm okay—"

But the flight attendant had gone.

Maggie frantically wiped blood and bile from the sink. Then her attention settled on the vomit-spattered toilet. If she was quick, perhaps she could climb in and flush herself right out of the plane before the flight attendant returned. The odds were low, but it might be worth a shot . . .

Yet *another* knock. This time, it was accompanied by a droll voice she knew only too well. "This better be good."

"Go away!" said Maggie. "I didn't ask her to get you!"

"Listen, that lady thinks your colon exploded. Tell me she's wrong."

"It's not that."

"Well, what is it?"

Maggie gave a convulsive shudder. "I'm *changing*!"

Laszlo did not reply for several moments. "Right. Well, I've never had to give this talk before, but here goes. You see, Maggie, when humans reach a certain age, their bodies undergo a series of awkward but amusing changes that doctors call—"

"Would you please shut the fuck up?"

"Okay, then."

"Is anybody else out there?"

"Nope. Everyone's fled."

Maggie opened the door a crack to see her Curse Keeper standing outside with an amused expression. She pointed to her right eye. "*Look!*"

Laszlo yawned. "Is *that* what this is all about? Having sexy cat eyes? Jagger would kill for those peepers."

"Oh yeah?" said Maggie. "Well, what about *this*?"

She opened the door another inch so Laszlo could see the hole near the crook of her elbow.

Another yawn. "Tape an aspirin to it."

At that moment, the worm reappeared like an eel peering from its grotto. Laszlo raised a curious eyebrow.

"Well, hello there," he purred. "Do you have a name? I'll bet it's Larry? Or maybe Phil. You could definitely be a Phil."

"It doesn't have a name, and I don't want it to!"

Laszlo shrugged. "What do you want me to do? Did someone forget she's cursed?"

Maggie let out an involuntary sob. Yanking the door shut, she locked it once again. "I don't want you to do anything. I just want it to stop!"

Ten seconds passed before there was another knock. This one was a touch gentler.

"Open up, Your Highness."

"No."

"Come on. Just a smidge."

Maggie hesitated before unlocking the door and opening it a crack. A candy bar slid through the gap.

"What's that?"

"Toblerone. It's triangular. And delicious."

Maggie grimaced. "Who eats chocolate in an airplane lavatory?"

"You'd be surprised."

"Well, I don't want it!"

The Toblerone withdrew, replaced a moment later by a pair of designer sunglasses.

Here was something Maggie could actually use. The frames were too large for her face, but the lenses hid her eyes completely. Even better, no one would be able to tell she'd been crying.

Laszlo was still outside when Maggie finally reemerged.

"How do I look?" she asked tentatively.

The demon winked. "Like a star on the sly. Or brutally hungover. Your choice."

Maggie tried to smile. She returned to her seat and was surprised when Laszlo squeezed into the row and claimed the seat between her and Lump.

"You don't have to sit with us," said Maggie.

"Oh, it's fine," he said easily. "Who doesn't crave a middle seat by the shitter?"

Maggie sat down and buckled her seat belt. The flight attendant hurried over. "Everything okay, hon? We were worried about you."

"I'm fine. Sorry for taking so long."

"Not at all. Can I get you two anything?"

Laszlo spoke up at once. "I'll take some bubbly, and the lady will have . . . ?"

"Water," said Maggie.

"Coming right up," said the flight attendant.

"One more thing," said Laszlo. "I want to thank you for fetching me, Denise. You're a gem."

When the demon grinned, Denise turned an alarming shade of pink. She started babbling about it being her pleasure and she really shouldn't say anything but did anyone ever tell him he looked like Paul Newman? Not *The Verdict* Paul Newman but *The Long, Hot Summer* Paul Newman? Laszlo admitted he might have heard that once or twice. Denise nodded vigorously and opened her mouth to say something else before glancing at Maggie and promptly zipping it. Turning on her heel, the woman practically sprinted to get Laszlo a glass of "the good stuff."

Maggie had never witnessed a more puzzling sequence in her life. "Did you do something to her?" she whispered. "Something magical?"

"Yeah," said Laszlo. "It's called looking like Paul Newman."

"That's not magic."

"Give it a few years."

Maggie said nothing. Denise returned with their drinks and mentioned something about her wedding ring being a decoy to "throw off the creeps." She hurried away again, smoothing her apron and blushing furiously.

Laszlo glanced over at Lump. "How long's the little man been snoozing?"

"Couple of hours."

Laszlo poked Lump's shoulder. "He's really out."

"He has a gift."

"I guess so," said Laszlo, and he sipped his champagne. "You should take a page from his book. Some z's would do you good."

"How am I supposed to sleep with a fucking worm in my arm?"

Laszlo acknowledged this. "Yeah, I'm sorry about that. You don't deserve it."

Was a demon actually pitying her? Maggie hadn't cried in years and wasn't about to break the habit twice in one night. When she spoke, her voice was strained. "But what if I *do* deserve it?"

Laszlo shot her a glance. "Did you burn a witch and not tell me?"

"No. But all those sins . . ."

"What sins?"

"The ones I ate," said Maggie softly. "That's what we do, you know. For money. When one of the villagers dies, a Drakeford has to eat their sins. For the last nine years, that's been me."

She described the ceremony: the body and bread, the chase, the stones.

Shaking his head, Laszlo waved off her concerns. "Bullshit. None of that stuff makes a person wicked."

Her voice was soft, almost pleading, and she hated herself for it. "Are you sure?"

"Take it from me. You've got problems, but a stale loaf of bread isn't one of them."

Maggie hesitated. "There *is* something else."

"Lay it on me."

She fiddled with her water glass, then folded her hands in her lap. "When I was a kid, my mom got appendicitis and had to go to the hospital, and Dad wasn't so far gone by then that he couldn't look after us for a few days. Lump was just a baby, and he woke up one night with an earache. No matter what we did, he wouldn't stop howling, so the next morning we bundled him up and walked down to the village for medicine."

"Your dad could walk?"

"Not very well," said Maggie, "but he could still get along on crutches if he took it slow. It was summer, but he wore a hat and a long coat so people wouldn't see too much of him. He didn't want to frighten anybody. He said it would be okay."

Laszlo grunted. "Let me guess. It wasn't okay."

Maggie took a shaky sip of her water.

"What happened?" said Laszlo. "The whole village turned out?"

Maggie nodded.

"Pitchforks and torches? 'Kill the monster, kill the monster,' all that shit?"

"No."

"So what did they do?"

Maggie swallowed. "*Nothing!*" she whispered. "They just lined up along the road and watched. And when we left, they followed us. Getting home took hours. Dad fell a couple times. And whenever he did, the villagers kept on doing nothing. They watched him suffer and let a nine-year-old carry a baby up a mountain. They followed us all the way to the sign."

"So you made it home okay."

"We did," Maggie allowed. "But later that night I told Dad I *hated* the villagers. Every single one."

"Who wouldn't?"

"My dad. He said they were frightened and that frightened people did all sorts of dumb things. He said—and I'll never forget this—that fear made them 'forget their decency.' He said I could be angry, but that I mustn't give in to hating them. The villagers had lost their way. We could help them find it again."

Laszlo looked half-amused. "Oh yeah? And how'd that work out?"

"It didn't," said Maggie dully. "I hated those bastards then, and I hate them now." She looked soberly at Laszlo. "Does that make me, I don't know, an evil person?"

The demon snorted. "Evil? Hell no, it makes you *normal.* No offense to your pops, but he expects too much. You're Maggie the Mouth, not Maggie the Martyr. They should be grateful you just hate them. My dad would have turned them into jigsaw puzzles."

Maggie smiled in spite of the grisly image. "So your dad is some kind of big deal? Dimitri said you're 'highborn.'"

"That's the rumor."

"I didn't know demons had families," said Maggie. "Do you have brothers and sisters?"

"Four brothers, two sisters. Yours truly is the baby."

"So you're lucky number seven."

Laszlo sipped his champagne. "No one would call me lucky."

"Are you close with them?" asked Maggie. "Your brothers and sisters, I mean."

"What is this, twenty questions?"

"I'm just curious. I haven't met too many demons."

Laszlo shrugged. "Nah, we're not too cuddly. I'm only eight hundred and change, so I'm the youngest by, like, five or six centuries. My sibs are more like aunts and uncles, and they're not exactly the doting type."

"Are they Curse Keepers too?"

At this, Laszlo actually burst out laughing. "Are you serious? Curse Keeping's a *job*. Nobles don't have jobs. They rule big-ass domains, hunt endangered species, and murder their rivals in creative ways. Work is for servants."

"Then why do *you* have a job?"

"Simple. I'm not a noble."

"But—"

Laszlo headed her off. "They gave me the boot," he explained. "Long story. Don't want to bore you."

"It doesn't sound boring," said Maggie.

"I'm just kidding. It's a fantastic story."

"But you won't tell me."

"Bingo. By the way, I'm stealing your brother's cookies."

"Go ahead. He already ate his. A lady gave us those."

"Our new bestie, Denise?"

"No. A different woman. Another passenger."

Laszlo's demeanor changed. "Which lady?"

Maggie stood to survey the cabin. "I don't see her," she said, sitting back down. "Oh, wait. She said she's in row eight."

Laszlo clucked his tongue. "Let me see if I've got this right. Some gal sitting thirty rows up comes all the way back here to tinkle. What's more, she brings cookies along in case she can give them away to a couple randos?"

Maggie nodded. "What's wrong?"

"Depends. Did this lady have a tan sweater and a face like yogurt?"

Maggie's jaw hung open. "How did you know?"

Laszlo smirked. "She's a demon. So's her 'hubby.' I spotted them before we boarded. Let's have a look at these cookies."

Sliding the package away from Lump, Laszlo opened one end of the wrapper and tipped the contents onto his tray. Two gingersnaps slid out, each stamped with the airline's logo.

"They look fine to me," said Maggie.

Laszlo turned off the overhead light, then cupped his hands around the cookies so they were in a shadowy little cave. He studied them for several seconds before flipping them over. A grin broke out. "Thought so."

"Thought what?" said Maggie.

"They're bewitched."

"How do you know?"

"Magic symbols," he replied. "Invisible to humans, but they emit traces I can see in the dark. This cookie's a tracker. The other will have you puking for the next day or three."

"But why?" said Maggie. "What would demons have against us?"

Laszlo slid the cookies back into their package. "Against you? Nothing. They work for Androvore, and they're here to sabotage me. But we're going to teach that colossal prick a valuable lesson."

"Oh yeah? And what lesson is that?"

"To hire better goons."

CHAPTER 18
DIE ALPEN

To Laszlo's surprise, Maggie and Lump weren't the worst travel companions he'd ever had. That title belonged to a flatulent CrossFit devotee who'd spent an entire flight to Singapore extolling the virtues of box jumps.

The Drakefords were miles better. Lump could sleep through a transatlantic flight, and Maggie wasn't the worst conversationalist. More importantly, the two were game for some mischief. With Laszlo, that counted for quite a bit.

The mischief started with their descent into Switzerland. First, Laszlo applied a fresh coating of faerie essence to their passports—along with a discreet swipe on Maggie's eyelid—to expedite their passage through customs. He then turned his attention to the tampered cookies Androvore's goons had given the Drakefords.

When they disembarked, they found those goons lurking on the other side of customs. "Hubby" made a show of buying coffee, while "Kathy" waved to Maggie—who returned the wave but appeared preoccupied with Lump, who was moving with effort, groaning and clutching his stomach.

Right on cue, a concerned Kathy hurried over. "Is everything all right? Your brother looks sick."

"I don't know," Maggie said. "I've never seen him like this."

Kathy promptly introduced herself to Laszlo and said she knew an excellent doctor "right here in Zurich." Laszlo replied that this was a *private* matter, a *family* matter, and he would handle it, thank you very much.

They left the building and a flustered, indignant Kathy and loaded their luggage into a waiting taxi.

Laszlo told the driver to take them to the nearest hospital. After the cab dropped them, they made a stop at a neighboring park, where they broke the tracking cookie into pieces and fed it to some delighted geese. Then Laszlo hailed a second taxi, and they headed east, toward Liechtenstein.

Lump was practically giddy with excitement. "So what happens now?"

Laszlo eased back against the leather seat. "We relax, kiddo. Relax and take in the view."

And a gorgeous view it was, even by Laszlo's jaded standards. The Alps soared in the distance, their slopes a burnished copper beneath frosted peaks. The scene was downright majestic, but Maggie wasn't lapping it up. She was staring at Laszlo.

"Do you think it will work?" she asked.

Laszlo glanced over. "The only things they'll be tracking have beaks and gizzards. While our friends waste time in Switzerland, we'll rock out in Liechtenstein. So relax already. The baddies are on a literal goose chase, and no one else knows where we're going."

"Those kobolds in Central Park do," Maggie pointed out. "What if Madam Catfish interrogates them? They know *exactly* where we're going, and—"

"We can discuss it later," he muttered. The driver was watching them in the rearview with a puzzled expression. "Inside joke," he explained. "From a TV show."

"I don't know that show," said the driver in accented English. "But I like *Friends*. Phoebe is funny."

Laszlo nodded. "So silly, and yet so wise."

The driver pounded the steering wheel in agreement. "Exactly! Like Sancho Panza!"

"I've been saying that for years."

The topic of American television kept the man happily engaged. When they reached Liechtenstein, they encountered no border station or security clearance—just a cheerful *Welcome* sign as they crossed the Rhine. They might have been visiting any Swiss town.

And yet this was *not* a town, Laszlo reminded himself. Liechtenstein was a *country*. A country with a *sovereign*. A sovereign whose crown was missing! A crown whose location was in his pocket, mapped out on a flyer for reasonably priced guitar lessons!

The demon chuckled complacently.

"What?" said Maggie.

"Oh, nothing," he sighed. "Just one of those moments when you're in the Alps on a crisp October day and you realize the universe has your back."

When they reached Vaduz, Laszlo had the driver drop them at the national museum, a modest building on a street lined with shops, government offices, and a church.

Shouldering her pack, Maggie gazed up at a castle overlooking the town. "Remind me why we're going to this museum?"

Laszlo waved goodbye to the driver. "Research."

As its name suggested, the museum was dedicated to all things Liechtenstein. Laszlo had discovered it while doing some in-flight research. He had also learned that the original Herzogshut had vanished centuries ago, but a replica had been commissioned, using an old illustration as a model. According to Wikipedia, the Liechtensteinians (Liechtensteini? Laszlo wasn't sure) had gifted the replica to Prince Franz Josef II for his seventieth birthday. The demon could not recall his own seventieth birthday, but he was positive he hadn't received a ducal hat. Then again, in the Middle Ages people didn't need ducal hats to be happy. Some teeth and a hovel were sufficient.

The museum was small, and it did not take long to find what he was seeking. The Herzogshut was such a prototypical crown it was almost cartoonish. Within the case was a red velvet hat encircled by a gem-studded band topped by eight golden leaves. A plaque informed them the design was modeled after the imperial crown of Austria, but historical tidbits held little interest for Laszlo. He was far more intrigued by the list of its gems and pearls.

You sexy beasts, he thought, eyeing them through the glass. When they got their hands on the real Herzogshut, Laszlo would pocket the choicer baubles. After all, the curse's materia hadn't specified what *condition* the object had to be in. For all Laszlo knew, the Shin-Barkers were using the crown as a chamber pot. He glanced at the Drakefords. "Will you be able to recognize it?"

"It would be kind of hard to miss," said Lump.

Maggie agreed. A docent offered to show them a stuffed boar popular with tourists, but they passed. The three left the museum, bought sandwiches from a nearby café, and ditched their carry-ons in some storage lockers before hiking northeast. Once they'd passed Vaduz Castle, they consulted their map and followed a series of hiking trails that took them up into the Alps.

To say Liechtenstein was a small country was an understatement. The signs they passed posted distances not in kilometers but rather in the time it took to *walk* there. It would take about ninety minutes to reach the Shin-Barkers' cave, and that was mostly due to the terrain. As inbred mountain folk, Lump and Maggie were clearly used to steep climbs. As a city gentleman, Laszlo was not, and he required frequent breaks to catch his breath.

"What's wrong?" asked Lump during Laszlo's fourth such break.

"Nothing," wheezed Laszlo, "I'm simply admiring the view." He swept his arm over the valley. "Isn't it glorious?"

Maggie adjusted her backpack. "How can a demon be in such crappy shape?"

Laszlo mopped his forehead. "How dare you. I belong to the best gym in Manhattan."

"Yeah? And what do you do when you're there?"

"Drink smoothies."

"What about exercise?"

Laszlo considered a moment. "Does the elliptical count?"

"Apparently not."

Laszlo did not much enjoy being the butt of jokes. Still, Maggie had a point. He was finished with the elliptical and those silly rubber bands. Power smoothies too. Sitting down on a rock, Laszlo decided he'd be turning over a new fitness leaf as soon as he'd eaten lunch.

He doled out sandwiches before arranging their remaining spell-tubes on a patch of moss. There were four: a scarlet mist, a violet vapor, a pearly twinkler, and some ocher sludge. Laszlo claimed the mist and twinkler for himself and left the vapor and sludge to the Drakefords. Lump, naturally, wound up with the latter.

"Why do you get two?" Maggie asked Laszlo. "If anyone gets two, it should be me. I'm the only person who hasn't used one yet."

Laszlo took a bite of his sandwich. "Tough luck. I stole these babies. They belong to me."

"Um, I've been wondering," said Lump delicately. "Do you have any powers?"

Laszlo almost choked. "Excuse me?"

The boy indicated the demon's arsenal. "Powers of your own, I mean. Powers that don't come from a tube."

Laszlo flicked away a persistent beetle. "One or two," he said. "Nothing to shake the heavens, but a few in the vanishing and illusory line."

Maggie crunched a chip. "So that's how you disappeared in Ramble Cave."

He grinned. "You should have seen your face. Downright flabbergasted, if I do say so myself. Intensely gratifying."

"*Flabbergasted?*" said Maggie. "I beg to differ. Try *furious*. No more ditching us."

"Oh, I don't think that will be necessary," said Laszlo easily. "Those New York kobolds made the Shin-Barkers sound like a bunch of fops. Still, it never hurts to be prepared." Leaning over, he picked up a heavy stick and handed it to Maggie. "Here you go, DiMaggio."

She tested its weight. "Didn't he play for the Yankees?" A nod. "My dad hates them."

Laszlo shrugged. "Joltin' Joe had the prettiest swing I've ever seen. Even when he missed, the crowd practically had an orgasm."

"What's an orgasm?" said Lump.

Maggie stared daggers at Laszlo, who was momentarily lost for words. "A refreshment," he answered, and took a bite of his sandwich.

Mercifully, his cell rang before Lump could get in any more questions. Glancing at the number, he set down his sandwich and answered. "Hey, Clarence. You'll never guess where I am."

"You're in Liechtenstein!"

Laszlo almost dropped the phone. "How the hell do you know that?"

"You've got to get out of there," Clarence pleaded. "They're closing in!"

"Those wankers on our flight? We ditched 'em in Zurich."

Clarence took a steadying breath. "I don't know about any wankers. But apparently the assassin roughed up some kobolds in Central Park, and—"

"Hallooo!"

The greeting came from above and so startled Laszlo that he performed a reflexive somersault over the rock serving as their picnic bench. Scrambling to his feet, phone still in hand, he eyed a stranger on the path above and reached two swift conclusions. The first was that the man was *not* an assassin. The second was that he was a certifiable loon.

The fellow stood on the trail some thirty feet above them, elderly but hale with a wiry gray beard, an Alpine cap, and honest-to-goodness lederhosen. With his lively eyes and crooked grin, he might have been a gnome hobbling out to wish them good day. Raising his walking stick, he repeated his greeting and shook a garbage bag that clinked with cans and bottles.

Laszlo held the phone to his ear. "Clarence, I'll call you back. We've encountered some sort of mountain kook or hermit. Wouldn't rule out cannibal."

"Okay, but—"

Laszlo ended the call and watched as the stranger made his way down the trail, chattering pleasantly to himself in German. When he arrived at their picnic site, the man sat on a rock and removed one of his boots, which he proceeded to empty of pebbles and pine needles.

"Can we help you?" said Laszlo.

The man peered at them. "*Sie sind Amerikaner?*"

"Yeah, that's right. Americans."

The newcomer cackled and continued his rapid flow of German. When Laszlo signaled that they didn't follow, the stranger shrugged and offered to share a sausage wrapped in waxed paper. Laszlo and the Drakefords declined, then watched in silence as he carved neat slices with a pocketknife and sipped from a flask around his neck. When he'd finished his meal, he tossed the scraps in his bag and offered to take their garbage as well.

"Uh, sure," said Maggie, handing him their wrappers. "Thank you."

The man doffed his cap and then inspected its feather, which he seemed to find wanting. Frowning, he removed it from the band and replaced it with another from his shirt pocket before inquiring if they would like to join him on his journey down the mountain.

"Sorry," said Laszlo, "we're going the other way." He pointed toward the summit.

The man's smile faded. "*Hoch?*"

"Um, *jawohl,*" said Laszlo. "*Hoch.*"

The man shook his head emphatically. "*Nein, darfst du nicht. Das ist Unsinn. Der Berg ist gefährlich. Nicht gut nach Sonnenuntergang.*"

Laszlo got the gist. "Thanks, but we're good. *Auf Wiedersehen.*"

The gentleman pointed west, where the sun cast dramatic shadows across the valley. Laszlo nodded appreciatively. It really was very pretty.

"*Nein,*" the man barked. "*Die Stunde der Tiere kommt! Achtung. Tod auf Flügeln. Nachtkrapp!*"

This latest outburst brought a frown to Laszlo's face. He had no idea what *Nachtkrapp* meant, but it sounded lewd, and Lump was already puzzling over orgasms. Spreading his arms, the man capered about in a circle, snapping his teeth and making a grotesque sound somewhere in his throat.

Lump poked Laszlo. "Um. What's he doing?"

"No idea, but I don't think that flask is filled with Perrier."

The newcomer continued his bizarre performance. Now and again, he added a guttural howl followed by a shriek. "*Nachtkrapp!*"

Laszlo had heard quite enough. "Sir, there is a child present."

The theatrics ceased. The man eyed Laszlo suspiciously. "*Du bleibst?*"

"I've never *bleibst* in my life. Good day to you."

The old man squinted. "*Was?*"

"Good day, sir!" Laszlo snapped. He pointed at the man, then down at Vaduz, and repeated the sequence for good measure. *Get lost. Scram. Fuck off.* The meaning was so plain even a moron in a feathered cap couldn't fail to understand.

Shaking his head, their visitor made the sign of the cross, which Laszlo couldn't help but take personally. "*Sie sind ein dummer Mann und werden sicherlich gegessen,*" he muttered in an undertone. "*Möge Gott diese armen Kinder beschützen.*"

Laszlo shooed him away. "Yeah, yeah. Hit the road."

Doffing his cap, the man continued down the trail, muttering to himself every step of the way. The Drakefords watched him go with anxious expressions.

"What do you think he was saying?" said Maggie.

"Von Trapp?" said Laszlo. "Who cares. He's probably hammered."

"I wish I spoke German," said Lump wistfully.

"You speak English and Nerd. That's plenty. Come on."

The geezer belonged in an asylum, but he was correct about one thing: they didn't have long before sunset, when the Shin-Barkers would begin to stir.

The trio increased their pace as they continued upward, toward the peak labeled *Alpspitz* on their hand-drawn map. When they reached a fork in the trail, they did not turn left or right but continued straight upslope, as the Central Park kobolds had indicated.

The going was tedious, and the breeze picked up as the afternoon waned. It swept through the trees, sending pine needles skittering down toward the valley. Now and again, one of the Drakefords stopped to admire the castle far below.

Finally, a gasping Laszlo clung to a shrub. "It's just ahead," he wheezed, pointing. "See that tree? That's the entrance."

"You're sure?" said Maggie, turning to look.

"Is there another dead tree two hundred yards past the fork?"

"No, but are we sure those kobolds were telling the truth?"

"Are you kidding?" said Laszlo. "They would never steer the 'Alpha' wrong."

Lump blushed. "I really don't think they would."

"Here's the plan," said Laszlo, having regained his wind. "I'll pop in and look around. When I know it's safe, I'll fetch you and away we go. *Capisce?*"

Lump nodded, then asked what *capisce* meant.

"The same as 'orgasm.'" Maggie glared and took the curse folio he handed her.

The demon continued solo. Sure, he was tired, but the Alpine air was invigorating, and he was anxious to get the hell out of Liechtenstein. Clarence was always jumpy, but this time he sounded legitimately terrified. If there really was an assassin on Laszlo's trail, that could seriously jeopardize his plans.

The dead tree was enormous, an ancient evergreen that must have toppled years ago. It sprawled across the slope, its trunk bleached white by the sun. As Laszlo crept closer, he spied a cleft in the mountain camouflaged by branches. He looked around; no visible sentries. That made sense. Unlike the Ramble kobolds, the Shin-Barkers weren't living under a thriving metropolis. Security would be more relaxed.

Slipping under the branches, Laszlo peered inside the opening. The roof was a tangle of moss and little roots, but the floor was smooth stone that angled down into darkness. He inhaled and promptly held his nose. There wasn't enough pine resin in the world to overpower the stench of kobold. It was worse than the E train.

The things I do. Swinging his legs over the edge, Laszlo slid down feetfirst. At the bottom, he was faced with a network of tunnels illuminated by patches of bioluminescent fungi. The ceiling was low enough that he'd have to stoop throughout, but on the plus side, the fungi were charmingly psychedelic.

With a snap of his fingers, Laszlo Faded, just as he'd done beneath Ramble Cave.

The power was fairly standard among Class IIIs. While Fading wasn't genuine invisibility, it often amounted to the same thing. Laszlo did not *vanish* but *receded* to the point that beings ceased to notice his presence. Unlike invisibility, a proper Fading could extend to senses beyond mere sight. When Maggie had reached out in the cave, she'd actually touched Laszlo's jacket, but her brain hadn't registered the contact.

The power was not without its limitations, of course. Fading rarely worked in well-lit conditions, and it never worked when one was already the focus of attention. Still, it was a handy trick that had saved Laszlo's hide on many occasions.

He quickly prowled through a variety of caverns, some furnished with tables or beds, others packed with stolen goods, and there were even a few guardrooms complete with dusty weapons racks and drinking wells bored deep into the stone.

As he explored, Laszlo saw many things.

But he saw no Shin-Barkers.

It wasn't simply that he hadn't spotted any kobolds; he had yet to uncover any evidence of their recent presence. It reminded Laszlo of the Black Death. In those days, it wasn't uncommon to come across empty villages or even towns. In some cases, the locals had simply fled to escape the disease. More often, they hadn't gone anywhere. They were at home and usually in bed, where they languished in various states of decomposition.

Laszlo never robbed those houses—not even the manors. It was just too depressing.

He looked in one more cavern before chalking up the lair as abandoned. For whatever reason, the Shin-Barkers had forsaken their den for greener pastures.

With a sigh, Laszlo sat down on a tiny bench. His scheme hinged on boosting Drakeford hopes into the stratosphere—and he had to do it quickly. This Herzogshut business was looking like a goddamn debacle.

As he pondered this, Laszlo took out Androvore's hourglass and set it on his knee. A mound of small red grains sat in the collecting bulb. Another tumbled down the chute. As Laszlo watched it join the rest, he reflected that time was the greatest power of all. No demon—not even his mighty father—could halt its steady progress.

When Laszlo had finished pouting, he took a deep breath and retraced his steps. He found the Drakefords thirty yards from the entrance, hidden behind a fir tree.

The demon spread his hands. "No luck."

Maggie looked past him at the cavern entrance. "What do you mean? What did you find?"

"Nothing," said Laszlo. "The place is abandoned."

"But what about the Herzogshut?" asked Lump, cleaning his glasses.

Leaning down, Laszlo rapped his knuckles on the boy's blond head. "Anyone home? The Shin-Barkers ghosted, kiddo. They left. They'll have taken the crown with them."

Maggie got to her feet. "But where would they have gone?"

Laszlo shrugged. "Who knows? They could be partying on the Riviera in matching Speedos."

"You searched the whole place?"

The demon chewed his lip. "No," he allowed, "but it's a goddamn warren. Tunnels everywhere. Anyway, I don't need to explore every inch to know there aren't any kobolds."

Maggie fished her flashlight from her pack. "I'm going in."

Laszlo waved a hand in front of her. "Did you hear me? There's no point."

"What other options do we have? Turn around? Go home? Abandon our only chance to break the curse? Shin-Barkers or no Shin-Barkers, this is the only place I know of that *might* have a crown jewel."

Laszlo scanned the horizon. "It'll be dark soon."

"Why would that matter? You said the place is empty."

Following his sister's lead, Lump also brought out his flashlight.

The demon threw up his hands. "Fine. You want to waste time crawling through caverns, be my guest. But no crying when you come up empty. Deal?"

"Deal," said Maggie. Strapping on her pack, she made grimly for the entrance, flashlight in one hand, cudgel in the other. Lump scampered after.

The two climbed inside and slid down the stone slab. Laszlo followed, humming to keep himself entertained as the Drakefords explored caverns he'd already visited. The two were comically earnest, shining their flashlights this way and that and peering into wells like they were the Hardy Boys.

Laszlo checked his watch. Almost six. By now, they'd ventured even farther than he had and discovered no evidence of kobolds. No food. No recent fires. Even the turds were fossilized. He kicked one out of the way. "I told you. This place is dead."

Maggie hissed from an archway up ahead. "Come look at this tunnel. It's bigger than the others."

Laszlo reluctantly obliged, only to discover that Maggie spoke the truth. *Bigger* was an understatement. For the first time, he could actually stand like a civilized demon. Stretching his back, he sighted down a passage that was not only larger but covered with carvings not unlike hieroglyphics. Laszlo was impressed. Who knew kobolds could be so cultured?

"Where do you think it leads?" said Lump.

Laszlo's interest rekindled. "Someplace important," he muttered. "No more talking."

Leaving the Drakefords, he stole ahead to where the passage ended. This archway had a pair of heavy bronze doors that sagged brokenly on their hinges. Laszlo was about to venture in when his shoe struck something.

There was a skull at his feet.

The skull was roughly the size of a grapefruit and had unsettling canines along with a sizable hole in its cranium. Five vertebrae dangled from its stem like a tail.

Laszlo glanced about. There wasn't a single femur, rib, or pelvis to be seen. He almost laughed. *Of course* they would be missing! Intact kobold remains would have been far too normal. Those were for *other* Curse Keepers, Keepers with loving fathers and lenient bosses.

The Drakefords joined him. Laszlo motioned for quiet as he inspected the doors' mangled plating and hinges. What could do that kind of damage? A battering ram?

With growing unease, he looked into the chamber beyond.

It took a moment to fully comprehend what he was seeing.

The cavern was by far the largest they'd encountered, some eighty feet across, with a domed roof perhaps half as high. The floor was covered with the same glowing fungi as the tunnels. It illuminated a number of haystacks spaced evenly throughout the chamber.

At least that was what they resembled. A closer look revealed that the "haystacks" were made of countless skulls and bones carefully arranged into mounds the size of garden sheds.

Had they come across some sort of tomb or ossuary? His demonic vision pierced the gloom, and he saw a leather recliner on a dais. Laszlo was impressed. He associated recliners with eating buffalo wings and snoozing through Monday Night Football. The Shin-Barkers had seen greater possibilities. Their recliner was a throne.

And that throne was occupied. Laszlo hadn't noticed the skeleton at first, for it was small and slumped like a petulant child. The skeleton was missing an arm and its lower legs, but it most certainly possessed a head.

Upon it sat the Herzogshut.

CHAPTER 19
HIDE-AND-SEEK

"There it is," Laszlo whispered. "Right on that guy's melon."

Across the cavern, Maggie saw a leather chair atop a stony platform. It held a skeleton, skull tipped back to stare at the ragged black banners hanging from the ceiling. She could see that there was *something* on its head, but she couldn't say for certain.

She kept her voice low. "Are you sure that's it?"

"Of course that's it," said Laszlo. "How many crowns do you think these guys have?"

Maggie looked around at the piles of bones. "Do you think this was the entire clan?"

Laszlo nodded grimly. "I'd say the Shin-Barkers are toast."

"If they're toast, why are we being so quiet?" said Lump.

For such a brilliant kid, he could sure overlook the obvious. "Because something *killed* them," Maggie whispered. "Something made these piles."

Lump's mouth rounded into an *oh*. "What do you think it was?"

"How am I supposed to know?"

"Shh," said Laszlo. "Listen, as Curse Keeper, I can't get it for you. One of you has to grab it."

Maggie glanced back at the skeleton in the chair. "I'll do it, but you're coming with me."

The demon snorted. "Not a chance."

"You promised to protect us."

"That's right," said Lump. "You swore an oath!"

Laszlo made a face. "On a menu. But okay, fine. Hurry up, though. I don't like this place."

The boy nodded and readied his spelltube.

"What are you doing?" Maggie whispered. "You're staying put."

Her brother gestured at the dim and dusty passageway. "Here? Alone? Not a chance."

Laszlo took out one of his own spelltubes. "We'll all go, but *absolute silence* inside. We're just three quiet mice stealing a piece of cheddar."

In Maggie's opinion, they might as well have been mice as they scurried across the floor and picked a path among the mounds. She was careful not to touch these and kept an eye on Lump to ensure he didn't venture close to anything that could topple or break. A few stray bones were scattered about the floor, but most were quite small and could be easily avoided.

Despite the pledge of silence, Maggie felt they were making a terrible racket. The chamber was so deathly still that every breath, every rustle of clothing, seemed dreadfully conspicuous. She could not shake the feeling that they were poised on the edge of disaster. Now and again, she stopped and looked back to ensure nothing was sneaking up behind them.

When they reached the dais, they crept up its shallow steps and took in the little skeleton slumped in its chair. The crown was missing several pearls, and the velvet was torn, but there was no question that this was the long-lost crown of Liechtenstein.

Maggie's fear was replaced by a surge of excitement. Two days; two treasures. They were going to break this goddamn spell. Images flashed in her mind of the future ahead. Her eye and arm had returned to normal. There was her father, restored to the man he should have been. Would such things truly happen? Maggie didn't know, but a girl could hope.

Not now, she told herself sternly. *Focus on the task.*

Laszlo nodded for Maggie to take the Herzogshut. She gingerly lifted the crown from the kobold's skull and tried stashing it in her pack. No good. With the porridge pot already inside, there was no room. Leaving her pack on the ground, she gestured for Lump to turn around so she could stow the crown in his pack, layering it between some clothes. When it was safely nestled, she zipped up the compartment, spun him about, and grinned.

Lump beamed and looked to their Curse Keeper. *Can we go?*

Laszlo nodded and went to hand Maggie her backpack. As he did so, a crooning voice broke the silence.

"Fly me to the moon . . ."

The song was coming from Laszlo's pants. Dropping Maggie's pack, he fumbled in his pocket and brought out his phone, whose screen he tapped with frantic urgency. The song stopped, only to be replaced by an anxious voice bleating from the speaker.

"You never called back! I thought the assassin—"

Laszlo cursed and pressed a button on the side. This time, the phone powered off.

Silence returned. No one dared move. Instead, they remained frozen on the dais, staring at one another with appalled expressions. Maggie glowered at Laszlo, who looked uncharacteristically sheepish. *For all his blather about keeping quiet, the idiot forgets to turn off his phone? Unbelievable.* She had a strong impulse to brain the demon with her club.

But Maggie suppressed the urge. Instead, she remained perfectly still and silent, ears pricked for any sign of danger. Ten seconds passed. Twenty. Nothing crawled or slithered from the mysterious mounds. The caverns remained mercifully quiet.

Laszlo exhaled. "My bad," he whispered. "Let's go—"

Something dropped from the ceiling.

The something landed with a wet slap on the skeleton. Maggie stared at the object, struggling to make sense of its raw and glistening contours. Was it part of a goat? A sheep?

A skinless head landed beside it.

Definitely a sheep.

The three craned their necks. High above, the banners had begun to sway and tremble. Long black feathers fluttered down to the floor. Maggie's throat went dry as she stared up at the cavern's roof, unable to move.

She realized now that what she'd taken for ragged banners were actually the wings of huge creatures now descending on cords that appeared to issue from their bodies.

As the creatures were illuminated by the fungi's glow, Maggie gave a soundless cry.

Taking Lump's arm, she pulled him swiftly out of their path. The two stumbled blindly from the throne, frantic to put distance between themselves and these strange monstrosities. Seconds later, Maggie realized she'd made a terrible mistake; in her bid to get Lump away, she'd led him not down the dais steps but into the alcove behind the throne. Now they risked being trapped, cut off from the passage by which they'd entered.

She spun about, but as she was about to move, she found three ragged creatures landing silently on the dais. Even as they settled, their heads remained bowed, faces hidden behind folded wings. As they crouched upon the floor, they might have been a trio of black-robed monks engaged in a silent prayer.

Behind her, a voice spoke up, faint and trembling. "Maggie, I'm scared."

She nodded and reached back to stroke Lump's arm. "Me too."

Laszlo called out from somewhere in the chamber. The acoustics made it difficult to guess his location. "You two stay put."

Like we have a choice, thought Maggie. Clearing her throat, she tried to find her voice. "Laszlo, what are these things?"

"No idea," he replied, "but when I count to three, hit the deck."

Before Maggie could ask another question, the creatures rose to their full height. They were exceedingly tall—at least seven feet—with emaciated torsos covered in dull black feathers. Their upper limbs were bat-like, bony joints connected by folds of leathery skin; their legs were long and slender, the splayed feet tipped with six-inch talons. This was unsettling enough, but their faces . . .

They were nightmares from a Bosch painting: crow-like, with powerful beaks and eight milky eyes each. Those eyes were now locked upon the Drakefords. Hungry and alien, inscrutable and merciless.

A new breed of fear welled up in Maggie.

Not fear of attack or confrontation; she'd experienced that many times. This was more primal and chilling. The things standing twenty feet away did not care who Maggie Drakeford was or why she was in the cavern. They simply wanted to eat her.

"One!" called Laszlo.

Two of the creatures took a step toward the Drakefords. Maggie let her pack fall to the floor.

"Two!"

The creatures were only ten feet away now. They loomed over the Drakefords, huge and hellish, a pair of fairy-tale nightmares sizing up their prey. Maggie tightened her grip on the cudgel.

"*Three!*"

Maggie and Lump dropped to the ground as a phosphorescent flash rippled through the chamber. The creatures retreated several paces and wheeled to observe the new threat.

A dozen luminous butterflies flitted about the cavern before vanishing in a burst of pink sparkles.

Laszlo did not hesitate to make his feelings known. "Shit."

Yup, thought Maggie. Leaping to her feet, she brought up the club just as one of the creatures turned to make a lunging stab. The point of its beak impaled the wood like Styrofoam, and the club was ripped from Maggie's hand. Spreading its wings, the creature reared up and brought back its neck to deliver the death blow.

Something smashed behind her. A heartbeat later, torrents of red fire screamed past her ear and slammed into the creature's chest, lifting it off its feet. It tumbled in midair like a sparrow caught in a cyclone. When the flames vanished, all that remained was half a beak that fell with a clatter upon the dais.

A speechless Maggie turned to find Lump standing rigid, his arm still extended from hurling his spelltube to the floor. Shattered glass lay

about his feet, and he was breathing heavily. Laszlo's disgruntled voice
sounded from somewhere in the chamber.

"How are you doing that?"

Neither Drakeford had any idea. But there was no time to discuss
it, for the two remaining creatures had not taken kindly to their companion's incineration. One leaped off the dais, presumably at Laszlo.
The other made straight for Maggie's brother.

Seizing Lump's arm, Maggie heaved him aside just before the creature's beak sparked against the wall where he'd been standing. Their
momentum sent them spilling together in a heap near the throne. As
Lump scrambled up, Maggie made a dive for her backpack. She grasped
its strap; four talons slammed down upon it, nearly impaling her hand.

Maggie rolled aside before the other foot came down. Getting up,
she shouted at Lump to make for the passageway.

She ducked just as the creature sprang at her. It smashed headfirst
into the kobolds' throne, knocking the recliner and its occupant down
the dais steps. As the monster struggled to right itself, Maggie vaulted
over it and raced to catch up with her brother.

As they fled, Maggie wondered where Laszlo and the second creature had gone. She yelled the demon's name but got no reply. She kept
running.

Their creature had recovered and was in hot pursuit, its talons clack-
ing on stone as it chased them down the long passage adorned with
carvings.

As she caught up to Lump, Maggie shifted her focus to a second,
equally desperate objective.

Get small.

It was their only chance. They would never beat this thing in a
footrace. Its legs were longer, its stride swifter. But if they could reach
the tunnels where even Lump had to crouch, perhaps they could gain
the advantage.

Leaving the larger passage behind, Maggie shouted for Lump to take
the right-hand tunnel. It was the same one they had taken earlier, and
she wanted to work her way back toward the entrance. The last thing

they needed was to plunge blindly down paths unknown. They had to get out of these caverns, with or without their guide.

Lump darted through the smaller opening. Maggie went to follow, but a sweeping blow knocked her feet out from under her. She tumbled and crashed into some crates piled next to the archway. The impact left her shoulder numb, but she rolled aside just as the creature slammed into the wall. Crates exploded in a shower of splinters. Sprawled amid the wreckage, the panting monster scrabbled about for Maggie, who crawled frantically in hope of reaching safety. She cried out as a talon punctured her foot, but pulled herself forward and made a limping dash under the archway.

Lump was huddled ten feet beyond, pressed flat against the wall, as though it might hide him. Pale and rigid, he didn't respond when Maggie said his name. Taking his wrist, she dragged him along. Behind, they heard the creature croaking and hissing as it squeezed its bulk into the passage.

"Don't stop," said Maggie. "Keep going, no matter what."

Lump's voice was barely audible. "I thought it got you."

"Not yet."

"But—"

"Shut up and move!"

They ran. Swiftly. Desperately. Down tunnels, through storage rooms and workshops. And all the while they heard the monster in pursuit, its talons scraping on stone and an almost playful humming from somewhere in its throat. Occasionally, it let out a guttural cry that echoed throughout the caverns. Maggie wondered if it was calling to others.

The last cry had come several minutes ago. Now, the creature pursued them in silence, worming its way along with dreadful and dogged purpose.

Their exertions, combined with their fear, proved too much for Lump. As the Drakefords entered yet another chamber, he sagged and collapsed into a wheezing heap.

"I can't," he gasped. "I can't go any further."

Maggie shook him firmly. "You have to. Get up!"

"I can't—" His words were muffled by a fit of coughing. Clamping a hand over his mouth, she dragged her brother away from the tunnel to a shadowed corner where rusting cots were stacked like beds in some Dickensian orphanage.

"Shh! You have to be still, or it will hear you!" she pleaded in quiet desperation.

But Lump could not. Sweat blossomed like dewdrops upon his face and hands. He was shaking uncontrollably.

And then, from somewhere in the nightmarish labyrinth, Maggie imagined she heard that awful humming again. She glanced anxiously at her brother. Lump couldn't go any farther, and there was no way she could carry him through passages where she had to stoop or crawl.

Maggie cast her eyes frantically about the cavern. The trunks and lockers were too small to hide him, as were the niches carved into the rock. The best she could do was cover him with a mildewed blanket and pray. Pulling his backpack off, she turned his limp body to the wall. If he stayed motionless, the blanket would cover him. And if the universe was kind, the pervasive stench of kobold might just mask the scent of boy.

Maggie stacked three footlockers and huddled behind them to rummage through Lump's pack. There was nothing of real use, just the Herzogshut and some rolled-up clothes. Her spelltube was in the pack she'd left behind in the throne room. She could picture the vial stowed in a zippered compartment for easy access. She cursed silently.

Maggie did not know how long she crouched behind the trunks, ears strained for any sound in the darkness. The tomb-like silence had returned, more unsettling than any cries or humming.

Now she realized that the old man had been trying to warn them, that his peculiar display was an imitation of the horrors now hunting them in the dark—the Nachtkrapp.

Laszlo is worse than an idiot. She cursed again. He should have understood, and he had no excuse—an eight-hundred-year-old demon had had plenty of time to pick up some German. At least enough to understand when the natives were alerting him to local monsters.

As the minutes passed, Maggie's body grew stiff. A damp chill was seeping into her bones from the surrounding rock. She tried to massage some strength back into her legs and felt a sticky patch where blood had soaked into her shoe. The pain barely registered. All that mattered was whether she could still run.

Finding another weapon wouldn't hurt either. Risking a bit of light, she turned on Lump's flashlight and swept the beam along the piled beds and belongings. Surely there must be something she could use.

And there it was. In the corner, she spotted a wooden stand some five feet tall, with various hats hanging from little pegs. It was not the hats she noticed but the pointed metal spike at the top. The pole was screwed into a separate base and could probably be detached.

Flicking off the light, Maggie peered around the footlockers at the passage from which they'd come. The opening looked like a crude mouth cut into the stone. She watched it intently. When nothing crept forth, she crawled over to the stand and began unscrewing the pole.

She'd nearly finished when the back of her neck began to prickle.

The chamber felt inexplicably larger and colder, like a void was opening up behind her. With a final turn, Maggie lifted the sturdy pole free and turned to face the passage opening.

Something was crawling from it.

A frozen Maggie watched with dread as the monster issued noise-lessly from the confining tunnel and, once free, settled back on its haunches. It crouched for a moment in the darkness, nosing the air, before shuffling forward, its wings dragging on the stone like a tattered cloak. Maggie's eyes went to the cots and the blanketed mound that was her brother.

Don't move, Maggie pleaded inwardly. *Don't even breathe . . .*

Just then, a distant cry echoed through the caverns, mournful and inhuman. The creature whipped its head about, facing the passage. It crouched lower, tense and alert, seemingly poised to hurry back the way it had come.

Go. Leave us alone . . .

As if in answer, the creature thrust its head into the passage and made an inquisitive humming in its throat. Maggie crept back to hide behind the footlockers, clutching the pole to her hammering chest. Ten feet away, Lump peered out from his blanket. From his stricken expression, it was clear he hadn't realized they had company. Maggie put a finger to her lips.

He nodded, but then his eyes shot wide with alarm. Maggie knew what was coming and frantically shook her head.

Don't! You mustn't—

It was in vain. Her brother's cough shattered the silence.

Instantly, the creature backed from the tunnel and wheeled around, knocking over a stool. Talons scraped against stone as it scrabbled forward on all fours, making straight for where Lump was hidden.

Maggie did not hesitate. Rising from behind the trunks, she set the pole against her shoulder and braced to meet the monster's charge.

The impact sent her careening back into the cots, where she struck her head against a post. Metal rails clattered about her as she lay stunned amid the wreckage. As the din subsided, Maggie became aware of a gurgling nearby. Someone tugged furiously at her hand. Above her, a blurred form came slowly into focus.

Lump.

Her senses cleared. Coarse feathers brushed Maggie's cheek, and she recoiled, almost knocking her brother over. Rising to her knees, she looked down at the monster sprawled amid a nest of twisted iron railings. Maggie's spiked pole protruded from its back, near the shoulder blade. The creature let out a burbling hiss as it struggled to draw breath. That hideous beaked face craned to gaze up at her, the eight eyes blank and inscrutable. It gave another hiss and stretched a claw toward Maggie's ankle.

Lump pulled her out of reach. "Come on," he pleaded. "This is our chance!"

Maggie nodded, then doubled over in a spasm of sudden nausea. Vomit splattered on the broken cots and the monster tangled among them. The purge left a bitter taste, but it also cleared her head. Maggie retrieved Lump's pack from beneath the toppled footlockers before taking his hand and leading him onward.

"What about Laszlo?" said Lump.

"We can't worry about him right now. We have to get out."

Escape was her sole objective. She needed to see the sky, to breathe fresh air and get away from this infested hell. She decided then and there that she did not care for Liechtenstein.

Behind them was the sound of metal scraping against metal. The pair hurried forward, dragging Lump's pack and relying on Maggie's memory of the rooms they passed. When they reached an armory, she grabbed two small spears from a rack. Lump accepted his without comment.

Through the tunnels, winding this way and that. When in doubt, they chose the path that seemed to lead up. Maggie didn't stop to listen for pursuit. Forward progress was all that mattered.

Get in. Get out. Go home.

Lump whispered something. "What?" she said.

"Which way?"

Only then did she realize that they'd reached a literal crossroads. Most of the chambers had only two tunnels branching off them; this one had five. She quickly studied each opening, scouring her memory for some hint or clue that might lead in the right direction. She glanced uncertainly back at the way they'd come, wondering if they had taken a wrong turn.

Another cry sounded from somewhere in the darkness.

Maggie plucked a hair from her head.

"What are you doing?" Lump whispered.

Holding the hair by one end, Maggie moved to one of the archways and watched as it fluttered ever so slightly in the direction of the opening. As a baffled Lump watched, she repeated the process at the next archway. At the third, the air current was noticeably stronger and blew the strand back toward Maggie.

"It's this way," she said.

Another cry behind them, louder than before. Maggie and Lump pushed forward through the caverns, their spirits bolstered by the cooler, cleaner-smelling air that greeted them.

Two minutes later, they reached the entrance and scrambled up the slab of stone.

Once they'd pushed past the dead tree's branches, they found their breath misting in the frigid breeze that washed over the mountainside. Maggie stopped to gaze up at the night sky ablaze with countless stars, so vast and unconfined.

They were safe. If she'd been alone, she might have wept.

"Come on," she said, and they scrambled down the rough terrain to the spot where they'd waited for Laszlo earlier that afternoon.

"Should we move further away?" said Lump. "What if that thing comes out?"

"I doubt it will. I think I punctured a lung. And it's one thing to chase us through a labyrinth of tunnels, but out here?" She swept her arm over the landscape. "Shit, we could have gone anywhere."

"You don't need to swear."

"I'm a grown-ass woman who just impaled a monster with a hatstand. I'll swear if I want to. For example: at the moment, my foot is fucking *killing* me."

Maggie turned the flashlight on it. The wound's diameter was the size of a dime, and she could tell that it went deeper than it looked. She had a brief flash of the medicine cabinet back home. It would take more than iodine to fix this.

"I'm really sorry," said Lump. "But I still don't like it when you swear."

His earnestness made Maggie smile in spite of herself. "Got it. Your glasses are broken, by the way."

Lump nodded and held them up; the moonlight revealed a sizable crack across one of the lenses. "It happened when that thing crashed into us. It's okay for now—I can still see through the other one." Slipping the glasses back on, he leaned past Maggie to squint up at the cavern. "Do you think Laszlo's okay?"

"I hope so. Like it or not, we need him."

"And he *is* pretty funny," said Lump.

"Yeah—but more to the point, he's got money and our passports. Without them, I don't know how we'll get home."

"Why would we go home? We just got our crown jewels!" Hoisting his pack, he gave it a little shake and offered a coaxing grin.

Maggie sagged inwardly. She hated to pop his balloon. "You're forgetting something."

Lump's smile wavered. "What?"

"The *other* backpack. I left it in the throne room."

Understanding dawned on that round little face. "The porridge pot!"

Maggie could only nod. During the escape, she hadn't had time to think about it. Now, its absence ripped a hole in her heart, in the hopes that had been building. They'd taken a sizable step toward breaking the curse, only to take an equally sizable step back. Maybe two steps, when you factored in the time they'd lost coming to Liechtenstein.

Where the hell was Laszlo?

The Drakefords huddled together, tense and shivering as their sweat cooled. Lump clutched Maggie's arm, the way he had as a little boy. No cries escaped the cavern. There was no sound but for the wind.

As they waited, Maggie replayed the events in the throne room. She could picture her backpack on the dais, her hand reaching for it, only to jerk back as the creature stamped down. Of course, she couldn't truly blame herself—the act was pure reflex—but she did wonder if she had doomed them. What was the point of escaping those monsters if it cost them their only chance at breaking their curse?

Maggie turned suddenly to Lump. "Can you find your way back to town?"

He blinked. "Why would I have to do that?"

"Yes or no?"

"I think so, but—"

She got up and hefted one of the spears they'd taken from the caverns. "I'm going back in. I know right where the backpack is."

"But those creatures—"

"—aren't in the throne room. They won't be expecting us to come back. Coming back would be stupid."

Lump wholeheartedly agreed.

"But we need that pot," she said pointedly. "We've got no chance without it. Besides, we can't just leave Laszlo behind."

Her brother considered a moment. "Do you think he'd come back for us?"

Maggie tested her weight on her injured foot. "Doesn't matter. We're not him."

"Well then. I guess I'm coming too."

"*No.*" The sharpness of Maggie's tone caught Lump off guard. "No, and I mean it. You stay here. If I'm not back in an hour, you get to town. Find the police. Knock on doors. Wake someone up if you have to. Tell them you need help and want to speak with the American embassy."

"Why?"

Because that's what they do in books. "Because they'll get you home."

Lump looked ready to hyperventilate. "But what would I say? How would I explain—"

"You're the smartest person I know," Maggie reassured him. "You'll figure something out. Hopefully, it won't come to that."

"But—"

She kissed her brother's sweaty blond tangles. "I love you, Lump, but now I need you to shut up and do what you're told. You're not going in with me, and that's final."

There must have been real steel in her voice, because this time Lump didn't argue. Instead, he hugged his sister and gazed up at her with an expression of fierce and boundless love.

Maggie didn't look back as she trudged up the slope. She knew he'd be watching like a puppy left by the roadside. She kept her eyes fixed on the tree sprawled across the cavern's entrance. By moonlight, its branches were spindly and grotesque, a desiccated insect clinging to the mountainside. And beyond? A house of horrors. She tightened her grip on the spear.

She'd nearly reached the tree when the sound of a snapping twig made her freeze. Something was crawling out of the cavern.

There was no place to hide. She crouched and kept still among the brambles and scree. With luck, she'd be mistaken for a shrub.

Another snap. Maggie tightened her grip on the spear.

A figure staggered out from the shadows and doubled over in a fit of coughing. In one hand, it clutched a phone. The other held a backpack.

Maggie stood up. "Laszlo!"

The demon gestured for patience until the coughing stopped and he was able to hawk a sizable loogie. When this was done, he sat heavily on a rock and started fiddling with his phone. Maggie hurried over.

"Are you okay?" she asked. "Are those things dead?"

"Don't know, don't care." Holding the phone to his ear, Laszlo wiped spittle from his chin and glanced at her spear. "What are you, a Zulu?"

"It's a weapon, jackass. I was coming to rescue you."

He snorted derisively. "Oh yeah? Where were you twenty minutes ago? My suit's filthy, and I took a beak to the cubes."

Maggie grimaced. "Your *cubes*?"

"My balls, sweetcakes, my cojones, my nectarines, my—" A woman's voice squawked from the phone. He sat up. "Hello? Uh, *sprichst du Englisch?* You do? Great. I need the best room you've got. Tonight. Something with lots of marble and room service and a bidet like a fire hose." The demon rubbed his neck while the woman ran through several options. "The Imperial Suite sounds perfect," he said. "Oh, and when I get there, I'll need a bucket of champagne and the number of a morally casual masseuse . . ."

Maggie listened in mounting disbelief as Laszlo provided his credit card number.

"Are you planning a party?" she asked sarcastically.

The demon placed his hand over the phone. "A funeral."

"Whose?"

He tossed her the backpack. "Mine."

Stooping, Maggie picked up the bag, whose canvas had been torn and pierced in several places. While Laszlo finalized his reservation, she unzipped the main compartment. There, nestled among some clothes, were the crumpled remains of a magic pot.

A lump formed in Maggie's throat.

"*Haferbrei-Topf . . .*"

She stared in hopeful silence, but no steam trickled from within; no porridge burbled over that battered rim. Not a single glorious drop.

The porridge pot was ruined.

CHAPTER 20
ROOM SERVICE

It was nearly midnight by the time Laszlo stood beneath the rejuvenating downpour of a five-star shower.

Getting to the hotel had been quite the ordeal. First, they'd had to hike down that miserable mountain and retrieve the luggage they'd stowed. Next, a tense and silent ride back to Switzerland, where they consulted a discreet and expensive physician to look at Maggie's punctured foot. Nine stitches later, yet another car ferried them to their final destination: a world-class resort overlooking Lake Zurich.

Laszlo installed the Drakefords in the cheapest room available before retiring to his suite. The imperial was an absurd indulgence—and one he could not afford—but what did it matter? Laszlo was going to die. And not some cushy mortal death, either. No, he would be melted down in an iron funnel and discarded like an abandoned Big Gulp into the Primordial Ooze, where his essence would mingle with the demonic *hoi polloi*. It might be millennia until he respawned as a *druude*, the lowest form of demonkind, little better than an amoeba. Laszlo sighed. He'd miss having opposable thumbs. They were so handy.

For example, they helped him set down Androvore's hourglass and retie his plush bathrobe. Laszlo simply adored hotel bathrobes and had stolen many in his day, but he did wish the belts would stay put. There you were, swaggering about like Cary Grant, when the belt would come undone and the robe would fall open, transforming a would-be god of leisure into a pasty schlub with frizzled chest hair. One day, some genius would invent a self-cinching bathrobe and make a fortune.

But that genius, alas, would not be Laszlo. The Drakeford quest was dead in the water and with it his brilliant scheme. There wasn't any point pretending otherwise. His ploy required great gobs of hope, mountains of the stuff. Things had been moving in that direction, but now it had dribbled away like so much porridge.

Peering out of the living room window, he took a swig of Dom. The view and the bubbly were world class, but in his present mood Laszlo couldn't fully appreciate them. He glanced at his watch: almost two. His company would be arriving any minute.

Remote in hand, he powered on the suite's absurdly large flat-screen and scrolled directly to the adult-entertainment options. He selected a movie and watched distractedly as the opening credits began to roll.

A knock sounded. Tossing the remote on a sectional, Laszlo sauntered out toward the entry. He opened the door with a flourish.

"And *you* must be Helga . . ."

The name died on his lips. Standing before him was not a six-foot Austrian with spectacular breasts and conversational English but a pair of cursed American rubes dragging their luggage.

"Oh, for fuck's sake. What do you want?"

"Who's Helga?" asked Lump.

"No one," said Laszlo. "A friend." Leaning forward, he peered over the humans to scan the corridor.

"We need to come in," said Maggie.

Laszlo barred the doorway with his arm. "Not a chance. Beat it."

"It's *important*."

"So is Helga."

But Maggie Drakeford was not to be denied. Ducking under Laszlo's arm, she entered the suite followed by Lump, who nearly walked into a sculpture as he goggled at the chandelier. "Wow. Do you have this whole place to yourself?"

"Yes, and you can't stay."

But Lump had already kicked off his shoes. He wandered past his sister. "What's that music?" he asked. "Are you watching something?"

Laszlo's eyes shot wide open. He dashed after Lump, elbowing the kid aside as he rounded the corner and made a diving leap for the remote. Snatching it up, he frantically mashed the buttons. To his infinite relief, the music stopped. Dropping the remote, Laszlo exhaled and turned to apologize for launching the kid into a ficus.

He found Lump standing ten feet away, staring at the television with a puzzled expression. "What is this?"

Laszlo let out a yelp. His button mashing had been in vain. Instead of turning the TV off, he had merely paused the movie.

At that moment, Maggie walked into the room. Her gaze went immediately to the screen. "Lump, cover your eyes!"

But Lump did not. Instead, the boy stared at the frozen image with an expression of mingled curiosity and wonder. "Is that man delivering a pizza?"

Laszlo stalled. "Is he carrying a pizza?"

"Yes."

"Then there's your answer."

"But he's not wearing pants," Lump observed.

Why were remotes so goddamn complicated? "It gets very hot in Southern California. In the Valley, pants are optional." At last, he found the necessary button and pressed it. The screen went black. Laszlo set the remote carefully on the coffee table.

"You're such a pig," said Maggie.

Laszlo folded his arms. "Well, excuse me. Did I *ask* for company?"

There was a second knock at the door.

Maggie clucked her tongue. "Apparently, you did."

"You two stay here," the demon ordered, and hurried to the door. This time, he used the peephole.

Not even a fish-eye lens could distort the platinum perfection beyond. Sweeping back his hair, he opened the door with an attempt at his previous mojo. "And *you* must be Helga . . ."

The woman nodded and looked him over. "Well, well," she purred. "A handsome client."

"Guilty as charged," said Laszlo. He glanced over his shoulder. "Um . . . there may be a slight hiccup."

Helga's smile took on a slightly fixed quality. "Hiccup?"

"Problem," Laszlo translated. "Just a teensy one. Nothing two consenting adults can't work around."

"What is this problem?"

He cleared his throat. "My niece and nephew are here."

The smile vanished. "*Schwein!*" she hissed. "*Schweinehund!*"

Before Laszlo could explain, luscious Helga turned on one stiletto heel and marched away in a swish of sequins. When Laszlo offered to call her a car, she did not even break stride. With a scornful laugh, Helga informed him the agency had his credit card information; the client would certainly be paying for a car, along with a boatload of francs for her time and trouble. A forlorn Laszlo watched her go.

As she boarded the elevator, the demon backed silently into the suite and began contemplating a double murder.

Maggie's head emerged from behind the ficus. "Where's Helga?" she asked innocently.

Laszlo glowered and stalked back into the living room, where he found Lump taking a package of cookies from the minibar.

"Put those back," Laszlo ordered.

"But I'm hungry! We never ate dinner."

As if on cue, the boy's stomach gave an audible growl. Muttering to himself, Laszlo snatched up the room service menu and called for two burgers, truffle fries, a roast chicken, and three packs of Davidoffs. He tossed the menu to the Drakefords. Maggie chose salmon, and Lump asked for veal in cream sauce because he'd never tried veal and was feeling "adventurous."

Once the order was placed, Laszlo set the phone back in its cradle and eyed the pair with simmering impatience. The ciggies couldn't come fast enough. Taking up his champagne, he parked himself in an armchair. "So," he said. "What's so important you had to ruin my date?"

At the word *date*, Maggie raised an eyebrow but merely said, "The porridge pot is broken."

Laszlo swirled his champagne in a snide and patronizing manner. Did he have it in him to commit murder? He'd like to think so. "I know it's broken," he said coldly. "I was there. I'm the guy who fetched it after getting pecked in the wee-wee."

Lump giggled.

"Right," said Maggie. "So our magic item's gone, and we thought— or rather *assumed*—that our quest is hopeless. But what if it isn't?"

Laszlo gestured wearily. "Get to the point."

"What if we can get another magic item?"

"Brilliant," said Laszlo. "Should we order it from Amazon or Target?"

"Sarcasm won't help things."

"Well, too bad," he snapped. "You seem to think magic items are easy to come by. Getting the skinny on that pot was a lucky stroke. We won't get that lucky again."

Lump piped up. "Our plan isn't luck. It's a calculated risk."

"Is that so?" Laszlo took a swig of champagne. "Okay, let's hear it. What's going to save my—uh, *our*—asses?"

The siblings spoke as one. "Signora Bellascura."

Laszlo drew a blank. "Who?"

"Signora Bellascura," Maggie repeated. "Dimitri told us about her. Remember? She's that really old demon who's the authority on the Magi?"

Laszlo pondered a moment. He did vaguely recall Dimitri mentioning someone who fit this unappetizing description. "What about her?"

"Dimitri said she lives in Rome."

"And . . . ?"

Maggie shot Laszlo one of those *can you really be so dense* looks he found so irritating. Could *she* complete the Monday crossword in under eleven minutes? He thought not.

"Well," she continued, "if Signora Bellascura's been around for thousands of years, she'll probably have some magic items, won't she? And Rome's not so far away."

Lump held up a train schedule. "The concierge gave us this. We can be in Rome today!"

Laszlo flicked his gaze from one Drakeford to the other. "Have either of you met a five-thousand-year-old demon?" he asked coolly.

The humans confessed that they had not.

"Well, take it from me—they're not as sweet and cuddly as yours truly. Compared to them, I barely even register as scary."

Maggie's gaze went to his bathrobe. "That's hard to believe."

"What I'm getting at," continued Laszlo, "is that Signora Scallopini isn't going to open the door and invite you in to browse her collection. She'll probably just eat you."

Lump looked oddly intrigued. "Do demons actually eat people?"

"Depends on the demon. Some went pescatarian."

"We're not asking her for charity," said Maggie. "We have something valuable to trade."

Laszlo raised an eyebrow. "Your *soul*, Maggie? I didn't know you had it in you. Then again, I'm not sure cursed souls are in demand—damaged goods and all. There might even be a lien."

"I have no intention of selling my soul."

"Then you don't have anything she'll want," the demon said with a shrug.

"But we do."

"And what's that, pray tell?"

"We know where one of the Lost Magi is located."

Laszlo leaned back in the armchair and appraised the Drakefords for a solid minute. He didn't know whether to be impressed by their determination or appalled by their naivete. Nevertheless, the gears in his brain were now easing into motion and building up speed. At length, he clucked his tongue.

"What you're proposing—"

"Is inspired!" cried Maggie.

"—is insane."

Lump looked disappointed. "You don't think it'll work?"

"I didn't say that," replied Laszlo. "It *could* work. It *might* work. But it's one helluva dangerous play."

"More dangerous than hide-and-seek with those monsters?" said Maggie.

"Much more. Everything depends on this Signora . . . what's her name?"

"Bellascura."

Signora Bellascura. Laszlo turned the words over in his mind. In his opinion, old people shouldn't be allowed to have such sexy names. It was misleading. Indecent. His thoughts were interrupted by yet another knock at the suite's door. There stood a middle-aged gentleman beside a cart piled with covered platters. The demon scribbled his signature, eyed the man's depressing uniform, and doubled his tip.

Laszlo laid out the platters and Lump's extra sodas before inhaling a cheeseburger. Maggie tucked into her fish.

"So," she said, "do you think Rome's worth a shot?"

Laszlo swatted Lump's hand away from his fries. "Maybe. I need to ping Dimitri and get the skinny on this Signora."

"But Dimitri doesn't even remember we visited." Lump forked up a piece of veal.

Laszlo shrugged. "No biggie. I'll tell him I came across the name and figured they might have crossed paths."

Maggie took a sip of water. "I thought you'd be excited. What are you so worried about?"

"Worried?" said Laszlo. "Why would I worry about waltzing into the lair of an ancient demon and announcing we have valuable intel to swap for a magic item? An item she'll have to cough up on the spot, while getting nothing but our promise to spill the beans at some point in the future? Why would that worry me?"

Lump looked from one to the other. "I don't get it. Why would the Signora have to wait? Why wouldn't we just tell her?"

Maggie caught on and rubbed her temples in a manner that would have made Dimitri proud. "Laszlo's right," she sighed. "We can't divulge the Witchstone's location, at least not right away."

"Why?"

"This Signora's a demon, Lump. What if she claims the Witchstone, or even steals it, before we can break the curse?"

Laszlo rang an invisible bell. "*Ding-ding-ding*, we have a winner!"

Opening a pack of Davidoffs, the demon lit one and left the Drakefords to their meal while he slipped out onto the terrace for a think. He settled in a chaise and gazed out at the lights of Zurich mirrored in its famous lake.

Yes, the Drakefords had come up with an interesting idea. The Signora wasn't far, and she'd almost certainly have something useful. And they did indeed possess something she might value. But the risk! Once she learned of the Witchstone's existence, there was nothing to prevent her from prying its location from their screaming lips. That she could do this, Laszlo had no doubt; age and power were strongly correlated in demons. There were exceptions, naturally, but as a rule the older the demon, the more formidable they were likely to be. It only made sense; they'd had more time to rise in the ranks, acquire mortal souls, even devour the essences of other spirits.

Blowing a smoke ring, Laszlo called Dimitri's private number. It went directly to voicemail. Laszlo cocked an eye at the phone and tried again. Once more, he heard that gruff and familiar voice. "You have reached You-Know-Who. If you like to leave message, wait for beep . . ."

Laszlo ended the call and stared out at Lake Zurich. It wasn't like Dimitri not to answer his private number. Those who dealt in exotic goods had to be accessible day or night. He checked the time. It was barely 7:00 p.m. in New York. He braced himself with a long drag from his cigarette and called a different number. The phone barely rang before someone picked up.

"Hello?" said a tremulous voice.

"Clarence, it's me."

A delighted squeal. "*Laszlo!* Are you okay, are you—"

Laszlo detected organ music in the background. "Clarence, where are you?"

"Coney Island. Anita surprised me for my half birthday and—"

"Who's Anita?"

"Supervisor Thatcher."

Laszlo searched his memory. "I thought her first name was Storgo."

"She prefers Anita."

"Of course she does. Is Anita with you now?"

"No. She went to powder her noses."

"Good. Listen, I have a question. Have you ever heard of someone named Signora Bellascura?"

"What a pretty name. Is she Italian?"

"She's a demon, you boob. Lives in Rome."

Clarence sounded hurt. "Well, how am I supposed to know? Anyway, it sounds like she's embraced the culture. It doesn't ring a bell, but I'm hardly in the know. Maybe she's in the TDD."

"What's that?"

"Terrestrial Demon Directory. You know, that big red book you got when you joined."

Laszlo tried to recall that bleary evening a century earlier. All he remembered was some business cards, a box of thumbtacks, and more pencils than he'd ever use. "Uh, sure. Only I don't have it with me."

"Oh, the TDD's all online these days," said Clarence brightly. "There's a portal. Excellent UI, and mobile friendly. Of course, you'll have to create a user account and—"

"Clarence, can you just look her up?"

"Sure thing, but—*sweet Georgia peaches!* Anita's coming back!"

"Make an excuse to get away."

A note of panic entered Clarence's voice. "What should I say?"

"Anything."

Things became somewhat garbled as the goblin shark apparently shoved his phone into his pocket. "Oh, hello, Muffin—don't you look beautiful! Please excuse me—I have to tinkle."

This declaration was followed by a jingling of coins that kept pace with Clarence's rapid footsteps. Every so often there was an "oof!" coupled with a hasty apology. Moments later, Laszlo heard the bang of a door followed by the rattling of a latch.

"Okay, I'm back," panted Clarence.

"Smooth getaway," said Laszlo. "Where are you?"

"Men's room, far stall." There was a lengthy pause. "My gosh, Laszlo, you should see this place. It's like a pipe burst."

"Never mind the ambience." He exhaled a plume of smoke. "Look up Signora Bellascura."

"Traditional spelling?"

"Oh, for the love of—"

"Okay, okay! Give me a sec to hop on the dark web . . . Speaking of, did you ever buy anything on Silk Road? They had the most amazing deals on vitamins . . ." Laszlo did not reply. Clarence's narration continued. "Pulling up the TDD. Entering username . . . There we go. And now for my secret password . . ."

Laszlo's ears pricked up. "What is it?"

"I am *not* telling you my password!"

"Ten to one it has 'Anita' in it."

There was an indignant sniffle. "It's Anita666," Clarence muttered, "but I'll be changing it the minute we hang up. Now, let me find this Signora . . ."

Laszlo paced up and down the terrace while Clarence did his thing. He looked back at the living room. The Drakefords had finished their own dinners and were now settled on the sectional eating Laszlo's fries. He couldn't help but chuckle. A few hours ago, they'd been trapped in an underground death maze, and now they were committing petty food larceny. Humans really were resilient.

For a moment, Laszlo almost felt guilty about what he was going to do to them.

The moment passed.

Clarence's voice returned. "Jeez Louise . . ."

Laszlo stopped pacing. "Find anything?"

"Lots. And it's all bad."

"Meaning what?"

"Meaning you shouldn't get near this lady. This Signora's a bona fide crime boss, Laszlo. She's got fingers in all sorts of pies. Smuggling. Soul bartering. Assassinations . . . It says here she's suspected in the disappearance of a dozen high-ranking officials and even some members of the *Daemadùna*!"

"And that's all spelled out in the TDD?"

"Yes!"

Laszlo scoffed. "Then it isn't true."

"Why not?"

"Because the Hierarchy would have shut her down, that's why."

"Maybe," came the doubtful reply.

Laszlo glanced sideways at his phone. "You don't agree?"

"Well, I mean, you *could* be right. But maybe the bigwigs decided it's not worth it to mess with her. Do you have any idea how old she is?"

"Not a day under five thousand."

"Yes!" Clarence squeaked. "That makes her one of the oldest demons on the terrestrial plane. She'll be terrifying, Laszlo! Almost as bad as your father! Please tell me you're not seriously thinking of contacting her."

"I might be."

"*Why?*"

"Because I need something, Clarence."

"What could you possibly need so badly?"

Laszlo briefly told Clarence about the Drakeford Curse's materia and the porridge pot they'd acquired in Central Park, only to see it destroyed in Liechtenstein.

"Well, that pot wouldn't have done you any good anyway," said Clarence.

Laszlo flicked his cigarette over the railing. "No? Why not?"

"It's a Class E item: an Enchanted Curiosity. That's only a step above Peddler Trinket."

"So what?"

"Well," said Clarence, "it's common knowledge that you need something of at least Class C quality for anything involving a curse."

"*Common knowledge?*" exclaimed Laszlo. "How would anyone know that?"

"Page thirty-six of the Rules and Regulations manual."

Laszlo lit another cigarette. "Let me guess. They gave me one at orientation?"

"Yes. It has an oxblood cover and smells like an abattoir."

Closing his eyes, Laszlo dimly recalled tossing a smelly book into a dumpster while ducking out of work to see Jack Dempsey wallop Georges Carpentier in Jersey City. The Frenchman never stood a chance.

"Whatever," he said. "Is there an address for this Signora?"

Clarence sucked his teeth. "Laszlo, please . . ."

"Is there an address or not?"

Amid numerous warnings, his colleague grudgingly passed on the instructions for how one might make contact. The process was absurdly tedious, but Laszlo filed it away before asking if there was any news about Androvore's goons.

"Nothing," said Clarence. "Not a peep."

"What about the catfish lady? Is she in that TDD thing?"

Clarence started coughing. "Laszlo, I need to get out of this stall. The smell . . ."

"Man up."

"I'm not a man. I'm part goblin shark, and my snout's acutely sensitive!"

"C'mon, buddy. Just a quick little search. You know I'd do it for you."

The word *buddy* seemed to give Clarence a second wind. "Okay. Let me see if I can sort the entries by head type."

"There you go," said Laszlo. His gaze followed a smoke ring as it disintegrated. What he really needed was a cocktail. A cocktail and Helga. Sweet, sweet Helga . . .

"Sorry," said Clarence. "There's a gar-headed demon who lives in Paraguay and a slew of carp-headed spirits in the East China Sea, but I'm not finding a catfish. Are you sure she wasn't a grouper? There's a grouper-headed demon who works at Google."

"Forget it," said Laszlo. "Thanks for looking. I gotta run."

"Be careful, Lasz—"

Ending the call, Laszlo leaned against the terrace railing and finished his smoke. He saw that, back inside the suite, the Drakefords had eaten most of his fries. Lump looked ready to pass out.

Laszlo thought over what he'd just learned. The situation wasn't hopeless—there might even be some opportunities. This Signora sounded like someone who could offer far more than a magic trinket. Clearly the woman was dangerous and had little love for the Hierarchy. Someone like that would have resources and contacts that were out of his league. If he played his cards correctly—turned on the Laszlo charm and so forth—the Signora could be a valuable ally for a dashing young demon who might need to disappear.

Old ladies had always found Laszlo irresistible. He recalled a Hapsburg he'd seduced back in the seventeenth century. She was no looker: a bewigged and liver-spotted thing with a lazy eye and the family jaw. An unsettling thing, that Hapsburg jaw. Like nuzzling an anvil. The weekend hadn't been a joyride, but he'd soldiered on, hadn't he? He knew what he was doing.

But would the Signora help him?

Laszlo didn't see why not. In addition to his looks and charm, he had three aces up his sleeve. One was the Witchstone. The other two were inside on the couch.

Lump was dead asleep against his sister when Laszlo slipped back into the suite. Glancing over, Maggie pressed a finger to her lips and nodded at the lights. The demon caught her gist and dimmed them. She slipped a pillow under Lump's head and came over to Laszlo.

He pointed at the nearly empty plate of fries. "Those were mine."

Maggie winked. "We left you three. So what's up? Are we going to Rome?"

"Possibly. I'm heading down to the bar to think it over."

"I see. Do you always drink when you make decisions?"

"Yes."

"Okay," said Maggie. "Then I'll go down with you."

Laszlo grunted. "And leave Baby Bro all alone?"

"He's not a baby. He's eleven, and fast asleep in a hotel that's so fancy I'm afraid to even use the toilet. He also defeated an entire kobold clan and incinerated a monster. We're safer with him than he is with us."

Laszlo eyed the human boy sleeping on the couch. Maggie had a point. He still couldn't figure how Lump had managed to snag the badass spelltubes while Laszlo was stuck with bubbles and butterflies. He turned back to Maggie. "Ever had a martini?"

"Do I look like I've ever had a martini?"

Laszlo sized her up. "You strike me as more of a moonshine gal. But okay, Country Mouse, saddle up and we'll head down in five. This should be fun." Smirking, he strolled off to the bedroom to get dressed.

There were no decisions to be made, of course. He and the Drakefords would be on that ten o'clock train for Rome. Laszlo simply craved a cocktail—and the chance to screw some lucky human(s) into oblivion. Helga had been denied him, so he needed someone else. Female, male, a bit of both; Laszlo didn't care. As far as he was concerned, the equipment didn't matter, so long as the individual was energetic . . . and, preferably, married. Laszlo simply adored the married ones; they were so grateful!

If Maggie wanted to tag along and soak up the ambience, that was fine by him. She was a big girl and could make her own choices. In fact, Laszlo was counting on it.

CHAPTER 21
COMPULSION

Maggie dried her palms on her jeans in what was rapidly becoming a habit. Why was she so nervous when she should have been enjoying herself? Here she was, ensconced in a private booth at an exclusive nightclub in the Swiss fucking Alps.

Not that she had any other nightclubs to compare it to, but it was a truly stunning venue, with recessed lighting and a long, sinuous bar that looked like it had been carved from a single slab of malachite. Techno pulsed from invisible speakers; in a purple suit and headphones, the DJ swayed to the beat and did whatever else DJs did. The place was *exactly* what Maggie had wanted it to be, and yet . . .

"Something wrong, Your Highness?"

Maggie glanced up at Laszlo. The demon was sitting across from her, so relaxed and in his element he might have been the patron saint of nightlife. He was already on his second martini, the drink delivered by a server who flushed crimson when Laszlo held his gaze a second too long. He unthreaded an olive from its fancy toothpick and popped it in his mouth.

"Please don't call me 'Your Highness,'" said Maggie. "I don't like it."

A smirk began to surface but faded when Laszlo saw that she was serious. "Fair enough," he said, and turned his gaze to her drink. "Want something else? A martini's a tall order for a rookie."

"It's fine," she replied. "I'll drink it."

"You don't have to."

"I *want* to."

Laszlo held up his hands. "You're the boss. You know, this may come as a shock, but the point of these places is to have *fun*."

"Really? I thought it was to help you make decisions."

"Made it," he said. "Roma, here we come."

Maggie sat up with excitement. "Really?" she said. "You're on board?"

"We'll take the ten o'clock train," said Laszlo. "The idea's insane, and we'll probably die in terrible, awful ways, but it's the only plan we've got."

"Thanks. I think."

Laszlo inclined his head. "And seeing as this might be our last night on Earth . . . cheers." The demon clinked his glass against Maggie's and took a languorous sip, his eye wandering to the other patrons sitting at the bar or clustered in stylish groups at nearby tables.

Maggie took a tentative sip of her martini, refusing to grimace as lukewarm vodka spread like a stain across her tongue. Setting it down, she leaned back and tried to let the tension unspool from her shoulders. She might have felt painfully out of place, but at least her foot was better, her curse mark wasn't acting up, and there was plenty of faerie essence on her eye. That was something.

When they had gotten to the hotel, she'd checked the Zurich doctor's work and discovered that his stitches were no longer necessary; the wound had already healed, just like her arm had aboard the airplane. She took another sip of martini, determined to put that awful flight out of her mind. The last thing she needed to think about was things growing or multiplying beneath her skin.

She forced a smile. "So what's the secret to having fun in places like this?"

Laszlo shrugged and surveyed the bar. "Depends on what you want."

"Meaning?"

He flicked his gaze back to Maggie. "There's only three reasons people come to a place like this."

"Excellent," said Maggie, student to the end. "What are they?"

Laszlo held up a finger. "Reason one: to get laid."

She blushed and waved him onward. "Let's skip to reason two."

"Fair enough. The second is to convince people that you *could* get laid if you wanted to. It's popular with newlyweds and men who drive Miatas."

Maggie was almost afraid to ask about the third. But she did.

Laszlo held up his cocktail and studied it by candlelight. "Reason three: to savor a drink and ponder the great mysteries of life."

"Really?"

"No, it's to get laid." She had to laugh. The demon chuckled himself and chewed another olive. "Money, clothes, cars, jewelry. They're just fancy feathers to convince the flock that you're the bird to mate with. Humans may tell themselves they've gone out to dance or catch up with old friends, but really, they want to get their rocks off. They can deny it all they like, but it's the unvarnished truth."

Maggie shifted uncomfortably. "You make us sound like animals."

"You are," said Laszlo cheerfully. "But you've also got souls, which is why my kind finds you so irresistible. And really, being an animal isn't a bad thing. The trouble starts when humans pretend they're something else."

Maggie spoke up as the song changed to something with a heavy bass. "What do you mean?"

The demon shrugged. "Laws punishing natural instincts; governments and churches forcing people to be things they're not. It's hilarious, really. Billions of self-hating fools trudging through life believing their very existence is a sin. Everything's just another loyalty test to satisfy the demands of some touchy, all-powerful authority. Call me crazy, but God seems to have a lot in common with your average Mean Girl." He shook his head. "And people accuse demons of being prideful."

"Oh, you've got plenty of pride," said Maggie. "In fact . . ."

But Laszlo's gaze had already drifted over her shoulder to settle on a man and two women at a table twenty feet away. As Maggie turned, she saw they were Beautiful People of the sort whose faces sold movies and magazines. All three were staring at Laszlo with an intensity that could have set something on fire. It would have made Maggie run for the hills. One of the goddesses—a stunning Black woman who must have been a fashion model—gave the demon a playful little wave.

A grin broke out on Laszlo's face. "Oh, you saucy minx," he muttered to himself. "The things I'm going to do to you . . ." He raised his glass in acknowledgment.

Maggie felt the atmosphere changing. An electric current had entered the mix, unsettling and—she blushed to admit—somewhat arousing.

Maggie had read her share of books and sneaked her share of movies, seen couples in Kingston making out in public, but she'd never witnessed people expressing their desires so openly, so unapologetically. She might have been seated between two converging storm fronts.

Looking at the other woman, Maggie could not help feeling a touch indignant. "How does she know you're not with me?" she said. "Not that I would *ever* . . ."

Laszlo pried his gaze from Cleopatra. Reaching across the table, he patted Maggie's hand sympathetically. "A sea sponge could tell we're not together. Anyway, I don't think our friend's the type who really sweats the competition."

Maggie made a noise of acknowledgment, uncertain whether she should be insulted or relieved. Regardless, she was officially a third wheel. She quickly checked the time. "Maybe I should look in on Lump."

"Oh, no you don't," said Laszlo. "The kid's just a few floors away, and you left a note. If he needs anything, he'll call. Let's not run up the white flag quite yet. I thought Country Mouse wanted new experiences."

Glancing about the club, Maggie nodded reluctantly.

Laszlo considered her. "I mean, you're what? Eighteen?"

"Almost twenty."

He whistled. "Time you got out a little. What's the point of breaking a curse only to lead the most boring life this side of Winnipeg? C'mon, girlie. Show some spunk."

Maggie forced another smile but said nothing. Staring into her martini, she found herself wishing she truly belonged somewhere.

Surely there must be a place in this world where Maggie Drakeford could relax and feel at home.

What would it be like to stop being scared and anxious all the time? To stop spending every second in a state of doubt or distress? God knew she'd tried. Over the years, Maggie had run more miles than she could count, toiling up and down the mountain until her lungs screamed and her vision blurred. The goal was simple: to punish her body so relentlessly that her brain had no choice but to sink into dreamless, untroubled sleep. Christ, what did that say about her?

She ran a finger around the rim of her glass. "Can I ask you a question?"

"Fire away."

"If you could be anything, what would you be?"

Laszlo blinked. "Come again?"

"I mean, did you always want to be a Curse Keeper?"

At this, the demon laughed in a way Maggie had never heard before. There was nothing sardonic or performative; he was, quite simply, happily amused. Had she just gotten a glimpse of the real Laszlo? Maggie couldn't say. But whatever it was, she liked it infinitely better than the glib and cocksure playboy. With a rueful smile, Laszlo set down his martini and laced his fingers in an attitude of quiet reflection.

"I'll take that as a no," said Maggie.

The demon shot her a piercing look. "Let's just say I'm pulling for you."

"Meaning?"

"When you break the spell, we'll *both* be free of the Drakeford Curse. And yours truly has some plans in mind." He paused. "Any idea what you'll do?"

Maggie hesitated. "I don't want to jinx anything. We still have a long way to go."

The demon raised an eyebrow. "You're living with a full-fledged *curse*, and you're worried about piddly little jinxes? Come on. Humor me. What's next for Maggie Drakeford?"

Exhaling, she took a moment to watch the multicolored lights playing on the ceiling.

Maggie had gone to the trouble of earning her GED and taking college admissions tests, but she suspected that was simply to show her mother she had the capacity to leave. Deep down, she knew nothing was going to change—not with her father in his condition, or the symptoms that were beginning to overtake her.

Had she ever truly entertained the idea that she could have a different life? Not silly daydreams but serious thought. What if they really did break the curse? What if there was nothing binding her to the Witchwood any longer? What if Maggie could leave Schemerdaal and never look back?

As she pondered this, Maggie became aware of an itching beneath the bandage on her left arm. Coincidence? Or was the Drakeford Curse reminding her that it was still present, thank you very much, and had no intention of leaving? She rubbed it, wincing slightly at the pressure.

"I don't know what's next," she said quietly. "I've thought about college, but maybe a job would make more sense. Whatever it is, it would be far away from Schemerdaal."

"Well," said Laszlo, "let me know if you need any suggestions. I've lived all over the world and can tell you where to avoid. For example, cross the Barbary States right off your list."

She had to smile. "Hmm. I'm not sure they call them that anymore."

"Well, they should. I've never been treated so rudely. Robbed blind, stripped naked, and left for dead near Tripoli. They even took my camel—"

"I can't picture you on a camel."

Laszlo ate another olive. "Don't. I'm through with them."

"How long ago was this?"

The demon gazed into the middle distance and tried to recall. Soon he was counting on his fingers. "Early 1700s," he replied at last. "Maybe the 1600s. Never been great with centuries."

"And you're barely eight hundred," Maggie teased. "Think what it must be like for the Signora."

"No, thank you. I'm doing my best *not* to think about her. That's what these babies are for." Hoisting his martini, Laszlo downed the rest in a single gulp before holding up a finger to his admirers.

Cleopatra was getting impatient and had started lobbing ice at Laszlo.

Maggie flicked a cube off the table. "Kind of pushy."

"You say 'pushy,' I say 'decisive.' Mind if I just pop over and . . . ?"

"Have at it." Maggie sighed. She knew perfectly well he'd go regardless.

Laszlo slid smoothly out of the booth. "You're a peach."

A peach? Maggie supposed that one could be called worse—a crabapple or a ginkgo berry—but something about a peach rankled. It was a plump and docile fruit, long suffering. The sort of fruit that spent all day preparing another person's dinner and hoping they'd show up to eat it. Maggie wasn't a peach. She didn't know what she was, but it sure as hell wasn't a peach . . .

Sipping her martini, Maggie closed her eyes and let the music wash over her. This song was louder than its predecessors. Much louder. Oceans of energy. It invaded her head, driving her thoughts away so effectively she gave herself up to it. The beat was like a sledgehammer, heavy and relentless. Machinelike. Primal.

Maggie kept her eyes closed as she took another sip. The martini was growing on her. It wasn't so bad. None of it was.

When she opened her eyes, Maggie found the DJ looking at her. He pointed and flashed a grin, still swaying to his music. She dropped her eyes. What did that smile mean? Was he being friendly? Was he hitting on her? Or maybe, as a consummate entertainment professional, he was just happy that she appreciated his music? He adjusted something on his turntable, still dancing; his movements were never flashy or self-conscious. Just a smooth, effortless rhythm. Goddamn, he looked cool.

What would it be like to talk to someone like that? Or, she allowed herself to wonder, maybe even *kiss* someone like that? She'd never kissed anyone, much less a hot European DJ in a purple suit. Did she have the courage?

Hell. No.

Maggie giggled and took another sip of martini. A soft buzzing started in her head, not unlike that little mosquito she'd heard when she'd tangled with the Ruyter brothers. It was mildly annoying, but the music helped to drown it out. In any case, it wasn't the frantic droning from the subway. What had *that* been about? The poor guy was practically hypnotized, and all she'd done was look at him.

Yet another sip, and this time she tried to appreciate the sensation of the liquid trickling down her throat.

Maggie had really never thought of herself as a *woman*, at least not in any sort of sexual way. She'd never imagined herself as a person others might find attractive or desirable. But she was doing so now. And she found that she liked it.

An older woman was trying to talk to the DJ, leaning forward in a flirtatious manner that showed off her cleavage. Maggie swallowed and glanced down at her own chest. *Not too bad*, she assured herself. *Some respectable B cups tucked away in there.* The DJ would appreciate that. He wasn't wowed by Botox and silicone. He liked natural girls who read mysteries, wore sensible underwear, and clocked five-minute miles.

Maggie sighed and closed her eyes once again. Really, it didn't matter what the DJ liked. She didn't want to become best buddies—she wanted to touch him, to kiss him, to feel his warmth next to her own. That was the mortifying truth.

It grated her that Laszlo had been right, but there it was. As she privately owned her desires, Maggie felt a surge of embarrassment, even shame. *This is ridiculous*, she thought. *Sex shouldn't be shameful.* It was a completely natural desire, a fundamental instinct ingrained into almost every living creature.

But Maggie's misgivings didn't go away. Neither did the buzzing in her skull.

It was all so complicated, and Maggie was new to it all. Best to keep things simple. She would simply focus on the music, and the music was taking her mind to exciting new places. For the time being, that was enough. She'd enjoy her drink and lose herself in the sound. Best of all, she wouldn't have to talk to anyone.

"Hello?" said a voice.

A man was sitting across from her. Not the sexy DJ but a white guy in his thirties wearing a half-tucked dress shirt and an unknotted tie that hung around his neck like an eel. It was a statement: *I'm a suit, but a suit that parties.* Maggie had noticed him earlier at the bar with what looked to be several male coworkers, doing shots and making quite the commotion.

He pushed a shock of brown hair off his forehead. "Mind if I sit?" Maggie couldn't place the accent.

She looked over at the table of Beautiful People, only to find it empty.

"Your friend left," the guy said, and tapped his nose significantly. What was that supposed to mean? "Want another drink?"

She realized that her martini glass was empty. How long had she been sitting here?

Signaling to one of the servers, the stranger spoke in rapid German. The server looked at Maggie expectantly. "Order something," said the man. "We have a tab."

The buzzing mosquito nudged her to say yes, but Maggie overruled it. "No, thanks."

The stranger looked as though he'd never heard anything so disappointing. "It's barely two thirty! Come on . . ."

But Maggie declined a second time. The server strode away.

"Are you, like, antifun or something?" the guy moaned. "Shit. You must be English."

"Nope."

"*American!*" His grin revealed teeth a size too small. They made him look like a giant baby. "Excellent," he said. "I love America. I'm Jan, by the way."

"Elizabeth."

"What brings you to Zurich? And who's that guy you were with?"

"A family friend," said Maggie coolly. "We're here on family business."

Jan laughed. "Well, your friend is the fucking man! Did you see who he left with? You know who that was?"

"Let me guess: someone famous."

He said the woman's first name, as if that were more than sufficient to identify her. Maggie found it vaguely familiar but simply shrugged.

"Jesus," said Jan. "You must not get out much."

"There's an understatement."

He scooted closer, across the banquette. Maggie did not move, not even when his cologne invaded her nostrils. She noticed that one of his lower shirt buttons had come undone, revealing a slice of a pale stomach, soft and hairless. His face was inches from her own, flushed and glistening; his watery eyes had almost no eyelashes. His breath was strangely pungent; not rank but alien. His hand brushed hers.

"I was watching you," he said, in a tone that implied it was a compliment. When he grinned, his lower jaw jutted forward, revealing those tiny teeth. Beneath the smile, Maggie sensed a healthy dose of hostility and entitlement. She wondered if Jan was aware that he hated women.

She also wondered why she didn't recoil.

But Maggie didn't. She remained at the table. Whatever fear she might have experienced—fear of being on her own and drunk, fear of this repellent man—had been muffled by the buzzing growing ever louder in her skull. Perhaps another martini was in order. The mosquito was in favor of it; so were the bees who were rapidly joining the party.

She watched Jan finish his drink. Patrón, he called it. Tequila. So that was the smell on his breath. Again, he offered to buy her a drink. This time, Maggie accepted.

She started in on the martini as soon as it arrived, and listened to him drone on about work. Meanwhile, the buzzing in her head intensified. It was as it had been on the subway; her brain, a veritable hive of activity, roiled with whispers and quiet suggestions that would not be ignored. Somehow, Jan's words managed to filter through the noise.

Jan was a banker. He and his team had been working like dogs—"fucking dogs"—on some sort of proposal. An IPO, whatever that meant. His bank had won the deal, and Jan was team lead. "A *big* fucking win," according to Jan. The group had stayed in Zurich to celebrate. Two of his colleagues were still at the bar, looking hapless and confused. The fourth—a new kid from HBS—had puked and gone back to his room, the pussy.

Jan's monologue was punctuated by stretches of silence; Maggie was too busy listening to the bees to be much of a conversationalist.

At length, the banker sniffed and glanced at his drink as though it repulsed him. "We should have gone to Berlin," he muttered. "Zurich *sucks*." His face darkened momentarily, and he banged his glass on the tabletop.

Jan was losing steam, and the bees feared he might leave. That would never do. The hive was growing impatient; they did not care if Maggie found her companion engaging or attractive. Jan was a means to an end.

Sliding over, Maggie brushed her shoulder against his. "Where are you from, Jan?"

He stared blearily at the DJ. "Utrecht. Ever been?"

"No."

"I don't get you, Elizabeth. You don't really talk. You don't know supermodels. But you're hanging out *here* on a Sunday night. Are you some kind of alien?"

"Maybe," allowed Maggie. She smiled and laid her hand over Jan's.

He blinked at it stupidly. "No, seriously. Are you like a pro or something?"

"A pro?"

"You know. A hooker."

"No," she said bluntly. "I'm not a *pro*, Jan. I don't want your money. I just like you. I like you very much."

Maggie heard herself talking; it was as if she listened to a stranger. Something else was speaking with her voice. She supposed it must be the bees.

Another force had taken the wheel, and her consciousness—her sense of agency—had been consigned to riding shotgun. Maggie wasn't certain she liked giving up control, but she had no choice in the matter.

The hive had a will of iron. And it knew what it needed.

Jan slapped his cheek. "I need to wake up. Long fucking week." Sitting up, he suddenly turned to Maggie. "Hey. Come with me."

"Where to?"

"The bathroom."

She raised a flirtatious eyebrow. "Someone needs help going tinkle?"

There was that laugh again—the laugh of a man-child who'd been coddled all his life. "Ha! That's right. I need help. If you're nice," he said leeringly, "I'll let you hold it."

Slipping out of the banquette, Maggie followed Jan past the bar and through a pair of velvet curtains to a dim corridor lined with three red doors. One was ajar. Inside the dimly lit bathroom, incense burned on a shelf decorated with vintage photographs.

Jan closed and locked the door.

"So . . ."

Shoving him against the door, Maggie pressed her body against his. Jan grunted with surprise but immediately kissed her, jamming his tongue in her mouth. Some corner of her consciousness found it revolting and invasive, but the hive didn't care.

Hands that did not seem to be hers unbuckled his belt. Jan made a growling noise and pawed at her breasts, worming a hand up her shirt and under her bra. Her brain registered it all with clinical detachment.

There was nothing enjoyable or erotic about what Jan was doing. There didn't have to be. The curse needed Bearers; any donor would do.

Dragging her fingers along his crotch, Maggie tugged at the zipper. Jan moaned and sagged against the door, making it bang and rattle in the frame. He was a big man, well over six feet, but Maggie pulled him up with startling force and pushed him against the opposite wall. A picture fell from one of the shelves and shattered.

Wrapping his tie around her hand, Maggie pulled his head down so his ear was level with her lips. "Your pants," she whispered.

"Ouch!" Removing his hand from under Maggie's shirt, Jan gingerly touched his earlobe. A spot of blood came away on his finger. He grinned and licked it away. "Did you bite me, you naughty bitch?" Laughing, he tried to take Maggie by the hand. "Let's go to my room."

She squirmed out of his grasp and backed away to shrug off her blazer, then tossed it on a basket of hand towels and unbuttoned her shirt. When she spoke, her voice was low and almost unrecognizable to her ears. It was sensual and commanding, and tired of playing games.

"We're not going to your room, Jan. I'm not interested in cuddling. I'm interested in fucking. Now do what you're told."

Jan obeyed at once. For all his bluster, he was the type who got off on taking orders. The bees knew that, even if Maggie didn't. Swaying slightly, he unbuttoned his trousers and shoved them down to his knees. The briefs came next, and there he stood, like an overgrown man-boy awaiting a physical. Maggie glanced at the pale slug peeking out from his shirt hem.

She clucked her tongue. "That won't do, Jan. Don't you find me pretty?"

Looking down, Jan flicked his member as though it were a faulty light bulb. It did not respond. "Shit," he muttered. "Don't worry, it happens sometimes . . ."

Bending over, he rifled through his trouser pockets until he came up with what looked like a cigarette case, and opened it to reveal a rolled-up plastic bag containing several pinches of white powder. There was also a small metal tube, which Jan offered to Maggie. "One-hitter," he said. "Good stuff. Nothing funky."

She declined and listened to the bees.

Jan shrugged and unscrewed the tube's cap before thrusting it up his nostril. He inhaled sharply, then tottered back, almost tripping over the toilet. Steadying himself against the wall, he blinked several times as a slow grin came over his face.

Maggie looked down at his erection: mission accomplished.

Seconds later, he cackled and staggered the few steps toward her, pants bunched about his ankles. He pushed her against the sink and tugged off her unbuttoned shirt.

Maggie undid her jeans and shoved them down, leaning back against the sink as Jan mauled her breasts. She watched things unfold with surreal detachment, a mere spectator to someone else's experience. And yet some part of Maggie's mind knew that wasn't true.

The nearly naked girl was *her*, Maggie Drakeford, and this wasn't some make-believe dream . . . but a very real and tangible nightmare.

She tried to speak up, but the bees weren't having it. The buzzing in her head had reached a wild, feverish pitch. Jan was grinding against her now, grunting like a boar. The oaf tried lifting Maggie onto the sink but nearly fell over again. Maggie spared him the effort. Hoisting herself up, she leaned back against the mirror. Jan began tugging clumsily at her panties. Maggie gripped the sink for balance.

There was a knock at the door.

"It's taken!" barked Jan, as he thrust against Maggie. He was nearly inside her when he suddenly stopped. "Shit. I don't have a condom."

"It's okay," this new Maggie cut in. "I'm on the pill. Besides, I want to *feel* you . . ."

"Yeah, but—"

Seizing him by the hair, she kissed Jan as though overcome with passion. This time, it was *her* tongue exploring *his* mouth, while her legs closed about him like a vise, drawing Jan closer to the promised land. She felt a searing ecstasy in the curse mark upon her forearm, in the worms wriggling and straining beneath her skin. Jan moaned and thrust his hips forward. Somehow, the idiot missed.

Another rap at the door.

Maggie's flesh was burning now, every nerve afire as sweat ran between her breasts. Jan started to turn toward the door, but she held him fast.

"Ignore them!" she whispered. "Ignore them and *fuck* me . . ."

The knocking grew sharper. Jan opened his eyes. For a moment, he stared at Maggie in hazy confusion as she took firm hold of his hair. Then his gaze went to her left arm.

The banker's eyes shot wide. He tried frantically to pull away, but Maggie held him fast with her legs. He stared in horror at the bandage, whose fabric was pulsing and bulging, straining to the breaking point.

With a sudden tear, the tendrils in Maggie's arm burst through the bandage. There were twelve now, each well over a foot long and covered with barbed hairs. They whipped wildly about before seizing hold of Jan's neck and pulling his appalled face to Maggie's.

When their noses touched, she exhaled a cloud of pungent yellow mist. Jan choked and sputtered as he inhaled it. Seconds later, his pupils dilated to an inhuman degree, and he stood compliantly as Maggie's right hand took hold of his erection and guided it toward her.

The hive in her head was ready to explode. The buzzing became a roar whose meaning was perfectly clear.

The curse must feed.

The curse must survive.

There must always *be a Drakeford!*

It was then that the bathroom door swung open.

Instantly, the tendrils released Jan and retracted into Maggie's forearm. Free of their hold, the banker sagged heavily to the floor.

The buzzing in Maggie's head subsided, and her own consciousness rose slowly to the surface. Confused and breathless, she stared dazedly at the person in the doorway.

Laszlo?

Slipping inside, the demon closed and locked the bathroom door before walking over to nudge something with his shoe. His voice was preternaturally calm. "Who's your friend?"

She leaned forward from her perch—*why am I on the sink?*—and saw a large, bloated man sprawled on the tiles with his pants and underwear bunched around his ankles. Only then did Maggie realize that she was practically naked herself. With a soundless cry, she slid off the sink and tried to cover her body.

Laszlo sighed and turned to face the wall. "Oh, relax." His voice was dry. "I didn't see anything I haven't seen in the past ten minutes. Except for the tentacles. I'll confess those were new."

Heart hammering, Maggie tugged up her jeans—and as she did, she noticed her forearm. The bandage was gone. A dozen holes, each the diameter of a pencil, had appeared within the boundaries of her ever-expanding curse mark.

Taking a deep breath, Maggie forced herself to look at the man on the floor. "Oh my God," she whispered. "What the hell am I doing?"

Laszlo turned back around and looked at him too. "Never mind that right now. First, we have to deal with this prize. Who is he?"

"I-I don't know," stammered Maggie. "Tom, maybe? I think he said he's a banker."

"I assume the blow belongs to him?"

Laszlo pointed to a plastic bag of white powder on the floor.

Maggie scoured her memory but came up blank. "It must be his. It's definitely not mine."

"No," said Laszlo. "You don't strike me as a raging cokehead. Pull yourself together, and I'll take care of 'Tom.'"

While Laszlo went to work, Maggie put on the rest of her clothes. Her bra was half-off, and her panties were torn. She saw toothmarks near her left nipple. Her hands wouldn't stop trembling. She managed to button her shirt and spotted her blazer on a basket of unused towels. For the next twenty seconds she splashed cold water on her face and tried to rinse the taste of blood and alcohol from her mouth. Shutting off the tap, she turned and shot a horrified glance at the stranger Laszlo was now easing onto the toilet seat.

Did I do this?

She watched in a daze as Laszlo arranged the man like a mannequin in a window display, seated on the closed toilet, his glazed eyes fixed on the ceiling. His pants stayed around his ankles, and one of his hands rested on his naked crotch. Finally, Laszlo took the man's belt and cinched it loosely around his neck.

"What are you—"

Laszlo held up a finger as he checked the man's pulse. Then, satisfied, the demon used a hand towel to pick up the bag of cocaine and plant it, along with a metal case and tube, on the nearby shelf before wiping down the sink, the mirror, and any other surface she and this man might have touched.

Finally, Laszlo refolded the towel and placed it back among the clean ones. "Ready to go?"

Maggie stared at the tableau. She noticed, in a detached fashion, that a framed picture lay on the floor, a crack across its glass. "Are we really going to leave him like this?"

The demon appraised his handiwork. "What's the big deal? A guy came in for a sniff and a wank. He's not the first; he won't be the last. And unless you have a better idea, we need to bolt." When Maggie did not speak, he unlocked the door with his elbow and looked out into the hall. "Coast's clear. Come on."

Tearing her eyes away, Maggie followed Laszlo out into the corridor. Her arm ached; she was shaky on her feet.

Music pulsed beyond the velvet curtains ahead. It triggered a jumble of memories, like images viewed through distorted glass. *A handsome DJ. Herself sitting at a fancy banquette talking with the man they'd just left in the bathroom. His name wasn't Tom; it was Jan. A tongue down her throat, grasping hands exploring every inch of her body—*

"I think I'm going to be sick."

Laszlo was busy doing something to the bathroom's doorknob. At her words, he hurried over and put an arm through hers. "Nope. No one's getting sick."

"Are you sure?" said Maggie. She desperately wanted him to be right.

"Positive. You're going to keep it together until we're back in the room. And then you can puke to your heart's content, take a nice hot shower, and put all this behind you."

Maggie glanced back at the bathroom door. "What about him?"

"Banker Boy won't remember shit. And if he does, I guarantee he'll never tell anyone."

She nodded dumbly, fighting tears as they slipped through the nightclub and made their way to the elevator. Thankfully, the car was empty.

The two rode in silence. The elevator was slowing when Maggie finally spoke.

"That was my first kiss."

Her affect was flat. There was no emotion in her tone. It was a simple statement of fact that she was trying to process. She didn't expect Laszlo to respond. Even so, the demon looked somewhat chastened. Reaching over, he took her hand and clasped it within his own. The two stared at each other's reflections in the elevator doors.

"Don't say anything to Lump," said Maggie with a tremble in her voice. "I won't."

"And don't leave me like that again."

When the doors opened, Laszlo squeezed her hand. "Never."

CHAPTER 22
URBS ÆTERNA

Maggie managed only a few hours of sleep before Laszlo had them up and rushing to the train station.

As soon as they got back to the suite last night, she'd brushed her teeth three times and taken a scalding-hot shower, scrubbing her skin raw with a washcloth. Afterward, she sat naked on the edge of the bathtub and stared numbly at her enlarged curse mark, wondering what else might be lurking in her body.

She had witnessed her father's decline. She'd always known a similar fate awaited her. But until the past few weeks, that had been an abstract problem, something she'd have to confront someday. Now that day had arrived. And unless Maggie was mistaken, her symptoms were taking hold much earlier and more intensely than her father's.

Maggie was good at compartmentalization. She imagined a small box in her mind and put last night in it. Even as she did, little details came back, bobbing to the surface like secrets she'd tried to drown. Maggie hoped that man was okay. No one deserved what had happened to him, no matter how obnoxious they might be.

The only saving grace was that Lump managed to sleep through everything. Her brother had no clue that Maggie and Laszlo had even left the suite. The kid really had a gift.

She closed the box, pushed it to the back of her mind, rebandaged her arm, and tried to get some sleep.

Now, on board the train to Rome, she embraced its much-needed distraction. New York's subways had nothing on this sleek red bullet flying down the Italian Peninsula. Their connection in Milan had been somewhat hectic, but Maggie was enthralled by the spectrum of people and cultures—bustling families, solitary students, businesspeople tapping away on phones. So much activity in one place. She realized that, instead of being intimidated by such scenes, she was beginning to find them energizing.

There was a downside to their travels, however—a pair of knockoff designer eyeglasses Laszlo purchased for Lump to replace the ones that had broken in Liechtenstein. They were the only pair in the shop whose prescription was in the ballpark—but the frames were so absurdly huge and colorful that he bore an uncanny resemblance to Elton John, whose picture was on display. Maggie thought her brother looked ridiculous; Lump himself was delighted.

Once aboard Trenitalia, they claimed seats arranged in facing pairs. Laszlo nodded off almost immediately, while Lump buried himself in an Italian travel guide that he'd begged the demon to buy. For her part, Maggie reviewed their curse documents and tried to ignore the throbbing in her left forearm. She was reading over the materia when a stab of pain made her suck her teeth.

Lump looked up from a page on aqueducts. "What's wrong?"

"Nothing," she lied. She could feel the tendrils wriggling and twining under her skin. Now and again, they strained against the bandage, and her arm went numb to the shoulder.

Lump glanced at the materia. "Have you memorized it by now?"

Closing her eyes, Maggie recited softly, "'Something loved, something hated, something found, something fated, the blood of saints, the wealth of nations. Last but not least, a spark of creation.'" She opened her eyes. "Easy enough. But we still don't know what we're supposed to do with them. We need the ritus."

"Maybe the Signora will know something."

"Maybe," said Maggie. She gazed past Lump as hills and little towns rocketed past the window.

"You think they'll have gotten our postcards?"

She blinked. "What?"

"Mom and Dad. Do you think the postcards will have reached them?"

"Probably not. It's only been a few days."

"We should write another," said Lump thoughtfully. "We could tell them about the Alps and truffle fries and aqueducts." He pointed to his book. "Did you know some aqueducts are two thousand years old, and they still work? It's kind of amazing."

His enthusiasm made Maggie smile, but she couldn't help thinking that, even old as they were, aqueducts were newer technology for the Signora Bellascura. The demon had been walking the Earth when humans were beginning to scrawl symbols in Tigris mud. Compared to her, Laszlo was a newborn.

The demon in question dozed across from them, his head resting against the window. For a being on the brink of annihilation, he looked pretty peaceful. Maggie wondered what he'd gotten up to when he'd left her at the nightclub. Whatever it was, it appeared to have worked.

When they'd barged into his suite last night, Laszlo had been mired in self-pity—snappish and sarcastic, determined to go out in a blaze of debauchery. When they'd shared their idea about the Signora, he'd expressed doubts before heading off to smoke on the terrace.

The Laszlo who returned was markedly more optimistic.

The Laszlo in the nightclub verged on effusive—whatever he'd sneaked off to do—and had confided in and truly rescued her. Still, he was a demon, and she couldn't quite bring herself to trust him.

He had to be hiding something.

As if reading her mind, Laszlo cracked a brilliant blue eye. The two looked at one another for so long that it became a battle of wills.

The demon blinked first. "Lira for your thoughts?"

Maggie kept a poker face. "I was just thinking about the Signora. I wonder what she's like."

Laszlo produced a roll of breath mints. "Mento?"

"No, thank you."

"Are you sure? They're the 'Freshmaker.'"

"I don't even know what that means."

"Suit yourself." Laszlo popped one in his mouth and gave a long stretch before flopping back against the seat. "I've never met the Signora, but I've rubbed shoulders with some of the old-timers. They turn up for my father's parties. Satan, Mammon, Lilith, Belial . . . so many geezers. They should serve prunes."

Lump looked up from his book. "I love prunes. We have them on Christmas."

"My condolences," said Laszlo. "What I mean is this Signora will probably be old fashioned and expect us to kiss her wrinkled behind. So don't speak unless you're spoken to. I'll do the talking. You two can just sit there and look . . . mortal."

"And how do we do that?"

"Be needy, dumb, and vulnerable. That's the way my dad likes 'em. Mortals make him feel powerful. This Signora won't be any different."

"So who *is* your father, anyway?" asked Maggie. "You haven't told us his name."

Laszlo glanced from one to the other. "Really? I could have sworn I mentioned it."

The Drakefords shook their heads.

"My father's Baal," said Laszlo. "Or *Lord* Baal, I should say. I assume you've heard of him."

Lump cocked his head. "I've heard of Beelzebub. Are they related?"

At this, the demon's face darkened. Leaning forward, he jabbed a finger at Lump. "Let's get this straight right now. There is no 'Beelzebub.' That name's nothing but a slanderous falsehood. I could sue you just for saying it."

Lump looked abashed.

"What are you talking about?" said Maggie. "Even I've heard of Beelzebub."

"Oh, but you haven't heard of *Baal*? The Grand Duke of Gluttony?"

"No."

"Lord of Carrion?"

"Sorry."

"Disseminator of Gout?"

Maggie smiled uncertainly. "Is that really a thing?"

Laszlo shrugged and stared out the window. "It's pretty new," he conceded. "The good titles were claimed ages ago."

"But what does your father have to do with Beelzebub?" asked Lump.

Laszlo eyed the Drakefords suspiciously. "I already told you. *There. Is. No. Beelzebub!*"

"Okay," said Maggie. "Fine. Then why have we heard about him and not Baal?"

"You really want to know?" She nodded. The demon looked like he'd been sucking on a lemon. "All right," he muttered. "Fine. I'll tell you. It all began when a certain bigwig—we'll call him Lite-Brite—didn't like my dad calling himself Baal Zebul. That means 'Lord of the Manor,' which we can all agree is perfectly normal and classy. But Lite-Brite thought Dad was getting too big for his britches. So what does that asshole do? He starts a rumor with the Israelites that my dad's name is actually Baal Zebub—'Lord of the Flies'—which might as well be 'Lord of the Turds.' Well, everyone thought this was *hilarious*." Laszlo assumed a patrician bonhomie. "'Evening, Baalzebub!' . . . 'How goes it, Baalzebub?' . . . 'I accidentally swatted one of your subjects, Baalzebub. Hope you don't mind, old chap' . . ."

The demon trailed off into peevish silence.

Lump raised his hand. "Question: Does Hell have flies?"

Laszlo shot him a withering look. "What do you think? It's *Hell*."

A nearby passenger set down her beverage and eyed them. Laszlo glowered at her. "Just drink your Pellegrino, lady."

She scowled and looked the other way.

Maggie's face was sympathetic. "Well, I'm sorry I brought it up. I had no idea it would strike a nerve." A pause. "Remind me never to ask about your mother."

Laszlo looked glum. "Mom was just a consort. Succubus, probably. Never met her."

"So your brothers and sisters . . . ?"

"Oh, we all have different mothers. Dad's never gotten hitched. People think he's angling to marry Lite-Brite's daughter."

"Why?" said Maggie. "To get revenge for the name?"

"I wouldn't put it past him. But it's probably to get closer to the throne. 'Grand Duke' is nice and all, but it ain't 'King.'"

Lump was riveted. "Hell sounds kind of fascinating."

"If you like soap operas," Laszlo said dryly. "Hell's pretty much just *Dynasty* with a lot of murder and magic."

"What's *Dynasty*?" asked Maggie.

"A soap opera from the eighties. Just picture a bunch of rich people in ridiculous outfits having affairs and wrestling in koi ponds."

She cracked a smile. "I'd watch that."

Laszlo opened his mouth to reply but stopped and did a double take. He reached into his pocket and pulled out the stolen jar of faerie essence. "Rub some on that eye. You're looking a little *Exorcist*-y."

A horrified Maggie asked if she could use his phone camera as a mirror. What she saw left her speechless. Since the train had pulled out of Milan, her right eye had changed dramatically. The entire iris was now pale yellow, the pupil a snakelike slit.

She put a hand to her mouth.

Laszlo began singing softly. "*Ch-ch-ch-changes . . .*"

Lump leaned over to get a peek, but Maggie pushed him back. "Don't," she warned. Turning away, she covered her eyelid and the surrounding area with the waxy essence. Her skin began to tingle.

"Take it easy with that stuff," said Laszlo. "A little goes a long way."

"How does it look?" she asked, returning the jar and his phone.

"Um . . . like it always does?" said her brother.

"Of course it does," groused Laszlo. "She practically spackled it." The demon held up the jar. "This isn't lip balm. If we run out, we'll get stopped at customs."

"I'll get stopped if I'm a total freak show," said Maggie.

Laszlo waved away her concerns. "All I'm saying is don't use so much. And if you think you're a freak show, you should see Clarence."

The loudspeaker announced that they'd be arriving at Roma Termini in *quindici minuti.*

"So do you know your way around the city?" said Maggie.

Laszlo shrugged. "Well enough. I killed some time here in the seventeenth century. Or maybe the fifteenth. When did Michelangelo die?"

Lump consulted his travel guide. "1564."

"Anyway," the demon continued, "I was here when Micky kicked it.
And I popped back a few centuries later for the premiere of *La Dolce Vita.*"

"Is that a movie?" said Maggie.

Laszlo scoffed. "A *film*, my dear. A classic film. The premiere was a
hoot. Some guy challenged the director to a duel."

"Why?" asked Lump.

"For making something entertaining, I guess."

"But why is that bad?"

The demon looked amused. "Because people work themselves into
a tizzy over anything new or fun. Humans have this kick-ass world, and
all you want to do is flog yourselves silly. Pure insanity. Don't ever be a
flogger, Lump."

"I won't," he said resolutely.

Laszlo suddenly straightened. "Actually, flogging reminds me of
something."

"What?" said Maggie, a little dubiously.

"Rome means the Vatican . . . and the Vatican means the pope."

Maggie waved him on. "And the pope means—"

"*Priests!*" Laszlo hissed. "Nuns. Clergy by the dozen. Churches on
every corner. There's probably holy water in the drinking fountains!"

"Okay, okay. You don't have to get hysterical."

"I'm not getting *hysterical.* Rome's a minefield! You should be massaging my feet and fanning me with palm fronds for taking you behind
enemy lines."

Lump looked puzzled. "If Rome's so dangerous, why would the Signora live there?"

But Laszlo had sunk into a sulk. Crossing his arms, he stared out
the window, a grimace spoiling his Hollywood looks.

The pouting continued until they were rolling their luggage through Roma Termini. Maggie was too busy taking in the station's atrium and bright advertisements for perfumes and fashion houses to be bothered.

They had just left the crowds behind when Lump tugged at her elbow. "I have to pee."

Maggie glanced around and spotted a men's room twenty yards away; her brother dropped his backpack and trotted off. She nudged Laszlo. "Go with him."

The demon scoffed. "And do what? Show the kid how to aim? You're the one who keeps insisting he's not a baby . . ." He stared past Maggie's shoulder with an unsettled expression. "On second thought," he muttered, and walked briskly toward the bathroom, the ebony curse folio tucked under his arm.

The reason for this soon became clear: A group of Catholic clergy was coming through the concourse. Leading them was an elderly priest wearing a violet cap and robes. He leaned on a cane. Several travelers hurried over to pay their respects. The man listened with his head cocked before offering his blessing. Maggie realized the old priest was blind. She also realized she was squarely in the procession's path.

Grabbing their luggage, Maggie got out of the way.

They had nearly passed her when the man stopped, as though he'd struck an invisible barrier. Turning, he fixed his clouded eyes upon Maggie, who was near a newsstand. The intensity of the man's gaze was startling. It reminded her of Dimitri, the way his attention was like an x-ray. The priest's expression wavered between curiosity and wariness. After several moments, he approached her. His attendants quickly caught up, looking as puzzled as Maggie.

The priest stopped an arm's length from her. His voice was soft and solemn, its edges sanded by age.

"*Hai una macchia su di te, signorina,*" he intoned. "*Hai un pesante onere.*"

"I'm sorry," said Maggie. "But I don't understand."

This did not dissuade him. "*Sei troppo giovane per questo onere,*" he continued. "*Non è colpa tua. Non chiudere il tuo cuore a Dio. Sei ancora sua figlia.*"

She smiled awkwardly, aware that a small crowd was gathering. Shuffling forward, the old priest touched his fingers gently to her cheek and spoke in an undertone. "*Roma è la città eterna. Urbs Æterna. Devi stare attenta, signorina. Le cose vecchie vivono qui. Vecchi appetiti. Rimani fedele a Dio.*"

With this, he offered her a blessing and continued on his way. His attendants followed, more than one casting a disconcerted glance back at Maggie. The crowd dispersed, except for a young man wearing a blue hoodie under a blazer. Even before he opened his mouth, she could tell he was an American.

"Are you okay?" he asked. "You look a little spooked."

"I'm fine." She tucked some hair behind her ear. "I just didn't understand him."

The young man grinned and adjusted his glasses, which Maggie thought suited him nicely.

There was nothing of Jan in this boy, and for some reason the mosquitoes and bees remained quiet. She took in his black hair, the hint of stubble, the warm brown eyes with their glint of ready humor. How old was he? Not much older than she was. His hoodie said *Columbia* in pale-blue letters.

"Are you a student?"

"I guess this makes it kind of obvious," he said with slight embarrassment, indicating the sweatshirt. "But yeah, I'm spending the semester here. My parents decided my 'horizons needed broadening.' You?"

"Just visiting. Do you have any idea what that priest said?"

Columbia laughed. "Priest? That was a bishop. You can tell by the purple on his vestments. My Italian's pretty pathetic, but I caught something about Rome being eternal and full of old things with old appetites. Oh, and he wants you to be careful and stay true to God. So . . . I guess you should behave yourself."

The young man wagged a finger before realizing just how dorky it looked and shoving his hand in his pocket. Maggie was happy to find she wasn't the only one feeling nervous.

He nodded at something beside her. "Who's this?"

Maggie looked down to find a far-too-chipper Lump at her elbow.

"I'm Lump," he replied.

"I like your glasses."

"Thanks. They're designer."

"I can tell," said Columbia.

"So who are you?"

"Jason Berman. Lump's an interesting name. What's it short for?"

"George. Are you bugging my sister, Jason?"

The boy gave Maggie a helpless look. "I . . . wasn't trying to."

Maggie glared down at her brother. "Don't be rude. A priest stopped to say something, and he—Jason—translated. Where's Laszlo, by the way?"

"In a stall. He decided as long as he was in there, he might as well 'lighten the load.'"

She winced. "Got it." She wondered if her spelltube had the power to transport her brother to a parallel universe.

Jason cleared his throat. "So how long are you going to be in Rome? There's a million gelato places, but I think I found the best one and—"

"We're not staying long," said Maggie, and was immediately embarrassed by how terse she sounded.

"Oh," said Jason. "That's too bad. I mean, it's okay if Lump wanted to come along too. I don't mind."

Maggie found herself smiling. There was something undeniably pleasant about talking to this boy, something easy and comfortable. It didn't erase the horrors from last night, but it helped. Oh, why did Lump have to come back so soon? Why couldn't she have five minutes alone to talk with someone her own age? Not some drunk banker in a club, or someone from Schemerdaal who'd been raised to hate all Drakefords. A *nice* guy. A *normal* guy.

"That's really nice of you," she said, and meant it. "But I don't think I can."

Jason looked poised to retreat; then he stopped and collected himself. "Listen, I don't normally do this, but could I get your number? It's just that you seem really nice, and my therapist says I can't be so shy. She says I need to ask for what I want, and what I'd really like is your phone number. Maybe I could call you and we could, you know, talk . . ."

"You don't even know my name," she said over her brother's giggling.

Jason looked mortified. "Shit. I totally forgot to ask. Oh my God, I feel like an idiot."

"I don't think you're an idiot. My name's Maggie."

Jason repeated it and smiled as though pleased by its ring. "Well, Maggie. Could I call you sometime?"

"I'd like that, but I don't have a phone."

He was clearly surprised but didn't ask why. "Okay. How about an email?"

Maggie felt like crawling under the newsstand. "Um. I don't really use email very often. My parents are kind of . . . what's the word?"

"Luddites?"

"Something like that. Maybe you could give me *your* info, and . . ." She didn't want to be rude, but she also didn't want to lie. She knew perfectly well she'd never call Jason or write him. They would never cross paths again. He was like that couple in Schemerdaal the day of the Schuyler wake—something fascinating but not to be indulged.

With a sense of awkward anxiety, she watched as he jotted his name, email, and phone number on a page ripped from a journal. Folding the sheet in half, Jason handed it to her and smiled like a person who understood he'd been dismissed. "Goodbye, Maggie."

"Goodbye, Jason." She watched as he strode off to the station's exit. He did not look back.

"Who was that loser?"

Maggie turned to see Laszlo wiping water off his hands.

Lump went into reporter mode. "His name's Jason Berman. He goes to Columbia. He asked Maggie for her number because his therapist said it would be good for him."

The demon snorted. "Ah, yes. An American student visits Italy to bask in the culture and learn a little art history. Has he grown a mustache? I'll bet he has. Something sad and wispy?"

"He did *not* have a mustache," Maggie snapped.

"Well, he did need to shave," put in Lump.

She flicked his ear. "Shut up."

Teasing Maggie seemed to brighten Laszlo's mood. Chuckling to himself, he took one of the suitcases and led them toward the exit. "I don't see why you're so touchy. A college creep came sniffing around. It happens."

Maggie walked with brisk purpose. "He wasn't creepy. He was nice."

"Please. I only got a glimpse, but I already know he listens to the Doors and writes cringe-inducing poetry. A corduroy blazer? What kind of kid owns a corduroy blazer?"

"A nice one."

"And a *therapist*," Laszlo crowed. "Hoo boy. You sure can pick 'em!"

Maggie shot him a glance. "Don't *you* have a therapist?"

"That's different. I have real problems."

"Yes. You're an asshole."

The demon cackled as they walked out of the terminal. The street was lined with taxis. "C'mon, let's grab a— Oh my God, you have to be *shitting me*!" In an instant, Laszlo reversed course and herded the baffled Drakefords back inside the station. "Walk," he ordered. "Don't run. Don't look back. *Just move.*"

"What's the matter?" Maggie's voice was urgent. "What did you see?"

"Our pals from the plane are here."

Maggie stepped up her pace. "*What?* Kathy?"

Laszlo nodded. "She and Hubby are out there."

"You're sure it was them?"

Not replying, he hurried them down a concourse as crowded as any in Manhattan.

"But that's impossible," she panted. "How could they know we'd be in Rome?"

"No idea," Laszlo muttered. "But it isn't good."

The three burst through a side door and trotted half a block to grab a taxi. Laszlo tossed their things in the trunk and told the driver to take them to Madama Lucrezia. The driver nodded and hit the accelerator.

Turning to Laszlo, Maggie lowered her voice. "Who is Madama Lucrezia? I thought we were going to the Signora."

The demon was busy messaging someone. He sent the text with an angry tap of the screen, then checked to see if they were being followed. His leg was bouncing like a jackhammer.

Taking out two cigarettes, he offered one to the driver, who happily accepted. Laszlo lit up, inhaled deeply, and promptly exhaled in Maggie's face. She coughed and fanned the air. With a distracted apology, he lowered the window half an inch.

Maggie had more pressing concerns. "How could Kathy have known we'd be at the train station? Who knew we were coming to Rome?"

Laszlo took another drag as the driver honked at a ridiculously tiny car that had darted in ahead of them. His voice was sheepish. "Just Clarence."

"Well then," said Maggie crisply. "I guess we know who betrayed you."

He shook his head. "Nope. Clarence would never do that."

"Why? Because you inspire such loyalty?"

Laszlo held up his phone to reveal a text string.

> Clarence, did you betray me?

> What?!? I'd never do that!

"Oh, well, that settles it," said Maggie dryly. "If Clarence says he didn't, then he must be telling the truth! As we all know, traitors are famous for their honesty."

Laszlo merely shrugged. "Clarence isn't a rat."

The driver made a sharp turn, sending Maggie careening into Lump. Getting about in Rome was a chaotic ballet, an arena where drivers played a never-ending game of chicken. Compared to this insanity, Manhattan was a country lane. Maggie gripped Lump's arm as a Vespa came speeding toward them. The street was much too narrow, they would collide, they would—

The Vespa rocketed past. Maggie exhaled and let her brother go.

Mercifully, the rest of their ride was uneventful.

The driver left them on the sidewalk with their luggage near what looked like a museum and a small park; an old woman in a headscarf was scattering bits of bread to a cooing crowd of pigeons. A poster on a nearby wall advertised an exhibit at the Palazzo Venezia. Beside it, a uniformed guard stood at an archway, smoking a cigarette and looking rather bored. In the distance were some official-looking buildings and a much larger park, whose terraced steps were packed with people enjoying the afternoon sunshine.

"Are you sure we're in the right place?" asked Maggie.

But Laszlo didn't answer; he was too busy writing on a postcard. Frowning, he crossed out several words and scribbled in something else.

Lump tried to peek. "Is that for the Signora?"

Laszlo waved the card to dry the ink. "It's for Madama Lucrezia. We give it to her; she gives it to the Signora."

"Who's Madama Lucrezia?"

Laszlo nodded at a statue of a woman tucked in a corner between two windows. Maggie hadn't even noticed it. Now that she had, its random location puzzled her.

She walked closer for a better look. One arm was a stump, and the features were so worn that they were mere indents in the stone. It was vaguely unsettling, something like an unfinished doll. Its face reminded Maggie of the corpses she'd seen on dining tables in Schemerdaal, the ones whose mouths wouldn't quite close.

"How is this going to contact the Signora?"

"No idea," Laszlo told her. "But those are the instructions. Madama Lucrezia's one of the 'talking statues of Rome.' Any one of them can supposedly get word to the Signora." Reaching up, he stuck his postcard to the statue's bosom with some chewing gum. "Voilà! Message sent!"

Maggie expected the guard by the archway to object, but he didn't seem to care. Evidently, this wasn't unusual.

Lump sat on one of the suitcases. "Now what?"

"We hang here," said Laszlo. "Clarence said the Signora will be in touch. Or she won't. When you're five thousand years old, you get to make the rules."

"Wait," said Maggie. "We're following Clarence's instructions?"

"Yes, ma'am."

She stared in disbelief. "The same Clarence who betrayed you? The one who's obviously working for Androvore?"

Laszlo asked Lump to roll their luggage over to the little park. When he did, the demon shot Maggie an impatient look. "I told you. Clarence isn't a rat."

"How else could Androvore know we'd be in Rome?" Laszlo said nothing. "Okay," continued Maggie. "Let's pretend Clarence is innocent. What if his phone is bugged? For that matter, what if *your* phone is bugged?"

"What do you know about surveillance? You live in a shack."

"I read spy novels," said Maggie. "And this statue is what they call a 'dead drop.'"

Laszlo eased down on a bench by their luggage. "Well, bully for you. Give the girl some microfilm."

Maggie sat down beside him. "Laszlo, if your boss's lackeys knew we'd be in Rome, they probably know who we came to see. And if everyone knows that statue is how you contact the Signora, don't you think they'll come here? They're probably on their way."

He lit another cigarette. "Maybe," he allowed. "But Rome has *six* talking statues, and I picked this one out of a hat. We've got time."

She fidgeted. "What if they have people posted at every statue? What if we're being watched *right now*?"

Laszlo opened his mouth to answer before turning to look behind them at the woman who'd been feeding the pigeons. She was now sitting on a bench talking quietly into a phone. A pair of beady eyes met Maggie's. Brandishing a pudgy fist, the woman extended her forefinger and pinkie like a pair of horns. Bracelets jangled as she shook her hand at Maggie.

Lump sounded puzzled. "What's she doing?"

A more relaxed Laszlo gave him a smile. "Warding off the evil eye. No biggie. It's not like it works."

But Maggie was appalled. "How would she know about my eye?"

"She doesn't," said Laszlo. "These old-world biddies think everyone has the evil eye." He returned the woman's gesture while doing something obscene with his tongue. Scowling, the woman gathered up her things and went to take refuge in a nearby church.

There was the sound of a powerful engine behind them. Laszlo and the Drakefords swiveled as an enormous silver limousine came to a halt beside the park. The passenger door opened, and a tall, powerfully built Black man in a gray suit stepped out. Without a word, he took their bags. Laszlo followed him back to the car with Maggie and Lump trailing uncertainly behind.

The Drakefords' Keeper shot them a wink. "And to think you were worried."

"How do you know he doesn't work for Androvore?" Maggie whispered.

"Easy. His goons would never drive a '66 Pullman."

The man stowed their luggage in the trunk. When he spoke, it was in perfect, accented English. "You know your cars," he said to Laszlo.

The Curse Keeper grinned. "My good man, I know luxury."

The mysterious man opened the back door and gestured that they get in. Maggie saw a spacious interior with two rows of facing leather seats and a black partition that hid the driver. "If you please," said the man. "Your enemies will be arriving shortly. I assume you'd like to avoid them?"

"Good assumption." Laszlo gave Maggie and Lump an encouraging shove. Laszlo took the seat opposite them and immediately started examining the bar, which held a selection of liquors and cordials in crystal decanters.

To Maggie's surprise, their escort joined them, taking the seat next to Laszlo, and the limo eased into motion. His face was almost sculpted, with flawless blue-black skin wholly free of wrinkles. The hair near the man's temples was gray, but the eyes that met hers were ageless. He gave a courteous nod before turning away.

"The Signora received your message," he said to their Keeper. His voice was a solicitous baritone. "I presume you are Laszlo?"

"That's right."

"Laszlo Zebul," the man confirmed. "Youngest son of His Fiend-ishness Baal Zebul?"

Laszlo shot the Drakefords a look of pride. "Exactly. Not Zebub. *Zebul*," he told them. Then, to their host: "Laszlo Zebul, at your service."

"I am honored."

"Don't mention it. By the way, what's your name?"

"My name is unimportant."

As he said this, the man reached across and casually tapped Lasz-lo's shoulder. There was a flash of light, and Laszlo stiffened before slumping unconscious against the console. His human guise drained away like a stopper had been pulled. What remained was a handsome, blue-skinned demon whose forked red tongue protruded from a slack and senseless mouth.

Maggie grabbed his wrist and tried to feel for a pulse. Lump gasped. "What did you do to him?"

Their host opened his hand and showed them a slim device. "Your companion is unharmed," he assured her. "As for you—the Signora does not permit visitors to know the location of her residence. If you wish to continue, you must wear these."

He handed her a pair of what looked like eyeless executioner hoods. Maggie threw a desperate look at Laszlo, but he was already snoring. She tried to swallow. Their host waited patiently for their answer, his expression calm and attentive.

At last, she found the courage to speak. "And if we don't, you'll let us go?"

The man's smile was inscrutable. "You misunderstand me. I never said the young mortals could leave. I merely asked if they wished to *continue*."

Maggie went cold. She looked first at the man, then at the hoods on her lap. "So . . . leaving isn't an option?"

"I regret to say it is not."

CHAPTER 23
SIGNORA BELLASCURA

The hoods were disorienting and uncomfortably hot. Maggie held Lump's hand and tried to keep her breathing slow and steady.

She couldn't say how long they'd been driving. It might have been two hours or twenty minutes. No one had spoken, not even their host. They changed directions many times, and the final turn led to a long, winding descent.

At last, the limousine came to a stop.

Maggie heard two doors open. There were footsteps. Lump's hand slid out of her grasp as he was pulled away. Strong arms took hold and lifted her from the car like she was another piece of luggage. She knew better than to try and take off the hood.

The air outside was as warm and moist as a greenhouse.

"Lump, are you all right?" she called, and her voice echoed in some vast, vaulted space. Another cavern—or perhaps a grotto; she heard water trickling nearby. Maggie was heartily sick of being underground.

Her brother's reply came from somewhere to her left. It was unintelligible.

A hand settled on Maggie's shoulder. "I will guide you," their host said close to her ear.

They walked fifty feet or so over hard and rocky terrain, then ascended a series of winding steps that seemed carved directly into the stone. At one point, Maggie slipped. When she caught herself, her palm scraped a rough surface that was slick with slime and moisture.

After they had been climbing for several minutes—again, in utter silence—it occurred to Maggie that she should have been counting the steps. Here she'd been lecturing Laszlo about spycraft and dead drops, and she wasn't following the basics. You had to file away all the knowledge you could. It might be the key to a daring escape.

It was comforting to think of these things—they represented a kind of optimism, a belief that all was not lost, that they could still get away. But deep down, Maggie knew it was a pointless exercise. These were not the kind of people one escaped.

She'd realized it while speaking with their guide. It was his calm that snuffed her hopes; that quiet, unflagging courtesy. The quiet ones were always the most dangerous. Ten years of sin-eating had taught her that. But no one in Schemerdaal gave off an aura like this soft-spoken, perfectly dressed man. If Maggie had spotted him at a wake, she'd have turned right around. The dead could keep their money.

Maggie stumbled a bit at the top of the stairs. Her guide steadied her and led her into a smaller space; to her relief, Lump was soon there too. His hand found hers. A gate closed, and she realized that they were in an elevator.

The ride seemed endless but was probably only several minutes.

The gate was opened and the Drakefords were marched, still hand in hand, down a long hallway.

Next, they were led through a door. Maggie felt a soft breeze and, through the hood, heard a fountain at her right. Somewhere above, a violinist was practicing scales.

Maggie was led to a chair and seated. The hood was lifted away.

She found herself in a spacious courtyard whose gardens were in full bloom, despite it being October. Lump was seated in a chair on Maggie's left. Their eyes met, and when each saw that the other was unharmed, they took in their surroundings with silent wonder.

It was the loveliest garden Maggie had ever seen. Countless

ornamental plants and trees—blue wisteria, rosebushes, cypress, even
olive—were tucked inside walls of pale stone whose columned terraces
dripped with flowering vines. Above, the first stars of the evening were
setting out their lights in a pure lilac sky.

It took a moment for her to register how quiet things were. There
was the fountain and the violin, of course, and the soft chitter of birds
and insects. But she heard no honking or traffic, no drone of passing
planes. They must have been deep in the countryside. As she absorbed
it all, something heavy slid over her foot.

Maggie froze. It was a snake, six or seven feet long, with an intricate
pattern to its amber scales and a large, wedge-shaped head.

She did not even breathe until the tip of its tail had passed. Even
then, all that moved was her eyes, following the snake as it slithered
toward a nightjar by a rosebush. The bird plainly saw the predator but
made no attempt to fly away.

Maggie hissed at it to move, but the bird remained stubbornly in
place. She watched, hoping that the serpent was blind or stupid.

It was neither.

The strike was far too quick for the eye to follow. The nightjar vanished within the snake's coils.

Then, to Maggie's horror, other snakes emerged from neighboring
shrubs and flower beds—vipers, asps, a twelve-foot cobra, others she
could not name. They streaked across the flagstones and converged in a
writhing conclave, hissing and snapping before honoring the killer's claim
to its prey and going their separate ways. Lump whimpered in his throat.

"It's okay," Maggie whispered. "Keep still and they won't bother you."

Her brother observed that the nightjar had kept still, a fair point.

Clearing her throat, she called out to anyone who might be listening. "Are you doing this just to scare us?"

No one answered. Maggie turned to look behind them. More to-
piary; marble statues of a faun and satyr. No sign of the man from the
limousine. By all appearances, the Drakefords were alone.

A lamp among the trees began to glow, as did others throughout
the gardens, emitting a golden light that limned the leaves and flowers.

"Maggie," said Lump. There was fear in his voice.

She turned back to see what was wrong. When she did, she realized they were not alone and never had been.

The blue wisteria flanked by cypress trees had vanished. In its place was a woman seated in a throne-like chair, flanked by identical twin girls. The woman looked to be in her late thirties and wore a sleek business suit and a necklace whose platinum pendant displayed a serpent devouring its own tail. Her shining black hair hung in a braid over one shoulder. Her skin was dark, her lips were full, and her eyes were like polished emeralds. She was, without question, the most striking individual Maggie had ever seen.

The twins did not resemble the woman. They looked to be eleven or twelve, with brown hair and sallow faces. Their dresses were the only remarkable thing about them: ornately embroidered silk, puffed sleeves, hooped skirts, and tapered waists. If one of the girls hadn't blinked, Maggie might have taken them for mannequins from a museum.

The woman looked from Maggie to Lump and back again. The expression on her face was neither hostile nor welcoming. It was full of curiosity.

When she spoke, her voice was like brushed velvet, wondrously soft and tinged with an accent that was impossible to place. "I am told you only speak English."

"Yes, ma'am," said Maggie.

"I do not care for English," remarked the woman. "It is harsh and unpleasant."

"I'm sorry, ma'am."

"Why do you apologize?" she said dryly. "Are you its creator?"

"No, ma'am."

The woman looked to the twins and repeated "ma'am" with a pronounced nasal twang. The girls smiled. "That word will not do," she told Maggie. "I am the Signora Bellascura. You may call me Signora."

"Yes, Signora."

"And who are you? Your companion did not mention your names in his message."

Maggie swallowed. "My name is Margaret Drakeford, Signora. And this is my brother, George Drakeford. We're from America."

"I gathered. Why are you here?"

Maggie glanced at the palazzo. "May I first ask after our companion? Is he all right?"

The Signora sniffed. "You keep poor company. That one is a liar and a rake. Many years ago, he seduced a girl and left her heartbroken. Do not trouble yourself with him."

"I'm afraid I have to."

The woman cocked her head a fraction. "Are you making demands of me?"

"No, no, ma'am—I mean Signora. It's just—if I was in his shoes, I'd want someone checking on me."

A glint appeared in the ageless eyes. "You are loyal."

Maggie sighed. "I suppose I am. Sometimes I wish I wasn't."

"Loyalty is an admirable quality," said the Signora. She looked at Lump, and her demeanor softened. "Those glasses are fabulous—where did you get them?"

Lump cleared his throat. "Milan."

"Of course. You have style, young George. But are you loyal, like your sister?"

Maggie's brother looked like he was about to faint. "Yes, Signora. I-I'd like to think so."

The Signora muttered something in Italian. Her attendants looked amused but retained their silent composure. "Let us get down to business. I assume you have come seeking to apprentice here."

"I apologize, Signora," Maggie answered carefully. "Did you say 'apprentice'?"

The lady's smile faded. She looked at Maggie as though she found her uncommonly stupid.

"Apprentice," she repeated. "That is the word in English, no? *Apprendista*. One who studies and serves a master. You wish to study magic and serve me, yes? You wish to apprentice."

The Drakefords exchanged confused glances. "I'm sorry," said

Maggie, even more carefully, "but I think there's been some sort of misunderstanding."

The Signora steepled her long fingers. "I should say so. I am not accepting new students at present. Your companion has misled you. But I am curious who taught you such arts in America. I know it is not this Laszlo. Is it that pretender Qasim? If so, you are wise to seek a different master."

Maggie was at a loss. "We don't know any Qasim. George and I were homeschooled."

"I see. So your parents are the magicians."

Lump piped up. "No, Signora. But our mother did want to be a history teacher."

Now the Signora was the one at a loss. Leaning back, she appraised the Drakefords with an air of simmering curiosity. "I do not understand. Why would two magical humans come here if not to apprentice?"

It felt like a trick question. Maggie shifted uneasily. "Signora, we're not magical."

When that beautiful face darkened, she understood Laszlo's warnings about ancient demons. The atmosphere became charged, even saturated with dangerous energies. The hairs on Maggie's arms and neck lifted as though a current ran through them. A chorus of soft hissing filled the courtyard.

Maggie did not dare break eye contact with the Signora, but peripheral vision told her the flagstones were now swimming with movement. Lamplight glistened on millions of gliding scales. Maggie could not guess how many serpents were converging upon them—hundreds at least. Maybe thousands! She felt them twining sinuously about her feet and ankles.

The Signora raised a finger in warning. "I say this only once. Never lie to me, Margaret Drakeford. Do you understand?"

Maggie could barely speak. "Yes, Signora."

This was all her fault. It had been her idea to come to Rome, her idea to seek the Signora's assistance and work out some kind of exchange. She had no clue what sort of predicament Laszlo was in but an all-too-vivid idea of what was about to happen to her and Lump.

The demon had promised he'd do all the talking, but he wasn't here. It was just Maggie and Lump, on their own and out of their depth. This was not the time to be witty or clever. That was what Laszlo would have done, but she sensed that it would not have had the desired effect on the Signora. Besides, Maggie wouldn't even know where to start being clever. She couldn't outsmart someone like this. There was only one thing to do: lay down her cards.

"I don't know anything about magic, Signora. But we did come seeking your help. Our family has been cursed for almost four hundred years."

The Signora remained impassive. "I am not fond of curses. Too often they go astray. But they have nothing to do with me. This is between your family and the Hierarchy's so-called Society."

Serpents were now coursing about the Drakefords in such numbers that Maggie's feet were completely buried. The sensation of the reptiles rubbing against her socks or venturing up the leg of her jeans made her want to scream.

"I appreciate your point, Signora. But there is a reason we came to you. We believe our curse involves something that may be of interest. We were hoping to perhaps work out a trade."

Amusement glittered in the Signora's eyes. "And what is it you hope to get from me?"

"We need an item to help us break the spell," Maggie explained. "Something magical. And we were told you might have things of that nature."

The woman laughed. "Tell me, Margaret Drakeford. Did you sell your soul? Was that how you acquired your magic?"

Again, Maggie was at a loss. "Signora, I am truly sorry, but I do not understand what you mean. The only magic that I know of would have come from the Drakeford Curse."

Something coiled around Maggie's upper calf. Revulsion washed over her.

The Signora was studying her closely. She muttered something to the twins, and the girls nodded. Then the Signora drew a symbol in the air with her finger—a symbol that burned away in golden flames, and Maggie saw a sheet of vellum that hovered before the demon. Its surface was covered with dense script, penned in red ink. At the bottom were two blank lines awaiting signatures.

The Signora looked at Maggie expectantly.

"Is that a contract for my soul?" asked Maggie. When their hostess nodded, she said, "No, Signora. I am not willing to trade that. Not for anything."

The Signora's eyes flicked to Lump. "Your brother, then? I must confess I have never bartered with one so young."

Maggie shook her head. "No Drakeford is selling their soul."

The demoness waved her hand as if this was the answer she expected. The contract dissolved into smoke. "Then there is nothing more to discuss."

She rose from the throne-like chair. As she did, the sea of snakes surged forward until it nearly reached Maggie's knees. Lump cried her name, and she turned to see her brother buried to the waist. Before she could speak, something slid onto her lap.

It was a bloated viper, heavy as a car battery. It propelled itself up her body. Soon its tongue flickered against her straining throat.

"Please," Maggie gasped. "Just hear me out!"

The Signora Bellascura gazed down at her. "It was a pleasure to meet you, my dear, but I have other engagements, and sadly, you have nothing to offer me." She turned away, her attendants following.

"No?" Maggie practically shouted. "*What about the Lost Magi?*"

The demoness stopped cold. "What could you possibly know of them?"

The viper at Maggie's throat seemed to be waiting too.

"We know where one is!"

The Signora locked eyes with her. "If this is a trick, my dear, you will wish I let the serpents have you."

Maggie twisted her head away from the snake. "No trick!"

A grim smile appeared on that matchless face. "Very well."

The Signora made a shooing motion. At once, the snakes abandoned

Maggie and Lump, slithering away in every direction until there wasn't a single reptile in sight.

An eerie tension settled over the courtyard as the Signora once again took her throne.

"Tell me, Margaret Drakeford. Are you a good storyteller?"

Maggie could not lie. "No, Signora."

"Then you must become one, for tonight you are going to tell me a story about the Lost Magi. You are going to reveal everything you know about them and how you came to know it. You have never told a more important story, my dear. Do we understand each other?"

"Yes, Signora."

"Begin."

Night deepened as Maggie spun her tale. She related how Ambrose Drakeford had come to the American colonies; how he had had a woman burned for witchcraft and she had laid a curse upon his family. She told the Signora about generations of the Drakeford Curse, appearing earlier and earlier as the years passed. She described the bizarre formation known as the Witchstone, the Drakeford graves, the sounds and smells. And finally, Maggie explained about Laszlo and the trip to Manhattan that convinced them that the Witchstone might be one of the Lost Magi.

After she was finished, there was a long silence.

"Who was the person who made this connection?" asked the Signora.

"I'd prefer not to say."

"Why is that?"

"I'm afraid you might harm them."

"Ah," said the ancient demon. "Once again, the girl is loyal. Tell me, did you get my name from this individual?"

Maggie hesitated. "Yes."

The Signora gave a delighted chuckle. "And how is Dimitri?"

Maggie felt her muscles relax. She had not wanted to reveal Dimitri's involvement but had been terrified to lie. "He's well—or at least I think he is. Dimitri was very kind to us. Right before we left, he swallowed a pill so he wouldn't remember our conversation. The Witchstone—the whole story—frightened him."

The Signora smiled wryly. "Men and their pills." She paused. "Is that the end of your story, girl?"

Maggie swallowed. "Not quite. After we left Dimitri, we've been searching for items—materia—to help us break the curse. We got a magic porridge pot, but it was broken by some monsters in the Alps."

The mention of monsters seemed to intrigue the Signora. "What did they look like?"

Maggie shuddered reflexively. "Like giant crows or ravens, but they walked like humans."

"Nachtkrapp. I'm surprised you were not eaten."

"It wasn't pleasant," she said flatly.

"Maggie stabbed one with a spear," added Lump. "She saved my life."

The Signora clucked her tongue. "Loyal *and* brave. The list of virtues grows. It is most unfortunate that Laszlo Zebul is your Curse Keeper."

Maggie was inclined to agree. Silently.

The demoness sighed in disappointment. "His father clearly has no use for him," she said to herself. "Any ransom would be pitiful."

Ransom? Maggie dared to venture a question. "So you're not going to kill him, then?"

At this, the Signora laughed long and well. "Kill the son of *Baal Zebul?* Are you mad, girl? Baal is destruction incarnate. Even I would not dare such a thing. No, your Keeper will be spanked and sent on his way. Even so, I'd hoped for payment."

"You were going to blackmail Laszlo's father? You just said he's destruction incarnate!"

The demon waved away Maggie's concern. "Pfft. Ransoms are common among our kind. It is not my fault the son of Baal Zebul finds himself my hostage. The boy should have been more capable. His father knows this. But now that I learn he is a lowly Curse Keeper . . . it's clear that the family has no greater plans for him." The demoness drummed her fingers. "This Laszlo must be useless everywhere but the bedchamber . . ."

Maggie had no idea what to say to that. Fortunately, her hostess did not appear to expect a response. The Signora had fallen into private musings. For their part, the twins continued to stand with perfect posture, hands at their sides, their expressions serene.

At length, the demon came back to herself, blinked, and looked at the Drakefords as though surprised to find them still present. "Is there more to the story?"

"No," admitted Maggie. "That's pretty much it."

"Well, I did enjoy the tale. Entertaining, yes, but of no use to me."

Maggie straightened in her chair. "*No use?* Forgive me, but why not? I thought you were interested in the Lost Magi. I thought you wanted to find them."

"There is nothing I desire more," the Signora agreed. "But unfortunately for you, I have reason to believe one of the Lost Magi is located in Asia."

"What about the other one? Dimitri said there were two!"

"Indeed. But the other is not your Witchstone."

"How can you be so certain?"

"Because I know where it is."

Maggie stared at the demoness. "T-that's not possible!"

"Precisely. This 'Witchstone' of yours is not what you believe it to be."

"But we have photos! On Laszlo's phone—he took pictures. There were inscriptions!"

The Signora Bellascura looked dubious. At length, she produced a slim phone and pressed a button. "It's me," she said to whoever had picked up. "Yes, I am aware I'm speaking English." A pause. "You forget your place, Marcel." Maggie and Lump could now faintly hear rapid Italian from the voice on the other end. The Signora rolled her eyes. "Stop groveling. What is the state of our young Zebul?" She listened as her lackey made his report. "Very well," she said. "Bring him here, along with his phone."

Marcel continued asking questions, but the Signora lost her patience and flung her phone at the fountain. It struck a marble porpoise and sank. "I hate those things. They have poisoned the world." She eyed Maggie suspiciously. "Do you have one?"

"No, Signora."

"Good! Stay away from them. Your mind will go to—what's the word? Oats? No—*mush*! That's it. Your mind will go to mush. Like Marcel's. I am taking his away."

The Signora sat in discontented silence, awaiting Laszlo's arrival. The twins did not move a muscle. Maggie and Lump shared an anxious glance.

At last, a door opened somewhere in the courtyard, followed by the squeaking rattle of something being rolled over the flagstones.

Two men in tailored suits were pushing a scaffold set atop a dolly. The scaffold was perhaps eight feet tall and supported an iron cage that slowly twirled upon its chain. The cage's occupant was naked and so cramped he was forced to crouch knees to chin, with his head bent at an awkward angle. The Signora's men rolled the dolly in front of their mistress before steadying the cage.

Maggie found herself staring up at Laszlo's royal-blue ass.

In spite of the view, she was relieved to find their Keeper alive and well. The cage rotated slightly, and the two made eye contact.

Laszlo was remarkably composed. "We will never speak of this."

"I give the orders here," commanded the Signora Bellascura. "You know who I am, so we will not bother with introductions. Do you have anything to say for yourself, Laszlo Zebul?"

The demon squirmed to get a better view of his captor. "Yes, I do." His voice was as urbane as ever. "I was told you were a lady of a certain age and assumed you'd be, shall we say, somewhat wrinkled and haggish. I see now that I was mistaken. I owe you an apology, Signora Bellascura." His voice warmed. "You are *not* haggish. On the contrary, you are the sexiest woman I've ever seen."

The Signora burst out laughing and did not stop until a tear ran down her perfect cheek. One of her attendants presented a silken handkerchief that she used to dab her eyes. "These ones are always the same," she informed the group. "A little flattery, a little charm. They slip into your heart and bed, only to disappoint you."

"Disappoint?" said Laszlo, with some confidence. "I've studied Tantra."

The Signora held up one hand; to Maggie, it looked like she was holding an invisible ball. Smiling at Laszlo, she began to tighten her hand into a fist. Iron groaned as the cage contracted. Laszlo gasped as the metal bars pressed into his flesh with such slow but relentless force that Maggie feared he'd be crushed.

"Please!" she cried out. "You're hurting him."

The Signora raised an eyebrow. "Why is his well-being of such concern to you? Do not tell me . . ."

Maggie caught her drift and recoiled. "What? Eww!"

"I can second that 'eww,'" said Laszlo. "Signora, there's no need to—"

The Signora's tone became that of a prosecutor. "Do you recall a young lady by the name Isabella de Castignole?"

"Um . . . should I?"

"Handmaiden to Lucrezia Borgia."

"Sorry. My memory isn't what it used to be. I blame Timothy Leary."

Again, the demoness curled her fingers inward. Metal squealed as broken bolts rained upon the flagstones. The Signora cocked her head. "Are you certain?"

Laszlo's answer came quickly. "Five foot two, brown hair, blue eyes, decent figure, atrocious dancer, but enthusiastic in the boudoir."

"That's better," said the Signora. "Lucrezia was my pupil, you wretch, and very fond of that poor girl you seduced. That poor girl who fell in love with you . . ."

"I never asked her to love me."

"And you left her . . ." continued the Signora.

"I never promised to stay."

The Signora Bellascura sighed. "Promises are interesting things, no? The ones we make; the ones we do not. You deny making a promise, and I see you are being truthful. Well and good. But *I* did make a promise, Laszlo Zebul. I swore to Lucrezia that if you and I ever crossed paths, I would not forget her Isabella. And here you are. Fate has a sense of humor, no?"

"Yes. And I don't like it."

Their hostess considered him. "Whatever shall we do with you?"

"I'll make amends," offered Laszlo. "What about a pilgrimage? Yes, a good old-fashioned pilgrimage to Isabella's final resting place. I'll pay my respects, apologize for any bruised feelings, and come clean about some missing heirlooms."

"It's a start," said the Signora. "What else?"

"I'll commission a florist," invented Laszlo. "That's right—a fresh bouquet on her grave every week for a year!"

"A thoughtful gesture, but a decade would be better."

"Done."

"And . . . ?"

Laszlo considered. "What's more timeless than an ode dedicated to her memory?"

"Are you a gifted poet?" inquired the Signora.

"God, no."

"Again, you are being honest. Yet that will not do."

"Ah," continued Laszlo, "but what if I offer a prize to *actual* poets? Real starving-artist types with lots of debt and turtlenecks. Who needs cash more than they do? One of them is bound to write something that will do her justice."

The Signora Bellascura nodded. "Very well. I expect a pilgrimage and the first bouquet within a week. You have a month to commission and publish a poem of suitable quality."

As the demons negotiated, Maggie wondered if Laszlo would disclose that he might well be crucibled before he could make good on his promises. That he kept his mouth shut came as little surprise.

Finally, satisfied, the Signora waved her hand, and Laszlo's cage dissolved into smoke. With nothing to support him, he fell onto the dolly, where he groaned and massaged his buttocks. Maggie averted her eyes.

The Signora ordered one of her men to fetch a robe for Laszlo. "Now we turn to the present. Margaret tells me you are her family's Curse Keeper, and that their curse involves a monument you believe to be one of the Lost Magi. She says you have photos of this."

Laszlo nodded. "On my phone."

A man Maggie assumed was Marcel produced the phone. The demoness inspected several cracks in the screen.

"Kobolds," Laszlo explained. "Not my fault."

The Signora rolled her eyes. "What is the password?"

Maggie committed it to memory.

A moment later, the Signora was swiping through various screens. When Marcel leaned in to help her find the photos app, she slapped his hand and demanded his iPhone, which she promptly flung into the fountain. She watched it sink, then returned her attention to Laszlo's screen.

"Who is the woman in this photo?" she asked.

Laszlo shrugged. "What does she look like?"

"Blond. Impressive bosom."

"Oh, that's Helga. We were supposed to have a date."

The Signora frowned and swiped. "What's this?" She held up the phone.

Laszlo squinted. "Central Park."

The Signora tutted. "No sense of composition."

He began to defend his photography skills as the Signora breezed through five or six more pictures. Abruptly, she stopped and brought the phone so close that her nose nearly touched the screen.

One of her men returned with a kimono for Laszlo, who snatched it with a haughty glare before shrugging it on. Meanwhile, the Signora had turned the phone sideways and was squinting at the image.

Laszlo cleared his throat. "You can, uh, pinch to zoom."

"Do not start with me," the Signora told him. But she pinched. A moment later, her expression became deeply puzzled. She swiped to the next picture and the next, peering close with unblinking focus. Her frown deepened.

"This is not possible."

"Excuse me, but what isn't possible?" asked Maggie.

The Signora smacked the screen with the back of her hand. "This! This is not possible!" Glaring at Laszlo, she shook the phone at him. "What are you playing at?"

"Nothing!" said Laszlo. "I didn't know anything about that stone until we talked to someone-I-don't-want-to-name-because-I'm-afraid-you'll-hurt-him."

The Signora gestured impatiently. "I know it is Dimitri."

Laszlo gasped and whirled on the Drakefords. "You told!"

Maggie shook her head. "The Signora guessed!" In any case, she was not about to be reprimanded after her ordeal with the snakes.

The Signora dismissed her men, leaving only the twins to attend her. Holding up Laszlo's phone, she pointed at the screen. "You took these? You have seen this object in person?"

"Yes."

"What did it feel like?"

Laszlo blew out his cheeks. "Honestly, it felt like raw power. Mountains of it. That thing's an atom bomb."

The Signora's eyes slid over to Maggie and Lump. "And you. You live near this Witchstone? You and your people before you?"

"Yes," said Maggie. "Our family's been there since the seventeenth century."

The Signora murmured in Italian to the twins before addressing her guests. "Well," she said, "at least one mystery is solved."

"Um, what mystery is that?" asked Laszlo, at sea.

The Signora gestured at the Drakefords. "The origins of their magic. Their family has been absorbing the stone's energies for generations. Surely you sensed it."

"Of course," said Laszlo. "I simply wanted to do more research before jumping to any conclusions."

The Signora made a sound of disgust. "You must be blind."

"Actually," he said to the Drakefords, "this *does* explain a few things."

"Like what?" said Maggie.

"Hmm, I don't know. Maybe it explains how all of Lump's spelltubes end up being *fucking amazing*. I get moths, and he gets flamethrowers? It isn't fair."

At that, Lump had to smile. "Well, I did tell you I was a hero."

"Zip it."

The Signora looked seriously at Laszlo. "This is a joke, yes? The son of Baal has not possibly lowered himself to using party favors."

Laszlo bridled. "Not all of us have your powers, Signora."

The demoness wore an expression of mingled scorn and pity. "A second mystery solved. I had been wondering why Lord Baal permits his son to work like a peasant. Ransom? *Ha!*" she spat. "I would have to pay *him* to take *you!*"

Despite herself, Maggie realized that she felt sorry for Laszlo. There he was, stark naked under a borrowed kimono, being ridiculed by an ancient, gorgeous demon in front of her mute attendants. Somebody had to defend him.

Unfortunately, that someone would have to be Maggie.

"We'd never have made it this far without Laszlo," she declared.

The Signora looked her over. "I do not agree. Perhaps I was hasty in dismissing the possibility of a new apprentice. I see vast potential before me. But that is for another day." Her attention shifted back to Laszlo. "Larger matters are at hand. Either I am mistaken and one of the Magi is not in Siberia, or you have a far greater problem than you know."

Laszlo sagged. "Please don't say that. I don't need more problems."

The Signora rose from her chair. "Do not despair, Laszlo, son of Baal. I have lived a long time. In my experience, big problems often lead to bigger opportunities."

She swept down a path along the edge of the courtyard, followed by the twins, Laszlo, and the Drakefords. Soon they had reached a tower—a simple, crenellated turret perhaps six stories tall, adorned with flowering vines. The Signora unlocked its door with a key produced from her robes and swung it open before looking back at her guests.

"Well?" she said. "Are you coming, or aren't you?"

CHAPTER 24
THE LOST MAGI

Laszlo and the Drakefords followed Signora Bellascura up the winding staircase. Laszlo wasn't thrilled to be climbing stairs; his knees ached, along with everything else, including his pride. That crow cage had been painful on several fronts.

He was still mulling over the Signora's theory that the Drakefords had been absorbing magic since they could crawl. In retrospect, Laszlo had to admit he should have realized something was up. The odds of Lump stumbling upon *two* superpowered spelltubes were not merely low; they were infinitesimal—he himself had used hundreds of the things, and the best had launched a disgruntled ferret at a Parisian bill collector. Yes, the ferret had gotten the job done, but it was hardly an explosion of self-guided energy whips.

The universe was unjust.

Still, the mechanics were intriguing. Had Lump amplified the tubes' effects, or did the tubes trigger magic that was already in him? Was he the chicken or the egg?

This made Laszlo realize he hadn't eaten anything since that cheese-and-tomato sandwich on the train from Milan. *A cheese-and-tomato sandwich?* What was wrong with him? Next time, he'd order prosciutto.

Next time . . .

Laszlo was running out of "next times." He knew this the way terminal cancer patients come to realize that they are dying. It no longer matters what treatments the doctors prescribe; the cancer isn't going to stop. The starkness of it chilled him.

To his surprise, he found himself empathizing with his Curse Bearers. After all, time was their enemy too. A Drakeford lived each day knowing that it brought them closer to an unspeakable fate. How Maggie must dread each morning, not knowing what fresh horror might await her.

It was a curious thing. Before last week, he'd never given time much thought. He'd had oceans of the stuff, a bottomless supply. But that was coming to an end. His life was measured in grains now, and every minute another tumbled down the hourglass.

Speaking of which, where was it? The last time he had seen it was when he had woken from his nonconsensual nap to find himself caged in what was obviously a torture chamber. Scanning the room, he'd spotted the hourglass on a stretching rack, along with the Drakeford Curse file and their luggage. In the dungeon's dimness, its glow had pulsed like an evil heartbeat.

Goddamn. What Laszlo wouldn't give for another week.

Another week and a different outfit. Flowery kimonos had never been his thing.

Still, he wasn't about to complain. He recalled too well how the Signora had flexed her hand and forced the crow cage tight around him. Their hostess was terrifying, but for all her scorn, Laszlo could tell she found him amusing. That was all the opening he needed.

He tried to keep his eyes on that magnificent caboose as the Signora climbed the steps above him. Unfortunately, the twins were in the way. They were creepy, like the girls who kept popping up in *The Shining*. Three times Laszlo had tried to make it through the movie, but he always bailed at the lady in the bathtub. Ghosts were the worst. Even ones in makeup.

When they reached the tower's third story, the Signora stopped to unlock an iron-bound door. Standing on tiptoe, the twins kissed their mistress on each cheek and scampered over the threshold. Laszlo glimpsed a cobbled lane shaded by windblown cypress trees; it led toward a castle on a promontory. He tried to see more, but the Signora closed the door and relocked it.

Laszlo looked back at Maggie to gauge whether he was hallucinating. Her stunned expression assured him he was not. The twins had indeed skipped off into Brigadoon.

"So," he said. "Do we get to ask questions?"

"No," said the Signora, and continued up the tower's stairs.

And those stairs were getting broader. The higher they climbed, the larger the tower seemed to become. At the beginning, they'd had to ascend in single file. By the fourth story, the four of them could climb side by side. And it wasn't just the width of the staircase that grew with each floor; the number of steps was increasing as well. No more than twenty had separated the first and second stories. No less than one hundred separated the top floors, and each was broad as a church pew.

Laszlo was a wheezing puddle as they climbed this final flight. The Signora was not. Neither were those cardio freaks, the Drakefords. It was beyond irritating. He wondered if he could sue his health club for fraud. Laszlo adored frivolous lawsuits.

Thoughts of lawsuits vanished as they reached the very top of the tower.

The space was shaped like an enormous hexagon, topped by a glass dome whose curving sides met at a point hundreds of feet above the marble floor. Each side of the hexagon held a separate landscape. Laszlo had seen his share of big places—Hell teemed with McMansions—but this was on a different level entirely. Not even his father's palace could claim to have more than one sky above it.

For the first time in recent memory, Laszlo was in awe.

The six separate and distinctive skies were partitioned by ribs that converged at the dome's apex. Laszlo turned slowly and took them in: a twinkling nightscape, a rose-gold dawn, an overcast afternoon, a winter sky aswirl with snow, and another where rain was drumming on the glass. The final sky was a dull and lifeless red, the color of oxidizing blood.

Laszlo gazed at this one the longest before he noticed the Signora Bellascura looking at him.

"Do you miss it?" she said.

Laszlo smirked. "Nope. I've always found Earth more appealing. I'm a sucker for variety." He gestured at his phone in her hand. "By the way, any chance I can have that back?"

Instead of giving it to Laszlo, the Signora handed it to Maggie. "I am entrusting this to you, my dear. Do not return it to him until I give permission."

"Yes, Signora Bellascura."

Laszlo glowered at Maggie. "Well, well. I never pegged you as a kiss-ass."

She simply slipped the phone into the inner pocket of her blazer. At the same time, Lump raised his hand to ask a question.

The Signora looked him over. "You are not at school, boy."

"Sorry," he said. "I was just curious if we'd get a chance to go in there."

He indicated one of the six huge doors, each for a side of the hexagon. They were as different as the skies they led to, and each bore a unique symbol at the center. When Laszlo found he couldn't recognize a single one, he added *get library card* to his mental to-do list. He'd never follow through, of course, but the idea that he *intended to* educate himself on mystic symbols had to count for something.

The door Lump was interested in was positioned beneath the dawn sky and looked to be made of smoked glass stamped with a silver seal.

"No," she replied. "We will not go through that one. Not today. But should fate lead you back to me, I promise you will pass every threshold."

Laszlo gave the boy a nudge and nodded toward the door beneath the dead red sky. It was made of iron and had a seven-pointed star engraved upon it. "I'd skip that one."

The boy gave it an unsettled glance.

The Signora led them to the door located beneath the gray and overcast sky. It stood over twelve feet tall and was wrought of hammered bronze. The elaborate seal at its center was encircled by a serpent biting its own tail.

As they stopped before it, Laszlo craned his neck once more to gawk at the six contrasting skies. "I've got to ask. Is this some kind of trick?"

The Signora turned to him. "I do not understand the question."

Laszlo gestured up at the dome. "How are you doing this? Are these skies just fancy screen savers, or do these doors actually lead there? Because if they do . . . damn!"

The demon's voice was pure ice. "Let me make something very clear, Laszlo Zebul. You will never speak of this tower or its contents to anyone. This tower does not exist."

Laszlo made a courtly bow. "Signora, you have my word."

The demoness fairly cackled. "You think your *word* is good enough for me?"

She beckoned him closer. After a moment's hesitation, he obliged and stood warily as the Signora murmured a spell in the same tongue his father used on high holidays. Few of the ancient words made sense to him; it was like speaking Old English to a modern Londoner.

Then the tip of the Signora's forefinger began to glow like the lure of an anglerfish. Laszlo was tempted to make an *E. T.* joke but managed to hold his fire. The Signora didn't strike him as a Spielberg fan, and pop culture references never landed with the Drakefords. Those two hadn't seen shit.

Leaning forward, the Signora tapped her glowing finger against Laszlo's forehead and throat. A pleasant tingling blossomed at each location. In another life, she'd have made a dynamite masseuse.

He tried to keep things breezy. "So what happens if I accidentally let something slip?"

The Signora stroked his cheek. "You will not be able to, my love. Should you even *attempt* to speak of this tower, you will be turned into a nightjar and become a permanent resident of my gardens."

"Really? That doesn't sound all that bad."

The Drakefords exchanged significant looks but said nothing when Laszlo pressed them.

The Signora set the spell on Maggie and Lump before turning back to the door. She placed her palm upon its seal. As she did, the golden serpent released its tail and glided inside the seal, whose intricate design appeared to serve as a maze. The snake navigated a complex and unerring path before slithering into a hole that appeared at the maze's center.

Laszlo whistled. "Seriously, who designs this stuff?"

But the Signora's attention remained fixed on the seal. When it began to glow, she gave the door a gentle push, and the massive thing swung inward as easily as a garden gate.

Crossing the threshold, the Signora led Laszlo and the Drakefords down a paneled corridor that opened onto a gallery whose scale dwarfed anything one might find in the Louvre or Smithsonian. It was larger than a football field and enclosed by a vaulted ceiling adorned with frescoes. Gray daylight streamed through immense windows in the far wall, illuminating thousands of paintings and tapestries.

From their elevated vantage some thirty feet above the floor, they could appreciate the staggering volume of treasures on display. The room was less an art gallery than a warehouse, with little paths winding among countless chests and crates stacked in pyramids that nearly reached the ceiling.

There was a muffled thump behind them. Laszlo turned to find that the door had closed. A moment later, the atmosphere within the gallery began to change, as though the entire space had been sealed and pressurized. He thought of asking the Signora what was happening, but their hostess was already descending the staircase down to the gallery floor.

Once there, Laszlo followed her down a path that snaked between bookcases teeming with scrolls and leathery tomes. The floor was cold beneath his bare feet. Everything around them smelled of age and dust and wealth beyond calculation.

Laszlo stopped and did a double take. "Is that *Guernica*?"

The Signora did not break stride. "As you say."

"That can't be the original, can it?" he panted, hurrying after her.

"As you say."

Their hostess led them all the way down to the far wall. Its windows overlooked an old city that straddled a sinuous river spanned by stone bridges. As he scanned the city's squares, streets, and rooftops, Laszlo realized *old* was an understatement. He didn't see a single car, telephone line, or cell tower. The city was like something you'd find on a movie set or at a well-funded Renaissance fair. His gaze went to a formidable-looking fortress across the river. Something about it looked familiar.

"Is that . . . ?"

The Signora Bellascura nodded. "The Castel Sant'Angelo, yes."

Lump pressed his face to a window. "Wait," he said. "Is this *Rome*?"

"Indeed," said the Signora.

Maggie joined her brother at the window. "But we were just there. Where are all the cars? Is this another picture?"

"It can't be," said Lump. "There are people moving."

Laszlo turned to the Signora. "What year is this?"

Shading her eyes, their hostess peered beyond the Castel Sant'Angelo to a distant construction site, where hundreds of workers swarmed like ants over ramps and scaffolding.

"Judging by Saint Peter's, I should say mid-sixteenth century."

Lump nearly swooned. "We're in the *past*?"

The demoness nodded. "Of course. If one wishes to steal from the Signora Bellascura, they cannot simply break into my vault." She scoffed at the very idea. "No, they must enter the proper *place* at the proper *time*. And that, my young friend, is not so easy to do."

"Easy?" said Laszlo in disbelief. "It's impossible. Space-time portals are crazy unstable. Even if you have the power to make one, they only last a few seconds."

The Signora turned on him. "Who told you this?" she demanded. "That ridiculous Hierarchy? I did not take you for a believer."

"I'm not," said Laszlo, flushing a darker shade of blue.

A scornful laugh. "Really? Tell me, Laszlo Zebul, what 'class' of demon are you?"

Laszlo found himself fidgeting. "Uh, I guess . . . I mean, if I had to say . . . maybe something in the vicinity of . . . Class III?"

The Signora's contempt was palpable. "You let them brand you," she sneered. "They tell you what you are, and you accept it? You climb their little ladders? I expected more."

"In my defense, I'm terrible at climbing that ladder," said Laszlo. "With my genes, I should be at least a Class VI or VII."

The Signora snapped her fingers under his nose. "Wake up! A favored slave is still a slave. What happens when you reach 'Class IV,' eh? A few more powers?" She made a face of utter disgust. "Where is your spirit? Can you not see the Hierarchy for what it is? The Lords of Hell have created the very tyranny they rebelled against!"

The demoness waved a hand. At her command, black curtains swept across the wall of windows. Renaissance Rome disappeared and the gallery was plunged into darkness, save for pockets of light from lanterns scattered amid the hoard.

Stalking past Laszlo, the Signora went to a towering structure draped with gray silk. "Nothing is impossible for those with the vision and will to bring it into being."

She pulled at the gray silk. As it pooled upon the floor, a brilliant light filled the gallery, so dazzling that Laszlo had to squint at the enormous object in its midst. The Signora spoke a command, and the radiance dimmed until only a shimmer remained.

Laszlo took in what looked like the base of a massive ebony column. The top had broken off, and only the first twenty feet or so remained. Some force had apparently warped the column, twisting its contours into shapes that muddled its architecture.

He and the Drakefords stared in silence at the bizarre formation looming over the Signora. She might have been Dr. Frankenstein displaying her monster.

Maggie, looking very pale indeed, pointed to the symbols and characters chiseled into its base. Her voice was barely a whisper. "It's another Witchstone."

The Signora gazed up at her colossus. "Mine is prettier."

Laszlo remained skeptical. "They don't feel the same," he said. "Signora, I sensed the Witchstone's presence long before I could see it. I'm not getting the same vibes here."

"Naturally," she replied. "This artifact's power has been channeled to more useful purposes than radiating magic. You say my portals are impossible. This says otherwise." She patted the monument with something like motherly affection.

"So that's one of the Lost Magi?" said Maggie.

"Indeed. You are standing in the exalted presence of the Priestess."

"Priestess?" said Laszlo. "I haven't heard anything about a priestess."

"*The* Priestess," said their hostess pointedly. "Each of the Magi came to be known by an epithet: the Judge, the Wanderer, the Shepherd, the Scholar, the Monk, the Warrior . . . and this is the Priestess. She is beautiful, no?"

Laszlo eyed the tortured form. "Stunning."

"And you said the other is somewhere in Siberia?" said Maggie.

The Signora nodded. "The Wanderer," she said. "I am sure of it."

Laszlo threw up his hands. "Wait. If there are two Lost Magi, and one of them is *here*, and the other one's in Russia, then what the hell is the Witchstone?"

"A mystery," replied the Signora. "Your 'Witchstone' should not exist, my friend. So either it is something else, or we have a second scandal on our hands."

"A second scandal?" said Maggie. "What's the first?"

The demoness's face had an expression of contained excitement. "The War of the Magi!" she exclaimed. When this failed to awe her guests, she sighed and looked to Laszlo. "Does the son of Baal Zebul know anything of their history?"

Laszlo blew out his cheeks. "Just what Dimitri told us. He said they were an order of human sorcerers who angered the Lords of Hell and were hunted down. Five were destroyed; two were never found. The two who vanished became known as the Lost Magi. Everyone wrote them off, except for some kooks who insisted they'd holed up someplace waiting for their followers to revive them. I think that's the gist. Between us, it was *quite* the story."

"Yes," said the Signora. "And the story is true—but conveniently incomplete. For example, do you know who these Magi were? Their identities?"

Laszlo shook his head. "Dimitri just said they were sorcerers who lived in Alexandria? Um . . . why are you looking at me like that? What am I missing?"

"You tell me, Laszlo Zebul. Had you ever heard of these Magi before?"

"No," said Laszlo.

"How curious," said the Signora. "An order of human sorcerers who commanded such power they were a threat to all demonkind, yet younger generations have never heard of them. Why does no one speak of this war? Why is it a secret?"

Laszlo shrugged. "Who knows? Maybe the Magi made the Lords look bad. They don't take kindly to that—believe me, I have personal experience."

"You are not far from the truth," said the Signora gravely. "What if I told you that the Magi were *not* human sorcerers? What if I told you they were *demons* who had rejected Hell and allied themselves with mankind?"

"But why would they do that? I mean, humans are our bread and butter." He shot an awkward glance at the Drakefords. "No offense."

"None taken," said Lump.

Maggie was silent.

The Signora took a step toward him. "They rejected Hell and the Hierarchy because it was their *choice* to do so. And that is the point! The Magi were old and powerful spirits. They had taken part in the Great Rebellion. Any one of them could have claimed a seat among the aristocracy, yet they did not. They rejected any law dictating how demons must live and whom they must serve. The Magi served no master other than the desire for knowledge—and it pleased them to share their knowledge with those capable of absorbing it. A school was founded in Alexandria, and the Magi accumulated followers. The Lords of Hell were furious. The Magi's defiance undermined their authority. And that was not all. The Magi were sharing forbidden knowledge with mortals—knowledge that the Lords of Hell preferred to keep for themselves."

"They sound like Prometheus," said Lump. "That Titan who stole fire from the gods and gave it to mankind."

"Yes," said the Signora. "But the Magi are no myth, my boy. They existed. And they had become a problem Hell could no longer overlook. The Lords united and declared war upon the Magi." The demoness gazed

up at the looming monolith over them. "Leviathan devoured the War-
rior in the Red Sea. Lilith and her harpies slew the Judge. Mammon and
Belphegor tore the Scholar to pieces, while Belial's hounds tracked the
Shepherd into the Astral Plane and dragged him back to face judgment."

"That's only four," said Maggie. "What happened to the fifth?"

"Ah," said the Signora. "And here we come to it. The final Magus that
the Lords managed to hunt down was the Monk. He died alone, slain by
an ambitious demon eager to claim a seat upon the High Council. According to legend, this demon pursued the Monk into the Sahara, where they
battled among the dunes. So fierce was their struggle, the sands melted to
glass and great chasms split the earth. The battle lasted far into the night,
but at last the Monk was broken and his ashes scattered on the wind.

"The victor returned to Hell, where the nobles hailed his conquest,
for the Monk was deemed among the strongest of the Magi, and to vanquish him in single combat was a worthy feat. Lucifer had no choice but
to reward this demon, for he had powerful allies among the Daemadùna—
the nobility—and many blamed Lucifer for ignoring the Magi for so long.

"The demon who slew the Monk was given lands and titles and the
greatest prize of all: a seat upon the Council. But in exchange for this
generosity, it was agreed that the War of the Magi would be forgotten.
No one speaks of it, lest they incur Lucifer's wrath."

Laszlo shifted uneasily. The tale was a hoot and all, but a few of the
details were making him more than a little uncomfortable.

Maggie gave voice to Laszlo's thoughts. "Forgive me, Signora. Are
you saying this demon made it all up? That our Witchstone is actually
the Magus he claimed to have destroyed?"

"Let us weigh the evidence," said the Signora. "The Priestess is before
you, and the Wanderer lies far to the east. Of this, I have no doubt. Of
all the Magi to be hunted down, only the Monk's death had no witnesses. On this basis alone, it would make him the most likely candidate
for your Witchstone. And then there is the identity of the demon who
claims to have slain him. For me, this removes all doubt."

"And who was this demon?" asked Maggie Drakeford.

The Signora smiled. "His Infernal Grace Baal Zebul."

CHAPTER 25
COLLATERAL

The Signora's proclamation was met with silence.

Laszlo had guessed the truth when she mentioned the titles heaped upon the demon who claimed to have slain the Monk. Now, two thousand years later, Baal Zebul was a *Grand* Duke—not merely one of the Seven Lords of Hell but the closest thing Lucifer had to a rival.

At first, the revelation made Laszlo want to curl up on the ottoman in this time-hopping vault on the cusp of the Renaissance. He felt so tired and empty he could easily have slept for a week. A year. An age.

But another part of Laszlo's mind, a darker corner of his psyche, was fixating on something else. For the first time in his existence, he wanted revenge.

Vengeance had never been Laszlo's thing. It came with too much baggage. Over the centuries, he'd seen it devour humans and demons alike; too often, it became an insatiable obsession. Why waste time on something that got in the way of more pleasurable pursuits?

But the feeling Laszlo was experiencing went far beyond humiliation.

Pieces were gradually clicking into place—pieces that cast the last hundred years in a profoundly different light. It was no accident that Laszlo had ended up as a Curse Keeper. Dimitri's intuition had been correct: Bazilius had been an overachiever, too curious and diligent. He had uncovered something amiss about the Drakeford Curse, something that was meant to remain hidden. That discovery led to his death, but only after he'd been forced to surrender the ritus whose instructions provided the Drakefords a chance—however slim—of breaking the spell and exposing Baal's dirty little secret.

Laszlo's father wasn't one to leave things to chance. Once Bazilius was gone, he'd used his influence to install the most incompetent replacement imaginable—a Keeper certain to shirk his duties, neglect his Curse Bearers, and allow the Witchstone to gather moss in the Catskills. What better candidate than his disappointing son? The realization that he had been his father's patsy whipped Laszlo's fury into a silent inferno.

"So your *father* is behind all of this?" His head cleared, and he saw Maggie looking at him with anger and a tiny bit of grudging sympathy.

He tried to muster a smile. "It certainly looks that way, doesn't it?"

"Laszlo, I'm sorry." This came from Lump, and the boy actually sounded like he meant it. He came over and sat on the ottoman. "Did you have any idea?"

The demon shook his head. "I wish I could say I was in on the joke. But no. I had no idea what the Witchstone was—much less that I was my father's handpicked stooge." He almost laughed. "Do you know what they say about poker?"

Lump did not.

"The saying goes: if you've been at the table for thirty minutes and can't spot the sucker, then the sucker is you. Well, I've been at the table for a hundred years and never had a goddamn clue. They'll need a new term for someone like me. How does 'überdupe' sound? Too German?"

Even the Signora seemed to take pity on him. "I know your father, boy. You are not the first to be taken in by him. All of Hell believed he slew the Monk. And unless I am mistaken, Lord Baal believed it too."

Maggie looked up from whatever private thoughts had been keeping her occupied. "Why do you say that?"

The Signora shrugged. "Only one who believed he had slain the Monk would claim to have done so. The alternative is too risky; if the Monk turns up, the lie falls apart. No, given your tale, I am confident

Baal only learned of the Monk's survival fairly recently—almost certainly in the last few centuries. If he had discovered it earlier, he would have destroyed your 'Witchstone' and kept his secret safe. If that proved impossible, he would have hidden the stone where no one could ever find it."

"Then why didn't he?" asked Maggie.

"Your curse, girl. The instant it was invoked, the Witchstone became a Curse Object. And once that happened, Baal could not touch it. It was beyond his influence."

"But why is that, if he's so powerful?"

"The scope of a curse's magic is very narrow," the Signora replied. "But within that scope, its power is absolute. For all his strength, Baal cannot break your family's curse or destroy the Witchstone at its center. I do not believe he could even lay a finger on it if he wished to cause it harm. No. His only option would be to ensure that the Monk remained trapped in the Witchstone, unlooked for and forgotten. To do that, he must prevent your curse from being broken."

Inside Laszlo, the past and present were reconfiguring themselves. He was so disturbed and preoccupied that he only noticed Maggie when she was standing mere inches away.

All sympathy was gone. Instead, her expression had darkened, and her voice simmered with rapidly escalating rage. "So do I have this right?" she seethed. "Your father's been the one sabotaging my family? He's the one who murdered Bazilius and stole the ritus? And I'll bet anything he's the reason we lost Ambrose's records in that fire. It's all a big joke to him, isn't it? Even if we get our hands on all the things we need, we don't have a clue what rites to perform. *The Drakeford Curse can't be broken!* And it's all because of your *fucking father?*"

For an instant, Laszlo thought she might hit him. What was more, he had a peculiar hunch that if she did, the blow might be fatal. He had to admit that, ever since the Signora suggested the Drakefords might have powers of their own, he had found himself growing wary of them. Lump had managed to kick ass with a pair of spelltubes. Maggie was far more formidable. She had seen and experienced things that Lump had not, and this told in every aspect of her being. Furthermore, she had also absorbed eight more years of the Witchstone's energy. Who knew what she would be capable of if that power was harnessed and developed? Laszlo understood now why the Signora was so interested in Maggie Drakeford.

The revelation made him afraid, and just a tiny bit jealous.

Laszlo held out his hands in a plaintive gesture. "Maggie, I didn't know."

"Well, you should have," she shouted. "You're a *fucking idiot!*"

There was nothing the demon could say in his defense, so he folded his blue hands in his lap and settled in for a thorough tongue-lashing.

Fortunately, the Signora spoke up before Maggie could build a head of steam. "I have a proposal."

Laszlo and the Drakefords looked expectantly to the demoness, who was now lounging on a settee near the Priestess. She might have been a cat conversing with three juicy mice. "You came here because you need something magical," she said. "An item to meet the requirements of your curse's materia."

"Yes, Signora," said Maggie.

"What are the rest of these requirements?"

Maggie recited the remaining materia from memory. The Signora listened attentively and gave a slight nod when she had finished.

"Very well," she said. "I can provide an item that will meet your needs. I can also provide instructions on how to combine the materia to remove the Witchstone's remaining enchantments. I suspect these directions will be an adequate replacement for the missing ritus."

"How can you know that?"

"Because your curse's materia uses the same ingredients that were required to resuscitate the Priestess."

The look on Maggie Drakeford's face was one of pure astonishment. "I'm sorry. Are you saying you have another copy of the ritus? You actually know what we have to do?"

The Signora considered a moment. "This 'witch' wanted your ancestor to complete her task, yes?"

Maggie nodded. "It's the whole reason for the curse."

Their hostess turned to consider the monument behind her. "Well then. It sounds as though she had already unraveled the first six layers of enchantment and was interrupted before she could complete the seventh. I have in my possession an exact copy of the directives the Priestess entrusted to her acolytes. It took us a thousand years to decrypt them, but what else are imps for?"

Laszlo sat very still, careful not to betray his excitement. It had never occurred to him that they could actually get their hands on the ritus.

After they'd left Dimitri's—the instant the Drakefords entered that ice cream shop—Laszlo had phoned an associate of his, a master forger who lived in Brooklyn. Ansel might have screwed up the Monet Laszlo had tried to sell to Dimitri, but he possessed stores of vellum, parchment, and paper stock that went back hundreds of years. His craft required it. And the "Monet incident" meant that he owed Laszlo a favor.

In fact, Ansel was, at that very moment, preparing a false ritus that would be delivered to Clarence within the next twenty-four hours. Wouldn't the Drakefords be delighted when Clarence, who they already knew was assisting Laszlo, called to report that he'd "discovered" a copy of the ritus in the Society archives? Their hope would soar off the charts.

Now, all of that was beside the point. A real ritus was available—or something just as good.

Laszlo had a trickster's brain, and it had just received information that unlocked new and greater possibilities. Fresh calculations were required, of course, but the demon thought he spied a path through the treacherous wood before him. A narrow path. A dangerous path. But when did he ever shy from a little risk?

He was watching Maggie closely. While the Signora spoke, the girl had raised her arms like a hopeful fan following a game-winning shot at the buzzer. The excitement, the anticipation. Her entire face came alive.

Such a different person from the almost naked girl he'd found in the nightclub bathroom, frightened, shaking, and confused. And Laszlo had come to the rescue. He had fixed things and whisked her away. He recalled the look in her eyes on their elevator ride, as she gazed at his reflection in the mirrored doors. Lonely. Grateful.

Against her better judgment, Maggie Drakeford wanted to trust him.

Her salvation required it.

It took all of Laszlo's self-control not to smile. *My oh my, how the game has changed . . .*

In the here and now, Maggie let out a gasp. "You've got the rites and you'll let us have them?"

A slow smile bloomed on the Signora Bellascura's face. "That is not how I operate, my dear. In exchange for my assistance, you will summon me when you attempt to break the curse. Once you have completed your ceremony, the Witchstone and its contents belong to me."

Maggie did not even hesitate. "Done. How do we summon you?"

The Signora gestured that she approach. Once she did, the demoness removed a jade ring from her hand and slid it on Maggie's finger. "Say my name, and I will come to you."

Maggie rubbed her thumb against the ring. "And then we're even?"

"No," said the Signora coolly. "If you succeed in breaking your family's curse, I shall require a favor."

Maggie hesitated. "What kind of favor?"

"Its nature will be decided at a future date."

The statement snapped Laszlo into the present. "Maggie," he said. "Be careful. Only a fool agrees to an open-ended contract—"

The Signora whirled upon him. "Do *not* meddle in my affairs!"

Even Maggie seemed to chafe at Laszlo's advice. "I'm not a child. I can make my own decisions." She met the Signora's eyes. "I'll agree so long as the favor only involves me—and does *not* involve my soul."

"Done."

Laszlo swore inwardly. The Signora's response had come too quickly for comfort; she already had something in mind.

"And now," said their hostess, "we come to the matter of collateral."

"Collateral?" said Maggie. "I don't understand."

Laszlo smiled grimly. "The Signora needs a guarantee that you'll summon her, as promised."

Their hostess nodded. "Precisely. And since neither the girl nor her brother will stake their souls, someone else must supply the collateral." She looked at him expectantly.

Laszlo squirmed under that formidable gaze. "What do you want from me?"

The Signora held out her hand. "Your *sarkyra*, my love."

He stared. "That's a joke, right?"

Maggie looked from one to the other. "I don't understand. What's a sarkyra?"

"The closest thing I have to a heart," Laszlo explained. "It anchors my spirit in this body. Signora—I can't give up my sarkyra. It would kill me!"

"Not immediately," she replied unconcernedly. "You have several days to break the curse, yes?"

"Until Thursday." Laszlo glanced at the eager Drakefords. He wondered if they had any idea that he was the only one on the clock.

"Then you have nothing to fear," the Signora assured him. "I have seen demons last a week without their sarkyras." *Not Class IIIs*, Laszlo thought. "When Margaret summons me, I will return it to you. Do we have a bargain?"

Laszlo's mind raced as he felt the watchful eyes of Maggie and Lump. Without the Signora's instructions, they had no chance whatsoever to break the curse. And without that possibility—or the siblings' belief in that possibility—Laszlo's master plan would be for naught.

But his sarkyra!

Laszlo was vain in many ways, but he did not overestimate his strength. Without his sarkyra, he wasn't certain he'd make it out of Rome, much less cling to life until Thursday.

Maggie's voice was iron. "You owe us this."

Closing his eyes, the demon nodded in reluctant agreement. "Okay," he said. "You have a deal. But first, we'll need to see the item and the instructions for the Priestess."

"Of course," said the Signora. The demoness snapped her fingers, and an inlaid box flew to her hand from beneath a Caravaggio. Setting the box on her lap, she raised its lid to reveal a pair of silken slippers with padded soles.

Maggie peered at them with interest. "What are these?"

The Signora dangled one between her fingers. "You have heard of seven-league boots?"

"Of course," said Lump. "From folktales. When you put them on, every step takes you twenty-one miles. Are those really seven-league boots?"

She laughed. "Of course not! Such boots are far too valuable to throw away on a curse. No, these were fashioned long ago as prototypes. Essays before the novel, yes? Their makers called them 'seven-rod slippers.'"

"What's a rod?" wondered Maggie.

Lump's reply was automatic. "Five and a half yards."

"How the hell do you know that?"

Laszlo reminded Maggie that Lump had rattled off the population of Liechtenstein.

"Why wouldn't I know it?" said Lump indignantly. "Our atlas has a whole list of archaic measurements. They're right there in black and white!"

Maggie examined the slippers. "So every step takes you almost forty yards," she said to herself, before looking up at the Signora. "Can I try them out to be sure they work?"

Their hostess nodded approvingly. "One should always test the merchandise."

Laszlo chewed his lip. He couldn't interfere, of course—the Signora would feed him his own tongue—but Maggie's arrangement was giving him an ulcer. Nothing in Heaven, Hell, or Earth was more expensive than a favor to be named later. He objected on sheer principle.

He watched uneasily as Maggie removed her shoes and pulled the slippers over her socks. Careful not to lift either foot, she pivoted ninety degrees to face an open stretch of floor that ran parallel to the windows; then, with two quick breaths, she put one foot in front of the other.

She vanished and reappeared almost instantly beside a statue of Heracles. Spinning on her heel, Maggie turned back to face them, her delight visible from precisely one hundred and fifteen feet away. She took a step toward them and reappeared beside an astonished Lump. Despite everything, Laszlo found himself smiling. Her joy was contagious.

"I guess they work!" She bent down to remove the slippers, ignoring Lump's demands that he get a turn. "And they'll qualify as materia?"

"Of course. I want your curse broken as much as you do."

"Oh, I doubt that," said Maggie with a smile, and returned the box to the Signora.

The demoness chuckled. "Don't be so certain, my dear." She patted the monument that loomed above them all. "My Priestess has opened doors I never thought possible. What else will she be capable of when she has the mighty Monk beside her?"

"Wait," Laszlo cut in. "Once the curse is broken, won't the Witchstone be destroyed? Wasn't the whole point of the witch's spell to bust him out of there?"

The Signora Bellascura's face was serene. "Let me worry about these details."

Lump cleared his throat. "Um . . . we still need a holy relic."

This was dismissed out of hand. "I do not traffic in such things. But," she added with a wink, "I will say that you could not have come to a better city. Use your ingenuity, my boy. Or your new toy." She handed over the box containing the seven-rod slippers; Lump clutched it to his chest.

Then the Signora turned to Maggie. A scroll materialized in the woman's open hand, along with a necklace. "Here are the instructions for removing the final enchantments upon your Witchstone. I cannot guarantee they are identical to your curse's ritus, but let us say I am optimistic."

Maggie took them in her hands and inclined her head in gratitude. "Thank you. And the necklace?"

"A gift, Margaret. Loyalty and courage should be rewarded, and you have demonstrated poise under difficult circumstances. It gives me pleasure to meet a young woman with such qualities. If you succeed in breaking your curse, perhaps you will find it useful."

Laszlo could have sworn Maggie blushed. She slipped the necklace over her head.

To his eye, it wasn't much to look at: a silver chain whose tarnished pendant exhibited a woman's profile. Still, it was always nice to get a freebie.

The demoness gave the girl a pointed look. "When the time comes, you will call for me."

"I will, Signora. I promise."

"Good." Those catlike eyes flicked to Laszlo. "And now for the collateral."

Laszlo nodded queasily. He assured himself it was just a temporary inconvenience, a necessary step in his master plan. He told himself many things, but none changed the fact that he was breaking out in a sweat. Other demons might have done without their sarkyras for a few days, but they were probably of greater rank and power. Could a Class III even survive the process?

Rising from the ottoman, Laszlo beckoned for Lump and placed a hand on the boy's shoulder to steady himself. With his other hand, the demon loosened his ridiculous kimono.

Maggie and the Signora watched in an expectant silence, their expressions inscrutable. Laszlo winked. "Here's looking at you, kids."

Focusing his will, Laszlo reached within his body. He was a spirit, after all—his flesh was simply borrowed matter to give him earthly substance. His hand parted skin and muscle, cartilage and bone, to take hold of the sarkyra inside his rib cage.

He shuddered as his fingers made contact—the sarkyra was egg size, with a pitted, metallic texture—and positively groaned when he felt it pulse within his grasp.

Laszlo's knees gave out, and he sagged heavily against Lump. The boy tried to brace him upright, but the best he could manage was to ease the demon onto the ottoman.

Once seated, Laszlo's mind cleared somewhat, and he hunched forward, gathering himself for what was coming.

The room was silent.

The extraction was worse than anything he could have imagined. The initial pain was sharper than a stitch and kept ratcheting up. Each escalation recalled various traumas he'd experienced: everything from a recent beak to the groin to an unplanned rectal aboard a faulty carousel. And it wasn't just physical pain. The experience also included pangs of inconsolable malaise, ennui, and other angsty French terms. It was like reading Camus.

The sarkyra did not want to come out. It resisted his initial, feeble attempts and only began to shift when Laszlo gave a forceful yank accompanied by an involuntary scream. But it slipped free at last.

Now, cradled in his hand, it was like a small, pulsing meteorite whose fissures gleamed with blue fire. He looked down to watch his chest close up, flesh and bone knitting together, leaving a scar of the sort one saw on boastful cardiac patients.

Mopping his brow, Laszlo took an unsteady breath and held his sarkyra up to the Signora.

She plucked the object from his palm. The instant her fingers made contact, Laszlo began writhing on the ottoman and slid to the floor. *The pain!* He might have been hooked to jumper cables.

His seizure stopped the instant the Signora placed his sarkyra in a jewel box. Clammy and trembling, Laszlo crawled back to the ottoman and clung to it as though it were a life raft.

Lump tried in vain to help him up.

Laszlo waved him away. "I'm okay . . . Just give me a minute."

The Signora stroked the box in her lap. "Thank you, Laszlo Zebul." She surveyed the three of them. "I believe that concludes our business."

"Not yet," he panted. "I have a request of my own."

She cocked her head. "Is that so? And what is this request, young Zebul?"

Laszlo turned away from the Drakefords. "It's personal, Signora. For your ears only."

Maggie, who had been looking both grateful and concerned for Laszlo's health, snapped out of it. "No," she said firmly. "Signora, I have a right to hear anything he says."

Laszlo's laughter came out in hoarse gasps. He honestly didn't know where he found the strength. "My heart's in a *box*, and you still don't trust me?"

Her face softened. For a moment, she looked hesitant and conflicted.

"My request doesn't have anything to do with either of you," he rasped, pressing his advantage. "It's for *me*. Something *I* need. Something the Signora can provide."

"Do you swear?" said Maggie anxiously.

Spittle flew as Laszlo lost his temper. "Are you serious?" he managed to hiss. "Not everything is about poor Maggie Drakeford!"

The blood drained from her face. For an instant, he was afraid that he'd overplayed his hand—but Maggie mastered herself and merely nodded to him before leading Lump up the path toward the gallery entrance.

When they'd gone, a bone-weary Laszlo managed to haul himself up so that his back was against the ottoman. The Signora gazed down at him; the Priestess towered behind her.

Her rich voice almost sounded amused. "And what is it you want from me?"

Laszlo told her. And then he told her why.

When he'd finished, the Signora appraised him a moment before kneeling to smooth the damp hair from his forehead. Her exquisite face hovered inches from his own.

"I misjudged you, Laszlo Zebul."

He almost managed a smile. "How's that?"

The Signora nodded. "There is more to you than I suspected. You are very much your father's son. Should you survive, I will be in touch. My organization could use you."

Laszlo cleared his throat. "And my request?"

She kissed him lightly on the lips, leaving behind a smell of jasmine. "Granted," she whispered. "With pleasure."

CHAPTER 26
THE HOTEL AUGUSTUS

Maggie, Lump, and Laszlo were summarily returned to Rome the same way they had left it. Only when the car finally came to a stop were they allowed to remove their hoods. The limousine this time, Laszlo informed them, was a Bentley; their escort, a plump, grandmotherly woman who somehow exuded such an air of menace that Maggie was even more frightened than she had been of the ebony-skinned man.

As their escort removed their luggage from the Bentley's trunk, Maggie touched the weathered pendant around her neck. She was proud to have earned it—proud that she'd held her own, proud that she'd kept herself and Lump alive. They'd departed the Signora's with everything they'd come for, and more besides.

But it hadn't come cheap.

She had quickly agreed to the Signora's terms; given the state of Maggie's eye and the pain throughout her arm, she was willing to pay almost any price. The ride had given her ample time to turn over the possibilities. What would be demanded of her, and when?

As she so often did, Maggie compartmentalized.

The deal had been struck. Now they were here, at the Piazza Navona. There was no point in second-guessing herself. The more pressing concern was Laszlo's health.

Their Curse Keeper was a mess. His condition had been in steady decline ever since he'd removed his sarkyra. When they'd left the Signora's tower, his demonic form had been looking rather sickly. His human guise was even worse: sallow skin, glazed eyes, and a patina of sweat that he mopped continually with a pocket square. Grumbling, he took his time walking away from the Bentley and, as soon as he could, claimed a table at a café where patrons were enjoying the morning sunshine.

Laszlo eyed the waiter suspiciously before ordering in Italian; then he shooed the man away as though his continued presence was intolerable. Donning sunglasses, the demon slouched low in his chair and raised his waxy face toward the sun.

Maggie took a seat beside him. "You don't look so great. Maybe a table in the shade would be better."

"And maybe *you* should boil your head."

"You don't have to be grouchy."

Laszlo's voice became a shriller version of her own. "'You don't have to be grouchy.'"

"Fine," said Maggie. "Be a jackass."

"Lump," the demon croaked, "could you straighten my sunglasses? I'd do it myself, but I'm feeling somewhat wobbly after my selfless act of heroism."

Lump adjusted the glasses half a centimeter.

Laszlo tried to pat his arm but missed entirely. "You're a good egg. I'll never forget your clumsy attempts to steady me after I literally wrenched my heart out for you children."

"I'm not a child," snapped Maggie.

The demon sniffed. "Compared to me, you're a babe in diapers. A puling papoose. The merest stripling."

"Isn't a stripling a boy?"

"Oh, I see. So a girl *can't* be a stripling? And I took you for a feminist. By the way, I ordered pastries for the table, and you haven't even thanked me."

Maggie checked her temper. "I didn't know. That was very nice."

"Too late."

Lump placed his napkin on his lap. "Thank you, Laszlo."

"You're welcome, dear stripling."

The waiter returned with juices, a French press of coffee, and a basket of sugar-dusted zeppoles. He said something to Laszlo, who merely scowled.

Maggie leaned forward when the man had gone. "You're being rude."

Laszlo merely tilted his head back to bask in the sun.

It was a perfect October day, with a crisp bite in the late-morning air. She took in the piazza, its towering obelisk and misting fountains. *If I ever get the chance*, she thought, *I'm coming back here and taking my time.* There was something about the buildings and light, the way old and new coexisted, that felt more like home than any place she'd been.

"What are you thinking about?" asked Lump, licking powdered sugar from his fingers.

"Androvore's goons," Maggie lied. "I mean, they could be anywhere. Maybe we shouldn't be sitting in the open."

"You're such a worrywart," groused Laszlo. "Why do you think I had them drop us here? This is tourist central, sweet cheeks. It's the last place they'll look. See that fountain over there?" He gestured limply. "That was in *Angels and Demons*."

"I assume that's a movie?"

Laszlo stared like she'd just asked if the Earth was flat. "It's a Dan Brown *thriller*, you backwoods hick. A ripping yarn, rife with errors, but titillating nonetheless. Spoiler alert: Ewan McGregor's the villain."

"Who's he?"

Laszlo squirmed with irritation. "Oh my God. I just can't anymore. Rent the movie, you fucking rube. It's directed by Ron Howard. I assume you know who he is."

Maggie grinned and shook her head.

"Sweet guy, but he curses like a sailor. Can't take him anywhere."

"That's super interesting, but what's the plan?"

The demon shot her a churlish look. "The plan for what?"

"For getting our hands on a holy relic and going back to New York?"

Laszlo waved her away. "Sure, leave the brainwork to me when I'm not even caffeinated. Lump, be a good human and prepare my coffee."

The boy peered at the carafe. "How does it work?"

Laszlo sniffed. "It's a French press. You press it. I'd do it myself, but in my present state my wrist might shatter."

Lump didn't need to be asked twice. He pushed down the plunger and beamed as its fine mesh forced the coffee grounds to the bottom. "Cool."

"Isn't it, though?" said Laszlo. "Next week, we'll cover fire and flint tools. Now, fill that cup and don't be stingy with the cream. And when you've finished, pop a few zeppoles in my mouth." The demon indicated some sugared balls of dough in the basket that resembled doughnut holes. Lump had already had a few.

Maggie let Lump fix Laszlo's coffee because her brother was enjoying himself, but she drew the line at hand-feeding. "Nope," she said. Taking the zeppole, she dropped it on Laszlo's plate.

The demon stared at her. "Someone's true colors are showing. A gal learns she's got a *teensy* bit of magic, and she starts acting like the Queen of Sheba."

Maggie bit into a zeppole herself. "Is that what this is about?" she said, brushing powdered sugar from her lips. "You're jealous?"

"*Jealous?* Of you? *Ha!*"

Maggie poured herself some coffee. "Okay. Let's get it out."

"Get what out?"

"The sulking and self-pity." She added cream and sugar. "And that stupid face you make when you pretend to be having 'deep thoughts.' It doesn't work, by the way. You look like a halibut."

Laszlo took another zeppole. "A halibut should be so lucky. And if I'm upset, it's because I have a right to be. I've been electrocuted, stuffed in a cage, and *then* learned that my father's been using me as his stooge for the past hundred years. Am I missing anything?" He made the halibut face. "Oh yeah! I also handed over my *heart* to a criminal who will probably use it as a bocce ball!"

Maggie adopted a more mollifying tone. "And we do appreciate that. Truly."

But Laszlo was off and running. "Did the Signora give *me* a gift? Some cuff links, or a nice pen? No, she most certainly did not—"

"But she did give you *something*," said Lump. "What did you ask for?"

The demon glared. "Is your name Laszlo Zebul?"

"No."

"Then mind your fucking business."

"Jeez," muttered Lump. "Sorry for asking. Can I try a little coffee?"

"Try absinthe, for all I care."

Before her brother could ask what absinthe was, Maggie poured him a splash of coffee, to which he added enormous quantities of cream and sugar. To no one's surprise, he pronounced it delicious.

"Well, we still need a plan," said Maggie, finishing her own. "And here's your phone, by the way. It's been buzzing all morning." She fished it out of her blazer and handed it to Laszlo, who took one look and promptly thrust it back at her.

"Sixty missed calls. I can't deal."

"Well, what do you want me to do?" said Maggie.

The demon shrugged.

Maggie didn't have much experience with phones, but it seemed intuitive enough. She tapped the button for voicemail and held the thing to her ear. The messages began in a shaky whisper and got progressively louder.

"Laszlo. It's YKW—You-Know-Who. Give me a ring-a-ding."

"Hey, big fella, it's your wingman. Call me for the 411."

"*Comandante*. It's your *mejor amigo*. Where are you?"

"Laszlo, it's me, from the place Anita says I shouldn't mention. Listen, I overheard a certain someone with a flaming head tell Flagella in Accounting that 'the target is in Rome' and they should 'prepare to make final payment.' I think he was talking about the A-S-S—"

"Sorry! Got cut off. Continuing previous message: A-S-S—"

". . . I hate AT&T. Continuing: I-N. Got that? I repeat: A-S-S—"

"Forget it! I hate this pho—"

"Laszlo! Call me! I'm so worried I'm getting hives!"

The messages weren't all from Clarence. There was one from

"Michelle in Saratoga," another from "Phoebe from that underground thing in Tribeca," and a third from someone named Serge who said Laszlo owed him six hundred bucks for gas, tolls, and getting his cab out of the impound lot. Maggie reported this while Laszlo sipped coffee and popped zeppoles in his mouth.

"Is that all?" he asked glumly.

She looked at the screen. "No. There are six more voicemails from Clarence, along with one hundred ninety-two texts."

Laszlo waved the phone away. "Just stow it."

"Are you sure? Clarence sounded kind of hysterical."

"Clarence always sounds hysterical."

"Okay." She slid it into her blazer pocket. "But how are we going to get a relic? I mean, what's the definition of a relic, anyway?"

Laszlo shrugged. "A holy artifact. Usually from a saint. You know, the Toe of Saint Wilbur or something like that. The holiest of holies, and all that jazz."

"So it's something we'll probably find in a church," said Maggie. "What about the Vatican? Won't they have lots of relics?"

The demon laughed and promptly grimaced in pain. "Are you nuts? Security at the Vatican's insane."

"Well, what do you have in mind?"

Laszlo fanned himself with a napkin. Overdramatic or not, he really wasn't looking well. "Did we rip a tiara off a queen's head? No. We hunted down a long-lost crown in Liechtenstein." He inspected the remaining zeppoles. "That's what we need. Nothing fancy or high profile—just something to check the box."

Lump weighed in. "Would the internet have a list of relics?"

"No idea," said Laszlo. "But I need to lie down, or I'm going to pass out and shit myself. Hopefully in that order."

Maggie leaned in and looked at him. "Are you joking?"

He removed his sunglasses, and she winced. His eyes were completely bloodshot, and the skin around them was bruised. He looked far worse than when they'd first sat down.

"Okay," she said, going into crisis mode. "Let's figure something out."

Standing, she scanned the piazza for a hotel and spotted one just a hundred yards away. She told Lump to get the bill while she checked to see if there were any rooms available. There were not, but the hotel did direct Maggie to a nearby establishment on a side street off the piazza.

She sprinted there and explained, as best she could, to the woman at the desk that they needed a room so her uncle could lie down. They'd checked out of their hotel that morning, but now he was feeling sick. No, no—they didn't need a doctor. He had diabetes, this had happened before, he just needed to rest. If the hotel had a room available—*anything*—she would be so grateful. The woman shrugged and allowed that they might have a room, but it had not yet been cleaned. No problem, said Maggie—that would be perfect.

Hurrying back to the café, Maggie found Lump anxiously hovering over Laszlo, who had sunk so low in his chair that he was practically sliding off the edge. People at nearby tables were watching with curiosity and concern.

"It's fine," Maggie announced to the café at large. "He's diabetic. Just needs to lie down." Taking Laszlo's wallet, she removed a hundred-euro bill and plunked it on the table before heaving the demon to his feet. "Lump, grab his phone and the bags."

The three made quite the spectacle as they left the Piazza Navona.

The woman at the hotel looked dubiously at Laszlo when they struggled through the door, and asked again if they needed a doctor. Maggie shook her head, shoved money across the desk, and promised to be out by this evening. After pocketing the cash, the woman handed Maggie a key to a room on the second floor.

It was both small and a complete mess: bed unmade, water on the bathroom floor, empty wine bottles cluttering the dresser and bedside table. Maggie simply shook out the bedspread, flung it over the sheets, and helped Laszlo out of his jacket and shoes.

Within minutes, the Curse Keeper was unconscious, his breath slow and labored while perspiration beaded on his feverish skin.

Maggie soaked hand towels in cool water and draped them over Laszlo's forehead and neck. The demon was so delirious that his disguise was slipping; he was a shifting hybrid of his human and demonic selves. His skin was a patchy blue and his teeth had sharpened to points.

The Drakefords observed in somber silence.

"What should we do now?" said Lump anxiously.

"Let him rest. Meanwhile, help me repack. We have to travel lighter."

The two spent fifteen minutes winnowing down the contents of the suitcases to the bare essentials. These they transferred to their backpacks, including the Herzogshut, the seven-rod slippers, the Signora's instructions, and anything that could be used to identify them. Everything else—extra clothes, Maggie's paperbacks, even Lump's beloved travel guide—was tossed back in the suitcases they'd leave behind.

Maggie checked Laszlo's phone. It was almost noon on Tuesday. He'd said they had until Thursday before the hourglass ran out, but that was misleading. According to the Signora's instructions, the rites to remove the Witchstone's enchantments had to be performed between moonrise and midnight. In practical terms, that made Thursday irrelevant; the spell had to be broken Wednesday night. Maggie paused a moment. Was that Wednesday as in *tomorrow*? She pulled up the phone's calendar. There was no escaping it. Not only did the Drakefords have to get back to the Witchstone by tomorrow evening, but they had to do so with all of the curse's materia in their possession.

Maggie steadied her breathing. Whatever happened, she mustn't panic. Panic would sink them. No, the sensible thing to do was sit down and work things out. The bed was taken, but there was a desk with a pad and pen by the room's only window. Perfect.

Using Laszlo's phone, Maggie searched the average flight duration from Rome to New York, then factored in how long they'd spend going through customs, getting a car, and performing all the other little steps that ate up precious minutes. The notepad was soon covered with calculations. The entire trip—from getting to Rome's airport to arriving home in Schemerdaal—would take roughly eighteen hours. Next, she searched for available flights. The results had her swearing under her breath.

"What's wrong?" asked Lump from his spot on the floor.

Maggie looked at the screen in frustration. "Time. Our only chance to complete the ceremony is tomorrow, between moonrise and midnight. We have to leave Rome by two o'clock this morning, or we'll never get there in time."

"Okay. So what's the problem?"

She handed over the phone. "The last flight to New York is at nine thirty tonight. There isn't another until eight tomorrow morning, which is too late. We've got to somehow get a relic and make the nine thirty, or we're finished." She twisted the ring on her finger. "I don't see how we can pull it off."

Lump checked over Maggie's calculations. "Did you include the time change?"

"What?"

"New York's six hours behind Rome."

Maggie nearly smacked her forehead. She was an idiot! She was so anxious that she'd forgotten, and it made all the difference in the world. They could take the first flight tomorrow morning and still make it back in time! Leaning over, she pulled her brother into a ferocious hug. "You're a genius!"

He blushed. "If you say so."

Hope rekindled. They could do this.

After picking their flight, the Drakefords did extensive relic research. Laszlo's phone was a revelation. Yes, they'd used the computers at the Kingston Library, but those were slow-motion dinosaurs in comparison. Maggie couldn't believe how much information was just sitting out there, neatly compiled and organized.

She and Lump pored over databases listing every relic in Rome along with its location. They came up with a few rules: no famous relics, because those locations would probably be overcrowded and crawling with security; no relics that sounded large or cumbersome. Once they had a preliminary list, they looked to see which were closest and, if they could, took virtual tours of the locations.

As they worked, Maggie hummed with adrenaline. She was proud of the swift and systematic way she'd been tackling problems under pressure—replacing a crushed magical porridge pot, making a binding deal involving magic, nursing a heartless demon, tracking down a relic. It felt good to be on point.

She surveyed their list. "What do you think about heads?"

Lump looked up from the phone. "Sorry. Are you talking about *actual* heads?"

"They shrink down over time, don't they? We could probably fit one in a backpack."

Lump looked at her as though she'd lost her mind. "Maggie, you're talking about a person's *head.*"

"Yeah," she barreled on. "A head they're not using anymore."

"But other people *believe* in those heads. Those heads are important to them."

She clicked the pen a few times. "Lump, this isn't the time to get squeamish."

"I'm not squeamish. It's not that. I just don't think it's right to steal something that gives so many people . . . I don't know. Hope."

Maggie scanned the list again. "That's touching," she said absently, "but if stealing a moldy skull means we get Dad back, then I'm stealing a moldy skull. If that's a sin, God can just add it to my tab."

Lump did not reply, which was never a good sign. Maggie saw him studying her from behind those ridiculous glasses. The kid looked like he'd just left a disco.

She raised her eyebrows. "What?"

"I want to break the curse too," he said earnestly. "You're not the only one who wants to save Dad. And it's not just him—I want *you* to get better!"

Maggie grinned. "I know you do. And we're *so* close! You've been amazing, Lump. Truly. I know I didn't want you to come along, but I was wrong. I'm so proud of you."

"Thanks," he replied, but he looked far from pleased. "I guess what I'm trying to say is that *I* want to be proud of me too. And I'm not sure I could be, if I stole something that people turn to and depend on when they're desperate. Even if that something's a skull."

A lovely sentiment, but her patience was fraying. "Lump, I get it. Seriously. And if there was a sweet and cuddly way to do this, I'd be first in line. But there isn't. Remember, the Signora's scroll doesn't say that the materia gets destroyed when we break the spell. For all we know, the relic might be fine! If it is, we'll return it along with an apology, okay? We're just borrowing it."

Lump was still unconvinced. "Yeah, but we're not borrowing this stuff from Walmart. These are *churches*—"

"Oh?" said Maggie sharply. "Is *that* what this is all about? That we're going to rob a church?"

He ducked his head. "Maybe."

She barked a laugh. "And what makes a church so special? We've got one in Schemerdaal. The pastor makes me say I'm low and vile before I enter someone's house. Then he stands aside so I can scurry in and condemn myself to Hell. And you know what I tell myself before I go inside?"

Lump's voice was barely audible. "No."

"'Get in, get out, go home!'" said Maggie. "I say it every time, Lump. It's my good luck charm. You know who taught me to say that?"

Another "no."

"Dad did. Because the one time he didn't 'get in, get out, and go home' fast enough, he caught a stone in the eye and it almost blinded him. When he fell, they just kept throwing stones. And when he didn't come home, Mom and I went looking. We found him in that creek near the turnoff. There was so much blood I thought he was dead."

Her brother's eyes were glistening behind his glasses. "Oh, Maggie. I didn't know."

"And that's okay. You weren't even born! But do me a favor"—and here, her voice hardened—"and take two seconds to consider that you don't know jack shit about what goes on with Reverend Farrow and the village. Mom shields you from all that, and she should. But if you want to get into it, let's get into it." Now her voice was steel. "The church has screwed us over for centuries."

"Not these churches," countered Lump, holding up the phone.

"A cathedral's no different than the dump we've got in Schemerdaal."

"Yes, it is."

"Really?" said Maggie. "So what makes it different? More gold? Higher ceilings? Stained glass? If that stuff matters, Las Vegas is the goddamn Holy Land."

Lump said nothing. A part of Maggie wanted to smack him, to shake some sense into his coddled head.

Instead, she sighed and held up their list. "They're all the same. Every church, big or small. And the people who run 'em? They act like they've got all the answers. And if you don't toe the line or fit the mold, then it's 'Fuck you, sinner. You're gonna burn . . .'"

"I don't like it when you swear." Lump sounded like he might cry.

"I didn't ask you to like it."

There was a groan from the bed. Maggie took a look at Laszlo, who hadn't moved since she'd laid him down: legs splayed, one hand resting on his stomach in a pose not unlike Napoleon. His appearance was fully human again but so wan and corpse-like Maggie prodded him in the ribs. The demon sighed and let out a warbling fart. The room suddenly reeked of rotten eggs. Maybe it was brimstone.

"Charming," Maggie said. "But at least he seems to be improving. Okay, we're set with the flights." She grabbed a fresh bandage and the jar of faerie essence from her backpack. "I'm going to take a shower. You go over the list and circle any relics your conscience might let me steal."

Lump nodded without making eye contact.

The bathroom was cramped, with a tiny toilet, a sink, a shower, and no lock. Maggie wedged a damp towel beneath the door before removing her clothes and bandage. Then she looked in the mirror.

Two more curse marks had appeared. One was under Maggie's left breast, near the bite marks left by that banker. It was already the size of a grape and warm to the touch. The other, larger mark was on her shoulder, teeming with blisters and swarming cilia.

She moved closer to the mirror. Her entire left forearm was scarlet now, pocked with a dozen dime-size craters. A grayish-pink tendril suddenly emerged from one, then retracted with a soft squelching noise.

She felt it moving against the bone, felt others stiffen at its touch, like a nest of proprietary eels. Most sickening of all, their movements were plainly visible to the naked eye—the skin bulged and roiled in a series of constant undulations.

She squeezed her eyes shut.

She compartmentalized.

She forced the nauseating, visceral sensation into the background by focusing on something else. Jason, that guy she'd met at the train station. The paper with his name and number was still in her wallet, which was pointless. She'd throw it away once she'd cleaned up.

In the meantime, she needed to take a shower.

It was a good decision. The water temperature topped out at cool, but that suited Maggie fine. She stood beneath the drizzle, careful to keep her hair dry.

Afterward, she dried off with a damp, threadbare towel, then dressed quickly and applied the new bandage to her arm and some faerie essence to renew the glamour that disguised her snake-slitted eye. There was no need to look in the mirror. She had seen enough for one day.

She came back out to find a nervous Lump sitting at the desk, holding Laszlo's phone as if it were a grenade. The phone started buzzing.

Maggie stowed the jar of faerie essence in her backpack. "Who is it?"

"I don't know," said Lump, "but they keep calling."

"It's probably Clarence." She took the phone and glanced at the number just as the call disconnected. "Yeah, that's him." The phone started buzzing again. Laszlo was still on the bed, semicomatose. "How many times has he called?"

"Seven or eight."

Maggie took the call. "Hello?"

"*Thank God!*" screamed a voice. "Wait . . . who is this?"

"This is Maggie Drakeford, Clarence. I almost feel like I know you."

"*It's a pleasure to meet you, but please get Laszlo!*"

Maggie held up a finger to silence Lump, who was trying to ask a question. "Laszlo can't talk right now. Can I help you?"

"You're in danger!"

Maggie snorted. "What else is new?"

"No!" shrieked the voice. *"You're in danger* right now! *They know where you are!"*

"Is that right," she said dryly. "Where am I, then?"

"The Augustus! Right off the Piazza Navona! It has a two-star rating on Expedia!"

Maggie snatched up the notepad. Two words were printed at the top of each sheet. They were the last two she wanted to see:

She looked through the window. Kathy and Hubby were heading briskly down the cobbled street, scanning the building numbers.

Maggie moved away a fraction too late.

Kathy's head snapped up. The two locked eyes. For a split second, Maggie did not see a middle-aged woman but a hellish face reminiscent of a snarling jackal. The demon darted into the hotel, her companion swift on her heels.

"Get out of there!" yelled Clarence.

Maggie rushed past Lump, shoving the phone in her pocket, and latched the door chain. Downstairs, she heard shouting, a woman yelling in Italian.

Heavy footsteps pounded up the stairs.

"What's wrong?" asked Lump.

She had just secured the chain when something slammed into the door.

The chain snapped taut. A hand scrabbled through the narrow opening, trying to grab Maggie's wrist.

The hand was anything but human.

CHAPTER 27
FIGHT AND FLIGHT

Laszlo was having a most remarkable dream.

He and the Signora Bellascura were lounging in Louis XIV's bed, sharing cream-filled zeppoles and listening to music on an antique Bakelite radio, when the program was interrupted by breaking news: the country of Liechtenstein had gone missing. The two demons cheered and clinked champagne flutes, then set them aside to begin a carnal extravaganza . . .

But something was warping the dream. Just as the Signora was slipping out of her teddy, the image became snowy. It was like those scrambled adult channels back in the 1980s. Laszlo remembered them only too well. He'd once spent an evening glued to his set, trying to spot a nipple amid the static.

Wait! The image was coming back.

A voice cooed in his ear. "Laszlo . . . Laszlo . . ."

"I'm here, baby . . . I'm right here."

"Laszlo!"

The demon's eyes shot open. What he saw was not a pair of soft, scented breasts but the panicked face of George Drakeford wearing Elton John glasses.

"Get out of my dream!" he yelled.

Lump shook him by the shoulders. *"Wake up, Laszlo! We're under attack!"*

As he was hauled into a sitting position, Laszlo blinked dazedly at a dingy hotel room. What a clunky dream segue. Where were they? He started to ask, but Lump gave him another shake and directed his attention to where Maggie seemed to be locked in heated battle with . . . the door.

Its chain was on but strained to the breaking point. Maggie threw her shoulder against the door, forcing it shut.

Instantly, it slammed back open. Laszlo saw what was trying to break in. The thing was hideous—unconscionably ugly, like a rabid jackal with a touch of mange.

It was also oddly familiar. Why was he thinking of the F train?

Tourists . . .

Thatcher's office . . .

Androvore!

Holy shit. One of Androvore's Class III goons was on the other side of that door, snarling to get at them. Laszlo congratulated himself. Cross-species facial recognition was no small talent, especially during REM sleep.

"Get up!" Lump yelled a second time.

Laszlo yawned. He noticed that someone had folded his suit jacket and placed it by the pillow. How thoughtful! Taking his time, he shook it out and slipped it on, then checked its inner pocket for the hourglass.

That thoughtful someone had also paired his shoes on the floor next to the bed. Laszlo slipped them on and methodically laced them up, just like Mr. Rogers used to. The man was one of the few people he admired. Making a career out of putting on cardigans while speaking in a nonthreatening manner? Brilliant.

Meanwhile, the scene had become an outright brawl; what the French used to call a *mêlée*. The door was ripped off its hinges and Jackal staggered into the room, where she collided with Maggie. The two were going at it, all right. Laszlo couldn't believe how tough Maggie was. There was simply no question; she belonged in the UFC. He whooped as she picked up Jackal by the neck, swung around, and smashed the demon into the absurd little desk. The varnished wood exploded with a gratifying crash whose impact was so great that it even shattered the window.

Jackal lay amid the wreckage, looking stunned.

"You might want to tap out," suggested Laszlo.

Meanwhile, another baddie had joined the fray—a taller Class III with a face like an outraged stork, who rushed into the room and seized Lump, who was trying to get in a few, bless him. Laszlo wasn't even sure they counted as punches; they were more like the little *excuse me* taps one once used to let strangers know they were hogging the pay phone. How he missed pay phones. They'd vanished right around the time neck pillows came on the scene. That couldn't be a coincidence.

Poor Lump. Storky slung him over one shoulder like a sack of yams and made to head out.

Laszlo waved farewell and returned to the action by the window. Sadly, that fight was kaput. Jackal had been officially KO'd. Maggie stood over her, breathing hard and looking rather feral.

Her attention snapped to Storky, carting her brother out of the room.

The girl extended her left arm like a Jedi about to use the Force. Laszlo always sympathized with *Star Wars* actors. Standing in front of a green screen while pretending to wield mystic powers had to be mortifying. There you were, a Juilliard graduate, forced to grunt and make faces as you battled enemies who would be added in postproduction. There wasn't enough money in the world . . .

Fortunately, Maggie Drakeford didn't have to pretend to use mystic powers.

She had real ones at her disposal.

There was a ripping sound as gray tentacles erupted from her forearm, bursting through her shirtsleeve in a spray of blood. They shot toward Storky, wrapping around the demon's neck like grappling hooks. Steam hissed from the places where the tentacles touched his flesh, filling the room with an awful stench.

Storky released Lump and collapsed onto the floor, where he

proceeded to writhe and gasp as he struggled to pry the tentacles from his throat.

Maggie stood over the suffocating demon. Lifting her foot, she stamped hard on his face. Then she did it again.

Laszlo heard something crack, and Storky lay still.

The demon broke out in applause. "Bravo! You're like Jason Bourne . . . but with tentacles!"

A wild-eyed Maggie stared at him as said tentacles retracted into her forearm. Then she turned to Lump, who was backed up against the wall.

His face was drained of all color. "Maggie," he whispered. "What happened to you! You're—"

"Cursed," she said flatly. "We don't have time for you to freak out, so get it together." She nodded over at Laszlo. "What's wrong with him?"

Lump did not answer at once. He was too busy staring at Maggie's left arm.

"*Snap out of it!*" she barked.

The boy blinked. "I-I don't know! I think he's sleepwalking."

"Oh, great." Maggie grabbed a stray pillowcase, wiped the blood from her arm and ragged sleeve, and threw on her blazer. She tossed one backpack to Lump before shouldering the other.

Then it was Laszlo's turn.

He giggled as she dragged him off the bed and yanked him to his feet. "Gee, you're strong."

Maggie shoved the Drakeford Curse file into Laszlo's arms before snapping her fingers under his nose. "Wake up! We have to go."

Laszlo could snap his fingers, too, and did so. "Lead on, Tinker Bell!"

Maggie let out a disgusted sigh and hurried down the stairs.

In the lobby, they found a woman cowering behind the front desk holding up a crucifix. Laszlo leaned over and gave her a friendly wave before the Drakefords ushered him out the door.

A small crowd had gathered in front of the Augustus, looking up at the broken window. Laszlo told them they'd missed a roaring good fight; Maggie grabbed his wrist and hauled him along like an unruly toddler. At first he resisted, but it was so much easier to just go with the flow.

"Where to?" he asked.

Maggie's voice was tight. "Somewhere else. Come on."

Laszlo whistled. "Looks like *someone's* a little crabby. I won't say who."

They had not gone another ten steps when the Drakefords stopped short. Maggie's fingers tightened on his wrist.

A delivery truck had turned in to an alleyway, revealing a figure who had been walking calmly, steadily behind it and now continued toward them.

Laszlo shaded his eyes for a better look and did a double take. "Hey! What do you know? It's Madam Catfish!"

There was no mistaking that bulky silhouette, the fur-trimmed coat, or the jowly face. This time, however, she had left the "dog" at home. Laszlo noticed that, without the handbag, her arms hung straight down and did not move in rhythm with her steps. It was a terribly awkward gait.

He offered a snappy salute. "Welcome to my dream!"

A prim smile appeared on Madam Catfish's face. She winked at him and kept coming toward them.

There was a sharp pull on his arm. Maggie had reversed course and doubled her pace. As they retraced their steps, weaving through the crowds, Laszlo gamely jogged along. Lump brought up the rear.

Back at the Hotel Augustus, Jackal had reverted to a bleary and disheveled Kathy, who leaned against the doorway. Hubby, behind her, was in even rougher shape: two black eyes and a nose like flattened putty.

Laszlo hallooed them as he and the Drakefords trotted past.

The longer they ran, the more his dream was breaking up around the edges.

For one, he was gasping and seeing spots in the corners of his vision. For another, Maggie kept saying things like "Wake up, jackass!" He came to a spluttering halt halfway down an alley lined with trash cans and dumpsters. An ungodly stench filled his nose. Could you smell things in dreams?

Maggie whirled on him. "*Come on!*"

Laszlo switched the ebony briefcase to his other hand. "Hold up," he wheezed. "Breath—catching—must!" Leaning against the side of the dumpster, he coughed up something icky before turning to his companions. "Do either of you have a cigarette?"

Maggie grabbed his sleeve. "Laszlo," she said. "We have to *move*."

He held up a finger for patience.

The fog was lifting. The dream was receding into memory, and the present moment took its place. *My sarkyra is missing!* he realized, and clutched his chest. And why were they in this disgusting alley? Why did the Drakefords have him running around like he was on *The Amazing Race*?

"Come on!" urged Maggie.

"Are *you* missing your ticker?" Laszlo snapped. "Give me a minute!"

Lump nudged his sister. "I think he's waking up."

Laszlo opened his mouth to reply—and instead vomited great gouts of bluish liquid, along with semidigested Italian pastries. He watched the mess slide down the side of the dumpster, dimly aware that a garbage truck was slowly approaching. Those guys were going to love him.

"*Laszlo!*" Maggie frantically gestured to the alley's entrance.

Wiping his mouth with the back of his free hand, he turned to see Androvore's goons trotting toward them. He and Kathy made eye contact. "That sweater's hideous," Laszlo said. "You look like a bowl of oatmeal."

Kathy flipped him the bird.

"What do we do?" whispered Lump. "We're trapped!"

The garbage truck was only fifteen yards away, and there was no more than a foot of clearance between its sides and the dumpsters that lined the alley. Old-world streets were not designed for modern sanitation.

Laszlo tried to bolster the boy's spirits. "Don't fret, Lump. They're just a couple of Class III pussies, no tougher than I am. Your sister whupped their asses once. She can do it again." He turned to Maggie, as though siccing a Doberman. "Maggie! Get 'em!"

She simply looked at him. "What the hell are you doing?"

"It's just a job," Hubby called to them. "Give us the backpacks and we'll go."

Maggie stood firm. "We're not giving you anything."

"Hear that?" said Laszlo. "Fuck off. And tell the other one while you're at it."

Kathy and Hubby drew a blank until they turned and found Madam Catfish approaching at her own leisurely pace.

Kathy held up a hand to stop her. "I don't know who hired you," she said, "but this is our gig."

Madam Catfish continued strolling toward them. She extended one arm almost limply, as if she expected them to kiss her hand. A moment later, forks of red lightning streamed from her fingertips, enveloping Kathy in a lattice of energy.

She exploded into oily globules that spattered Hubby's face.

Laszlo nearly peed himself. "*Jesus!* That's not a Class III. That's a *real* demon! Quick, Maggie—toss her the backpacks!"

Madam Catfish's piggish eyes bored into his. Her words were hollow sounding and spectral, not formed by physical vocal cords. "I'm not here for backpacks."

"Then what do you want?"

A cryptic smile. The woman continued toward them. Hubby made a break for it, sprinting as fast as his legs would carry him. Madam Catfish let him go with nary a glance.

Maggie yanked at Laszlo's arm. "She's the one Clarence told you about."

"What?"

"She's the assassin! *Run!*"

No one needed to tell Laszlo twice. At least, not again.

He bolted toward the garbage truck, yelling frantically for them to throw that shitbox in reverse. The driver, who had just seen a middle-aged woman turn into a Jackson Pollock, tried to oblige him. The truck careened wildly backward, smashing into dumpsters and sending them spinning. Laszlo used them for cover, hugging the walls and keeping as much industrial-grade steel as he could between himself and any stray death bolts.

Were the Drakefords keeping up? He didn't stop to check. The assassin wasn't after *them*.

He was nearly alongside the truck when it swerved in his direction, nearly pinning him to a dumpster that crumpled from the impact. Sparks flew. The truck came to a squealing halt, wedged almost sideways between the dumpster and a wall so that it blocked the alley.

Laszlo glanced back just in time to see a two-ton dumpster get blown ten feet into the air.

Madam Catfish continued walking calmly after him with her arm extended like Emperor Palpatine. He swore never to mock *Star Wars* again.

Two humans raced past him in a blur.

"*Come on!*" Maggie shrieked.

The Drakefords were scrambling under the garbage truck like a pair of recruits in basic training. Laszlo imitated them as best he could, flattening himself and dragging the ebony case as he crawled along.

The men in the truck were shouting at each other in Italian. One jumped down from the passenger side. Laszlo glimpsed a pair of sneakers and blue jeans before—*whoom!*—they were consumed in a flash of light. All that remained was a single smoking Adidas.

The other man was screaming now. Laszlo crawled faster. Then there was a terrible sound, high and discordant, as metal heated and burst. A wave of energy crackled over Laszlo, propelling him forward. He shot out from under the truck as if jolted by a cattle prod.

The Drakefords were already on their feet. Maggie heaved Laszlo up, and the three were off and running. No thought of destination or direction—just *get away!* as fast and far as they could.

They raced down a crowded street, trying not to plow into anyone. Some of the passing pedestrians were actually heading toward the alley to see what was going on. Maggie shouted at them to turn around and run. Several took her advice.

They ran another four blocks before Laszlo had to stop and catch his breath. Sirens blared in the distance. Behind them, black smoke curled up into the sky as daylight deepened to dusk. Laszlo winced, reached back, and felt his suit jacket. The material had been singed in forking patterns whose edges were hot to the touch.

Maggie was still galvanized. "We need to hide!" She pointed to a nearby church, where the faint sound of singing suggested that vespers were beginning.

Laszlo stared at her. "Are you insane? I can't go in a *church*!"

"Why?"

"It's taboo. I'll probably explode when I cross the threshold. And that's if I'm lucky."

"The assassin would never look for you in a church!"

"Well, that's one smart lady, because I won't be in one," said Laszlo. "You two go ahead."

He waved the Drakefords on and suddenly realized he was trembling.

It had nothing to do with the goons or Madam Catfish and everything to do with the loss of his sarkyra. Ever since he had deposited it in the Signora's hand, along with the nausea and weakness, he had felt a certain . . . ennui? Apathy? Or maybe it was hopelessness.

Whatever the word, its effect was insidious. Even with the new parts of his plan taking shape, it was hard to rally.

The demon sighed. Maybe it would be easier for all concerned if he just stayed put and waited for Madam Catfish to arrive. He had no doubt she was on her way.

There was a hand on his arm. Looking up, he saw Maggie Drakeford studying him with an expression usually reserved for lost children and addled seniors.

"We're all going," she said.

"You go," he told her. "Really, you'll be safe in there. *Sanctum sanctorum*, and all that."

Her expression intensified. "We're not leaving you behind, Laszlo."

The demon scoffed. "Why not? You think I'm a jackass."

"Yes," said Maggie. "But you're *our* jackass."

Lump squeezed his hand. "You really are."

Whether it was their touching loyalty or his cresting nausea, the demon was rendered speechless. He merely nodded and staggered onward, passing the church with a primal shudder.

This continued for another five or six minutes, until Laszlo begged to sit down.

Maggie chose a bench outside a tailor's shop in a quieter neighborhood a block from the Tiber. The sun had set, and the sky was a deepening blue wash with the occasional cloud obscuring the early stars. Laszlo gazed up at them dully. His singed clothes hung like rags; his breath came in struggling gasps. All he wanted to do was sleep.

After a few moments, Maggie urged him to get up, but what was the point?

Madam Catfish had tracked them from Central Park to Rome. They weren't going to outrun her. She was toying with them. Laszlo wondered what he could have done that pissed off Androvore so badly. Yes, he'd mocked that ridiculous name, but he could hardly have been the first. Besides, he'd ridiculed countless people over the centuries, and no one had ever hired a *fucking assassin* to get revenge. The Overseer had no sense of proportion.

Finally, the Drakefords managed to pull a groaning Laszlo to his feet. He was on the edge of another complaint when a bolt of red lightning annihilated the bench. It was blasted right through the shop window, where its melting iron ran like gravy over a display of dress shirts.

People scattered as Madam Catfish again emerged from an alley, electricity dancing about her fingers. She walked at the same languid pace and bore the same cryptic smile. It was like being hunted by a zombie mannequin.

There was nothing for it but to run. So they did.

They ran swiftly. Furiously. Down streets and across plazas, through alleyways and along the river. Laszlo was rapidly growing delirious. He tripped over a cobble. Stumbled against a street sign.

Maggie caught hold of his arm. Lump was yelling something.

He must see Madam Catfish, thought Laszlo. *Any second now . . .*

Closing his eyes, the demon braced for a bolt to blast him into oblivion.

But none came.

His mind reeled, and he could swear that he was falling. When he opened his eyes, he found that he was mistaken. Maggie Drakeford was dragging him over the cobbles, straight for the nearest building.

Laszlo didn't resist—he didn't have the strength.

Someone was standing in the building's doorway. Maggie shouted for them to make room. Laszlo closed his eyes as yellow light fell across his face. Another pair of hands seized him, and he was pulled over a threshold. The door slammed shut, and he heard a chair or bench being hauled across the floor. Someone hovered over him now, asking questions in soft but urgent Italian. Laszlo couldn't make out the words. The person knelt and took his hand. A man, judging by the size. Cracking an eye, Laszlo glimpsed a hazy figure with a band of white around his throat.

The demon blinked, and the figure came into sharper focus. He'd been mistaken. It wasn't a man holding Laszlo's hand.

It was a priest.

CHAPTER 28
FATHER ANGELO

"Shit," Laszlo muttered, "I'm seeing things."

The priest cocked his head. "*Sei americano?*"

"Sure. Why not?"

There was movement at the corner of Laszlo's vision. More sounds of wood sliding over tile. Shifting slightly, the demon saw Maggie and Lump dragging another bench past him. Such busy bees, those Drakefords.

His gaze drifted upward. Laszlo squinted. Was he still dreaming, or was the ceiling covered with fat winged babies capering about a faded blue sky?

"What's wrong with them?" he wondered.

The priest looked up too. He was crouching before Laszlo, a man in his early thirties with close-cropped hair and a trim brown beard. "Who?" he said. "The *cherubini?*"

"Their BMI's off the charts."

"I like them," remarked the priest. "They're my happy dumplings."

"Aha! You speak English."

"Yes. My studies once took me to San Francisco." He turned to Maggie, who had returned with Lump to check on Laszlo. "Does your friend need a doctor?"

"A doctor can't help him."

"May I ask why you're barricading the door?"

"Someone's after us," said Lump. "Well, really, they're after him."

All three looked down at Laszlo.

"Should I call the police?"

Maggie shook her head. "They can't help him, either."

The priest looked from one Drakeford to the other. "I don't understand."

"Our friend's a demon," said Maggie, crouching to touch Laszlo's forehead. "And he's being hunted by a much scarier demon."

"That catfish is at least a Class VI." Laszlo's words came out in a rush. "Maybe a Class VII. It isn't fair. She's flinging lightning bolts around like Zeus, and *I* can't even toast Wonder Bread."

The priest was at a loss. "Wonder Bread?"

"That's right. I tried once, you know. Couldn't even brown it. You know. *Bzzzz!*" Laszlo vibrated his hands as though trying to electrocute something.

"I think perhaps a doctor is best," the priest told Maggie.

She shook her head. "I know it sounds crazy, but it's the truth. A demon's after us, Father. I figured a church might be the one place where we'd be safe."

Laszlo snorted. "This isn't a church."

Maggie and the priest spoke in unison. "It isn't?"

"If this was a church, I'd be screaming in pain and one of those archangels, Gabriel or Michael—probably Michael—would be paddling my ass with a flaming sword."

The priest cleared his throat. "Sir, I can assure you that you are in a house of God. This church was built in the fifth century."

Another snort. "Demons *burn* in churches, my guy. If this is a church, why aren't I burning?"

"I couldn't say. Is it possible that you are not a demon?"

"Then how do you explain this?"

Laszlo dropped his human guise.

Gasping, the priest scrambled backward until he struck a pew. Laszlo sat up fully as the man sat and rubbed the back of his head. The two stared at one another.

"How's your head?" inquired Laszlo.

"It hurts. Are you going to kill me?"

"No. Just don't get lippy."

"I won't."

"You know, you move pretty well for a priest."

"I played tennis in *scuola superiore*." Laszlo was confused. "High school," he added.

The demon took this in as Maggie and Lump helped him to his feet. Breathing deeply, he took in the "house of God." He had to confess he wasn't all that wowed.

The church was tiny, barely the size of a modest barn. A single column of pews led toward a chancel whose sanctuary contained a modest altar and ended at an apse exhibiting a relief of the Virgin Mary. The images on the walls were obviously very old; some were so faded and cracked that their subjects could only be guessed at.

"Where is everyone?" asked Laszlo.

The priest got to his feet and brushed off his cassock. "I was closing for the evening when the young lady brought you in."

The young lady introduced herself. "I'm Maggie Drakeford, sir, and this is my brother, George. Thank you for your help."

The priest gave a little bow. "I am Father Angelo."

Laszlo cocked his head. "Aren't you freaked out that a demon is standing in your church?"

Father Angelo spread his hands. "This is a place of welcome. If the Holy Father is content to accept you, who am I to object? I am but His servant. Do you have a name, my friend?"

"Laszlo." He scrutinized Father Angelo. "So . . . you're not scared of me?"

The priest shook his head. "No. You gave me quite a shock, but no, I am not afraid of you."

The demon resumed his human guise and turned to the Drakefords. "*This* is what I'm talking about. Class IIIs are basically glorified imps."

As he spoke, a wind began to blow outside. Its moan quickly escalated to an unearthly scream. A hurricane had seemingly descended upon the church. Gales whipped past, making the candles gutter. The entire building trembled.

Lump gave a cry and scampered away from the front door. The planks were bending inward, timbers straining as though a giant were pressing against them.

Laszlo whistled. "Now *that's* a demon!"

Blood seeped under the door as a spectral voice whispered through the keyhole. "*Da mihi quod meum est, humilis servus Dei . . .*"

Maggie went pale and looked to Father Angelo. "What's it saying?"

The priest appeared equally stricken. "'Give to me what is mine, lowly slave of God,'" he murmured, his breath misting in the dim light.

The temperature inside was plummeting.

Laszlo exhaled a pearly cloud. "Just like *The Exorcist*. And here I thought that was just Hollywood fluff."

Father Angelo turned to him. "My friend, you may be on to something." The priest ran down the nave to a room off the chancel.

Now the blood was flowing under the door, staining several inches of the floor before gurgling back and advancing again. The door groaned ominously. A chunk of plaster fell from the ceiling, striking the floor as several candles went out entirely.

Laszlo turned to Maggie, who was holding the last of their spell-tubes. "Why didn't you take me to a cathedral? This is like the Motel 6 of churches."

Father Angelo came hurrying back, a leather-bound book in his hand and a determined look on his face. His expression wavered as he spotted the blood now boiling upon the threshold, but he clutched his crucifix and instructed the others to get behind him. Laszlo was happy to oblige.

The priest quickly located the passage he was looking for. Drawing himself up to his full height, he held out one hand in a gesture of denial.

"*Crux sacra sit mihi lux,*" he called. "*Non draco sit mihi dux! Vade retro Satana! Nunquam suade mihi vana. Sunt mala quae libas—ipse venena bibas!*"

He waited a moment, then repeated the words. His voice was reso-
lute. The blood at the door retreated like an ebbing tide before surging
forward—but this time it crashed against an invisible barrier.

"*Vade retro Satana!*" bellowed Father Angelo.

This time, the blood withdrew entirely and left no trace of its presence. The church's candles flickered back to life, and the room grew
warmer as the gale outside began to die away. The door, no longer warped
and poised to burst, settled back into its normal position.

But a voice slipped into their ears, soft and insidious. "*Non potes
effugere mortem*," it whispered. "*Ego ubique . . .*"

"*You cannot escape death*," Father Angelo translated. "*I am everywhere . . .*"

Laszlo shouted through his cupped hands, "Oh, really? Then why
are you out *there*, and we're in *here*?"

"Shh!" hissed Maggie. "Don't piss it off!"

But it was hard not to gloat. Laszlo thumped his chest in a territo-
rial display similar to those seen among the great apes. Unfortunately,
he'd forgotten about his sarkyra.

He yelped and his knees buckled. "It is all right," Father Angelo assured Laszlo, steadying him. "Whatever it was, I believe it has gone."

"Thank you," said Laszlo, only somewhat humbled. The priest acknowledged this. "So how long have you been a man o' God?"

"Three years. I am still quite new."

Laszlo clapped him weakly on the shoulder. "Well, you're a goddamn prodigy."

The priest said Laszlo was very kind, then asked him to refrain from
taking the Lord's name in vain. Laszlo said he'd try but couldn't guarantee anything—old habits and all.

"Sir?" Maggie spoke up.

"'Father Angelo' will do. Or simply 'Angelo,' if you prefer."

"Uh, thank you." She paused. "Father Angelo . . . would it be all
right if we stayed here tonight? We have to leave early in the morning,
but I'm worried that thing may still be outside."

Father Angelo went to inspect the door. "Of course you can stay.

But leaving may be more difficult. Ours is a humble house of God; this door is the only way in or out."

"I have an idea," said Maggie. "In the meantime—I hate to ask, but do you have any food? We've been running for our lives and haven't eaten since this morning."

The priest smiled. "Follow me to the grandest table in Italy."

That table was in the room off the nave where the priest had gotten his book, a space no larger than a cramped pantry. Its furnishings were minimal: a desk and chair, a small cot, one bookshelf, a lamp, a hot plate, and a cooler.

"You should go on strike," said Laszlo, looking about.

The priest merely chuckled and, using the hot plate, made a large batch of pasta tossed in olive oil. The Drakefords inhaled their dinner on the cot; Laszlo parked himself on the stone floor to purchase their airline tickets.

At this point, most of the Wednesday flights were fully booked and the only workable option was a 9:30 a.m. flight on Alitalia that would get them into JFK by Wednesday afternoon. Few seats remained, however, and their prices were insane. Between the passports, plane tickets, train tickets, taxis, clothes, cocktails, meals, the Imperial Suite, and unrealized appointment with Helga, this little excursion had run Laszlo almost thirty grand. Closing his eyes, he purchased the tickets. He only hoped they'd have a chance to use them.

When they'd all finished eating, Father Angelo stacked the plates in the tiny sink. The room reminded Laszlo of a prison cell. He made a joke along those lines, but their host merely smiled and said nothing was a prison if you chose to be there. While the demon considered this, Father Angelo asked how they had come to be in Rome.

Maggie shared the essentials of the Drakeford Curse and their desperate bid to break it by tomorrow evening.

The priest shook his head in disbelief. "Demons and curses. Exorcism rites! I never imagined I'd ever need to invoke such things."

"Well," said Laszlo, "you should tell your bosses about the exorcism. That shit worked."

"They'd never believe me," muttered Father Angelo. "Maggie," he went on, gesturing at Laszlo, "how does your friend figure into this quest?"

"Laszlo oversees the spell. He's the Curse Keeper."

The priest turned to Laszlo. "Is this desirable work?"

"It's a living."

Father Angelo gave him a pointed look. "And just so I understand . . . you are *helping* them break this curse you manage?"

Laszlo didn't like that shrewd expression. The priest had a bit of Dimitri in him. Fortunately, Lump came to the rescue.

"Laszlo's been amazing," he gushed. "We'd never have gotten this far without him. We have almost everything we came for!"

"I am delighted to hear it," said the priest, glancing at Laszlo.

"Actually," put in Maggie, a little anxiously, "I need to ask you something, Father Angelo."

The priest gave her his attention.

"We're still missing something," she continued. "We were planning to steal it when that other demon showed up. We still need it, but I would really prefer not to have to steal." She paused and in that moment looked at Lump. "My brother kind of opened my eyes there."

No sibling of Laszlo's had ever looked at him that way. The closest was when his sister Azabel had lent him her wyvern while she marched off to flay a neighbor whose cattle had grazed on her lands. Good ol' Azabel.

"What is this thing that you need?" asked Father Angelo.

Lump cleared his throat. "A holy relic."

The priest stared. "A relic of the Church?"

"Yes," Maggie broke in. "I don't know if it has to be from a particular church or if any faith would do. But yes, we need an honest-to-goodness relic."

"We made a list," added Lump. "We looked up every relic in Rome to find one we could take that wouldn't upset too many people."

Laszlo clucked his tongue. "You two did all that while I was sleeping? I'm impressed!"

"Nothing really famous," said Maggie. "No heads or anything."

The priest was clearly at a loss. "Uh, that was very considerate."

"But we *do* need a relic," she pressed. "If we don't get one, our family's situation is going to get a lot worse. It's already pretty bad."

Removing her blazer and rolling up her tattered, bloodstained left sleeve, Maggie showed Father Angelo her arm. Laszlo was quietly appalled. The entire thing, from shoulder to wrist, was now a flaming scarlet; two uneven rows of holes along the forearm glistened with secretions. Fortunately, their inhabitants—those tentacles, worms, tendrils, whatever they were—were being shy. He had no desire to lose the dinner he had just eaten.

Maggie pulled her sleeve back down. "Our dad's worse," she said urgently. "Much worse. You can't imagine how he's suffering. We're doing this for him."

"And I'm doing it for Maggie," said Lump.

Laszlo withdrew a step and leaned against the wall. Things were taking a melodramatic turn. Soon, there would be lots of "You're the best!" and "No, *you're* the best!" and he *would* have to vomit. The priest shot him a curious glance before returning to Maggie.

"Your community," he said. "Are they aware of your situation? Do they support you?"

Her laugh had an edge. "No, Father. I can't say they do."

She gave a shorthand version of the Drakefords' centuries-long work as Schemerdaal's sin-eaters. Laszlo thought she demonstrated remarkable restraint. He supposed it was to spare Lump the less pleasant details.

Even so, the PG version left Father Angelo stunned. "Sin-eating is not unknown to me," he said gravely, "but it is a very old practice. Obscure. The church has condemned it for centuries."

"Yeah," said Maggie. "Well, no one told Reverend Farrow."

There was a silence. When the priest spoke, his voice was gentle. "Do *you* believe you are lost, Maggie? Do you believe your soul is tarnished and cannot be redeemed?"

She looked down at her shoes. "I don't know what I believe."

"Listen to me," said Father Angelo. "You are a child of God, Margaret Drakeford. And He has not abandoned you. If anyone has lost their way, it is those who would heap their own misdeeds upon the innocent."

Another silence. Then Maggie met his eyes. "I appreciate your saying that, Father Angelo. Truly. But right now, we need your help. It's not my nature to ask, and you've already done so much. But we're desperate." She twisted the ring on her finger. "Do you know of *any* relic we can use? I can't promise to return it—I don't know if that will be possible."

Father Angelo exhaled and tapped his fingertips together. "You know this is a highly unusual—some might even say sacrilegious—request. I will have to give it some consideration. But first, tell me—how do you intend to leave this church with such evil awaiting you? You said you had an idea. If so, I would hear it." His face was serious. "If it's no good, I may have to call in the Vatican."

"No!" exclaimed Laszlo.

It took the demon a moment to realize there was a twinkle in Father Angelo's eye.

As Maggie shared her idea, Laszlo was annoyed that he hadn't thought of it himself. Lump wasn't the only Drakeford with brains.

"Ingenious," said Father Angelo. "This is truly a night of wonders. What time do you intend to leave?"

The demon finally spoke. "By six. Early, but not too early. Otherwise, our friend might have time to catch up to us at the airport. She seems to have a way of tracking us."

Father Angelo nodded and looked to the Drakefords. "Get some rest. The bed is small but not uncomfortable. In the meantime, I should like a quiet word with your companion."

Laszlo expected Maggie to protest, but she merely kicked off her shoes and lay back on the cot. Lump snuggled beside her. She had been through the wringer and looked it. Her eyes were already closing when Father Angelo beckoned Laszlo to join him outside.

He followed the priest as he went to reinspect the church's entry. To Laszlo's surprise, there were no traces of blood at the threshold, no lasting damage to the door. He wondered aloud if it had all been an illusion.

"I was thinking the same," said Father Angelo. "But then there is Maggie's affliction. That is no illusion and doesn't resemble any disease I've heard of. And of course, I am saying this to a demon." He gave a small, incredulous laugh. "Either I've gone insane, or I must accept that this is real."

"Sorry you let us in?" Laszlo asked.

"Quite the opposite."

The two of them settled into one of the pews. After a moment, Father Angelo gestured toward the altar. "My calling is one of faith," he explained. "My faith was strong before I ever encountered you or that evil presence outside. I did not need these experiences to believe. But now that I have had them, they have strengthened my conviction." He turned to the demon. "You have given me a great gift, Laszlo. I thank you for it."

"Happy to help."

Father Angelo raised an eyebrow. "Always a quip, eh? I sense conflict in you, Laszlo. You are wrestling with something." His eyes again grew shrewd. "Tell me, are the Drakefords wise to put their trust in you?"

Laszlo rested his arm atop the pew. "That sounds like an accusation, Father."

"It is not. But it would comfort me to know you are helping them. They care about you."

A snort. "The kid, maybe."

"Maggie too," said the priest. "They are counting on you, Laszlo."

Laszlo kept his eyes on one of the faded frescoes. "I'm aware. Believe me."

Father Angelo moved so he was squarely in Laszlo's sight line and gave a piercing look. "*Should* they be counting on you?"

"You heard the kid. They never would have made it this far without me."

"So he says."

"You sound a little dubious, buddy. Is this the 'he's a demon and you can't trust him' thing? If so, save your breath. I've heard it all before."

A noise of acknowledgment. "I see. Do you know where the word 'demon' comes from?"

"Yeah, yeah," said Laszlo. "The Greeks and all that."

"Yes. And for the Greeks, a *daimon* was simply a spirit. Only later was the word linked to evil."

"Good to know."

"Answer me this," said the priest. "Do you believe it is your purpose to defile and corrupt? That you are, by nature, a wicked and evil being?"

Laszlo laced his fingers behind his head and gazed up at the cherubs. "I don't know," he reflected. "Funny you should ask, though. Mommy Drakeford wasn't a fan of my being a demon. I told her she was being unfair—that demons were just freethinkers who'd gotten a bad rap."

"I suppose that's one interpretation," allowed the priest.

"Yeah, well, I've been giving it some thought." He paused, searching for the proper words. "I met a woman recently—crazy hot, just thinking about her makes me tingly—and she made it sound like I've spent the last century being a wimp. What's Italian for 'wimp'?"

"Pappamolle."

"Everything sounds better in Italian," remarked Laszlo. "Anyway, what she meant was that I've been letting others slap labels on me and tell me what to do. And that kind of hit home, because she isn't wrong. I mean, if demons are just freethinkers, what I do and how I do it should be *my* call. Maybe I'd rather teach kindergarten and breed Bernedoodles."

"It sounds better than managing curses."

"Yeah," said Laszlo, "but my gig generates misery and despair, human souls, and all that. There's power in souls. That demon outside? You don't get that badass without gulping down a few."

The priest gave this some thought. "If a desire for power leads one to commit wicked acts, perhaps it is not a worthy objective. There is more to existence—even for a demon—than simply acquiring more and more power."

Laszlo took this in. "How old are you?"

"Thirty-three."

"Damn. You're better than Dr. Nussbaum."

"Who's that?"

"My therapist."

Father Angelo smiled. "Well, I'd say a demon who sees a therapist is a demon who wishes to better himself. And that tells me a great deal, Laszlo . . . ? I'm sorry—do demons have last names?"

"Those with a pedigree. If you're Ooze spawn, they just assign one name. Most get stuck with 'Throk.' Don't ask me why."

"I see. So you don't have a last name?"

Laszlo braced himself. "I do. It's Zebul. As in *Baal Zebul*."

Father Angelo repeated it. "Hm. Sounds a bit like Beelzebub. Are you related?"

Laszlo sighed inwardly. Nicknames were like herpes; you could never get rid of them. "You could say that. Anyway," he continued briskly, "enough about me. Did you always know you wanted to be a priest?"

A laugh. "When I was in high school, all I wanted to do was play tennis and chase girls."

"Really?" said Laszlo. "I've been known to swing the ol' racket myself. How's your game?"

"Lethal." The priest's admission was matter of fact. "Do you still play?"

"Not for years. I took it up when Borg was the rage. Grew my hair out. Headband. Short shorts. The whole deal."

"You're braver than I am. I could never pull that off."

"Oh, I pulled it off," said Laszlo. "No matter my guise, I'm always pretty. People tell me I look like Paul Newman."

"You know," the priest admitted with a smile, "I wasn't going to say anything. You're vain enough. A *pavone*—a peacock."

"I guess," said Laszlo with a smile, "but we all need something. My looks are all I've got."

Father Angelo tutted. "If that is true, I don't think you'd be permitted in here."

Laszlo took a moment to mull the implication. "You think someone on your team gave me the green light?"

The priest shrugged. "All I know is that you are sitting beside me and the other one—the 'badass'—could not pass the door."

"So what you're really saying is that I'm *special*—"

The priest burst out laughing. "If you like."

Laszlo *did* like, and he found himself feeling better—*fuller*—more like himself than he had since surrendering his sarkyra. Twisting in his seat, he stretched his back and took in the rest of the church—including the confessional booth. "Do people still use those things?"

"Some," replied Father Angelo. "Older parishioners, mostly."

Laszlo took in the booth's paneling and the curtain shielding the confessor's compartment. "Can I give it a whirl?"

The priest stared. "You are full of surprises, Laszlo Zebul. You wish to confess to me?"

"Why not? It's cheaper than seeing Dr. Nussbaum."

"I assume you are not a baptized Catholic?" The demon stared at him. Father Angelo spread his hands. "Then, sadly, I cannot offer you the holy sacrament. But if it pleases you to sit in the booth and unburden yourself, I am willing to listen."

Laszlo didn't need to be asked twice. Jumping up, he hurried to the booth like it was the world's best roller coaster. He sat in the tiny space, taking in the vibes and inhaling the smell of wood polish. Father Angelo sat in the curtained compartment; his profile was visible through the metal grille.

"Should I start?" asked Laszlo.

"Do what you like. This isn't an official confession."

"Yeah, yeah." Laszlo took a moment to collect his thoughts and prepare his narration. He intended to sound just like Morgan Freeman. The man could make anything seem profound.

He drew a deep breath. "It all began when I came into consciousness on March seventeenth of the year 1212. My first sins were committed the next day, when I broke four of the Ten Commandments. Our neighbor's wife was quite the looker, you see, and . . ."

Laszlo talked. The hours crept by. When he finally left the confessional, it was five in the morning. Father Angelo came out from behind the curtain looking rather shaken.

"Oh, come on," Laszlo chided. "Was it really that bad?"

The man nodded uncertainly. "It might be. I need to look up several terms."

"Yeah," said the demon, stretching, "but you have to admit it was basically just lustful, thieving, blasphemous sort of stuff. I mean, what has two thumbs and never killed anyone?"

"You?"

Laszlo's face fell. "So you've heard that joke."

"Lucky guess." Father Angelo looked at his watch. "It's time to wake them. Before we do, I very much want to ask you a question."

"Fire away."

"Have you ever met an angel?" The priest was dead serious.

"In Vegas," said Laszlo. "Her stage name was Chablis."

"I'm not joking."

"I know you're not," said Laszlo. "You met a demon last night and exorcised another one, and now you're wondering: 'Does the other side exist? Seraphim. Cherubim. Those plucky thrones. Are they real?'"

"And?" Father Angelo's face was full of anticipation.

Laszlo placed a hand on the priest's shoulder. "I want to tell you. I really do. But . . . I can't."

A groan. "Are you kidding me? Why not?"

"Because you're a man of faith, Angelo, and a man of faith shouldn't need to ask."

With this, Laszlo offered a very wise and superior look before sauntering away to wake the Drakefords. Father Angelo muttered something in Italian and hurried after him.

The Drakefords were already awake. Maggie was busy reapplying faerie essence to her eye while a drowsy Lump brushed his teeth at the little sink. Father Angelo bid them *buongiorno* and excused himself for a moment while Laszlo asked if they'd gotten any sleep.

"A little," said Maggie. "How do you feel?"

Laszlo tapped the spot where his sarkyra should have been. "Shockingly, not that bad. Father Angelo's good company. You know, I meant to tell you earlier. That idea of yours? Hop, skip, and jump?"

"What about it?"

He nudged Lump aside to splash some water on his face. "It's fucking brilliant."

Maggie could not keep from smiling. "Thanks. But first, let's see if it works."

Father Angelo returned holding a jar that resembled a saltshaker. Instead of salt, however, it looked to contain a lock of white hair as well as something else.

"Eww," said Laszlo. "Are those . . . *fingernails?*"

"Yes," replied Father Angelo. "The hair and nails are from Saint Clare of Assisi. They were gifted to this church as a token of friendship some centuries ago—the rest are kept in her basilica." The priest glanced up at the ceiling. "If I am wrong in sharing them, I beg God's forgiveness. But in my heart, I believe that good will come of this." He hefted the container. "Will a few hairs and fingernails suffice?"

Maggie looked dangerously near tears. "Yes. If it's not enough, then none of it is. Thank you, Father Angelo. I don't know what else to say."

She embraced the priest, who laughed and also accepted a hug from Lump. Together, they opened the reliquary, and Father Angelo used tweezers to remove three fine hairs and two mummified fingernails, which he placed in a plastic sandwich bag.

Maggie accepted it gratefully and had Lump stow the bag in his glasses case.

"Well," said Father Angelo, "you have a flight to catch, and I must begin my day. You will write when you have broken your curse, yes?"

"*If* we break our curse," she corrected.

"*When*," he insisted. "Have faith, Maggie. I will pray for you."

The priest stood aside as she took the seven-rod slippers from their box and put them on, then reviewed the map they'd drawn after dinner last night.

Careful not to lift her feet, she pivoted to face due south.

"You have it memorized?" Lump asked, a little nervously.

Maggie nodded. Twenty-seven steps had been measured out on that map. Twenty-seven steps would carry them across the Tiber via the Ponte Sisto, to a location half a mile from where they stood. Once there, they'd take a taxi arranged by Father Angelo and head straight to the airport. With luck, Madam Catfish wouldn't even know they'd left the church.

"*Ciao*," said Maggie, and took a step forward. She instantly vanished.

Father Angelo promptly crossed himself. The three waited in tense silence for Maggie to complete the trial run.

Two minutes later, she reappeared several feet from where she had started. No flash of light, nothing conspicuous or glitzy; she was just *there*.

Lump hopped up and down. "How was it?"

"Okay," said a breathless Maggie. "I just need to be really precise with the angle I'm facing. I almost ended up in the river. Are you ready?"

He nodded and cinched his backpack more tightly. Crouching down, Maggie let him clamber up and get settled for the world's strangest piggyback ride.

One step—and the pair vanished.

Father Angelo shook his head. "A strange night, and no mistake."

"What's life without good stories?" said Laszlo. "Thanks, Padre. If you're ever in New York, give me a holler. I'd be honored to whip your ass in tennis."

"Do not be so confident, my friend," the priest said with a wry smile. "In the meantime, take care, Laszlo. I have faith in you. It is time you had faith in yourself."

As the two shook hands, Laszlo got the distinct impression that this priest had guessed his plans down to the last detail. Sheer paranoia, but it left him feeling unmoored.

Laszlo couldn't explain why, but he wanted this human to respect him.

Maggie reappeared a moment later without Lump or their backpacks. Massaging her neck, she eyed her Curse Keeper with grim resignation. "Let's get this over with."

"Sure you can carry me?"

Maggie rolled her eyes. "Get on and shut up."

Laszlo complied. Clutching the curse folio, he hopped on Maggie's back. She barely seemed to notice his weight.

As he got settled, Laszlo turned to the priest. "Quick! Father Angelo, grab your phone and take a pic—"

But he was too late. Maggie took a step, and they reappeared in an alley outside the church. A second later, they were on a street that ran along the Tiber. Each step brought them one hundred and fifteen feet closer to their destination.

Occasionally, Maggie and Laszlo appeared within sight of people who got the merest glimpse before the pair vanished again. Those bystanders would spend the rest of their lives telling friends they'd seen the ghost of a girl giving a full-grown man a piggyback ride. No one, of course, would believe them.

Three more steps carried them over the Ponte Sisto. They turned northwest and crossed several uneventful blocks until they arrived at the botanical gardens.

Once there, Maggie replaced the magic slippers with her sneakers, stowing the former in her backpack when Lump joined them from his hiding spot among some nearby trees.

Father Angelo's promised taxi was waiting around the corner.

Rome's streets were quiet at such an early hour, and they made excellent time. Laszlo handed the Drakefords their passports, which had been treated with the last of the faerie essence.

At Leonardo da Vinci Airport, a man at security was curious about the Herzogshut, but Maggie explained they'd bought it as a theater prop and showed him the seven-rod slippers for good measure. He smiled and wished them well, and they proceeded to their gate, where they tensely watched for any sign of the assassin.

Madam Catfish did not appear.

At 9:00 a.m., they boarded. The plane was packed. The three took their assigned seats in different rows until Laszlo did his thing and arranged for them to sit together. Lump took the window and Maggie the aisle, while Laszlo was wedged in the middle. The plane had not even taken off before the Drakefords were fast asleep. They reminded Laszlo of two weary knights returning from their quest, grails stowed in the overhead compartment.

Once they were airborne, Laszlo ordered a glass of wine. When the attendant set it on his tray, she inquired if anyone ever told him he looked like Paul Newman. Laszlo admitted that he might have heard it once or twice before. The woman smiled the sort of smile that said she'd be back, early and often.

The demon watched her go before shooting off a text to Ansel telling him the forged ritus was no longer required. When that was done, Laszlo took a slow sip of wine and directed his gaze out the window.

His plan was going to work.

And when it did, he would never forgive himself.

CHAPTER 29
BRING YOUR HUMANS TO WORK

For Maggie, the next ten hours were wonderfully uneventful. For one thing, she slept for most of the flight. For the rest, no tentacles burst from her skin, Madam Catfish hadn't found them, and they were returning to America with everything they needed.

As the plane made its descent into JFK, she tried to keep her excitement in check. The curse required additional materia, but those were ordinary, more personal items. The heavy lifting was done, and they even had step-by-step instructions for the ceremony. The instructions were in Greek, of course, but Laszlo had sent a photo to Clarence for translation.

Maggie wondered what would happen when they broke the curse. Would there be a flash of light? Would her father simply transform back to the man she remembered? Would her Drakeford ancestors finally find peace?

By midnight, she would know.

Her chief concern was the Witchstone itself. According to the Signora Bellascura, it contained an ancient demon who might prove to be far more powerful than Madam Catfish. The assassin had been bad enough. How would the Monk react, once released? Or would that even happen?

The Signora had her own plans for the Witchstone once the curse was broken. Maggie's hand strayed to her necklace. She realized that she looked forward to summoning the Signora and seeing her again.

And of course, there was the matter of Laszlo's sarkyra.

His flight had been less restorative. He too had slept, but dreams had left him twitching and groaning. When Maggie woke him before their descent, he peered groggily about the cabin and blotted beads of perspiration from his face. He explained, with a wave of his hand, that it was all due to his missing sarkyra and reassured them both—especially Lump—that he'd be fine once it was returned.

The three chewed gum during the descent, and Laszlo swapped seats with Maggie so she could squeeze next to Lump and marvel at Manhattan unfolding beneath them. The sight of all those skyscrapers was remarkable, as was the large green rectangle of Central Park. Maggie imagined the curmudgeonly kobold lurking by his hot dog cart, scowling at passersby, and had to smile.

Her pulse fluttered with excitement as they touched down and taxied to the gate. It was still fluttering when they joined the long line leading to Customs and Border Protection.

"Passports, please."

Laszlo handed them over. The agent swiped them through a reader and reviewed her computer screen. "You're arriving from Italy?"

"Rome," Laszlo told her.

"And you departed the United States for Switzerland last Saturday."

"Correct."

"Business or pleasure?"

"Pleasure," Laszlo replied easily. "I was showing my niece and nephew their grandmother's birthplace. A good trip."

"A great trip," put in Maggie. She smiled at the woman. "Have you ever seen the Alps?"

The woman sighed, "Not yet," and returned to the monitor. "Anything to declare?"

Laszlo submitted their customs declarations, and she asked if they were bringing any animal, vegetable, or biological matter into the United States, including pathogens or plant seeds.

"Not intentionally," he said dryly. "Are we free to go?"

"Not yet, sir. Please be patient."

The demon drummed his fingers on the countertop.

Is this normal? Maggie wondered. He was affecting an air of pleasant unconcern, but she wasn't fooled.

Studying the monitor, the agent frowned. Then she took a closer look at the three of them and typed something on her keyboard.

Moments later, two CBP officers in blue uniforms and bulletproof vests joined them. The agent showed them her screen and spoke in a soft but urgent undertone.

One of the officers turned to them. "Come with us, please."

"I don't understand," said Laszlo. "Is there a problem?"

The other officer's hand rested on his sidearm. "Sir, we're going to need you to cooperate."

"Sure thing, but can't you at least tell me what's—"

The man nodded to his partner, who ordered Laszlo to place his hands behind his back. The demon hesitated a split second before complying. A stunned Maggie and Lump saw other travelers whispering to each other or standing on tiptoe for a better view.

Once the handcuffs were secure, the officer snapped his fingers to get Maggie's attention. "Do we need to cuff you too?"

"No, sir."

"Smart girl. Come with us."

The officers marched Laszlo through a security door and led them all down a corridor to a sparsely furnished room, where they were ordered into folding chairs across from a plain wooden desk. The only other decoration was a wall clock.

One of the men seated himself at the desk while his partner tossed the Drakefords' bags into a corner.

"So what's this all about?" asked Laszlo impatiently.

"Your passports were flagged," said the officer behind the desk.

Laszlo chuckled. "There's nothing wrong with our passports, you syphilitic twat."

Maggie froze in horror. "Laszlo!" she said stiffly. "They're the *police*—"

"Nope. They're demons." He smirked. "I got a good whiff of Tweedledum when he put the cuffs on. I can smell Tweedledee from ten feet. They're just two more of Androvore's goons."

This seemed to amuse the first officer. He and his colleague started laughing. "Goons!" he chortled. "You say that like we're dumb."

"You are, you incontinent lickspittle."

"Who's the one in handcuffs?" the man needled. "Who's been traipsing around Europe carrying a *homing beacon*?"

Laszlo narrowed his eyes. "What are you talking about?"

The second officer reached inside Laszlo's suit jacket and removed the hourglass. He shook it playfully, like a toy maraca, before setting it on the desk. It gave off a sinister light.

"We took bets on when you'd figure it out," said Desk Demon, with no small delight. "I mean, the thing's glowing red, and our people keep showing up wherever you are. You had to catch on eventually, right? I figured Monday at the latest, but my partner had you pegged. Congrats, Oslük. You win."

Oslük grinned wider than should have been possible on a human face. "Thanks, Throk. Hooray for me!"

"Jesus, *another* Throk," Laszlo muttered.

"What was that?" said Desk Demon.

"Oh, nothing. Hey, Oslük," Laszlo said to the other demon, "take my advice and go celebrate. A little Red Lobster, some popcorn shrimp, the works. Live it up while you can."

Oslük glowered. "What do you mean, 'while I can'?"

Laszlo shrugged. "Because in a few hours you're going to be skinned alive and fed to my siblings. And I mean that literally, you gibbering ape."

"You're bluffing."

"I'm not," said Laszlo, adjusting the handcuffs. "I assume you know who I am."

"Oh, indeed, *Your Lordship*," sneered Throk. "I also know your daddy's done with you."

"Not quite," countered Laszlo. "Let's go back to that hourglass. See those grains up top? Every one of them belongs to my father. *He's* the one who requested a week from Androvore, and your boss agreed. But now you're telling me the hourglass was just a tracking device, and Androvore's going to *steal* the time he promised Baal Zebul? Hoo boy!"

Oslük licked his lips. "So what? How will His Lordship even know?"

"Well, I told Dad we'd be wrapping things up tonight. He's planning to attend the festivities. Don't you think he'll be curious when I don't turn up?"

Oslük shot Throk an anxious glance. "We didn't make any promises to Lord Baal himself. We're just following orders."

"Good luck with that," said Laszlo flatly. "Dad may not be my number one fan, but as someone familiar with his moods, I can assure you he's going to hit the fucking roof when he learns that a couple of Class III maggots interfered in family business. You do have some balls, gentlemen, I'll give you that. Not for much longer, mind, but you've certainly got 'em."

Silence.

The two demons looked at each other, then at Laszlo, then at the Drakefords, and finally back at each other once again. Maggie listened to the ticking clock and marveled inwardly at Laszlo's casual arrogance. It was simultaneously impressive and unsettling. He was too clever a liar, too effortlessly deceptive. Whenever she was tempted to write him off as a buffoon, he showed a competence that surprised her. Which was the real Laszlo?

Had she ever seen the real Laszlo?

Throk scratched a pimple on his chin. "We can't just let you go. Androvore would crucible us. He's an Overseer."

"And my father's a Lord of Hell," said Laszlo coldly. "Pick your poison, gents. In your shoes, I'd at least give the boss a ring and explain the situation."

Oslük gave his partner a hasty nod. Phone in hand, Throk hurried from the room.

Oslük promptly claimed the desk chair and jabbed a thick finger at Laszlo. "No funny business. Don't even think of making a break for it."

"I'm not going anywhere," said Laszlo. "I honestly can't wait to see what happens to you." He turned to the Drakefords. "How are you two holding up?"

"Okay," said Lump unconvincingly.

Maggie didn't answer. She was too busy watching the clock. It was almost three already. They only had until midnight to complete the ceremony at the Witchstone. Every minute lost seemed a catastrophe.

"Don't sweat it," Laszlo said easily. "We've got time."

Maggie fiddled with the Signora's ring. "Are you sure?"

"Positive."

When Throk returned, looking pale and greasy, he barely made eye contact with Laszlo. "Androvore wants to see you."

"Splendid. Is he coming here?"

"No. We're to bring you to him."

"To the office?" said Laszlo brightly. "Oh, goody!"

"Are we going too?" asked Maggie.

Throk chewed at his lip. "I forgot to ask."

"Of course they're going," said Laszlo. "It's Bring Your Humans to Work Day. Now, if you wouldn't mind removing these handcuffs, I'm feeling a bit confined . . ."

The captors *did* mind and stubbornly refused, even after Laszlo explained that he was missing his sarkyra. When they asked how it came to be missing, he assured them it was a thrilling tale they'd never get to hear.

The disgruntled demons packed up everyone's things and marched them from an elevator to a parking garage, where a still-handcuffed Laszlo and the Drakefords were crammed into the back seat of a police cruiser.

The trip into Manhattan went quickly. Lights flashing and sirens blaring, Oslük wove through traffic and edged along the shoulder. In spite of his missing sarkyra, Laszlo managed to maintain a lively chatter: Did the goons root for the Jets or Giants? What was the line for Sunday's games? Had they ever encountered Baal's Grand Inquisitor? Laszlo had met the Inquisitor once at a family retreat and assured them that the stories didn't do the creature justice.

"I mean, we're on *vacation*, and It brings a dissecting table!" he said, laughing. "Who *does* that? And so many tools! One of the kits had an eye spoon. Can you believe it? An *eye* spoon! And goddamn if that thing doesn't work. It's like a melon baller with . . ."

They headed up Third Avenue and turned left on Fifty-Third Street. Four blocks later, Oslük killed the sirens and pulled into another garage, where he made for the lower levels.

Laszlo rapped the bulletproof partition. "Guys, the elevator's by the loading dock."

Throk chuckled. "The elevator's for nobodies. There's a special lot for bigwigs."

"What?" cried Laszlo. "Nobody told me about—"

When he saw that the goons were enjoying his outrage, Laszlo leaned back to stew in silence. The cruiser drove right through what looked like a solid wall and proceeded down a dim ramp; it ended at a guard booth, where Throk showed his ID to a ghoulish-looking attendant. The whatever-it-was pressed a button, raising a gate not unlike a portcullis. The cruiser kept going, winding down a ramp that continued farther beneath the city than Maggie would have thought possible.

They parked in a lot illuminated with green torches. Oslük and Throk hauled the trio from the back seat and escorted them toward a stone archway whose lintel was etched with strange characters.

For explanation, she looked to Laszlo, but he was too busy muttering about the parking lot, the luxury cars it held, and the fact that some of his colleagues were apparently pulling in a lot more cabbage than he was.

Lump was wondering about the inscription too. "What does that say?"

"'The Ancient and Infernal Society of Curse Keepers,'" Laszlo recited from memory. "'Established 5036 BC. Our Reach Endless, Our Grasp Eter—' *Are you fucking kidding me?*"

Maggie froze. "What?"

Their Keeper was staring at a silver Aston Martin whose license plate read *G8LN5RK.*

"Does that say 'Goblin Shark'?" Lump was practically vibrating with excitement. "Didn't you say Clarence has the head of a goblin shark? Is he here? Can we meet him?"

"Yeah, yeah," Laszlo groused. "He can show you around while I chat with Androvore."

Maggie raised her eyebrows. "Shouldn't *we* be talking to Androvore too?"

"Definitely not."

"Because?"

"You want to get home by tonight, don't you?"

"Yes."

"Then let me handle him."

Laszlo did seem to know how to deal with his own kind, and Maggie knew that he had as much incentive to get to Schemerdaal as they did. The grains in his hourglass were running low. The demon desperately needed his sarkyra back.

And only Maggie had the power to make that happen.

They entered the building through a pair of glass doors and proceeded down several corridors, passing storage rooms, mail rooms, and other rooms lined with trash or recycling bins, until finally they reached another pair of doors that opened onto a massive space filled with cubicles.

The Drakefords stared at the busy office and its staff: squat imps in bellboy uniforms, birdlike demons and mammalian demons, scaly horrors with gibbon heads, and a bat-like fellow hunched over a copier, scratching his corduroys.

As Oslük and Throk led them onward, word spread that humans were on the premises.

Everyone hurried to get a glimpse.

Maggie saw a fiftyish, bespectacled demon with seven bulbous eyes and a lower body composed of blue tentacles appear in an aisle clutching some files. Her voice was appalled.

"Oh. My. God."

Laszlo spotted her. "Ms. Spiegel! How are you? Drakefords, this is my assistant, Freykka Spiegel."

"*Former* assistant," she corrected. "And did you say 'Drakefords'? As in your *Curse Bearers*?"

"That's right," said Laszlo. "I thought it was high time they saw the office."

Lump waved and introduced himself.

Ms. Spiegel nodded weakly, with a somewhat repulsed expression. Maggie thought she had some nerve, considering her own means of locomotion.

"*Laszlo!*" cried a voice.

There were rapid footsteps. Coming up behind Oslük was the oddest-looking creature she'd ever seen—a plump humanoid wearing a lavender shirt and natty suit tailored to accommodate its legs, which were shaped like those of a goat or sheep. Up top, it wore a pair of pince-nez clamped to an elongated, flat snout whose mouth was lined with naillike teeth. Beady black eyes twinkled with pleasure as its maw stretched into what Maggie assumed was a smile.

This peculiar being did not hug Laszlo so much as collide with him. Laszlo immediately tried to wriggle out of its frantic and surprisingly stubborn grasp. Maggie caught the strong scent of cologne.

The new demon's shriek was all too familiar. "They *handcuffed you!*"

"It's okay," said Laszlo, twisting himself so Clarence could not examine his restraints. "Really, Clarence, it's fine."

Clarence wheeled on Throk and Oslük. "*You're brutes!*"

"Move it, Stubby," Oslük growled. "His Fiendishness is expecting us."

"Hold up," said Laszlo. "Clarence, look after the Drakefords. Make them feel at home."

Clarence squealed with excitement and practically tunneled through Androvore's goons to get at Maggie and Lump. Seizing each of them by a hand, he declared that he'd be *delighted*, and would the humans like some cider or hot chocolate?

Maggie said that sounded fine, and Clarence whisked them away to a break room containing a kitchenette and several vending machines. There was only one demon there; it had the head of a mandrill and was reading the *Economist* over a cup of tea. At their boisterous entrance, the demon looked up from its magazine, stared at the humans, and quietly edged out of the room.

Clarence began rummaging in a cabinet. "I can't believe I'm meeting you in person. I mean, I already felt like I knew you, but—*bada boom*—here you are! Oh, my stars."

"Should we sit down?" asked Maggie.

"*Yes!* Dear me," he said with some embarrassment, "you'd never know I host professionally."

Maggie chose a table by the vending machines. "Was that before you joined the Society?"

"Oh, no," said Clarence from the cupboard. "I've been here for ages. I just moonlight a little at Olive Garden. You know, for the breadsticks."

"How interesting." Maggie checked the time on the wall clock. Almost four. Beside it was a bulletin board with an emergency exit diagram and an Urgent Notice regarding break room etiquette. Apparently, *someone* had been helping themselves to other demons' lunches, and this would *not* be tolerated. A handwritten addition suggested the culprit was named Todd.

Lump tapped Maggie's arm. "How long do you think it'll take to get home?"

"Three or four hours, probably."

Clarence was now exploring a different cabinet. "Cider or cocoa?"

"Whatever's easiest," said Maggie.

"Oh, it's no bother. We've got these pod thingies. French roast? Chai latte? Cocoa? Whatever you want! The convenience is a dream, but I'm not a fan of the plastic . . ."

A few minutes later, the demon bustled over with three cocoas. He distributed the mugs and napkins as if they were having a tea party.

"I want to hear everything," he whispered. "Liechtenstein. Signora Bellascura. *The assassin!* How did you get away? I haven't been able to sleep!"

"It's a long story," said Maggie. "But first—"

Clarence gasped as if he'd just remembered something terribly important. "Would you prefer my human guise?" he asked solicitously. "I should have checked right away. You're probably completely repulsed and too polite to say anything."

"You look fine," Lump assured him. "And your cologne smells like applewood."

The goblin shark blushed. "You like it? I got it for my girlfriend. She's into camping—well, more like *glamping*—and I thought it would remind her of bacon. I was watching *The Fellowship of the Ring*—the extended version, naturally—and there's that scene where the hobbits are cooking bacon, and it was just so cozy that—"

Clarence suddenly caught some kind of scent and whipped his head around. Three new demons were watching the humans through the break room window.

"This isn't the zoo!"

The heads withdrew.

"They don't mean to be rude," he explained. "It's just we don't get many humans down here."

"That's okay," said Lump. "But you were talking about *Lord of the Rings*. Are you a Tolkien fan?"

"A *fan*?" Clarence almost shrieked. "You are looking at a former junior secretary of the American Tolkien Society."

"You're kidding."

"I'm not. *Pedil edhellen?*"

Joy flooded Lump's face. He responded with a flurry of lyrical-sounding nonsense.

Clarence flapped his hands in delight. Leaping to his feet, he bowed so enthusiastically that his snout bonked the table. He said something equally nonsensical, which prompted Lump to rise, give a majestic bow, and respond in kind.

The two immediately fell into a spirited discussion that included whether Balrogs had wings, what the Blue Wizards were up to, and if Treebeard or Tom Bombadil was the oldest being in Middle-earth.

Fascinating as this was, Maggie felt she could make better use of her time. For one thing, she wasn't thrilled that Laszlo was off on his own. What if Androvore had him crucibled before they could break the curse?

From the way their Keeper described the situation, it sounded like this Androvore had swept onto the scene, reviewed the Society's books, and decided the Drakeford Curse was no longer worth their time. He was the reason Maggie and Lump had run themselves ragged trying to break it before they lost their Curse Keeper.

"Excuse me," she said, after taking a sip of cocoa. "Where is Malignis Androvore's office?"

Clarence was slightly preoccupied. "All the way down the corridor," he told her. "Big bronze door under the flat-screens."

She thanked him, and as she rose, he looked up. "What are you doing?"

"Heading over there," she replied.

"Oh, but you can't. His Fiendishness is very particular about appointments. You'll never get past his people. There's an army of assistants!"

Maggie chewed on this before walking over to study the emergency exit diagram. "Is this map to scale?"

Clarence replied that it was and resumed his conversation with Lump. "Personally, I think if you stretched ol' Smaug from tail to snout, he'd measure in at . . ."

She removed the diagram from the bulletin board. Neither Tolkien fanatic noticed as she measured the room's length in sheets of standard paper. Once she had a number, she consulted the emergency exit diagram to estimate how far it was to Androvore's office.

It was hard to ignore some of the diagram's details, like the rooms labeled *Soul Processing* and *Pain Enhancement*. For all its bureaucratic trappings and break rooms, the Ancient and Infernal Society was an outpost of Hell.

Its purpose was to profit from human misery.

A chilling reminder, but it didn't change the task at hand. Studying the diagram, Maggie mentally marked a spot by the bathrooms that was roughly 115 feet away from Androvore's office. Then she pinned the diagram back to the bulletin board and retrieved the seven-rod slippers from her backpack.

"Clarence?" she said.

The demon was busy showing Lump his Tolkien Society membership card. "Yes?"

"Would it be okay if I run out to use the ladies' room?"

"Of course. I'll show you where it is."

"No need," said Maggie. "I found it on the map."

"Righty-ho."

Magic slippers in hand, she left the pair to Tolkien and their cocoa.

CHAPTER 30
DISCLOSURES

Laszlo had to concede that the new boss was efficient. The Overseer had made many changes in a mere five days; so many that Laszlo had to restrain himself from quoting Genesis. It wasn't the time for jokes, considering that he might well be walking to his execution.

Nevertheless, the transformation was remarkable. Scylla and Kozlowski weren't the only Keepers to have vanished. He also counted Plibb, Steizll, Hanzo, Grooba, and Dave—and those were only the empty cubicles he passed. The whole office smelled of fresh paint, new blood, and even new plants. On every pillar were inspirational posters: *Suffering Spawns Success! Pain Prompts Performance! Make Mortals Miserable!* The guy was clearly a fan of alliteration. And exclamation points!

The most conspicuous changes had been made to the wall outside Androvore's office. Last week, it had been paneled in mahogany. Now, it looked like something out of Times Square. Bright screens covered every inch, forming a glowing mosaic of changing images and information. One screen showed a live feed of souls being tormented by demons of R&S—Rack and Screw. Another had a news program hosted by a succubus reporting on curse-induced tragedies around the globe. Stock ticker screens had live readings of individual curse performances. He saw one that benchmarked the MM&D output of various Society branches. New York's production was lower than its global counterparts, but there had been a recent performance uptick. Laszlo had no doubt that it was due to the flame-crowned demon now giving an interview on the largest screen of all.

There were at least a dozen unfamiliar demons sitting behind a curving wall of desks that barricaded the Overseer's office. Each was busier than a 911 operator.

As they approached, a carp-colored demoness wearing a headset and blocking the barricade's only gap motioned that they stop.

"He's expecting us," Throk told her.

Ms. Bluetooth glanced at his orthopedic loafers. "That's fantastic, but His Fiendishness is wrapping up an interview. You'll just have to wait."

Laszlo cleared his throat. "This is kind of a *time-sensitive* situation."

He received the sort of smile found on pharmaceutical brochures. "I'm aware—but don't you worry, Keeper 923. We'll have you in and out of there in five to seven minutes."

"Our business might take longer than that."

"So sorry. His Fiendishness has a four o'clock."

"With who?" demanded Laszlo. "This is *important*."

"I'm not at liberty to discuss the Overseer's appointments."

Standing on tiptoe, Laszlo craned his neck about the office. "Where's Thatcher? I want to talk to Thatcher, dammit!"

"So sorry, but Supervisor Thatcher is with the consultants."

"Consultants?"

"Yes, we've engaged McKinsey. They're interviewing key personnel."

"No shit. Do they need to speak with me?"

An amused glance. "That won't be necessary."

"You're a cold fish, you know that?" The assistant gave a little frown and shook her head emphatically. "Well, you could have fooled me," said Laszlo.

But Ms. Bluetooth wasn't listening. She flicked her headset to improve the connection. "Mario? Mario, are you there? Hi. It's me. The new gal screwed up the order. I wanted a *Cobb* salad. That's right. C-O-B-B. Bacon on the side. Thanks, babe." She ended the call and looked to Laszlo. "I'm sorry, were you saying something?" He simply shook his head.

Something brushed against his leg, and he looked down just in time to see a reptilian tail slither by. It belonged to an albino alligator some twenty feet long. An anxious-looking imp was controlling the beast—or trying to—by means of a leash attached to a spiked collar around its neck. As they passed, the alligator hissed and broke into a run, dragging the imp along as it made a sharp left turn and barreled down a row of cubicles. Moments later, there was a bloodcurdling shriek.

Laszlo wished he could cover his ears. "What the hell is that?"

"Productivity Gators™," said Ms. Bluetooth. "McKinsey came up with them. The sewer reptiles are blind but so sensitive to their surroundings they can tell if a potential meal is idle or dozing. We've turned local liabilities into assets," she added proudly. "Time theft is down eighty-three percent."

"Oh, for fuck's sake," said Laszlo. "Someone tell Pretentio Man-Eater it's the *humans* who are supposed to be miserable, not us."

Ms. Bluetooth flashed the sweetest of smiles. "You can tell him yourself."

As she spoke, the doors to Androvore's office opened wide.

Laszlo beheld the Overseer himself towering over a reporter and television crew. As Androvore bade them farewell, he noticed Laszlo and the two goons and gave Ms. Bluetooth an almost imperceptible nod.

She stood aside to let the trio pass. "Go right ahead, gentlemen. I'll be in shortly, so don't get too comfy!"

Laszlo privately wished a Productivity Gator™ would sink its teeth into her ass.

Throk and Oslük led him into a sprawling office that dwarfed the hotel suite in Zurich. Modern art and koi ponds abounded, along with sleek furniture designed by angsty Scandinavians. One wall stood out from the rest: it was covered entirely with instruments resembling seismometers, displayed in a neat and tidy array.

Sir Malignis Androvore stood behind a massive desk of stainless steel topped with white marble. Just how tall was the Overseer? Nine feet?

Ten? Laszlo gazed up at that leonine head and its crown of flickering white flames. The guy might have picked a ridiculous name, but he'd sure made some shrewd selections when it came to his body.

Oslük bowed to Androvore before setting Laszlo's hourglass and curse folio on the desk. "Anything else, boss?"

"No. Remove his restraints and wait outside."

"You want us to remove the cuffs?"

The Overseer was amused. "Do you fear for my safety?"

"No, Your Fiendishness. Of course not. It's just—"

"Take them off and sit him down. Keeper 923 looks dead on his feet."

Throk did as instructed, although he was none too gentle as he unlocked the handcuffs and pushed Laszlo into one of the chairs before Androvore's desk.

Laszlo rubbed his wrists. "Thanks, Chief. Fetch me a LaCroix while you're at it. Something with a little zing." Throk glowered but said nothing.

When he and Oslük had gone, closing the heavy door behind them, Androvore sat down and looked Laszlo over.

"I see your mouth still works. I'm not so certain about the rest. What happened to you, 923? If I didn't know better, I'd say you've had a trying week."

Laszlo made a show of looking around. "It's been busy. Looks like you've been busy too."

"Did anyone give you a tour?"

"Nope. Like those Productivity Gators™, though. Classy."

A chuckle. "Yes, I have a feeling they'd be fans of yours."

"Good thing my office has a door."

Androvore sighed and flicked a speck of dust from his desktop. "I regret to inform you that your office has been reassigned. So has Ms. Spiegel."

Laszlo wasn't going to give his boss the gratification of seeing him upset. "Well, I can't say that I'm surprised. You'd already reneged on our agreement."

The Overseer tutted. "Reneged? Do tell."

"Please," said Laszlo. "Your goons have been on my ass from minute one. You promised me a week, Androvore. A *Hell* week, but a week nonetheless. And what do you do? Give me an hourglass that lets them track me, harass me, *and* steal back the very time you promised. If that wasn't enough, a fucking *assassin* tried to Palpatine me in Rome."

"Palpatine?"

"It's a *Star Wars* thing."

"I see. I'll confess, I did hear about that little incident. Rumor has it you took refuge in a church. I refused to believe it. A *Zebul* siding with the Enemy?" The demon sighed. "Well, let's just say it doesn't look good—"

"My ass got dragged in there," said Laszlo. "And don't change the subject. You've been sabotaging me from the beginning. And when my *father* finds out—"

Androvore held up a clawed hand. "Let me stop you there."

"Why?"

"Your situation is humiliating enough without playing the daddy card again."

"Oh, really?" said Laszlo. "You think my father's just going to let it slide when he learns what you've been up to?"

"No. I think he's going to let this slide because he knows *exactly* what I've been up to."

In what was becoming an uncomfortably familiar routine, the Overseer passed him a sheet of parchment bearing the ducal seal.

SIR MALIGNIS,

RECEIVED YOUR FOLLOW-UP QUERY. OBSTACLES ARE AN EXCELLENT IDEA—WHAT BETTER WAY TO TEST THE BOY'S METTLE? YOU HAVE MY SUPPORT FOR ANY AND ALL, INCLUDING THE MORE EXTREME ELEMENTS. HAVE YOU CONSIDERED MAKING THE HOURGLASS A HOMING BEACON? JUST A SUGGESTION . . .

Laszlo closed his eyes. Honestly, why did he fucking bother?

There was a knock at the door, and Ms. Bluetooth entered. "Sorry to interrupt, but Mr. Z.'s standing by for your videoconference."

"He can wait," Androvore ordered. "Tell him I'll take it out of Jeffrey or Elon's time."

"Will do," said Ms. Bluetooth. The door closed.

"Mr. Z.?" said Laszlo.

"New initiative," said Androvore lazily. "Research suggests eighty percent of billionaires will barter their souls if it means subjecting rivals to supernatural torment. Naturally, moving first has inherent advantages. Once they learn we're already chatting with the competition, the pressure to commit skyrockets. It's basic game theory."

"Damn."

The Overseer spread his hands. "What can I say? I have a vision, 923. The Society has a virtual monopoly on curses, but it's never put that leverage to work. Why just *manage* curses when we can grow the entire market? Did you know that twenty percent of mortals would be willing to sell their souls to invoke a curse in moments of acute emotional distress? The number's even higher on Wall Street. Why don't they take the leap? The answer's simple: they don't know they can! They assume curses exist only in movies and comic books. I intend to change that."

Laszlo took a moment to ponder this. "Honestly, it's brilliant."

"You're too kind."

"I could help, you know," offered Laszlo. "I'm a natural-born salesman. Humans love me. Some even say I look like Paul Newman in *The Long, Hot Summer*."

"Have you looked in a mirror lately? I'd go with *The Verdict*."

"Nothing a tan can't cure," said Laszlo. "But seriously. I'd *crush* it as a salesman, especially if the incentives were juicy."

Androvore checked a notification on his phone. "At the moment, they couldn't be juicier."

"What do you mean?"

Setting down the phone, the Overseer gave Laszlo his undivided attention. "*Sell* me, 923. Convince me I shouldn't crucible you this very minute."

"No problem." Laszlo began to tick points off on his fingers. "First, the hourglass isn't empty, so you'd be violating our agreement. Second,

I'm about to demolish your performance targets. Last but not least, if you melt me down, you'll be pissing away the greatest opportunity of your Ooze-spawned existence."

The Overseer raised a flaming eyebrow. "What are you talking about?"

"*Sir* Malignis," Laszlo mused aloud. "Does that mean you're a Knight of Hell?"

"Not a knight," the demon growled. "A baronet."

"What's the difference?"

"Baronet's a higher rank," said Androvore proudly.

"That's cute," replied Laszlo. "I can never keep this stuff straight. Tell me, do baronets count as *lords*? I mean, are you a member of the peerage? Do you have a seat in the Daemadùna?"

A pause. "No."

"I see. So that makes you a commoner, correct? A mere dreg."

The Overseer replied in a stiff undertone. "Technically speaking."

"So, *technically* speaking, every member of the Daemadùna outranks you. No matter how weak or incompetent they might be."

Malignis Androvore narrowed his eyes. "What's your point, 923?"

Laszlo sprung the trap. "*This* is my point. If you start playing *with* me instead of *against* me, 'Sir' Malignis' could be 'Lord Androvore' by next Walpurgisnacht."

At this, the Overseer laughed so hard a paperweight vibrated across his desk. As his mirth intensified, the flickering fire about his head grew into leaping flames. They nearly scorched the ceiling before he recovered himself. "Forget salesman. I should keep you as a jester."

Laszlo blinked. "I'm sorry, but what was so funny?"

"You claimed that *you* could make *me* a peer."

"Not quite," he clarified. "Only Lucifer can elevate you to the peerage. But I guarantee His Infernal Highness will be happy to, once he learns the little secret I've discovered."

"And what's that, pray tell?"

"Now, what kind of salesman would I be if I just gave away the goods?"

"Ah, but you've miscalculated," said Androvore. "A good salesman stretches the truth within reason. You've overextended yourself, 923. Here you are promising a peerage, when you can't even complete the basic tasks I gave you."

"Is this about MM&D ratings?" Laszlo waved this away. "Pfft. That's as good as done."

"I've already had my laugh for the decade," the Overseer told him. "Allow me to direct your attention to those instruments. Top row, third from the left."

Laszlo squinted at the array of seismometers and located the machine that Androvore had indicated. Its spindly arms were busy tracing two lines near the bottom axis. "Is that the Drakeford Curse?"

Androvore nodded. "I didn't think it possible, but you've somehow managed to *lower* their misery and despair. We'll have to make you a case study."

Again, Laszlo dismissed this with a wave. "All part of the plan."

A chuckle. "I see. You have a 'grand strategy,' do you?"

"Don't sound so shocked."

"Humor me, 923. What's your angle?"

"Simple." As Laszlo spoke, a smile grew on his face. "I tricked my Bearers into thinking they only had a week to break the curse before it gets mothballed. They bought it, and for the past five days, we've been running ourselves ragged gathering materia. They have everything required, Your Fiendishness. All that's left is for you to release me so I can lead my stooges to the slaughter."

Androvore tapped the desktop. "If they already have everything, why do they need you?"

"Because I told them a Curse Keeper has to be present to 'certify' that the spell's been broken. They don't think the ceremony can start without me."

A grunt. "And once the ceremony's underway, you intend to disrupt it."

Laszlo nodded. "Right at the end, Your Fiendishness. Right when their hopes are highest . . ."

There was another knock at the door. It opened, and Ms. Bluetooth's perky face appeared in the gap.

Androvore shot her an impatient look. "Not now."

"But Mr. Z.—"

"*Out!*"

The door closed. Laszlo noticed a change in the Overseer's demeanor.

Leaning back, Androvore steepled his fingers as though deep in thought. "The MM&D ratings will skyrocket," he murmured. "What's more, you'll have prevented a Curse-Breaking Event . . ."

"Exactly," said Laszlo. "I'd be hitting *two* of the targets. You said I only needed one."

Androvore nodded to confirm that this was indeed the case. He examined Laszlo as though seeing him properly for the first time. "923, I'll admit you've surprised me. Perhaps I misjudged you."

"I hear that a lot."

"Well," said Androvore. "On to more important things. Namely, the matter of my being raised to the peerage. How much pull do you have with Lucifer?"

"Zero," said Laszlo. "Actually, it's probably less than zero. Lucifer and my family aren't super tight."

"Then how can you possibly help me?"

"Easy. I'll supply proof that Baal Zebul tricked Lucifer and the nobles and that he parlayed his deception into a spot on the Council."

Silence. "*You're kidding.*"

"I'm not. And when Lucifer has this proof, he'll use it to turn the Council against my father. With their support, he'll finally have the strength to eliminate the greatest threat to his reign. Can you *imagine* the rewards he'll heap upon the demon who makes this possible? Forget a baronetcy. He'll make you an earl. Maybe even a duke!"

Malignis Androvore stared at Laszlo for a full minute before he spoke. "You are playing an exceedingly dangerous game, 923. One that is so far out of your league I can't decide if you're comically desperate or clinically insane."

"Maybe I'm both. But that doesn't mean I'm wrong."

"So what is this 'deception' you've stumbled upon?" asked Androvore.

Laszlo wagged a finger. "Nope. Not a word until you let me finish what I've started. I've upheld my part of the bargain. You need to uphold yours."

"That's one option." The Overseer's smile revealed his canines. "But what if I just torture the secret out of you instead?"

Opening his shirt, Laszlo displayed the scar on his chest. "Good luck with that. I'm missing my sarkyra, amigo. I'll be dead at the first thumbscrew."

Understanding dawned. "That's it, then. I was wondering why you looked like something from the morgue. What happened to your sarkyra?"

"It's in someone else's keeping."

"Did you sell it to acquire materia for your Bearers?" said Androvore. "I hope not, 923. That would violate Rule 7A of the Keeper Code."

"Relax. My Bearers acquired everything themselves. The sarkyra's just collateral to ensure they make final payment. When they do, I'll get it back. No harm, no foul."

Androvore swiveled in his oversize chair to the wall of MM&D recorders. He looked to be deep in thought. At length, his basso voice formed a question.

"Am I really to believe you'd betray your own father?"

Laszlo held up the letter Androvore had shown him. "That depends. Are we talking about the father who signed off on having his son crucibled or assassinated? *That* father?"

"Fair point." Still, the Overseer did not look entirely comfortable with these developments. He rubbed a hand across his jaw. "I wish to make it unequivocally clear that I, Sir Malignis Androvore, would *never* betray Lord Baal or any other member of the High Council. But if I was to be made aware of some deceit—great or small—that affected His Unholiness, Lord Lucifer, it would be my solemn duty to report it."

It was Laszlo's turn to laugh. "What is this? Do you think I'm wearing a wire?"

The Overseer looked at him levelly. "It's a possibility."

"Want me to strip?" said Laszlo. "No problem. I love being naked."

"Kindly keep your trousers on. The chairs are new."

"Fine. But just so you know, no one else is listening." Androvore considered his wall of instruments. "Full disclosure?" said Laszlo. "Lying is kind of my thing. I do it for shits and giggles. But I haven't told a single lie since I walked in here. You already know that."

"Are you suggesting I rely on some kind of primitive machine to tell me whether someone is telling the truth? Don't be absurd."

Laszlo pointed at the wall. "Fifth row down, second from the left—you know, the lie detector camouflaged to blend in with the MM&D recorders? Now, its needle didn't so much as wiggle when you claimed it didn't exist, so either it's broken or the machine's been programmed to ignore your voice."

The Overseer said nothing.

"Listen," said Laszlo. "Time's ticking and Z-man's on hold. You can crucible me now, or you can release me and get the highest MM&D ratings in your portfolio, along with intel that transforms *Sir* Malignis into *Lord* Androvore. I know what I'd do."

Laszlo leaned back in his chair. He felt surprisingly relaxed. His case was sound, and he'd appealed to the one thing ambitious bootlickers like Androvore craved above all else: *advancement.* It didn't matter how well Androvore ran the New York branch or even if he took over *all* the Society's branches. He'd still just be an employee, a commoner, a *dreg* that crawled from the Primordial Ooze. How that must rankle someone like the Overseer. So strong, so capable, yet nothing more than a captain of someone else's yacht.

The instant Laszlo had mentioned a peerage, he knew he'd found the way to Androvore's sarkyra. Nothing surpassed that desire. Now that it had been kindled, he knew he was home free. Nothing could *possibly* screw things up now—

And then Maggie Drakeford appeared.

If nothing else, the girl knew how to make an entrance. She appeared out of thin air over the Overseer's koi pond. There was a splash and a startled yelp, followed by Maggie's leaping out of the water. Unfortunately, the seven-rod slippers made her vanish as quickly as she'd appeared.

A moment later, she was back. "Sorry!" she blurted. "I'd better take these off."

She pulled off the slippers and stood in her dripping socks. Her eyes went first to Laszlo, then to Malignis Androvore, who was rising from his chair.

As he stood at full height, his hair aflame, all color drained from Maggie's face. "Oh my God," she murmured.

To his credit, the Overseer did not betray one iota of surprise. He merely looked down at her with an expression of nonplussed curiosity. "And who might you be?"

"M-Maggie," she stammered. "I mean, *Margaret* Drakeford."

"And am I correct in assuming that you are human?"

"Yes, sir."

"I see. Well, Margaret the Human, welcome to the Ancient and Infernal Society, and thank you for uncovering a security flaw. We will address it. In the meantime, what can I do for you?"

Laszlo had to finesse the situation—head Maggie off, prevent her from doing or saying anything that could derail his plans. "Maggie," he said, his tone both calm and pleading, "everything's settled. Go back to Lump."

He looked intensely at her with all the feeling he could muster. *Don't argue, don't argue, don't argue . . .* Sadly, telepathy was a Class V power.

Maggie shook her head. "I'm sorry, Laszlo, but there are some things I need to say." She turned to Androvore. "Sir, I'm sorry to have barged in, but may I speak freely?"

If Laszlo had his sarkyra back, he would have smashed it with a hammer. At this point, the universe was simply laughing at him.

"By all means," said Androvore.

"Thank you," said Maggie. She stood very straight, one hand clutching the seven-rod slippers, the other cupped underneath to catch the water dripping from them. "Sir, I know that your organization doesn't believe my family's curse deserves your resources or attention. And I know that Laszlo's in trouble with you personally. Based on what I've seen, he probably deserves it."

Spots swam before Laszlo's eyes. He gripped the sides of his chair, curious if the sensation was mere vertigo or if his body was honoring his plea to self-destruct.

"We've been through a lot since Friday," Maggie continued. "We've done everything we can to give ourselves a shot at breaking this curse. And my hope is that we can do just that and also get it marked in your books as a spell that's been managed through its life cycle. Win-win."

Androvore shot an amused glance at Laszlo but said nothing.

"And Laszlo . . ." she added. "Well, he's been kind of a hero. I can't tell you how many times I chalked him up as a jackass or just a lying, lazy piece of shit, if you'll pardon the expression—"

"Of course," said Androvore.

"But he's *changed*." Her voice took on a note of wonder. "And *I've* changed too, and not just in the terrible ways the curse works. It's strange to think Laszlo could make me a better person, but he has. I've never been able to trust anyone. But I *trust* Laszlo. I might not want to, but I do. And so does my brother. All I'm asking is to please let us finish what we've started. We'll be out of your hair—uh, flames—in no time. You'll never have to hear about the Drakefords again. We're so close, sir. So goddamn close after all these years. *Please*."

Tears glinted in Maggie's eyes. Her petition was remarkably sincere, even moving—best of all, she hadn't mentioned Laszlo's father, the Witchstone, or the Lost Magi. In short, it was not an outright catastrophe.

Not yet, anyway. Laszlo had no idea how Androvore would respond to a human trespasser on the edge of his koi pond.

The Overseer came out from behind his desk. Maggie went even paler but nonetheless stood her ground, gazing stoically up at the demon as he loomed over her. To Laszlo's surprise, Androvore lowered himself to one knee so he could look Maggie in the eye.

"Miss Drakeford," he intoned. "You are a remarkable young woman, and I want you to understand that, in spite of any torments you or your family have experienced at our hands, it was never personal. The Society simply manages curses invoked by others. We carry out their instructions to the best of our ability, because that is our job. And while we have professional duties, that doesn't mean we can't rejoice when a Bearer shows that they're ready to meet their obligations, leave their curse behind, and start a fresh chapter. You *are* ready, Miss Drakeford, and I salute you for not only gathering the materia so quickly but overcoming the obstacles I placed in your way. As you yourself acknowledge, Keeper 923 has a talent for aggravating his betters. I suppose I must have wanted him to fail, and that was unprofessional. Please accept my sincere apology."

Maggie looked as stunned as Laszlo felt. "Um, of course, sir. Apology accepted."

"Thank you," said Androvore. "And now, I think the best thing I can do is step aside and let you complete your task without further delay."

"You'll call off the dogs?" she asked, hopefully.

"I will. I'll even lend you the police car. A few sirens are handy if you hit traffic."

Laszlo watched with fascination as Androvore sheathed his claws and took Maggie's hand gently within his own. Then the Overseer informed Keeper 923 that he was free to go.

It took a moment for the words to register, but Laszlo eventually lurched into motion. Maggie came over as he forced his weakened body from the chair and snagged the curse folio and hourglass from Androvore's desk.

Androvore led them out, ignoring Ms. Bluetooth's puzzled questions about the human. Snapping his fingers, he called Oslük over and told him to surrender the keys to the cruiser. This Oslük did, pressing them into Laszlo's hand with a not-too-subtle death stare.

"Thanks, sporto. No hard feelings." And Laszlo winked.

A massive hand settled on his shoulder; he almost tipped over. Androvore's voice purred in his ear. "I'm glad we could chat, 923. I look forward to the ceremony."

Maggie looked up at the Overseer. "You're coming, sir?"

The massive hand on Laszlo's shoulder tightened a smidgeon.

The mere hint of its strength was appalling. Androvore, if he wished, could tear off Laszlo's arm like a chicken wing.

The Overseer beamed down at Maggie. "I wouldn't miss it for the world."

"Fantastic," said Laszlo. "I'll text you the address."

Androvore playfully tapped the hourglass clutched to Laszlo's chest. "No need."

He managed a weak laugh and, ducking out from under Androvore's grip, led Maggie away.

Laszlo ignored the stares, waited for a Productivity Gator™ to pass, then hurried them to the break room, where they found Lump and Clarence engaged in animated conversation.

"Laszlo!" squealed Clarence.

Lump's eyes went to Maggie's handful of dripping slippers. "Where have you been?"

"She'll explain on the way," said Laszlo. "Lump, grab your shit and let's go. Clarence, walk us to that parking lot you've never mentioned."

Clarence was only too happy. He hurried along, chattering ceaselessly, even opening the car doors for each Drakeford like he was their chauffeur. Laszlo took the driver's seat and turned the key. The cruiser's powerful engine roared to life. With its lights and siren, they'd be in the Catskills in no time.

Laszlo lowered the window as Clarence came around to say goodbye. The goblin shark handed him a rolled-up parchment. "The Signora's instructions?"

"Yes sirree," said Clarence. "All translated and ready to go. I promised Lump I'd take him to the next Tolkien convention, once the curse is broken. He can borrow my Legolas wig."

Laszlo tried to scrub the image from his brain. "That's great. Listen, Clarence, we've gotta run, but I want you to know you've been a huge help. We couldn't have done this without you."

The goblin shark flushed maroon. "Shoot. It was nothing."

"No, I mean it. And one good turn deserves another. Do me a favor, and hold out your hand."

Clarence obliged with trembling anticipation. The trembling stopped as a vintage watch fell into his palm. Tiny shark eyes stared at the object in confusion.

"Recognize it?" said Laszlo.

The demon's shriek echoed off the walls of the parking lot. "*My watch!*" cried Clarence. "Oh, my sweet Breguet! Where on Earth did you find it?"

Leaning out the window, Laszlo spoke in a pointed whisper. "*Androvore's office!*"

Understanding dawned slowly on that innocent face. Closing his chubby fingers around the watch, Clarence made a fist that trembled with indignant rage.

"*That motherfucker.*"

CHAPTER 31
PRINCESS PRIMROSE

It was just past eight o'clock in Schemerdaal. The October evening was clear and cold, with a gibbous moon hanging high above the Catskills. As usual, the village was quiet. Aside from the occasional porch light and the neon sign at Earl's, it was country dark, without even a streetlamp to throw a ghostly halo on the road.

That suited Maggie just fine. She didn't need the locals wondering why she was driving a police cruiser.

Lump was riding shotgun so that Laszlo could have the back seat to himself. They'd been barely out of Manhattan when the demon had started shivering so badly his teeth actually chattered, and the car began to weave. Maggie made him pull over so she could take the wheel.

She flicked on the cruiser's brights as she turned off the main road onto the winding path that led to the Witchwood. Even blindfolded, she'd have known where she was. There was something about that particular turn—its angle, the bump, the crunch of gravel beneath the tires—that told Maggie she was *home*. It reminded her of when she'd been little and accompanied her parents on errands, back when her dad could still drive, still walk, still venture out in public. Small Maggie would nap on the ride back, curled up like a cat on the truck's warm seat. Even after the turn told her she was home, she would feign sleep until Gladys was parked and one of her parents scooped her up.

That was then.

Midnight loomed, and there was work to do.

Maggie knew that as soon as they pulled in, her mother would immediately want to sit them down for an interrogation. Once she'd heard Lump's account, she'd ask Maggie for a "private word" so she could express, in her cold, controlled way, how furious she was at Maggie for taking George. It was one thing to risk her own life, but to endanger a *child*?

The cruiser rumbled up the mountain, leaving a cloud of dust in its wake. From the corner of her eye, she could see the excitement and anxiety on her brother's face. Or what she could see of it behind his new glasses.

"Listen," Maggie said quietly, "Mom's going to have questions, but we don't have time for that right now. Afterward, we can answer all the questions she wants to ask. But until then . . ."

"I know," he replied. "I get it."

"I'm proud of you." Her voice was uncharacteristically warm. "When we found you in the trunk, I could have killed you! I thought you'd just slow us down. But we couldn't have done this without you, Lump. I really mean that."

Reaching over, Maggie squeezed his hand. Lump allowed a small smile to cross his face.

A voice, shaky yet indignant, came from the back seat. "Sorry, was someone speaking to me? I'm so woozy I can't be certain. Was that Maggie expressing gratitude for the heroic and *deeply personal* sacrifices I've made on her behalf?"

In the rearview mirror, Maggie saw a bent leg, with fingers drumming on the knee. "You've been okay," she said casually.

"*Okay?* That's not what you told Androvore!"

The Drakefords laughed.

"You know I'm kidding," said Maggie. "You're the best, Laszlo."

"Hmph."

Lump twisted around to face the back seat. "When this is over, maybe you could visit us. Stay for Christmas or something."

Another hmph. "*Christmas?* Oh, you're funny. Rest assured that when this is over and I've got my sarkyra back, I'm heading straight to Hedonism Two."

"What's that?"

"It's a resort for open-minded individuals and couples."

Maggie grimaced. "Honestly, Laszlo . . ."

But Lump sounded intrigued. "Can I come? I've never been to a resort."

"No," snapped the demon. "It's adults only. And I need a break from kids. No offense."

"How is that not offensive, Laszlo?" Lump protested. "I'm a kid!"

"Well, I'm not apologizing. I've been a fucking saint. My entire body probably qualifies as a holy relic. Hair. Fingernails. Even my—"

"We get it," Maggie interrupted. "Stop before I puke."

They rounded the final turn that brought them to the mountain's summit and the towering hedge that marked the Witchwood.

She brought the cruiser to a stop some twenty feet before the warning sign. There was the junk Laszlo had tossed out of the taxi—it seemed so long ago!—and, past that, the moss-covered giants that flanked the entrance to the Drakeford domain. Steeling herself, she stepped on the gas.

The cruiser plunged through the gap and into the shrouded darkness of the Witchwood. It jostled over ruts and roots, its headlights jittering over trees and little streams. Maggie noticed that her hands had started trembling. *Did you ever outgrow the need for your parents' approval?* she wondered ruefully. Perhaps those ties had their own peculiar magic, like a spell that could never be undone. Even after she broke the curse, Maggie doubted that she and her mother could ever be as close as they'd once been. Maggie was almost twenty now. She'd never be nine again.

The farmhouse came into view. The porch lamp hadn't been lit, but the windows were uncovered, and she could see firelight inside as well as a shadow moving about.

It froze as they pulled up.

The front door opened, and there stood Elizabeth Campbell Drakeford. She squinted at the cruiser's headlights, her expression closed and stony—until Lump threw open the passenger door and scrambled out.

With a happy shout, he bounded up the porch steps.

Mrs. Drakeford caught Lump and held him tight, as though she never intended to let him go. While he showed off his new glasses, Maggie opened the cruiser's back door for Laszlo, then got the backpacks from the trunk. Her mother simply looked at her as she went into the house.

She dropped the bags on the kitchen floor and removed her jacket and shirt. Her white tank top displayed her left arm in all its curse-marred glory. The skin burned from shoulder to wrist, and the muscles beneath throbbed with a dull and ceaseless pain.

It's go time. One by one, she found what she needed in the bags—the seven-rod slippers, the battered Herzogshut, the plastic bag containing Saint Clare's hair and fingernails—and recited the list of materia as she arranged them on the table.

"Something loved, something hated, something found, something fated . . ."

"Maggie?" said her mother.

"Not now," she replied without looking. "We don't have much time. Did you get our postcards?"

"Yes."

"And Lump left a note here too. So you knew where we'd gone and what we were trying to accomplish. The good news is we've done it. Or almost."

Her mother's voice was quiet. "Maggie, are you all right? Your arm—"

"Is ugly as sin and hurts like hell, but you get used to it."

"Do you want to—"

"*Concentrate?*" she snapped. "*Yes!* Very much so. Mom, you can ask all the questions you like after we've broken the curse. Until then, I need you to stay out of the way."

Laszlo shuffled into the house clutching a can of Scorchin' BBQ Pringles and the Drakeford Curse folio. His appearance was startling, even to Maggie. The demon's skin was waxy and almost translucent. Damp hair clung to his forehead, and those sparkling eyes had become lifeless marbles. He was a walking cadaver.

"Jesus," said Maggie, "you look horrible."

His voice was a low rasp. "You're too kind."

"Mom," she directed her mother, "Laszlo's sick. Help him lie down somewhere. And don't give him any grief. We couldn't have done this without him."

To Maggie's immense relief, her mother didn't argue. "I'll put him in your room," she said, and ushered Laszlo toward the stairs.

"Great. Laszlo, I'll grab you when we're ready." The demon merely coughed. Then Maggie looked to Lump. "Grab every portable light or lantern we've got, along with the folding table in the barn." Her brother nodded and hurried out.

She returned to their inventory: *Magic, jewels, relic. Check, check, and check.* All she needed now was the ordinary stuff.

Maggie had spent much of the three-hour drive considering this.

One of the four items was a no-brainer.

Within a battered wardrobe in the sewing room hung a variety of somber clothes, dating back to colonial times. Generations of Drakefords had worn them to work. Most were for adults, but there were a few outfits in children's sizes. Maggie reached for a girl's woolen dress. Pinned to it was a coif.

Maggie laid the coif flat across her palm. She remembered when she'd first worn it—shortly after her tenth birthday, when Tessa Mulder's grandmother had died from emphysema. There was a dark stain along the coif's edge, a reminder of Maggie's first outing as the village sin-eater. Rutger Leeuwen had done it. She knew because she'd glimpsed the man's pure elation an instant before the stone struck near her hairline. He knew he'd cast it true. Maggie still had the scar.

She hurried back to the main room and laid the coif by the slippers. Finding something hated was easy. The coif could have been replaced with so many things; the Drakeford house held many items capable of conjuring memories of pain or rage or a craving for revenge.

Love was trickier. Maggie had thought of a book, some well-thumbed paperback that had given her moments of pleasure and escape. *The Black Stallion, Jane Eyre, Anne of Green Gables, The Outsiders, Death on the Nile* . . . But the more she considered it, the more unsure she became. She had read these novels many times and cherished them, but would that register as *love*? A love strong enough to break a curse?

Lump bustled back in with the table and several kerosene lamps. He set them down and went to the kitchen, where they kept some flashlights and a battery-powered lantern.

Their mother came down the stairs, having finished settling Laszlo in the bedroom. She and Maggie made eye contact.

"Where's Dad?" asked Maggie curtly.

"In the back. Sleeping, I hope. The last five days have been hard on him."

"Yeah, well, they've been hard on all of us." On the mantel was a collection of pretty stones and quartz they'd collected over the years. *Something found?* Maggie examined the biggest and held it up as Lump walked by with the flashlights. "Did I find this or did you?"

Her brother shrugged.

Her urgency was curdling into panic. She'd risked everything acquiring ultrarare materia, and here she was, stumbling over the normal items. She'd had *five days* to brainstorm, five days to decide *exactly* what these objects should be. She could have discussed it with Lump or Laszlo or even the Signora; instead, she'd kept her own counsel, somehow convinced she'd get it right.

Maggie sat down in despair and stared at the fire, uncertain whether to laugh or cry.

"What's wrong?"

It was her mother's voice, calm and inquisitive.

"Not now, Mom. I need to think."

"Maybe I can help. Your father and I have been talking, and—"

Maggie's head came up. "I don't have time for this! Do you understand? I need to pick something I love, but I don't *love* anything! I'm nineteen, and there isn't anything in my life—nothing I own or can lay my hands on—that I can honestly say I love. It's pathetic."

Her mother remained unruffled. "May I make a suggestion?"

"It can't be something of yours," said Maggie wearily. "You're not cursed."

"No. But your father is." She paused and looked back to where his bedroom was. "You have no idea how much he's suffered."

Maggie spat back: "I'm the *only one* who knows."

"That isn't fair, Maggie. I've told you the choices I made."

"Yes, you have. You're one hell of a martyr."

Elizabeth Drakeford appraised her daughter for several moments before replying. "When I learned that you and George had left, I was furious," she said quietly. "I've never been so angry."

Maggie stared at the fire. "Yeah, well, sometimes other people get to make decisions."

Her mother continued, anxious to explain. "It wasn't that. It was fear. Fear—that's where anger comes from. I was *afraid*, Maggie. You'd gone off into danger, and there was nothing I could do. It's a parent's worst nightmare."

"Well, I'm not sorry," said Maggie matter-of-factly. "And Lump was a stowaway. I had no intention of bringing him."

"I'm not asking you to apologize," said her mother. "I'm merely explaining how it was. At first, I'd drive all night, looking for the two of you, knowing full well you were far away. Your father and I felt . . . helpless. But then—and this was his idea—we realized that perhaps there was something we *could* do. Something useful."

Maggie turned from the fire and met her mother's gaze. "What was that?"

"We'd heard the list too," said Mrs. Drakeford. "And while we couldn't get jewels or holy relics, we thought we could pull together some of the other things."

Maggie felt a mixture of impatience and curiosity. What could they have found that would possibly work? Would it be personal enough? "I don't know, Mom. I think maybe it has to be something of mine."

"It's the *Drakeford* Curse, not the *Maggie* Curse," said her mother with a touch of her old astringency. "Your father would like to contribute something. I think he's earned that right."

"Fair enough," said Maggie, a trifle embarrassed. "What is it?"

"Something we'd put away long ago. I don't know if it will work, but I'm certain it's something your father loves."

Her mother slid an old photograph across the table. The colors and vibrancy had faded, but the image was clear enough: Two boys with unruly brown hair, playing on the road just beyond the hedge. The older boy, who looked to be about nine, was pulling the younger one in a wagon, looking back at his passenger, whose face was suffused with the kind of uncomplicated happiness you could only feel at five or six.

It was a picture Maggie had never seen before.

The older boy's face was in profile, but she would have known that smile anywhere. It was not calculated to charm. Rather, it had an inward quality, a quiet generosity that took pleasure in someone else's joy. Something inside her ached. It had been years since she'd seen it.

"That's Dad," she whispered.

Her mother nodded.

"This is the first photo I've ever seen of him. Did you know that?"

"He hid it away. As you can imagine, it brings back difficult memories. He loved David so much."

The boy in the wagon. Uncle Dave. The Drakeford brothers looked alike, but David's face had a hint of mischief. One glance told you he'd have been a heartbreaker and hell-raiser—if he'd had the chance to live a normal life. Maggie saw the delight in his eyes. She could almost hear the whoop he was making. So much life in his face, such spark.

But that spark had gone out when he was her age. David snuffed it himself the day he found the Drakeford letters and learned that he was doomed.

Her mother broke the silence. "Do you think this could work?"

Maggie blinked her eyes a few times and nodded. "I do. Thank you."

"I came across something else too." Mrs. Drakeford produced a dried yellow flower, clearly some kind of keepsake. "Recognize it?"

By the age of six, Maggie had been able to identify every plant, flower, and tree in the Witchwood. "Evening primrose."

"Yes," said her mother. "But this one's special. I'm sure you don't remember, but . . . the two of us used to hunt for these. We'd go after sunset, when the fireflies came out. One night, we couldn't find any and had just about given up when you spotted this one standing all by itself beneath a rowan tree. You hallooed so loud they must have heard you in the village. Anyway, you refused to pick it. You declared that it was a 'fairy flower'—Princess Primrose—and she was specially there to pay her respects because she knew you were a princess too. How I laughed. You were so funny."

"I was?" *Funny* was not a word she would have ever used to describe herself.

Her mother's face brightened. Elizabeth Campbell Drakeford suddenly looked ten years younger. "Are you kidding? You had a sense of humor before you could talk. You were just born with it. Something would happen, and this little egg in diapers would turn and give me this wry look, like she wanted to confirm that I found it funny too. You were a riot!"

Maggie carefully picked up the flower. "So how did Princess Primrose end up getting mummified?"

Her mother sighed. "We visited her every night, but as the days passed, our princess began to wilt. One night I plucked her and put her aside as a keepsake for you, when you were older. When you asked where she'd gone, I told you she couldn't stick around forever—Princess Primrose had a kingdom to run! That seemed to satisfy you."

Maggie managed to keep a straight face. "So you *lied*."

"Hell yes, I lied!"

The two shared a laugh of the sort they hadn't in years. Maggie felt a weight lift from her shoulders. After twirling the flower's stem between her fingers, she placed it on top of the photograph. All that remained was *something fated*.

It occurred to her almost at once: *the Drakeford chest!* Together, she and her mother brought it up from the root cellar. Once it was on the table, that time capsule of futility and broken lives, Maggie rooted inside until she found what she was looking for: the very first journal entry by Ambrose Drakeford.

A Doom has been set upon me. As Maggie reread the line, it struck her that every Drakeford had been governed by those words since the day Ambrose had sentenced that poor woman to burn. Even as he had written them, his life and the lives of all his descendants had been set upon a course they could not escape. The letter was proof of that fate. The letter would do.

"This will work," said Maggie, and carefully put it with the rest.

She rose from the table then and considered the array of objects: the crown, the slippers, the relics, the coif, the photo, the flower, the letter . . . They seemed *right* to Maggie; they seemed *whole*. She would take these weapons into battle, and with them she would shatter the spell that had tormented her family for nearly four hundred years.

It was about goddamn time.

Collecting herself, bringing herself back to the present moment, Maggie turned to her mother. "Can I look in on Dad? I wish we could bring him, but you know as well as I do that the chair just can't make it."

Mrs. Drakeford nodded. "Take George with you. I'll pack all this up and check on Laszlo."

Lump was on the porch, looking solemnly out at the Witchwood. At Maggie's soft words, he turned and followed her to the back of the house, squeezing past the empty wheelchair and their mother's cot to where a hospital curtain hung from a track screwed into the ceiling.

On a stained mattress on a platform of old cinder blocks, their father lay on his side, facing the window, which had been opened to admit the cool night air. Moonlight illuminated wisps of steam that rose off his feverish skin. Every few moments, his bloated torso rose and fell like a bellows. A sheet covered his lower body, but his upper body was exposed.

Maggie and Lump were silent.

Their father's spine was hunched, his musculature grotesquely knotted. Half of his visible skin had peeled away, leaving patches of raw flesh that smelled of ammonia. What little skin remained was covered in spongy growths or weeping sores the size of cherries. No stranger would have suspected they were looking at a human being. Bill Drakeford might have been a diseased hog left half-butchered on a slaughterhouse floor.

"Dad?" Maggie whispered.

A faint grunt.

"Dad, it's us. We're home."

There was a long silence. Bill Drakeford did not shift position to look at his children but finally extended a scabrous hand in their direction. Maggie and Lump grasped it and held it gently between their own.

"Dad, we did it," Maggie whispered. "We got everything we need, and now we're going to the Witchstone to put an end to all this. You're going to get better."

"That's right," added Lump. "We're going to play chess and boo the Yankees. And I'm going to tell you all about Europe."

Maggie leaned closer, wincing at the heat radiating from her father's body. "One more thing. We're using that photo you gave Mom. You're going to help us break this thing. You and Uncle Dave."

Bill Drakeford started trembling. There was a muffled sob. His children held his hand a moment longer before they slipped away quietly, drawing the curtain behind them.

Laszlo had come downstairs in the meantime and was huddled by the fireplace, finishing off the last of the Pringles. Their mother had put everything in the backpacks, which were by the front door along with the table, lanterns, and flashlights.

"How is he?" asked Mrs. Drakeford.

Maggie tried to smile. "Okay," she said. "I think he's happy we're using the picture." She straightened up, purpose flooding her body. "Is everything ready?"

Her mother nodded.

As they put on their jackets, Maggie removed Signora Bellascura's scroll, Clarence's translation, and the last remaining spelltube from her backpack.

Her mother noticed it as they were loading up the truck. "What is that?"

Maggie raised the slim vial to the moonlight. "Magic."

Her mother considered the swirling mist. "What kind?"

"I don't know," said Maggie matter-of-factly. "That's half the fun."

"Do you need it to break the curse?" Maggie shook her head. "Then why are you bringing it?"

Their Curse Keeper was already sitting in the truck, waiting to head out. Thrusting the spelltube in her pocket, she turned to gaze out at the sprawling dark of the Witchwood. "Laszlo's not the only demon we'll be seeing tonight."

CHAPTER 32
SEVEN, THE SACRED NUMBER

Hold on, Laszlo. Just a little longer . . .

The demon repeated this mantra on the way to the Witchstone. It was not a pleasant drive. For one, the truck was a rusting shitheap more likely to disintegrate than get them where they were going. For another, Laszlo was wedged between Drakefords and able to see himself in the rearview mirror. He'd never looked worse. Not even during Fleet Week.

As the truck bumped and lumbered over the fields, Laszlo tried to focus on the Witchwood ahead. Within its shadowed depths was that awful stone. He could already sense it, but this time the feeling was different. It was as though the Witchstone was actively repelling him, as if they were two magnets whose poles were in opposition. Every yard the truck covered was draining him like a battery. Laszlo could not help wondering if the Witchstone was sentient, if it somehow knew his intentions.

He hadn't expected this.

"Faster," he croaked. "I'm slipping."

Maggie muttered something he didn't catch and stepped on the gas. The truck shot forward, but its rattling sprint ended a hundred yards later, when they hit a patch of mud that sent them skidding sideways. She managed to keep them from tipping over. When they stopped, the truck was mired in slop so thick that the tires—ancient things balder than Prince William—were unequal to the task. No matter how Maggie tried to coax and cajole it, the truck refused to budge.

"We'll have to walk from here," announced Mrs. Drakeford. "George, help Laszlo."

She and her daughter strapped on the backpacks and carried a folding table along with a number of kerosene lanterns. The demon leaned on Lump as the group began to squelch through the reeking mud, across little streams, and up a shallow rise toward a tangle of trees.

This was not the way they had gone last time; the Drakefords had chosen a longer, less strenuous route for Laszlo's benefit. There was less splashing and scrambling as they looped around and came at the Witchstone from the northeast, along a spit of rock and soil that bridged the labyrinth of streams.

It was an easier trek but also longer. Laszlo tried not to dwell on the time as they slogged through the dark and silent Witchwood. Even their steps and the leaves crunching underfoot had a smothered quality, as if the place itself were strangling the sound.

Laszlo stumbled and fell to one knee, retching like a sick dog while sweat dripped off the end of his nose.

Maggie crouched beside him. "We're almost there. You can do this!"

Nodding dully, the demon wiped spittle from his chin. After a moment, he nodded again, and Maggie pulled him to his feet with unsettling ease. He thanked her with a third nod—but frankly, it was humiliating to be manhandled like this.

They'd gone another thirty yards when Laszlo spotted it through a gap in the trees.

The Witchstone was awash in cold autumn moonlight. It utterly dominated the hilltop, looming over Drakeford graves like a monster ringed by the remains of its victims.

From this new vantage, the Witchstone looked even more sinister, if such a thing was possible—a collection of tortured forms and spires, a raging colossus frozen and transformed into a mountain of obsidian.

It was far more unsettling than the monolith in Signora Bellascura's tower. The Priestess was positively demure in comparison. The Monk was grotesquely deformed, as though time and the prodigious energies it contained had corrupted its fundamental character. Laszlo imagined a lunatic inside, hurling himself against the walls of his prison. What would happen when they started chipping away at the final layer of the spell?

Would the Witchstone hold?

A sudden fear came over Laszlo that things would fall apart at this last and most vital juncture. Desperation spurred him forward, and he moved stiffly with Lump's assistance toward the Witchstone. He was beyond caring if he stirred up the Drakeford spirits. Ghosts didn't hold a candle to Androvore or a missing sarkyra. And now, every second mattered.

When they reached the knoll where the Witchstone stood, Laszlo's skin began to prickle. It was like approaching an open blast furnace. The air had become like sludge, and a metallic tang had blossomed on his tongue. He feared he might burst into flames. He leaned against a headstone to gather his strength, grateful that its tenant made no protest.

The Drakefords did not seem to be affected the way he was, and in passing he wondered why. Then, catching his breath, he hissed at them to set up the lights.

They quickly arranged the lanterns in a semicircle around the basin that fed the mouthlike cavity in the Witchstone's side. Light bathed the surrounding graves.

Laszlo craned to look up at the jagged crown some forty feet above them. There was no chance the Monk was really that big, was there? The stone was just a fortress, right? An obsidian cocoon. *Jesus, I hope so . . .*

By now, the Drakefords had set up the table and arranged the seven materia in the order they would be used. Laszlo staggered over to Maggie, who stood by one of the lanterns, studying Clarence's translation of the Signora's scroll.

His words came out in gasps. "Call her," he pleaded. "Summon the Signora, or I'm not going to make it."

"What's he talking about?" asked Mrs. Drakeford.

"Someone helped us in Rome," Maggie explained. "She wants the Witchstone after the spell is broken, and we promised to summon her beforehand."

Her mother's brow furrowed. "Is this someone a demon?"

Maggie nodded. Before her mother could get in another question, she closed her eyes and touched the ring she'd been given. "Signora, it is time. Please come to us."

Long seconds ticked past. The wood seemed to grow even quieter; then Lump gasped.

About ten yards away, the earth was smoking as a symbol appeared upon it, so crisp and clear it might have been fashioned of white-hot wire: a six-pointed star set within a hexagon set within a circle. As the symbol blazed into being, seven figures materialized within. One was at the center, the rest at each of the star's six points. Silhouettes became shades; shades became flesh.

And then Laszlo and the Drakefords were looking upon the Signora Bellascura and six attendants.

The demoness looked as stunning as ever in a beautiful cocktail dress and a diamond-studded choker. Her attendants, tall men in black suits, held metal stands topped with polished bronze disks roughly three feet in diameter.

The Signora inclined her head to Maggie. "How nice of you to call. I was getting worried."

Maggie bowed. "Good evening, Signora. I'm sorry. We're running a little late."

Leaving the circle, the Signora came over and embraced Maggie like a daughter. "No matter. We are here now, yes?" She turned to Lump. "And how are you, my handsome George?"

The boy smiled shyly. "I'm fine, Signora. Well, more than fine. Excited."

Laszlo signaled in vain for her attention.

The Signora stroked Lump's cheek before turning to Mrs. Drakeford. "And is this your mother? What I would give for those cheekbones . . ." Taking the woman by the shoulders, she gave a kiss to each cheek. "Good evening, my dear—I am the Signora Bellascura. Your offspring delight me. I am so pleased I did not kill them. What are you called?"

It took Mrs. Drakeford a moment to find her voice. "Elizabeth."

The demoness beamed. "Charmed. We must have lunch one day—I

will have you to my club. But for now, business calls, and my assistants must take up their positions."

"Positions?" asked Maggie. "What exactly are they going to do?"

"Subdue our friend, of course." The Signora turned to the fearsome-looking Witchstone. "The Monk looks anxious to be free, no? He will not go willingly into another cell."

"Will it be dangerous?" Maggie's voice was uneasy. "Maybe the rest of my family should leave."

"Nonsense." The Signora indicated the bronze disks her men were setting up around the Witchstone. "Mirrors of Daedelus," she explained. "When the spell is broken, they will trap our Monk in a cosmic maze that will occupy him until he can be safely contained."

"You're certain?" said Maggie.

"Of course."

"It sounds kind of cruel," said Lump, as he helped Laszlo rest against a headstone.

The demoness laughed. "Humanity is so touching. Never fret, my love. Cruelty requires awareness. Our friend will still think he's dreaming."

"And who is this 'friend'?" inquired a deep voice.

Malignis Androvore emerged from the depths of the wood. The Signora's henchmen drew guns from beneath their jackets, strange-looking firearms whose barrels were etched with glowing runes. Laszlo assumed that whatever ammunition they fired would not be found at the local range. Androvore took in the weapons and those who held them. He did not appear overly concerned.

Signora Bellascura whirled on Laszlo. "Who is this?" she demanded.

The newcomer answered for himself. "I am Malignis Androvore. Baronet, Overseer, and head of the Ancient and Infernal Society's North American branch. And you are the Signora Bellascura. A known smuggler, assassin, and traitor."

"Traitor?" scoffed the Signora. "One cannot betray what one has never acknowledged."

"No matter," said Androvore, as he walked toward them. "The Lords of Hell rule all of demonkind, and I am their devoted servant." Coming to a halt, the Overseer directed a cold glance at Laszlo. "You neglected to mention that this . . . lady would be joining us."

Laszlo was so drained that he nearly rolled off the headstone. "Please," he gasped. "I can explain."

"You had better, Laszlo Zebul," said the Signora. "I am tempted to put you over my knee."

There's a thought. Aloud, he said, "I promise to explain, Signora, but first I must request the return of my sarkyra. Maggie honored the bargain."

The Signora gestured angrily at Androvore. "But this oaf—"

"I didn't know," Laszlo cut in. "Not when we spoke. It happened when we returned to New York. And," he added with a meaning look at the Signora, "Sir Malignis's interests have *nothing* to do with yours. He is here to observe my management of the Drakeford Curse."

She studied Laszlo for a moment. Then she faced Androvore. Her voice was pure ice. "Meddle with my business, and you'll wish you had never been spawned, you miserable dreg."

Smoke trickled from Androvore's nostrils. "Are you threatening an Overseer?"

The Signora turned to Maggie and Lump. "Let this be our first lesson," she said. "Little tastes of power can be dangerous. I've never heard of this fool, yet here he stands, swaggering about as though he is the one in control." The demoness addressed Androvore. "You do not matter, insect. You do not exist. I could have you killed for sheer amusement."

"And incur Hell's wrath?" said Androvore stuffily. "You underestimate my importance, Signora."

And there was the smile that had bewitched Laszlo, beautiful and withering. The Signora Bellascura laughed. "You think anyone is starting a war over *you?* There are a thousand Overseers, my friend. You are the definition of replaceable."

Laszlo waved weakly. "Sorry to interrupt, but I'm literally about to *die* if I don't get my sarkyra back . . ."

"Signora," said Maggie. "*Please.*"

The demoness eyed Laszlo. "Very well. I do not like surprises, but a deal is a deal."

She seemed to take forever to reach him. When she finally did, she removed something in a silk scarf from her handbag. She unwrapped it and held it out in the palm of her hand. His sarkyra looked as cold and lifeless as a lump of pig iron.

Snatching the sarkyra from the Signora's palm, Laszlo reached under his shirt and pressed it against his chest. The instant it touched his feverish skin, the demon felt his ribs part; the sarkyra sank through his flesh as though it were quicksand. It *knew* where it wanted to go.

Once the sarkyra was in position, a network of fine filaments would connect to it, rewiring the organ to the body it was meant to power. Laszlo shuddered throughout a sequence of electric shocks, like a furnace whose pilot light had rekindled.

And then the furnace caught.

Strength surged back into Laszlo, warm and delectable. His eyes glowed like moonlit pearls. Getting up from the gravestone, he noticed the Drakefords watching him with fear and concern. Laszlo winked at Maggie, then turned to the other demons present. His manner became that of a seasoned emcee.

"Signora Bellascura, thank you for upholding our agreement. Sir Malignis, my apologies for any misunderstanding. The Signora's assistance was vital, and I'm certain this evening's revelations will justify my dealings with those who operate outside the Hierarchy. I humbly ask for a truce—or at least mutual tolerance—until everything is made clear. Time is fleeting."

Androvore and the Signora glared at one another. Although it clearly pained the Overseer to do so, he gave her a small bow. The Signora merely rolled her eyes and gestured for Laszlo to move things along. Her men returned to their posts by the mirrors.

Rubbing his hands together, Laszlo trotted over to the Drakefords, who were standing in a rather tense and frightened-looking cluster.

He addressed the group at large. "Ladies and gentlemen, demonesses and demons, what an evening we have in store! We are gathered together to bear witness to the end of the Drakeford Curse, whose roots go back to 1665. This is a big moment, my friends."

He swept an arm toward the Drakefords. "Allow me to introduce our Curse Bearers, Margaret and George Drakeford, along with their mother, Elizabeth Drakeford, née Campbell. Cheering from home is Bill Drakeford, who couldn't be present due to numerous deformities and the challenging terrain—"

"Laszlo!" Maggie hissed.

The demon held up a hand. "The ceremonies will be brief," he assured everyone. "Following the opening incantation, Margaret will add the curse's seven materia in proper sequence to the Witchstone's basin, before breaking the spell with a clear and dramatic utterance of the *ultima verba*." His voice was low and thrilling. "Maggie . . . are you ready?"

She nodded hastily. "Yes. I think so."

Laszlo embraced her. "Relax. You'll do great," he whispered, and gave her shoulder a reassuring squeeze before turning back to the others. "We humbly request that there be no talking, interruptions, or flash photography during the ceremony. And while we're at it, let's set those phones to vibrate. If there happens to be any spirit activity, just ignore it. The ghosts might be shrill and rustic, but they're perfectly harmless."

With this, Laszlo bowed and moved to stand by Mrs. Drakeford, near the table of materia. The siblings had the floor.

Maggie shook out her hands. "Lump, just hand me the items as I ask for them. You know which is which?"

He nodded, his face so solemn it canceled out his glasses.

"Okay, then." Clarence's translation in hand, Maggie positioned herself by the bowl that protruded from the base of the Witchstone. She took a deep breath and read aloud, in a voice that rang throughout the clearing.

> Seven, the sacred number
> Strongest and eternal
> The last and final rite
> Twixt the moon and midnight
> Seven treasures, seven prayers
> Seven shields, seven layers

To hide you, to bind you
To shelter and to feed
To veil you from the Enemy
In time of greatest need
That time has passed, O Magus
Your acolyte is here
To cast away the seventh coil
And offer up thy spear

A hellish light ignited in the altar bowl. Waves of heat emanated from its depths, so blistering that Maggie initially recoiled. She braced herself, cleared her throat, and called out in a clarion voice.

"Something loved!"

Lump handed her a photograph. Maggie dropped it swiftly into the cavity. There was a phosphorescent flash and a plume of red smoke. A slight tremor ran through the earth, and a crack appeared in the Witchstone, as thick as Maggie's finger. A red light shone within it.

"Something hated!" Maggie cried.

She held aloft a small cap of stained and soiled linen. Her loathing for it was plain as she cast it into the bowl. A second flash. This time, ribbons of orange smoke twined up into the night. Once again, there were tremors beneath their feet.

Ghosts had begun to rise from the surrounding soil—translucent forms as warped as the Witchstone itself. Their faces were waxy smears. Only by their clothing could Laszlo distinguish men from women. The spirits drifted silently together and linked hands to form a spectral chain that encircled the Witchstone.

Despite these new arrivals, Maggie maintained her focus. *"Something found!"*

Taking a dried flower from Lump, she added it to their offering. There was a serpentine hiss, and the bowl's radiance brightened to pale gold. The spirits began whispering to one another as they circled the Witchstone in a clockwise procession. Laszlo tried not to look at them.

"Something fated!"

A green flash as Maggie dropped a yellowed piece of parchment into the bowl. More fissures appeared on the Witchstone. More light escaped from within, an emerald fire that bathed the surrounding trees in an eerie light.

"*Blood of saints!*"

Laszlo shielded his eyes as Father Angelo's gift was offered up. When the hair and fingernails were added, a brilliant blue light shone from the basin. The procession of ghosts moved faster, hands clasped, limbs stretching grotesquely as they cavorted about the Witchstone.

"*Wealth of nations!*"

This one hurt—Laszlo had forgotten to pry the choicer jewels off the Herzogshut, and it was too late now. He watched as Maggie added the ducal hat of Liechtenstein. Ghostly flames leaped up, and it vanished in a plume of purple smoke.

A cracking noise, and a fault line fractured the Witchstone down its center. Sprays of light gushed forth. The ghostly dance became almost frenzied; the spectral voices were a hellish chorus whose yowling frayed Laszlo's nerves.

Across the way, Androvore towered above the Drakeford graves. His attention was fixed not on ghosts or pyrotechnics but on Curse Keeper 923.

Their eyes met. Laszlo nodded.

Maggie's final cry was exultant. "*A spark of creation!*"

Joy suffused her face as she reached to accept the final item from Lump. As she turned, however, Maggie found her brother empty handed. He looked as confused as she was. Together, they looked to the table of materia for the inlaid box containing the seven-rod slippers.

The box was there.

It was the contents that were missing.

Only then did their eyes go to Laszlo, and the slippers dangling from his fingertips.

Pursing her lips in irritation, Maggie hurried to retrieve them. But as she extended her hand, the demon merely smiled and held the slippers beyond her reach.

"Not tonight, you trusting bitch."

CHAPTER 33
EXCRUCIARE

Maggie blinked in confusion at the grinning demon.

Yes, Laszlo was fond of jokes—but this was beyond the pale. She stared at that handsome face, so human but for the catlike gleam in his eyes.

"Laszlo," she said. "Give them to me."

There were those perfect teeth. "Sorry, Your Highness. This is my moment, not yours."

Maggie took a step forward. "This isn't funny."

"But it is," said Laszlo. "All this time you've been marching to my beat, opening your heart and spilling your sad little secrets. You thought you'd be the hero to break the Drakeford Curse. Between us, I think that's fucking hilarious. *Whatever* will you tell Daddy?"

Maggie thrust her hand into her blazer pocket, only to find it empty.

Laszlo held up the spelltube she'd been looking for. "Never hug a thief, Maggie. That's just asking for it." The demon twirled the vial around his thumb, and it vanished from view. "And here you thought *I* was the jackass!"

Her face burned with embarrassment. When she looked over, her brother and mother appeared to be in shock.

An awful stillness settled about the hilltop. The Witchstone still shimmered with amethyst light, but the generations of Drakeford ghosts had ceased their howling and now watched the proceedings in grim silence.

Maggie faced Laszlo, doubly determined. "You can't do this."

"I *am* doing this."

"I don't believe you!"

Their Keeper held the magic slippers up to the moonlight. "Neither did my boss. He couldn't believe anyone—not even humans—would be gullible enough to believe the spell had been 'scheduled for termination.' A curse being *archived*? How stupid can you get?"

"So it was just a lie?" croaked Lump. He sounded broken.

Laszlo chuckled. "Don't take it personally, kiddo. Sir Malignis had me dead to rights. Let's be real—for the last century, I've been the Society's sorriest employee. A perfect storm of negligence. His Fiendishness gave me six days to show him that I could inflict some serious pain on my Bearers. How am I doing, by the way?"

The demon grinned down at him. Lump could find no words.

Maggie could only find one. "*Why?*"

"Simple," said Laszlo. "Like it or not, I'm a *Curse Keeper*, Maggie. It's my profession. Why would I ever allow some inbred hicks to break the spell that feeds me? Your misery is my meal ticket. You think you're in pain now? Wait till you see what the curse does to Lump. Wait till you start popping out children!"

Maggie's response was close to a snarl. "*Never!*"

Laszlo howled. "Oh, Maggie. Did we forget about Zurich? The banker? The cocaine? You naked on a bathroom sink, begging a stranger to pump you full of little Jans. Any of that ringing a bell?"

"What's he talking about?" said her mother, with an edge.

But Maggie could not respond. Her head whirled with memories, with shame beyond description. She felt Lump's eyes on her and couldn't meet them. Her mother pressed for an answer.

"*Maggie?*"

The demon took it upon himself to elaborate. "You sure did raise a firecracker, Liz. I think Jan was having second thoughts, but Maggie wasn't taking no for an answer. She had her hooks in him—and I *do* mean that literally. Hope you like rug rats! You'll be a grandma in no time."

"Never!" seethed Maggie. "I'm *never* having children!"

The demon cocked his head. "You think that's *your* decision? Wake up, girlie. The *Drakeford* Curse needs *Drakefords*. Give it a month. You'll sneak off one night and come home with a brand-new Bearer in your belly. And once that one's off the teat, you'll climb in Gladys and head out to make another one. Maybe it'll be some nice guy who buys you dinner. Or maybe it'll be five guys behind a truck stop dumpster. The point is, Maggie, you won't have any choice in the matter. You'll be a prisoner in your own body. And it won't stop. You'll do it again. And again. And *again* . . ."

Tears streamed down Maggie's cheeks. "I won't," she whispered.

"Stop kidding yourself. This curse will have you squirting out Drakefords till you're so deformed not even the frat boys will look twice."

She dug her fingernails into her palms. "You're a fucking monster."

"Sorry," said Laszlo, "but *you're* the one and only monster at this party. I'm just a demon, remember? Or did you lose sight of that little detail? I could swear I told you. Did you think I was somehow *different* from all the other demons? Or did you convince yourself that we had a 'special connection' and you'd be the one to change me?" He shook his head in mock pity. "That's it, isn't it? Well, you know what they say about pride and falls. I can't remember the exact quote, but I know there's a 'goeth' in there. I love a good 'goeth,'" he added conversationally. "It's so biblical."

Maggie retreated a step—a cornered animal, almost mad with fear and desperation.

Then, like a Hail Mary pass, she had it: *the Signora!* The demoness was powerful; far stronger than Laszlo and probably even Androvore. The Signora wanted to teach Maggie, take her on as a pupil. They'd formed a bond. She'd even given Maggie the necklace and ring. Yes! The Signora would help—

But there she found no sympathy or solace. The beautiful face was a marble mask. The Signora Bellascura stood at a remove, arms folded, her expression impassive. She wasn't even looking at Maggie but past her, at the Witchstone.

"Signora . . ."

Those stunning green eyes were chips of ice. "This is not my affair, girl. My business is with your Witchstone."

Even as she said it, Laszlo continued, eager to resume their one-sided conversation.

"Did you know you're a cliché?" he remarked. "You like to think you're an original—the poor little sin-eater from Shitsville—but really, you're just two scoops of vanilla. A basic bitch vain enough to think she's special, yet dumb enough to put her faith in a demon. I still can't believe you fell for it."

Maggie's mother had heard enough. "Leave her alone!"

Putting a finger to his lips, Laszlo said, "Hush, Liz. I'll get to you in a minute."

A murderous rage was boiling in Maggie now. As Laszlo strolled toward her, the tentacles slid from the holes in her curse mark. They glided down her left forearm to her wrist like so many serpents, each covered with barbs capable of tearing the flesh off that grinning face. And Maggie *wanted* them to. She'd worked too hard to get this far. And while they dealt with Laszlo, she would snatch the slippers with her right hand and complete the ceremony.

With or without their Keeper, Maggie was going to break the Drakeford Curse.

Laszlo was five steps away. Now four. Maggie's whole being trembled in anticipation. The tentacles were tensed, readying themselves to strike. To rend. To kill.

Three steps . . .

Two—

Maggie's left fist rocketed toward Laszlo. As it did, half of the tentacles shot from her shirt cuff; the rest burst through her jacket sleeve, whipping forward to latch upon his face.

Only they didn't.

Maggie's hand met empty air, and the momentum made her slip, sending her careening into a headstone. She sprawled on the cold ground, stunned and panting.

"*Peekaboo!*" Laszlo strolled out from behind the Witchstone, juggling the magic slippers and Maggie's spelltube. "Didn't know I could do that, did you?" he said. "That little trick saved my ass in Liechtenstein. Then again, you didn't get to see it—you'd already skedaddled. It's not a major power or anything, but if you're creative, it can work wonders."

Then a garbled cry came from the woods.

"*Help!*" It was her father—and he sounded as if he was in terrible pain. How could he have made it out this far on his own?

Scrambling to her feet, she turned this way and that, scanning the Witchwood in vain.

A chuckle sounded behind her. "I'm also something of a ventriloquist."

Maggie spun around to see Laszlo leaning against a gravestone, a patronizing smile plastered on his face. She cursed and aimed another blow at him. The tentacles smashed against the stone, breaking a chunk from its side.

The demon vanished.

Someone cleared their throat behind her. Maggie turned to see the Curse Keeper leaning against a different grave, twenty feet away. "Falling for the same trick twice? I'm disappointed. Pro tip: when dealing with an illusionist, don't let him distract you."

A bead of blue light appeared in Maggie's peripheral vision. It hovered a moment, then zoomed at her like a wasp. Instinctively, she ducked and swatted as the light buzzed past her ear.

Then she looked for Laszlo, but the demon was no longer there. The instant she'd taken her eyes off him, he'd Faded, just as he'd done beneath Ramble Cave.

"*Coward!*" Maggie's scream died away into a sob. All the energy drained from her body, and she crumpled in the damp soil atop her ancestor's grave.

A shout pierced the ringing in her skull. Lump was running toward Laszlo—who had reappeared yet again. The demon was clearly amused and waited patiently before stepping aside at the last minute and sticking out his foot. Lump tripped and landed on the ground near Malignis Androvore. His glasses fell off, and he blinked at the demon's black hooves before craning up at the flaming head gazing down at him.

"*Don't hurt him!*" The cry came from Elizabeth Drakeford. She ran to Lump and pulled him away from Androvore, scooping him up before hurrying to Maggie's side. The three Drakefords huddled by the gravestone as Laszlo strolled toward them.

His luminous eyes were fixed on Maggie's mother. "You want the pain to stop?" he asked. "You want your husband back? Your children? A normal, happy life?"

Maggie felt her mother trembling. "Of course I do!"

"Okay," said Laszlo. "What are you willing to do?"

"*Anything!*"

The demon came closer. "Do you really mean that, Elizabeth? Or is that just something mothers have to say? I ask because this is a moment for brutal honesty. Do you want to take 'anything' back? Hit the reset button? Now's the time to speak up."

"What are you proposing?" said Mrs. Drakeford coldly.

Holding a slipper in each hand, Laszlo brought them slowly together. "Symmetry," he replied. "A witch's soul bought the Drakeford Curse. A mother's can pay it off. Sign your soul over to me, and I'll return the slippers. Into the bowl they go . . . and *voilà*! The curse is broken, and you get your family back."

"Don't!" cried Maggie. "It's a trick."

Elizabeth Drakeford nodded in agreement. "I'm not making a deal with you, Laszlo."

The demon smirked. "I see. So when you said 'anything,' what you really meant was 'Anything—so long as it doesn't cost me, inconvenience me, or make me uncomfortable in any way.' Do I have that right?"

"No."

Laszlo went on as though he didn't hear her. "I can't believe it! You just pulled a 'thoughts and prayers' on your own children. I mean, here I am literally handing you the means to *save them*, to spare your precious babies eternal torment, and you can't be bothered!"

"I didn't say that—" snarled Mrs. Drakeford.

"I tried to help," he said, talking over her. "I warned you about that word, but you had to go and fool yourself into thinking you really meant it. And now your darlings have seen firsthand that Mom is full of shit, that she'll promise the world so long as no one calls her bluff. Well, I'm calling it, you hypocrite. Right here and now. Put up or shut up."

Maggie saw her mother wavering. "Don't!" she pleaded. "He's a liar."

But Mrs. Drakeford's attention remained fixed on Laszlo. "I can't trust your word."

"You don't have to," he replied. "I have a contract."

The demon appeared to pluck something out of thin air—a crimson scroll that he unfurled and thrust at Elizabeth Drakeford, along with a golden pen. She took the document and examined it. The contents were written in a fiery script:

IN EXCHANGE FOR A PAIR OF SEVEN-ROD SLIPPERS, I, ELIZ-ABETH DRAKEFORD, DO HEREBY RELINQUISH MY MORTAL SOUL TO LASZLO ZEBUL. SAID SLIPPERS SHALL BE DELIVERED UPON RECEIPT OF THIS SIGNED CONTRACT. ELIZABETH DRAKEFORD'S SOUL SHALL BE FORFEIT AT THE TIME OF HER DEATH, AN EVENT IN WHICH LASZLO ZEBUL, AS AN INTERESTED PARTY, HEREBY PLEDGES TO PLAY NO PART, DIRECT OR OTHERWISE.

The scroll had two lines for signatures. One already bore Laszlo's flourishy autograph. The other was blank. A disclaimer was at the bottom, printed in tiny copperplate:

THIS CONTRACT WAS DRAFTED BY THE SIGNORA BEL-
LASCURA ON BEHALF OF LASZLO ZEBUL. HER LADYSHIP
GUARANTEES THE AGREEMENT'S TERMS BUT MAKES NO
CLAIM UPON ELIZABETH DRAKEFORD, WHOSE SOUL AND
ANY USES THEREOF ARE LEFT TO THE SOLE DISCRETION OF
LASZLO ZEBUL.

Beside this disclaimer was a wax seal of a serpent swallowing its tail.

Maggie glared at the Signora, whose stoic expression had not changed. "Is this what he asked from you?" she screamed. "*A contract for my mother's soul?* And you *made* it for him?"

"Don't blame the Signora," said Laszlo. "Diabolical Contracts are serious magic. *Way* out of my league." He turned to Androvore. "A Class V power, if I'm not mistaken. I recall you saying so when you drafted our own agreement."

The Overseer nodded. "Correct, 923. I'm pleased you were paying attention."

Maggie's attention remained on the Signora. "*How could you?*"

The demoness appeared bored with her outrage. "This is business, my dear. As I told you in Rome, the Witchstone is a Curse Object. I can only claim it once the curse has been broken. Breaking the spell deprives your Keeper of his living, and he requires a soul by way of compensation. This is a reasonable exchange. Frankly, I am surprised to find your mother so reluctant, particularly given the hour."

"I'm afraid the Signora's correct," said Laszlo. "Clock's ticking, Elizabeth. What's it going to be? The pen's in your court . . . or something like that."

Mrs. Drakeford stared at the contract. "I need time to think this over."

"But you don't have it." Laszlo swept his arm over the scene, directing her attention to the Witchstone, its glowing bowl, and the silent spirits watching them. "At midnight, this spell turns into a pumpkin. That bowl goes dark, some disappointed ghosts return to their graves, and the Witchstone gathers moss again. Everything your children have done will be for nothing."

"It's okay," said Maggie stubbornly. "We can try again."

The demon laughed. "You sure about that, Maggie? You're changing, girl. In the past week, that mark on your arm's become a mini hydra. And don't forget the eye. Mom's gonna have a heart attack when that essence wears off. What will you look like in a month? How about a year? You know as well as I do that the curse is speeding up."

She did not reply. Laszlo's words merely confirmed what she'd discovered in the Drakeford letters: the curse was starting earlier with each generation, afflicting its Bearers more severely. She thought of Lump. When would his first mark appear? How much longer would they be able to go out in public?

"Listen," Laszlo continued reasonably. "Even with my help, it was a bitch getting to this stage. You won't have a chance without me. How will you travel, Maggie? What will you do for money? How will you disguise your appearance? Where will you find crown jewels and magic items? Don't bother asking the Signora. That well's dry until she gets what she's been promised."

One glance at the demoness told Maggie he was right.

The demon looked at her mother. "This is it, Liz. Your only chance. One little signature . . . and the slippers are yours."

The contract trembled in Elizabeth Drakeford's hands. Maggie began to speak, but a sharp look cowed her into silence.

There were tears brimming in Elizabeth Drakeford's eyes. For the first time in living memory, Maggie saw her mother cry.

Pulling her children close, she addressed them in a shaky whisper. "Listen to me. There is *nothing* I wouldn't do for you. That's not the issue. I-I'm just worried it's a trick. I'm afraid I'll sign and you still won't get what you need . . ."

Lump was sobbing now. "Don't do it. We'll be okay!"

His mother looked fiercely at him. "But you *won't* be. I know that, George. I see it every day. I can't bear to watch you suffer like your father has. It will break me. It's torture!"

"Anyone have the time?" said Laszlo pleasantly. "Sorry, but I gave my watch to a goblin shark. Go figure. How long till midnight?"

"Sixteen minutes," replied Androvore.

Maggie gripped her mother's wrist. "Mom. Don't!"

Mrs. Drakeford looked deep into her daughter's eyes. "It's *my* choice, Maggie. A mother's choice." She paused. "My darling, I love you more than you can ever know." She lifted her head and addressed the Signora Bellascura. "I have your guarantee the contract will be honored?"

The demoness bowed. "To the letter."

With a grim nod, Elizabeth Drakeford kissed her children on the forehead and put pen to paper. Her signature blazed like fire.

"*Done!*" As Laszlo cried out, the contract flew to his outstretched hand. Spinning on his heel, the demon brandished it at Androvore. Then, with his back to the Drakefords, Laszlo hunched over as though struggling with something.

"What are you doing?" said Maggie.

"I signed the contract," said her mother. "Give us the slippers."

"Hold on," the demon grumbled. "They're really crammed in there! Ah, here we go . . ."

Then he turned and lobbed the magic slippers at the Drakefords. Maggie knew something was wrong the instant he released them. As they tumbled through the air, the delicate things began to come apart. Four scraps of silk landed softly in the dirt.

Maggie stared in disbelief.

The slippers had been cut in half.

Grinning broadly, Laszlo held up a pair of dressmaker's shears. Maggie recognized them at once; they had come from the sewing kit in her bedroom, where he had been resting.

Something within Maggie broke.

It had all been a waste: the quest, the toil, even her mother's unimaginable sacrifice. Every risk, every chance they took . . . meaningless.

She was dimly aware of her mother gathering up the bits of silk and making a frantic appeal to the Signora. But Maggie knew that was meaningless too. Technically speaking, Laszlo had honored the agreement: he'd returned the slippers after receiving Elizabeth Drakeford's signature.

Nothing in the contract required them to be whole.

Such a *stupid* thing to overlook. Maggie knew they would have caught it if they had had the chance to parse the language. But there hadn't *been* time, and that was the point. Laszlo had seen to that. He'd seen to everything.

And now he was gloating in the Witchstone's shadow, his face bathed in the light from its altar bowl. With triumphant glee, he displayed the contract for all to see, along with Androvore's hourglass.

"Ladies and gentlemen, we now have another matter to address. Last Friday, I myself signed a different Diabolical Contract—this one with Sir Malignis." The leonine demon inclined his head. "He gave me six short days to do one of the following: maximize my ratings, disrupt a Curse-Breaking Event, or procure a human soul. Meeting any one of these objectives would spare my life, and yet I will not-so-humbly observe that I have achieved *all three*." He brandished the executed contract at the Overseer. "Do you acknowledge that this is the case, Your Fiendishness?"

Androvore nodded complacently. "With pleasure. If I'd known you were this ruthless, I'd never have given away your office. No matter. We'll get you a bigger one."

"And our contract?" inquired Laszlo.

The Overseer opened his massive hand. A scroll materialized upon his palm. The demon displayed it, made a civil bow, then tore the scroll in half. As he did, the hourglass in Laszlo's hand dissolved into motes of light.

"That's settled," rumbled Androvore. "And now, you will make good on *your* promise, 923." The Overseer indicated the Witchstone. "What is this thing? And what is the 'secret' threat it poses to the Hierarchy?"

The Signora Bellascura lost her patience. "Laszlo! The time! Have you forgotten about the curse?"

Laszlo held up a finger. "One moment, Signora. I did make him a promise, and I assure you that it will not affect our own arrangement. Very well, Sir Malignis, here at long last is the juicy secret—"

"Not in front of that one," Androvore growled, hooking a thumb at the Signora.

"Your Fiendishness, she's the one who told me the secret."

The Overseer was discomfited. "Oh . . . very well, then. Out with it."

"Have you ever heard of the Lost Magi?" asked Laszlo solicitously.

Androvore considered a moment. "The name rings a bell . . ."

"Seven sorcerers," Laszlo prodded. "Lived in Egypt. Super powerful—until the Lords of Hell decided to eliminate them."

"Ah, yes. I remember now. Your own father slew one of the brutes. What was his name? The Monger?"

"The Monk," the other demon said wearily. "My father slew the *Monk*."

"That's it. What of it?"

"Well"—and Laszlo's voice was delicate—"it turns out my dad might have *exaggerated* a teensy bit." A pause. "The Monk was never slain, Your Fiendishness."

"How do you know that?" demanded Androvore.

"Because you're standing next to him."

The Overseer's shock was evident. He started to back away from the Witchstone. "T-that's impossible," he stammered. "Lord Baal slew the Monk ages ago. He couldn't possibly lie about something like that. Lucifer himself would—"

Androvore fell abruptly silent. Then, turning, he looked out into the night with an expression of growing but uncertain fear. A moment later, he dropped to one knee and bowed his head, reciting something sacred Maggie could not understand.

In turn, the Signora's eyes went to where the Witchwood's trees clustered thickly at the base of the slope. All color drained from that beautiful face. Clutching the necklace at her throat, the demoness spoke a word of command and promptly vanished in a flash of green flames. Her assistants disappeared with her. Only the strange bronze mirrors remained behind. One toppled and clanged against a headstone.

Even the ghosts ran for cover. They streamed over the ground like trails of silver vapor, each making for a different grave. Maggie pulled Lump out of the way as the spirit of Delphina Drakeford (1793–1841) sought shelter in the ground that held her remains. Mrs. Drakeford rushed back to her children, holding them tightly, as the three braced for whatever was coming.

To Maggie's surprise, Laszlo joined them.

Or rather, *almost* joined them. The demon's expression was enigmatic as he calmly positioned himself between the Drakefords and whatever was approaching. He stood with his back to them, apparently untroubled.

What's he doing? wondered Maggie.

But she had no time to give it deeper thought. Waves of force were washing over them now, making her curse marks burn and her right eye ache in its socket. Below them, the Witchwood swayed as though a storm approached. There were groans of twisting wood, the crack of branches, and even trunks snapping, as though a colossal war machine were bulldozing a path through the forest.

The trees before them began to shake and split, breaking free of the soil as though invisible hands wrenched them up by the roots. They toppled aside as a darker, man-shaped shadow emerged from the darkness. It marched steadily up the Witchstone's knoll, in no apparent rush. As it approached the summit, the shadow solidified into flesh.

Maggie's legs failed. She sank to her knees, as did her mother and brother. Now she understood what had happened to the nightjar in the Signora's garden. Death itself was approaching, and she could not run away. She could not even move.

Among those on the hilltop, only Laszlo remained standing.

He kept perfectly still as the presence approached. It was taller than a human—eight feet, at least, with huge black wings. Fear went before it like a bow wave. And not only fear but deep, reverential *awe*.

Its aura burned Maggie like a dark candle held too close to her mortal flesh. She dared not look directly at it; to do so was to stare at an eclipse. Still, she got the impression of a man, tall and handsome but also cruel and imperious. A demon not unlike Laszlo but chiseled from a colder and grander block of marble.

The being was dressed for war. Armor forged of fine black scales covered its muscled body like a serpent's skin. One huge hand held a jet-black greatsword whose blade flickered with pale fire. The other gripped a severed head, which it tossed to the ground with casual disdain. The grisly thing rolled to a stop at Laszlo's feet.

Maggie didn't recognize it at first. Every time she'd seen that face, it had been eerily composed. Now it bore a frozen rictus of terror.

The head belonged to Madam Catfish.

Laszlo took note of it before dropping to one knee.

"It's good to see you, Father."

CHAPTER 34
THE DUKE

Baal Zebul did not acknowledge his son's greeting. Instead, he prodded Madam Catfish's head with his sword. His voice was flat and lacked any hint of emotion. "This insect was spying on the proceedings. I believe it intended to kill you."

"An assassin," said Laszlo. "Androvore hired her."

Baal addressed the kneeling Overseer. "Is this one yours?"

"I could not say, Your Grace. Our assassin operates by possessing lesser demons. No one knows its true identity."

The head bore a blank, terrified expression. Had the demon been possessed when they first saw her in Dimitri's shop? Or had that happened later? Villain she might have been, but Madam Catfish was yet another pawn in the match between Laszlo and Androvore.

They were all kneeling—the Drakefords like prisoners, Androvore like a parishioner. But Laszlo's supplication was different: head bowed, one arm resting upon his knee, the other flung gallantly behind his back. He might have been a knight pledging his service to a maiden. Maggie wondered if this was Laszlo's way of poking fun at his father's formality.

A moment later, she realized she was mistaken.

Laszlo was holding something behind his back. When Baal's attention had shifted to Androvore, the object had appeared in his hand.

What was more, he was waggling it back and forth in an apparent bid to get Maggie's attention.

Unfortunately, the demon was kneeling in the shadow of a headstone, so she couldn't make out what he was holding. The fact that he was wagging it like the tail of an overexcited puppy didn't help.

"What an ingenious assassin," remarked Baal dryly. "Perhaps I should have spared its life. How curious that you went to such extraordinary lengths, Androvore. Would you say you've been an impartial observer in this affair?"

"Milord?"

"Did you hope my son would fail?" said Baal bluntly.

The Overseer hesitated. "Your Grace, based on the available evidence, I did not believe Keeper 923 was worthy of his position."

"That is not what I asked."

Androvore cleared his throat. "Upon reflection," he said carefully, "I did indeed desire him to fail. I did not regard Keeper 923 as a credit to the Society, nor to his exalted lineage. He also insulted me personally. Had he not been Your Grace's offspring, I would have slain him immediately."

Baal grunted. "I appreciate your candor."

"I live only to serve my superiors."

"Yes, I see that," said the Grand Duke. His unblinking gaze now fell upon his son. "And considering the obstacles you placed before him, how did 'Keeper 923' perform?"

"Exceeded expectations," said Androvore approvingly. "The boy has great potential."

"How generous."

The instant his father had turned to appraise him, Laszlo had gone perfectly rigid. Finally, Maggie could make out the mysterious object in his hand.

It was a scroll.

She took a second look to confirm what she was seeing—and yes, he was holding the contract for her mother's soul. But why would he wave it under their noses? Was he taunting them? After tonight, nothing seemed out of the question.

Laszlo's efforts took on a frantic quality.

Baal inclined his head. "You've done well, son."

"Thank you, Father. Your praise means the world, knowing that you signed off on all of this. An impossible task, goons, crucibles, assassins . . ."

"And yet you *survived*," said Baal, with a touch of asperity. "You overcame adversity. You proved yourself more capable than many believed. Including me, I admit."

"Yes, I'm positively giddy," said Laszlo. His voice was dry. "Unfortunately, all I have to show for it is a single human soul I can't touch for decades—a soul that required me to incur a serious debt to a serious person so she'd draft the contract on my behalf. I'd have done it myself, but apparently Diabolical Contracts are 'highly magical objects,' well beyond a lowly Curse Keeper."

Baal clasped the pommel of his sword. "You could have come to me for the contract."

"No time," said Laszlo. "And forgive me, Father, but what sort of fool begs favors from the very demon who signed his death warrant?"

"I'll assume your debt to the Signora," Baal announced. "After tonight, I do not think she will be eager to call it in. As for your rank, I will recommend promotion to Class V and supply the required essence myself."

"Thank you," said Laszlo. "I would like to craft my own highly magical objects for a change. The experience would be so novel."

Highly magical objects.

Maggie went rigid. She felt like slapping herself. How had it taken her *so long* to catch on? Throughout the exchange, she'd been listening to Laszlo and wondering at his manner. The whining was familiar enough, but not these technical references to her mother's contract; that was uncharacteristic.

Now she realized that he wasn't citing these details for his father; he was citing them for *her*. The demon was letting the Drakefords know, in the plainest terms possible, that the scroll could substitute for the magic slippers he'd destroyed.

Maggie was blindsided.

Everything Laszlo had done that evening—the depth of his betrayal, the violence of his words, the unspeakable pain he'd caused—*was on purpose*. That prick! He was far cleverer than she could have conceived.

Stealing the magic slippers had disrupted the ceremony and coerced her mother to sign away her soul. Acquiring that soul, then destroying the very item it was meant to purchase, was unimaginably cruel. The act must have sent his ratings into the stratosphere.

And now that Laszlo had saved his own skin, this insane and infuriating demon was trying to save theirs too.

Hope blazed anew in Maggie's heart.

The Witchstone's bowl still emitted a purple radiance, which meant midnight had yet to arrive. The spell was still active, still waiting for the final ingredient and the ritus's closing word.

Someone pinched her arm. Lump's eyes were elsewhere, but it was obvious that he had seen and reached the same conclusion. He turned his wrist so Maggie could read his watch's illuminated face.

11:49 p.m.

Baal's voice rumbled forth. "Good evening, Drakefords."

Maggie began to tremble when Baal addressed them directly. She tried to meet the demon's eyes, but something in her simply refused.

"Forgive me," he said. "I'd forgotten the effect my aura has on mortals."

The dark energy pouring off the demon slackened. Maggie's skin cooled, and she found that she could now look into that terrible face. So handsome and composed, yet ultimately artifice. She knew she wasn't looking at the "real" Baal Zebul. This was simply his most human guise, a mask he donned when visiting the mortal plane. She suspected that his true form, whatever it was, would be horrifying.

"This is our first meeting," Baal observed, "but I am well acquainted with your family. I have been watching Drakefords for centuries, since I learned of this strange monument in the colonies." He looked at the Witchstone. "Tell me, Androvore, do you know what this is?"

The demon did not reply at once.

Baal tutted. "This won't do. Overseers must be obedient."

"I am told it is one of the ancient Magi, Your Grace," Androvore answered carefully. "A base sorcerer known as the Monk."

"Correct. And do you know of my connection to the Monk?"

Again, a careful response. "That you vanquished him, Your Grace. That you slew the Monk in battle."

"Quite so," said Baal. "And I believed as much myself—would have staked my life upon it, but the Monk deceived me." He paused. "It always rankled that I never returned with a trophy. Lilith brought the Judge's head. Mammon wears the Scholar's fingers. Belial's hounds dragged the Shepherd before the Council. But in my wrath, I had destroyed my enemy utterly. Nothing remained of the Monk: no body or token to prove his death, beyond my testimony. Lucifer was never quite happy with this. Neither was I."

Laszlo let the scroll drop from his hand. It landed softly and rolled an inch or two toward Maggie. Did she dare reach for it?

"Naturally, I could not share my misgivings," Baal continued. "I scoured the desert. I searched far and wide for my enemy, employed every means of detection I possessed. It turned up nothing—and yet the Monk loomed within my dreams, a shadow on the horizon. It puzzled me. How could one I'd slain continue to plague me?

"Then tales spread of these 'Lost Magi' that eluded us in Alexandria. Some whispered that they'd hidden in sanctuaries of their own design. Impregnable. Undetectable by demonkind. These rumors roused my curiosity. Perhaps they could explain the Monk's disappearance."

Lump's watch read *11:51*—nine minutes to midnight.

The glowing violet bowl was only twenty feet away. Could Maggie snatch up the contract and make a dash for it? She considered first the severed head, then Baal's fearsome sword. Maggie would probably meet that blade before she could reach the basin. But . . .

Baal went on, his deep voice rolling through the clearing. "The other Lords deployed scouts. They searched for the 'Priestess' and the 'Wanderer,' each hoping to lay a prize at Lucifer's feet. I cast a wider net. *My* imps were not confined to Africa, Asia, or Europe. They scoured the entire world—Old and New—with orders to report *anything* that hinted of magic."

His voice grew proud. "And so it was a scout returned and requested a private word. He had found a strange monument in the New World, a curiosity of considerable power. As he described the stone, I suspected my search was over. When I beheld it for myself, all doubt vanished. The Monk was *here*," Baal growled. "Right within my reach, and yet I could not touch him!"

Without warning, the Grand Duke struck at the Witchstone.

His greatsword was so swift, and the blow fell with such strength, that it brought Maggie to the brink of nausea. What had she been thinking? She couldn't possibly hope to get past him.

Yet for all the power behind it, Baal's blade did not even graze its target. Its edge slammed to a halt an inch from the Witchstone, repelled by some invisible force. Mastering the recoil, he glowered and lowered his sword.

"Powerful magic lay upon the stone," he said darkly. "Not only the Monk's enchantments but a *human* spell. I'd arrived a century too late—the Witchstone had become a Curse Object. Naturally, I looked into this spell and its Keeper, a crippled dreg named Bazilius. He was harmless, a glorified clerk who knew nothing of the Witchstone's true nature. So long as the curse remained in place, no one would be any the wiser."

"So you sabotaged us," said Maggie.

She was sure she had *thought* those words, not spoken them aloud. They hung, small and thin, in the night air. Maggie wondered if they would be her last.

Surprisingly, the accusation did not trouble Baal.

"It didn't require much," he replied easily. "An occasional fire, the odd atrocity. Your ancestors were so impressionable! I planted visions in their dreams. As the curse ravaged their bodies, it was a simple matter to convince them that unspeakable desires were welling in their hearts too. They came to believe they'd committed terrible crimes: Assault. Murder. Incest. Cannibalism." His tone grew warmer, even amused. "It became something of a game. I could slaughter a villager for sport and leave the corpse for a Drakeford to find. Witnessing their discoveries gave me pleasure, but the most gratifying aspect was that your ancestors believed themselves responsible. Their agony was exquisite!"

Like a knife in the heart, Maggie recalled the letters she'd read, those devastating accounts in which Drakefords confessed to terrible crimes they'd never actually committed. It had broken their minds and driven them further into darkness, until they begged their loved ones to lower them into a hole from which they could not escape. Even her father had begun pleading to be locked away. Her uncle David had committed suicide because of that looming fate.

It was a cruel trick beyond imagining, and Baal had been playing it on the Drakefords for centuries. *He'd done it for sport.* Maggie's left arm began to boil with movement as rage came to mingle with the fear that consumed her.

The Grand Duke sighed. "I admit that keeping the Monk's survival a secret was not forthright, Androvore, but as you see, no harm came of it. My orders were to eliminate a threat to the Hierarchy—and so I did. My efforts removed the Monk from the chessboard. So long as the Drakeford Curse was in effect, he would remain trapped in a prison of his own devising. The Hierarchy's ends were achieved, even if the means were somewhat unorthodox. Would you agree, Sir Malignis?"

There was an edge to the question.

The Overseer took the hint. "It would be difficult to argue otherwise, milord."

Baal chuckled. "You're a political creature, Androvore. No wonder you've risen quickly. Great things await if you avoid future missteps—perhaps even a peerage."

Androvore's relief was palpable, as was his muted delight. It was clear he had been expecting punishment, perhaps even execution, for learning the Grand Duke's secret.

In his place, Maggie would not have let down her guard.

"Bazilius is to blame for our present dilemma," Baal continued. "Had he simply fulfilled the basic requirements, he'd still be alive. But the dreg took it upon himself to question why the curse was growing stronger with every generation. He worried that this might undermine the invoker's intent and wondered if the Witchstone was to blame. Its power was becoming apparent, and Bazilius feared it might be amplifying the curse's effects. In this, he was correct.

"Unfortunately, his intelligence exceeded his judgment. A wiser Keeper would have realized there was nothing to be done and left things alone. But Bazilius was stubborn. He looked into the Witchstone's origins and consulted a Society expert on Curse Objects. Obviously, intervention was required."

"So you killed him," said Maggie, no longer as afraid. "After making him remove the ritus."

Baal shrugged. "If Bazilius had let matters alone, the Witchstone would have ensured the curse became unbreakable. He would have kept his life and his job, while I reaped the satisfaction of knowing that the Monk's sanctuary had become an inescapable prison. But this Bazilius was a stickler, even when it brought him into conflict with his superiors. A fatal flaw, wouldn't you say, Androvore?"

"Yes, milord."

"Indeed. With Bazilius gone, I'd hoped that replacing him with my son would solve two dilemmas: I'd be rid of an expensive nuisance, while his laziness and debauchery ensured the curse would remain intact."

Laszlo looked over his shoulder at Maggie. "And you wonder why I see a therapist."

Baal smirked. "My plan worked to perfection. Laszlo behaved just as predicted, and neglected the curse to the point that its Bearers did not even know it had a Keeper." His chuckle ended in a wistful sigh. "But good things never last, do they? The branch installed an Overseer to whip things into shape. This demon's opinion of my son's performance was less charitable than my own."

Androvore spoke up. "Milord, if I'd had any notion of your wishes, I would never have interfered."

Baal waved off his concern. "Not at all. We had different objectives, Androvore. Your concerns were perfectly in order, as was your letter to apprise me of the situation."

"Thank you, milord. Once again, I must reiterate that had I known—"

"But you did *not*," said Baal with some finality. "If I'd wanted to prevent you from taking action, I'd have made my desires clear. I chose a different route. I wondered if this was the test my hapless son required. Desperation is a matchless teacher. And look at what we've achieved, Androvore. We've almost made a demon of him."

Laszlo cleared his throat. "Almost?"

"Indeed," replied his father. "You remain laughably soft and sentimental. Here you are, constructing an elaborate charade to convince Androvore you're an evil genius capable of inflicting unimaginable pain on his Bearers."

"And I'm *not* an evil genius?" wondered Laszlo.

"No. What you are is a lazy, moderately clever scoundrel who's become oddly attached to the mortals he's meant to torment."

Laszlo sounded touched. "That may be the nicest thing you've ever said to me."

Baal smiled down at his son. "I'm not a common dreg, boy. You cannot deceive me."

Androvore was confused. "Deceit, milord? I'm sorry, but I don't understand."

"Clearly not," said Baal. "I'll explain in simple terms. My son has *tricked* you, Androvore. He has played you for a fool. He navigated your trials rather elegantly, did he not? Laszlo didn't meet *one* of your conditions; he met them *all*. And now that he's won the game, my son intends to humiliate you."

The Overseer stiffened. "Is that so? And how does he plan to achieve this?"

"By undoing what he's done," replied Baal dryly. "Surely, you must realize that a Diabolical Contract would make a suitable replacement for the magical item my son destroyed. If that contract *somehow* fell into his Bearers' hands," he said pointedly, "it would enable them to complete the ceremony. Laszlo gets his victory, and so do the humans. The only loser is you."

The flames about the Overseer's head were burning rather intensely. That leonine face turned to glare at Keeper 923. "Is this true?"

Laszlo cast his eyes down coyly. "A gentleman never tells."

"And what did you think would happen after I learned of your little scheme?" demanded Androvore. "Did you expect me to look the other way?"

"No," answered Baal. "My son expected the Signora Bellascura to eliminate you—an unwelcome witness to her dealings—the moment her business was concluded."

Laszlo sighed. "You make me sound so calculating."

"It's a compliment," replied his father.

Androvore was growing apoplectic. "This is an outrage!" he roared. "Lord Baal, as a senior officer of the Hierarchy I demand satisfaction. Keeper 923 may be your offspring, but—"

"But *nothing*." Ball's voice was ice. "Blood will tell, Androvore, and you have been outclassed. Accept it. Learn from it. *Evolve*."

A pause. "And if I cannot?"

"Then a promising career will end prematurely. In any case, after tonight, 'Keeper 923' will no longer be your problem. I have other plans for him."

"And what of the Drakeford Curse?" said Androvore.

By way of answer, Baal walked over and casually plucked up the scroll Laszlo had dropped. Then he held it out to Maggie. "The young lady will break it."

Maggie looked up at that domineering face. Was this another trick? She couldn't see what Baal had to gain. Yet it was impossible to trust him. And there was something deeply distasteful about accepting charity from the being who had destroyed generations of her family for sport.

Laszlo hissed at her, "What are you waiting for! There's only—"

"Forty-eight seconds," said Baal calmly. "Midnight looms."

Maggie accepted the scroll.

Nothing stood between her and the glowing purple bowl of the Witchstone. She looked one last time at her mother and Lump, whose faces were drawn and anxious. Lump whispered for her to hurry.

Now that the moment was here at long last, why was she finding it strangely difficult to proceed?

She willed herself forward, dimly aware that the Drakeford ghosts were once again emerging from their graves. The spirits formed no ring this time but simply watched as their descendant made her way to the offering bowl.

Maggie trembled from the October chill, from excitement, from a nagging fear that this was yet another deception. As she reached the Witchstone's altar, she looked down into the basin and found herself staring at a nacreous liquid, silvery and luminous.

She took a deep breath.

She held up the Diabolical Contract.

Crying, "*A spark of creation!*" she let the scroll drop into the bowl.

There was a flash of red flame and a whiff of brimstone as the dreadful thing was consumed.

When it disappeared, a tearful Maggie completed the ritus with a single triumphant word. "*Eleftheria!*"

Freedom!

One small word, and yet it meant everything.

Even though it was intended to bring an end to the Monk's imprisonment, Maggie knew that it was also for her. She was the beneficiary—Maggie, her father, Lump, and all the Drakefords who had gone before. *Eleftheria* meant freedom from suffering, from isolation, from the maddening dread that each new day would be worse than the one before.

The instant it left her lips, a white brilliance erupted from the Witchstone's basin.

Blinding pain shot through Maggie's left arm and exploded behind her right eye. She stumbled back. Someone caught her as she fell— Laszlo—and she pulled free.

Her mother and brother raced to meet her, leading her to a headstone and easing her down.

"Are you—Maggie, what's wrong?" her mother asked.

But Maggie couldn't reply. Her jaw had locked, and she writhed in the dirt as the Drakeford Curse went through its death throes. Lump was also affected, albeit far less intensely. His hand gripped Maggie's shoulder, squeezing every time a convulsion racked his body.

Mrs. Drakeford dragged first her son, then her daughter, from the Witchstone, whose many fissures blazed with light. The radiance was dazzling and extended far into the wood, bleaching the trees into twisted skeletons.

Through the waves of pain, Maggie felt a delicate touch, soft as gossamer and intensely cold. Opening her eyes, she beheld a ghostly figure crouching nearby. Its hand rested on her afflicted shoulder. Other ghosts were now approaching, like fragments of mist drifting on a breeze.

Slowly, slowly, the pain ebbed.

At the same time, hundreds of cracks formed on the Witchstone's surface. Huge chunks of obsidian were breaking off, like ice calving from a glacier. They toppled to the ground, shattering nearby headstones or embedding themselves in the soil. As the obsidian continued to fall away, the Witchstone looked less like a nightmarish sculpture and more like an organism hatching from an egg. There was a membrane beneath the stone, thin and translucent; and beneath it, living tissue laced with blood vessels.

And before this gruesome spectacle stood Baal.

The duke's bloodlust was rising. He paced before the Witchstone like a caged tiger, wings twitching as the flames around his sword kindled into an angry blaze. Wherever he walked, heat poured from him— fallen leaves began to burn, and Maggie feared that some of the trees might ignite.

Laszlo had apparently reached a similar conclusion, for he backed away from his father. Stopping short of the ghosts, the demon said to the Drakefords: "Now might be a good time to run."

Even as he said it, a ring of fire erupted about the base of the Witchstone's hill. The flames were so high Maggie could see nothing of the wood or landscape beyond. They were trapped.

Baal ceased his pacing to address them. "Long ago, the Monk robbed me of rightful victory. This is a night for vengeance long denied.

You shall all bear witness. And when it is done, when the Monk has bled his last, I will toss his head at Lucifer's feet and lay to rest the rumors that have plagued me." Turning from them, he resumed his vigil.

Climbing slowly to her feet, Maggie removed her jacket. Shriveled, withered tentacles dangled from her bare left forearm; the entire arm looked like it was covered in necrotic flesh, black and puckered. She touched it. The arm was numb, as was her eye, but at least she was no longer in pain.

A cool and comforting mist was settling about them. Looking around, Maggie realized it was her ancestors. The ghosts were forming a circle about the living Drakefords, whispering quiet words of gratitude as they sought to shield their descendants from the hill's inferno.

By now, the Witchstone had shed most of its outer layer. It looked like a hideous heart anchored in a basin of splintered obsidian. Twenty feet tall it stood, pulsing and pumping as luminous liquid sloshed over the basin's rim. Baal stood before it, silhouetted against its radiance.

Unable to contain himself any longer, the demon roared and struck at the Witchstone with his sword. This time, there was no curse or protective spell to repel his blade. It sheared through membrane and tissue, cleaving an eight-foot gash in the Witchstone's side. Liquid spurted from the wound, streaming down even as the blade set the heart, too, afire. Pale flames tore along the membrane, consuming it and the fleshy layers beneath.

The massive heart disintegrated like a paper lantern catching fire.

Leaping upon the obsidian rim, Baal looked down into the Witchstone's core. So much smoke and ash were billowing up he might have been standing upon a meteor strike. Dispersing the fumes with a sweep of his massive arm, Baal raised his sword high as though to destroy his enemy with one decisive blow.

But the stroke didn't fall. The demon's sword arm dropped a fraction before he emitted an unearthly howl that chilled Maggie to her core.

Before her eyes, the Grand Duke was devolving into something else entirely, something primal and carnivorous. She would never have associated that terrible cry with the urbane and imperious figure who'd addressed them mere minutes before. She shivered as the howl trailed off into laughter.

"The mighty Monk!" sneered Baal. He lowered his sword into the smoking crater and brought up something large and cumbersome. It was a huge skull crowned with curling horns and strands of lank white hair. The horns looked like those of a goat or ram, but the skull's size gave it a prehistoric quality, like some relic of the Ice Age.

Baal let the skull fall back into the crater. He looked disdainful and disappointed. Once again, he had been robbed of the contest he'd been craving.

Stepping down from the rim, the Grand Duke sheathed his blade and nodded to Androvore. "Gather up the bones and obsidian, along with the Monk's weapon. It is saturated with magic, as are the young humans. They will make useful servants."

Servants.

Had Maggie heard that right?

She suddenly felt the force of Baal's gaze. The Grand Duke's aura had resumed its potency, and now that his attention was directed upon her, Maggie was transfixed. She found herself unable to move.

While Androvore stood upon the crater that held the Monk's remains, Baal appraised Maggie and Lump like something he might salvage from a disappointing evening.

Laszlo hurried toward his father, waving his arms. "Dad," he said. "Slow down. You don't want these two. Trust me."

But Baal was already striding toward the Drakefords. They were frozen in place, as was their mother; Maggie heard her mumbling "no" again and again, as though trying to rouse herself from a nightmare. Laszlo was trying his best to intervene. Under different circumstances, the image might have been comical: a cub nipping at the heels of a wolf.

But the wolf would not be distracted. As Baal approached, the Drakeford ghosts streamed forward, in an attempt to hold him at bay. The demon took no notice, and the spirits broke upon his armored chest like a wave. Regrouping, they tried again to form a barrier, but the demon marched right through them.

He had nearly reached Maggie and Lump when Androvore gave a startled shout. Baal halted and turned back toward the Witchstone's remains. When he did, his hold upon the Drakefords was broken.

Maggie's eyes flicked to Androvore standing atop the crater's rim. The Overseer looked troubled. "Your Grace, I think something is—"

There was a flash, thin and silver bright. Androvore stiffened as a blade swept across his neck. Legs buckling, the Overseer toppled off the crater, a fiery liquid gushing from the stump where his head had been.

CHAPTER 35
SWORD AND SPEAR

Once more a horned skull rose above the crater. This time, however, it was attached to a humanoid skeleton in a tattered cowl and robes. As the figure stepped upon the Witchstone's rim, Maggie realized it must have been twelve feet tall. The weapon it held looked like a bronze quarterstaff with a long, tapering spearhead at each end. The blades sliced the air as the figure spun the weapon in one hand and then the other, as though reacquainting itself with its balance.

A cold smile appeared on Baal's face. He called out in a strange, sibilant language: clearly a challenge of some sort. The Monk responded by leaving the crater and descending the hill.

Turning from the Drakefords, Baal wrenched his greatsword from its scabbard. The weapon ignited at once, hellfire leaping from the blade as he closed upon his enemy.

The clash was deafening, a collision of sword and spear that dispelled whatever remained of Baal's hypnotic hold. Maggie's mind was clear now, and it was screaming at her to get as far from the battle as she possibly could. She led her mother and brother on a scrambling dash down the slope. The ghosts moved with them, a possible buffer against the roaring flames that circled the hill. She hoped that shield would allow them to escape.

But as they neared the flames, Maggie saw the ghosts recoil and veer away. Apparently, this fire could burn spirit as well as flesh.

There was nothing for it; the Drakefords had to shelter behind one of the larger gravestones.

Their only hope was for the Monk to prove victorious.

A battle raged above them, among the Witchstone's ruins. The sound of clashing weapons made their ears ring. Watching from behind the headstone, Maggie was awed by the combatants. Their weapons were a blur, each maneuver executed with superhuman speed and precision— and the Monk was nothing but an animated skeleton.

The demons did not fight with only physical weapons. Electricity arced between them, dancing about their blades and causing smoke to rise from Baal's armor.

Amid the chaos, Maggie spotted a smaller figure—Laszlo, huddled behind a chunk of obsidian near Androvore's corpse. His hands covered his ears. As his father and the Monk made the earth tremble, he scanned the hill as though looking for the Drakefords.

Maggie waved to get his attention, against her better judgment.

He saw her at once. At the same time, the Monk's spear shattered his obsidian shield. Laszlo remained crouched, ludicrously exposed, before racing down the hill like a soldier breaching no-man's-land.

As he reached the Drakefords, he slid to a breathless stop. "No idea," he gasped. "I had no idea he would actually come . . ."

Maggie showed her confusion, but the demon merely shook his head, too stunned or winded to explain. Instead, he pressed something into her hand and darted off to hide behind a gravestone. He ran and hid, ran and hid, clearly determined to put as much distance between himself and the battle as he could.

As always, a coward, Maggie thought. She opened her hand and saw her spelltube. Why had Laszlo put himself at such risk to return it? These weren't kobolds or Nachtkrapp above them; these were among the most powerful beings in Creation. A spelltube was useless here. Perhaps he'd done it to soothe his conscience and satisfy some bizarre personal code: *I may have taken the slippers, your mother's soul, and the spelltube—but I also returned them, so you can't be mad at me!*

Laszlo wasn't simply a coward; he was a coward with some kind of motivation she didn't understand. Of course, he was the only demon she knew who saw a therapist.

She slipped the vial into her pocket.

There was a bellow from above, atop the hill. Dozens of tentacles had burst from the ground to entangle Baal. As Maggie watched, she realized that they were not tentacles but roots and creepers drawn from the surrounding wood. The Grand Duke could barely move.

The Monk, on the crater's edge, appeared to be regenerating even as it worked its spell. Flesh and sinew covered the bones now, so that it resembled a freshly skinned carcass. Baal had said the area was saturated with magic; did the Monk draw power from the place it had been imprisoned for so long?

She realized then that it was not the Witchstone's magic that flowed within her and her brother; it was the Monk's. They had been absorbing his energy ever since the Witchstone deteriorated to the point that it could escape. An odd feeling of kinship welled up inside her, and she hoped with all her heart that the Monk would vanquish their common enemy.

It was looking likely. The Monk stood tall, dark, and bloody beneath the moon. One hand was upraised, its fingers flexed like claws. Roots pinned Baal's wings to his sides, and he snorted and bucked like a mad bull, trying to wrench free while maintaining a grip on his sword.

As the tendrils tightened, Baal's struggling grew weaker and gradually abated until it ceased altogether. The demon lay immobile on the hillside.

Triumphant, the Monk leaped from the crater's rim, his weapon poised to impale.

But as he descended, there was a flash of fire, and Baal broke his bonds like cobwebs. The Grand Duke's sword swept up in a murderous arc. Maggie cried out as blade met target. A spray of dark blood, and the spear fell from the Monk's grasp to clatter against one of the Signora's mirrors.

Baal stood panting over the Monk. Raising his sword high, the demon brought it down with hideous force upon the great horned head. Maggie cried out as the otherworldly skull shattered.

Then something caught her attention.

Ten yards away, Androvore's corpse gave a violent twitch. And another. Yes, decapitated bodies could do all sorts of unsettling things, but this went beyond anything she'd ever read. Then the Overseer's hands took firm hold of the smoldering grass. Maggie was both horrified and enthralled as Androvore's headless corpse levered itself up from the pool of fiery blood and stood tall. The Monk's spear flew to its outstretched hand.

The sound of its impact caught Baal's attention, and he turned to face this newly risen challenge. His face darkened. Spitting on the crushed skull, the Grand Duke shouted something in the strange tongue of his kind. As for the Monk, it merely shifted the weapon from hand to hand, testing this new body it had claimed. That it lacked a head did not appear to be an issue.

Once again, the Witchwood trembled and rang with the clash of combat. The two were well matched; there was no question Baal was stronger, but it was equally clear that the Monk was more patient and skillful. Baal launched furious offensives, and the Monk dodged or parried blows with uncanny speed and anticipation. When opportunity presented, one of the Monk's blades flicked out like a serpent's tongue to slash Baal's face or test his armor—the point was clearly not to injure the Grand Duke so much as to enrage him.

Maggie felt the heat behind them growing less intense—Baal was summoning the wall of hellfire. Swaths of pale flame swept up the hill like living things, enveloping the demon in a swirling inferno.

She yanked at her mother's sleeve and yelled above the fire's roar: "*This is our chance! We have to run!*"

And run they did. Scrambling downslope, the Drakefords breached the ring of charred and smoking terrain. They'd almost reached the first stream when Maggie thought to look for Laszlo.

All she could see was the burning hilltop where Baal was hammering his foe into submission.

The Monk had been driven into a corner. Crouching low, he spun his spear into a blur, fending off his opponent. The hellfire coursing about Baal was so hot it was melting everything around it. With a furious blow, he dashed his opponent against an oozing slab of obsidian. The Monk sank into the stuff like a mammoth stumbling into a tar pit. Within seconds, half his headless body was submerged.

As Baal stepped back, the flames coursing around him flickered out. The demon hissed something, and a wind came screaming from the north, so strong and cold it might have been straight from the Arctic.

The Drakefords lay flat, shivering, protecting their heads, as the icy gale swept over the hill. The stream instantly froze. Leaves and branches swirled and battered them in a stinging cyclone. Maggie felt her ears pop. A moment later, the air pressure plummeted, and she struggled to draw breath.

Atop the hill, the obsidian had frozen, and the Monk was trapped in solid stone, unable to free himself. As Baal advanced, the Monk brought up his weapon in a feeble attempt to ward off the coming blow. It was to no avail. The spear clattered harmlessly aside with the Monk's severed hand still clutching the haft.

Baal did not pause to gloat. Rising to full height, the Grand Duke reversed his sword and plunged it hilt deep into the Monk's exposed and vulnerable chest.

"*Maggie!*"

Lump and her mother were on their feet, beckoning for her to join them. She took a step—

And an electric jolt slammed into her body. She staggered and grabbed hold of a nearby sapling to keep her balance.

Pain, so much pain— A searing ember had buried itself in her chest. The agony was almost unbearable and crested until she felt she would surely burst into flame. She heard screaming. It was her own.

Then, miraculously, the pain receded to a level she could manage. Panting, gasping for breath, she knew that her mortal frame had been strained to the breaking point—and it had held. Now, she felt the ember's fire spreading through her, sharpening her reflexes, flooding her body with inhuman strength.

Another consciousness melded with her own, ancient and alien but not hostile. They did not share a language, but Maggie could sense this newcomer's thoughts. Unlike the Drakeford Curse, the Monk had no wish to dominate or control Maggie; instead, she felt her earlier kinship magnify a hundredfold. The Monk had always been a part of her, she realized again, for as long as she'd been alive. This joining only strengthened the bond.

Maggie heard her name again. "Run back to the truck," she told her mother and Lump. "Get as far away as you can."

"What are you talking about?" cried her mother. "Come with us!"

"Go on," Maggie told her. "We'll be okay."

Her mother stared. "Who is 'we'?"

Maggie simply turned away.

The hilltop was dark against the dark sky. All the lanterns had been broken, all the fires snuffed by that unholy wind. The smoldering trees sent up lazy curls of smoke. And there was Baal, a solitary figure standing above the headless body of Androvore. Reaching down, the demon removed the blade embedded in Androvore's corpse as if it were the sword in the stone.

Resting the weapon upon his shoulder, he turned and scanned the hill with eyes like distant stars. His gaze settled upon Maggie.

"Véya-sùl Monakós?"

Is that you, Monk?

Maggie felt an encroaching chill in the air. The Drakeford ghosts were again approaching. She sensed what they wished to do and welcomed it. One by one, the spirits entered her body, their essences mingling with the Monk's and her own. As they joined with her, Maggie felt a profound sense of resolve and solidarity.

Atop that hill stood the architect of all their pain and persecution. For centuries, the Drakefords had been utterly alone, frightened and powerless among the vast forces arrayed against them. All the family had lacked was a vessel strong enough to contain their collective love and hope, and the power they needed to defeat their ageless enemy.

Now they had a vessel to galvanize them, and its name was Maggie Drakeford.

Baal repeated his question. "*Véya-sùl Monakós?*"

When Maggie spoke, the voice that came forth was neither male nor female, old nor young. Its tone was calm and courteous.

"*Sùl-aveska Maëda.*"

It is Us.

Maggie extended her arm, and the Monk's spear flew to her hand. As she caught it, the weapon contracted to a size more suitable for a human. Its weight and balance were eerily familiar; she might have trained with it all her life.

Baal leaped high off the hilltop. For a moment, he seemed to hover in the air some eighty feet above her. As the demon reached his zenith, his wings fanned out wide, veiling the stars beyond. Then he dove toward the ground, building speed like a bird of prey. When he'd nearly reached the hilltop, the demon banked suddenly at Maggie, skimming over gravestones with his sword extended: a cavalier riding down a foot soldier.

Maggie stood her ground. Thrusting her arm forward, she held the spear upright and waited. The Grand Duke screamed toward her. He was nearly upon Maggie when she snapped the spear sideways. A glowing seal appeared in the air before her, ten feet across with symbols around its perimeter.

When Baal struck the seal, his momentum instantly reversed. He rocketed backward, shattered a gravestone, and smashed into the hillside. For a moment, he lay stunned amid the broken granite. But the moment passed.

Turning toward Maggie, Baal glowered and extended his hand. Electricity leaped from the demon's fingertips just as it had with the assassin in Rome. But instead of obliterating its target, the energy was drawn into the Monk's weapon; the spearheads, like a pair of lightning rods, channeled it into the weapon's haft.

Power flowed from the spear into Maggie. Unlike the ember, it was pleasantly warm and invigorating. She watched as Baal again regained his footing. Some of his strength had just become their own.

And Maggie intended to use it.

Baal returned to hand-to-hand combat, bearing down upon her with terrifying ferocity. But Maggie had the Monk to guide her, and found herself using the spear with the same prodigious skill she'd witnessed earlier from a distance. The proficiency was simply second nature.

Back and forth they went—Baal on the attack, Maggie defending, wielding the weapon in either hand or using both at once. She feinted, parried, and countered. As before, the Monk's skill was superior, but Baal's strength told. Sweat poured off her as she found herself making a grudging retreat through the Witchwood.

Once they were among the trees, moon and starlight vanished. The darkness was nearly total, but here again she had an otherworldly advantage: her vision was enhanced by the Drakeford ghosts sharing her body. She perceived her surroundings as the spirits did, and theirs was a world of perpetual twilight with gray grass, pale birch, and silver streams.

Through this landscape came Baal. A nimbus of dark energy surrounded the Grand Duke, forcing branches and trees aside in a frenzy of warping and snapping wood. The demon was almost upon Maggie. She ducked as the greatsword swept above her head. The blade embedded in a tree, which ignited at once. Wrenching it free, Baal brought the sword down again. Maggie parried, but the impact buckled her right wrist and nearly hammered her into the undergrowth. Baal kicked out and Maggie was sent flying backward, tumbling over a bank and landing hard in a rocky stream.

Stunned, she lay a moment in the water before scrambling up the other bank. The Grand Duke was not far behind. As soon as his foot touched it, the stream hissed and began to boil. He crossed it in two long strides, pursuing Maggie as she made a desperate bid to get free of the confining trees.

She needed space to maneuver; Baal was too strong to fight in close quarters.

As she reached the wood's edge, Maggie saw her mother and Lump perhaps a hundred yards away, running over the muddy turf toward Gladys. Lump stumbled along, exhausted and undoubtedly frightened out of his wits. He tripped and fell. Their mother stopped to help him.

A surge of adrenaline filled Maggie.

Death approached.

Maggie spun about just as Baal lunged for her. Her weapon caught the demon solidly in the shoulder, piercing the scales of his armor. Before he could react, Maggie brought up the other blade in a vicious slash that might have decapitated the Grand Duke had he not jerked away. Even so, the spearhead sliced his chin and bit into bone. Baal stumbled backward, clutching his face as flames flickered from the wound.

He looked past her to the open fields beyond, and understanding dawned in an instant.

Baal knew now what Maggie was protecting.

She lunged to impale her opponent—but with her wrist sprained, she could only use one hand. The strike was a fraction slower than it might have been, and the spear pierced a rock, nothing more.

Bounding past Maggie, the Grand Duke left her behind. She whipped about in time to witness a spectacle that brought a cry from her lips.

Baal was already airborne, flying silent as a glider as he gained swiftly on her mother and brother. Mrs. Drakeford had reached Gladys and was trying to get the truck started. Lump was limping toward her, an injured rabbit unaware that an eagle had him in its sights.

Maggie tore after the Grand Duke, covering ground faster than any human. She shrieked her brother's name, and he turned just as Baal snatched him up by the collar. Lump kicked and struggled, but it was futile. Baal dangled his body just a few feet off the ground as he sped over the terrain. Then the demon banked and soared up into the night sky.

Maggie hurled the Monk's spear so hard her shoulder nearly popped from its socket. The action was a reflex, pure instinct, oblivious to danger; it hadn't even occurred to her that she might accidentally hit Lump. The weapon raced toward its target like a missile.

Moments later, it struck home, narrowly missing him as it impaled

Baal's shoulder and the black wing behind it. Roaring with pain, the Grand Duke flung away his captive and tried to wrench the weapon free as he tumbled from the sky.

But Maggie's attention was on her brother. Lump plummeted like a stone dropped from a skyscraper. And she was too far away—she'd never get there in time.

Maggie felt the Monk take control of her actions. As she ran, she swung her arm skyward and cried out a word older than the Earth itself. A column of wind screamed up into the night, engulfing Lump and tumbling him about, tearing off his jacket as it slowed his momentum. Seconds later, he landed with a thud in a patch of scrub not far from Gladys.

Mrs. Drakeford was already out of the truck. Lump rolled onto his side, clutching his knee. As Maggie raced over, she saw that her brother had lost a few teeth and broken his nose. Then again, he was alive and semiconscious. Their mother asked if he could wiggle his toes. When he did so, she sobbed and hugged him to her.

As her mother helped Lump back to the truck, Maggie returned to battle.

She faced the Witchwood once more and raised her uninjured arm. The Monk's spear came whistling toward her from the darkness.

"Jesus!" hissed a voice.

And there was Laszlo, sprawled on the ground, just as Maggie caught the weapon. He'd been right in the weapon's flight path.

Maggie eyed him coldly. "I thought you'd run away."

Laszlo coughed. "I'm trying. You idiots won't let me."

"Go ahead," she snapped. "Don't let us mortals keep you."

Laszlo's tone grew urgent. "You don't understand. My father will be coming back. He won't stop."

"I'd say we're holding our own."

The demon was almost pleading with her. "Maggie, you will not win this fight."

Maggie sighed. "Be useful and help us with Lump."

Even as Laszlo grumbled about needing to flee, he gave her a hand getting her brother into Gladys's back seat. Mrs. Drakeford started the engine.

They all heard the disturbance coming from the Witchwood: frantic birdcalls and the snapping of branches. Hundreds of crows took flight from the distant treetops.

Something burst from the forest. Not a black-winged warrior but a monstrous wolf. It streaked toward them over the open fields, faster than a racehorse.

As soon as he saw it, Laszlo took off running. Not away from danger this time but *toward* it. Maggie watched in shock as the demon waved his arms and tried to intercept the monstrosity. The closer it got, the more sense she had of its appalling speed.

She shouted to her mother to stay put. There was no point trying to flee; Gladys could never escape that thing. Better to hold firm and make a stand.

Maggie tried to keep calm as she walked forward, weapon in hand. The Monk was still with her, of course, but now she sensed some indecision. Its own body had been destroyed, and without it, the Magus was too weak to defeat a being as strong as Baal. Yet if the Monk continued using the mortal as a vessel, it was unlikely she would survive.

The wolf slowed to a lope and eventually halted some distance away when it noticed Laszlo in its path. Laszlo did not even come to the beast's shoulder, but he nevertheless advanced, hands raised in a gesture of appeal and surrender. The demon was speaking rapidly in words Maggie could not catch. The wolf bared its teeth, and flames dripped like slaver from its jaws. It was nothing but fire, she realized. An inferno cloaked in wolfskin.

Laszlo was growing frustrated. He raised his voice. "Father, will you *please* listen to me? It doesn't have—"

With a snarl, the wolf cuffed its offspring. The blow wasn't meant to kill; it was a reprimand. Even so, the force sent Laszlo tumbling like a rag doll. He came to a stop ten yards away and did not move.

Growling deep in its throat, the monster advanced upon Maggie. As it neared, she saw that while its aspect was wolflike, its build was heavier, its muzzle shorter, and tusks like a boar's protruded from its lower jaw. The claws were more like a bear's than a wolf's or a dog's. No, Maggie decided, the creature was *not* a wolf.

It was a nightmare.

And this nightmare did not run or spring. It advanced slowly, like a battleship, well aware of the terror it generated and its ability to weaken prey. The beast was just twenty feet away when it stopped.

Observing Maggie, its piggish eyes gleamed with triumph. Its voice was thick with bloodlust.

"Monakós."

The word was first and foremost a summons, a call to execution. But there was respect in it too, regard for a worthy adversary. Baal Zebul would grant a swift death. The Monk had earned that much.

The Monk stirred in response. The Magus was weary, and long confinement within the Witchstone had further sapped its strength. Baal was offering it an *end*; not a happy or triumphant end, but one that was definitive . . . and not without honor.

Maggie wasn't having it.

A woman died for you, she told it fiercely. *People called her a witch, but I don't know what she was. I don't even know her name. But that woman sold her soul to ensure you came back. She burned in fire for you. She be-*lieved *in you, and you will* not *disrespect her by just lying down to die. You will run. You will survive. And when you're strong again, you will make her sacrifice worth a damn.*

There was a hesitation. The Monk was not concerned for itself; its concern was for its host and her family.

Maggie shook her head. *Do you honestly believe he'll spare us when you're dead?* Go. Run! *I'll do what I can to give you a head start.*

The comforting heat in Maggie's chest abated and then was gone. The Drakeford ghosts remained, but with the Monk's departure, that sense of ancient power and boundless skill was now missing. Then, after a moment, something else took its place and filled the void. It was a different sort of strength than the Monk's: warm and familiar, quintessentially and undeniably *human*.

Maggie found that she was crying.

Something took her hand. Looking over, Maggie perceived the Monk standing beside her. Without a body, its spirit appeared as waves of heat shimmer distorting the air.

A growl sounded across the way. The wolf leered down at the Monk, hungry and expectant. "Come forward," it rasped.

But it was Maggie who took the step. She looked up at the monster through her tears. "Not yet," she whispered. "I'm not finished with you."

Pale fire dripped from its jaws. "*Finished?*" it roared. "*You?* You're nothing without the Monk, girl. Who are you to defy a Lord of Hell?"

The girl in question held up a vial.

"I'm Maggie Drakeford."

When she crushed the spelltube, Maggie went off like a living bomb. Energy exploded from her body and the spirits within her, a screaming tsunami of rage and grief, a lust for vengeance against the demon who had tormented her family. It was Baal who'd made the Drakefords pay for his failure; Baal who'd poisoned their minds, exploited their pain, and prolonged their unbearable suffering.

Such crimes had a price—and the bill had just come due.

The recoil slammed Maggie backward against Gladys—but that was nothing compared to the destruction that went before her. The blast's shock wave leveled everything for hundreds of yards, including the hill on which the Witchstone had stood. All that remained were burning tree stumps and smoldering streambeds whose water had been vaporized.

There was no sign of Baal or Laszlo, or even the ethereal Monk. The instant Maggie had broken the glass, Baal had flown backward, a tumbling kite caught in a hurricane. As for Laszlo, the last she'd seen, he'd been lying face down in the grass. Now there was no sign of him.

The Drakeford spirits were gone too. Maggie had felt them vanish the moment she'd detonated. Whether they'd been destroyed or set free, she couldn't say. But tonight, her ancestors had learned they were innocent of crimes that had haunted them for centuries, and they had claimed their vengeance. Maggie suspected that was enough to bring peace to anyone. Even a ghost.

Blood trickled into Maggie's eyes as she slumped against Gladys's running board. She tried to blink it away before tilting her head back and using her thumb. As her vision cleared, she beheld a fiery form miles above her, blazing like a comet in the heavens.

Her mother was tending to her when a second comet appeared. Maggie watched it streak across the midnight sky, in pursuit of an enemy it had chased for two thousand years.

CHAPTER 36

THE LETTER

Maggie opened her eyes and found herself staring at her bedroom ceiling. She could have drawn it from memory—the blackened beams, the peeling paint with a section that looked like Australia. She had woken up to that view over seven thousand times, but this was the first occasion she had ever considered it beautiful.

The light told her that it was midmorning. She tried sitting up, but her right wrist was sprained and her muscles filed a formal complaint. This was something past *weary* or *sore*; even *bone tired* didn't do it justice.

"You can sleep," someone said. "There's no rush."

Her mother sat at the foot of the bed.

With painful effort, Maggie forced herself into a sitting position. She wasn't certain how to bring up the previous evening. "Are you okay?" she began. "You didn't get hurt?"

"I'm fine," said her mother. "Just a few cuts and bruises."

"And Lump?"

"He's pretty banged up, but his spirits are good. I've never seen him happier." Maggie managed a smile and opened her mouth to continue. "George is fine, Maggie," her mother told her. "I really think you should look at your arm."

She hesitated. Then, when her mother nodded encouragingly, she brought out her left arm from under the quilt.

The last time she had seen it, the skin had been black and necrotic, the remains of the tentacles hanging limp. Now the skin was smooth and pale, with a scattering of freckles. No curse mark, no cilia, no holes with tentacles lurking beneath them. Maggie looked at her arm in silence for several moments before asking for her hand mirror.

Her mother brought it over, and in silence, Maggie studied her reflection. A full minute passed before she set the mirror aside and eased back against her pillow.

A pair of plain blue eyes had never been so stunning.

Maggie was determined not to cry. Not because she believed there was anything wrong or shameful about crying—but she knew that tears would release a flood of emotions that had been building inside her, and she preferred to hold on to them for a bit.

Her mother was looking uncharacteristically nervous.

"What's wrong?" said Maggie. "*We broke the curse.* I'm back to normal. Aren't you happy?"

"Of course I am." Her mother smoothed the bedcovers. "It's just—well, you know how complicated feelings are. Especially Drakeford feelings. I've been sitting here for an hour, wondering what to say."

"About what?"

Mrs. Drakeford shrugged helplessly. "About us," she said. "About life. About where things go from here." She paused. "Things haven't been easy between us, Maggie, not for years. Of course I don't have to tell you that, but I do want to tell you something else. When you started working for Reverend Farrow . . . well, I don't know what happened to me inside, but it wasn't fair to you. You were my child—and I pulled away when you needed me most." As she said this, Maggie's mother closed her eyes and exhaled a slow, shuddering breath. "I don't expect you to forgive me," she said quietly. "What I did was unforgivable."

Maggie stayed quiet, letting her mother explain. She knew how hard this was; Elizabeth Drakeford was not the type to admit mistakes, much less lay bare her feelings. Part of Maggie wanted to speak up, to dispel the awkwardness and extend an olive branch. But something held her back—the same thing that held back her emotions. This couldn't be rushed.

The two of them sat together. Outside, Maggie heard the honking of geese flying south.

"I don't know what happens from here," said her mother at length. "I suppose we'll just have to see how things go, now that we have a chance for something . . . different. But before we go downstairs, I did want to tell you—woman to woman—that what you did last night was extraordinary." Maggie squirmed uncomfortably. "You stood up for this family—for your father and brother, for all of us—and showed a courage I can't even begin to imagine." Her mother took a slow breath. "You are the *bravest* person I know, Margaret Drakeford, and you have been since you were a little girl. Whatever happens next, I wanted you to know that."

The dam holding back Maggie's emotions crumbled. "Goddammit," she muttered, and swiped at her wet cheeks.

Pulling her mother close, Maggie hugged her fiercely for a very long time. When the two finally let go, each had to mop her eyes. Maggie hesitated a moment, then voiced the question she'd been dreading.

"Any sign of Laszlo?"

Her mother gave a tiny shake of the head. "I'm sorry."

Maggie lay back against the pillow. It was the answer she'd been expecting, but hearing the news from someone else brought it home with a stark finality. Until that moment, some possibility—and the hope that accompanied it—still existed. But that was gone.

Thoughts of Laszlo triggered a tangled skein of feelings that Maggie would have to unravel. But again, the process would require time and a bit of privacy, and at present she had neither.

"Do you want to get up?" her mother asked. "I know a few people who are anxious to see you."

Maggie nodded and closed her eyes. This was supposed to be a joyous occasion—after hundreds of years, the Drakeford Curse had been broken! She had been healed, and Lump would never suffer. And then there was her father . . .

Of course a celebration was in order! *I wish*, she thought, *I could just jump out of bed and race downstairs, the way Lump does on Christmas morning.* Pure joy must be quite the feeling. But that was not who she was.

Maybe one day she'd be able to enjoy moments like this without a nagging sense of wariness or guilt. But she had spent nineteen years cultivating those emotions.

Maggie knew she had real work ahead of her, making sense of what had happened, learning how to move forward. She didn't mind the challenges ahead; in fact, she welcomed them. She just wished she'd gotten the number of Laszlo's therapist.

Finally, she and her mother descended the stairs.

She heard her father's voice before she saw him. Dad was out on the porch with Lump, who was breathlessly recounting their adventures. In the time it took Maggie to work up the courage to step outside, Lump talked about kobolds, pawnshops, room service, and Liechtenstein bird-monsters. Anyone overhearing him would have thought he needed urgent medical attention.

She opened the door. Her brother and father were sitting on sun-bleached Adirondack chairs with a chessboard between them. For a kid who looked like he'd been trampled by a rhino, Lump was positively radiant. "*Maggie!*"

She returned his gap-filled smile. "You spinning tales?"

"Yes," he said. "And for once, they're all true."

Bill Drakeford got up from his chair slowly, not unlike a hospital patient who'd been confined to years of bed rest. Maggie drank him in, comparing the man before her with the version in her memories. There was gray in his hair, and he was far thinner than she remembered. The shirt he wore—an old one her mother had never altered—hung loose on his frame. His face still bore scars from his work as a sin-eater, and his skin had the sallow cast of a shut-in.

But his eyes told the real story. They had a shine to them, a generous spark that no stone or scorn had ever been able to extinguish.

Silently, Maggie went to him and rested her head against his shoulder.

It smelled of sweat and flannel, and she could have soaked it in forever. "I've missed you."

"That's funny," her father said wryly. "I could have sworn I never left the house."

She tried to laugh, but what came out was something between a sneeze and a sniffle.

"Hey." He tipped up Maggie's chin so their eyes met. "Wherever I was, I'm not there anymore. I'm back where I belong, Maggie." He kissed her on the forehead. "And I have you to thank for it."

Lump was outraged. "What about me?"

Bill Drakeford laughed. "And you, kiddo. Although I'm not too happy about my bishop."

Cackling, Lump surveyed the chessboard. "Maggie met a bishop in Rome. I was peeing when it happened, but . . ."

The Drakefords eventually sat down for a long lunch, during which Maggie and Lump regaled their parents with highlights—relevant and otherwise—from the previous six days. Lump provided the energy and non sequiturs; Maggie supplied clarifications and something resembling a cohesive narrative. She also managed to steer her brother away from topics she preferred to address later. Among these were her debt to the Signora Bellascura, and the magic they had absorbed courtesy of the Witchstone.

Now that the Witchstone and the Monk were gone, Maggie wondered if that magic would dwindle, or fade like a sunburn. Deep down, she hoped it wouldn't. As for the Signora, she wasn't sure. Would the demoness contact her or simply choose to forget about the Drakefords and the Witchwood fiasco? Maggie touched the ring on her finger. She wouldn't blame the Signora for staying away. The demon and her attendants had arrived expecting a sleeping Monk, only to find a wrathful Lord of Hell.

Speaking of which . . . Maggie was certain that Baal had survived, but otherwise all bets were off. Assuming he hadn't vanquished the Monk, his secret was out. Would Baal seek revenge against Maggie and

THE WITCHSTONE

he family? She imagined he might, but he certainly had a bigger problem at the moment, and its name was Lucifer. She would worry about Baal another day.

During lunch, after the story was told, the four Drakefords made a unanimous decision: They were going to leave Schemerdaal as soon as possible.

They lived far from their closest neighbors, and the Witchwood was hidden by its hedge, but there was no telling what the villagers might have seen or heard last night.

Even so, Maggie didn't think the police would come knocking. Everyone in this lonely stretch of the Catskills knew about the Drakefords. They'd heard all the old tales and even created their own whenever the mood or drink inspired them. These weren't people who called the authorities. The authorities were *outsiders*, and outsiders triggered even more fear and suspicion than the Drakefords. Maggie's family might be devils, but they were *Schemerdaal's* devils, and Reverend Farrow knew how to keep them in line.

But those who lived down in Schemerdaal had never forgiven or forgotten anything uncanny that happened in the Witchwood. Each villager would bring an extra stone or two to the next funeral. It was their sacred duty.

Unfortunately, they would need a new scapegoat, because Schemerdaal's sin-eaters had just retired.

Tonight Maggie would burn the cedar chest with her ancestors' letters and their strange collection of items. She had initially thought of burying it near what remained of their graves, but she thought better of it. The Drakeford Curse was dead, and some things didn't deserve a memorial.

That afternoon, the Drakefords worked out the details of their plan. They would leave before dawn and be well away before anyone knew they'd gone. What they took would be minimal: necessary clothes, along with any special books or keepsakes. "We'll travel light," her father said, "and leave as much as we can behind." The Drakefords were not moving out of the Witchwood; they were moving the Witchwood out of them.

Their destination had not yet been decided. Lump suggested Rome, but this seemed impractical, even with his endorsement of the pastries. Mr. Drakeford proposed heading west. California had always exercised a hold on his imagination. In his darker moments under the curse, he often tried to picture tide pools and sea otters and the steady drum of waves upon the beach. Mrs. Drakeford said that they didn't need to settle on anything yet—just getting out of Schemerdaal would be enough for now.

Maggie had no preferences; she was game for anything, be it Rome, California, or Timbuktu. It was all good. Over the past six days, she had gotten a whirlwind glimpse of the world beyond Schemerdaal. Between now and her final breath, she intended to see the rest.

These thoughts kept her occupied as she set aside the things she'd be taking—the clothes and books; several journals with stories, poems, and bits of nonsense; and a piece of rose quartz from the mantel. The small pile on the bed struck her as simultaneously funny and tragic. Nineteen years barely filled a suitcase.

She was going through her desk when she caught sight of the letter.

It had been folded into thirds and stuck into a physics book. When Maggie saw her name, she had to sit down. She wasn't certain she wanted to touch the thing, much less read its contents.

It had to be from Laszlo, and he must have written it when he was in here, resting. Maggie pictured the demon sitting at her desk, chewing a pen and scribbling away while she was downstairs, combing the house frantically in search of the remaining materia.

Maggie stared at the letter for a solid minute before sliding it out from the book. She held it by one corner as though a scorpion might wriggle out. It seemed silly, after everything that had happened, but her instincts about Laszlo would always be on high alert. The ink on that letter had scarcely dried when its author had ripped out Maggie's heart and ground it beneath his heel. The demon had an uncanny sense of where to stick the knife and how to twist it—clearly a valued skill where he came from. Whatever complicated game Laszlo had been playing— and whatever its triumphant result—he had nevertheless inflicted real damage.

For all she knew, this letter was part of some grander scheme, a backup grenade to score points with Androvore in case they'd been needed.

Maggie wasn't sure she could handle any more pain from Laszlo.

Ultimately, curiosity trumped caution. She unfolded the letter and read it by her bedside lamp. The warm kerosene glow plus the demon's flawless script made it look like something one might find in a museum or an antique shop.

The language, however, placed it firmly in the present day.

Dear Maggie,

If you're reading this, that means you're still kicking. Congrats! I hope I'm kicking too, but there's a pretty good chance I'm not. If that's the case, you should know I did something heinous to your toothbrush in Zurich.

Just kidding. Or am I?

Let's get to it. Some shit went down tonight. Now that the smoke's cleared, I wanted you to know a few things . . .

First and foremost, I'm a goddamn hero. Seriously. Here I am, missing a vital organ, and instead of resting, I'm pushing through the pain to write a farewell letter. (That goddamn priest ruined me.) Anyway, all I request is that you sculpt a bust in my honor. Nothing big or expensive. Styrofoam is fine.

Second: I enjoyed my time with you. Drakefords are expensive, but you're not all bad. If Lump can stop speaking Elvish, I'd say the kid has a future. Liechtenstein needs him.

Finally: Let's talk about tonight's festivities. If things went smoothly, you probably hate me with a deep and abiding passion. I hurt you.

What's worse—I meant to.

Everything I said out there was planned. Trusting bitch. That banker in Zurich. Dumpsters. Frat boys. All of it. Tough stuff, and I know it hit home. I'm a con man, Maggie, and the name of the game is observation. I've had five days to study you. I knew what would hurt—and I went there.

I don't expect you to forgive me. In fact, when you found this letter, I'll bet you sat there looking all moody and wondered whether to open it. (I'm right, aren't I?)

Anyway, I'm not asking for forgiveness, because I'm not sorry. Not even a little. I did what I had to do. All I'm asking is for you to understand why I did it. If you can do that, maybe one day we can mend our fences. I don't know what that means, but I read it in a poem somewhere and I know that kind of shit impresses you.

Maggie, I gotta run. You and your mom are getting weepy downstairs, and that means we're almost ready to roll. Good luck tonight.

If I played my cards right, we both got what we wanted. If I didn't, and you're reading this, then you might be flying solo. That's okay, though—if anyone can land this plane, it's you.

Adios, amiga,

Laszlo

PS: Get that necklace appraised. There's a guy on Broome Street who knows about these things. He may not remember you, but you remember him, and that's something to build on . . .

A puzzled Maggie unclasped the Signora's necklace and examined it briefly under the light. She read the letter two more times before folding it up and adding it to the things she'd be taking.

When she was finished, she went downstairs to have dinner with her family.

Afterward, they played a round of hearts. It was a fun enough game with three players, but infinitely better with four.

For the first time ever, Maggie Drakeford shot the moon.

EPILOGUE

ONE YEAR LATER

Maggie stared at the prompt for what felt like the hundredth time. How could two sentences cause so much anxiety?

Reflect on something that someone has done for you that has made you happy or thankful in a surprising way. How has this gratitude affected or motivated you?

She typed something and deleted it. Tried again. Drained her coffee and looked out the plate glass window at the cabs and pedestrians. She checked the time. Nearly two o'clock, or what Susie called the dead zone, the lull between lunchtime and when local schools let out. Within the hour, Mulberry Sweets would start filling up, and Maggie would have to surrender the table.

Susie swooped in with the coffeepot. "Dare I ask?"

"You daren't." Maggie sighed as Susie refilled her cup. "You know, you don't have to wait on me. I can get my own coffee."

"It's your day off, girlie."

"Then I insist on paying."

"Your money's no gooood . . ." Susie sang in an operatic tremolo that always got a grin out of Maggie, then went back behind the counter, where she was tweaking a Halloween display. In the six months Maggie had been working there, she had yet to see her boss repeat a single arrangement. Susie was the Georgia O'Keeffe of candy.

Maggie returned to her essay. The shop's bell jingled as someone came in. She didn't look up until she realized the customer was heading her way, instead of going to the counter. Without a word, he sat in the opposite chair and placed a trilby on the table.

She cleared her throat. "Nice hat. Is it 1962?"

"I wish."

Maggie raised her head and took in the figure across from her. "You're . . . looking well."

"You too. I like the ink."

She had a full sleeve, from the top of her left shoulder to the base of her wrist. The tattoos were a swirling, scrolling panorama that included mountains and forests, cavorting kobolds, shadowy Nachtkrapp, a porridge pot, a crumpled crown, silken slippers, a Roman church, and Egyptian hieroglyphs; the Witchstone itself was inked where the curse had first marked her skin. Maggie was very proud of her body art. She'd commissioned a famous tattoo artist to design each one. Expensive, but worth it.

Naturally, the newcomer fixated on what he *didn't* see. Maggie expected no less. He gave a disappointed whistle. "Well, that's downright cold."

Rolling her eyes, Maggie bared her left shoulder, which was dedicated entirely to a portrait whose demonic subject flashed a mischievous smirk.

"There he is," said her table companion. "Handsome devil, but the eyes are too sinister."

Maggie shrugged her shirt back in place. "I'd say they nailed it."

Susie wandered over and said in a careful voice, "Hey, there. Maggie, do you know this fella?"

"It's fine," she told her boss. "He's kind of an old friend."

Susie looked the man over as if she found this somewhat difficult to believe. Maggie didn't blame her. He might have strolled off a yacht in Monte Carlo. "Well, Mr. Friend, can I get you anything?"

"Chocolate shake," he replied amiably.

"What size?"

Maggie answered for him. "Large. Mediums are for indecisive pussies."

Susie's eyebrows nearly shot into orbit. "*Excuse me?*"

"It's an inside joke."

"Hoo boy! My girlie's got a mouth. Who knew?" Susie laughed. "Okay, Mr. Friend, one large and definitely-not-for-pussies milkshake coming right up."

Mr. Friend thanked her. Those bright-blue eyes assessed Maggie's neck, which bore traces of a summer tan and was conspicuously absent of jewelry.

"I take it you found the letter." At her nod, he asked, "So was Dimitri helpful?"

"Extremely. He contacted a collector and negotiated the deal. Didn't even charge a commission."

Mr. Friend's fingers drummed with curiosity. "How much?"

"Thirteen million."

The drumming ceased. "You're kidding."

"Nope. Who knew one little coin could be so valuable?" said Maggie.

"Fuck me, I should have swiped it."

Maggie shrugged helplessly. "Oh well."

Mr. Friend sighed and gazed out the window. "Where you living?"

"Around the corner," Maggie replied. "We bought an apartment in one of Dimitri's buildings. Nice place. It has toilets and everything."

Mr. Friend watched a bike messenger coast past the window. "I didn't know Dimitri owned real estate."

"Dimitri owns half of Nolita."

"Well, I guess I can stop feeling guilty about those spelltubes. You didn't tell him, did you?"

"Didn't have to. He already knew."

Her companion raised an eyebrow. "How's that? He took those memory scrubbers."

Maggie spoke slowly to ensure maximum comprehension. "In the twenty-first century, stores have these things called 'security cameras' that record everything that happens. Dimitri recognized us the moment Lump and I walked in."

Mr. Friend grimaced. "Was he pissed?"

"Not really," said Maggie. "Dimitri says it's just the cost of knowing you. He was happy they made a difference."

"That they did," said Mr. Friend. "You guys sound tight."

Maggie put the laptop to sleep. "We are. He comes over for dinner sometimes, and Lump helps out at the shop. He loves it."

An amused grunt. "I'll bet. How's ol' Lump doing?"

"Crushing sixth grade as we speak," Maggie answered. "He tested into some baccalaureate program. The school practically pays him to go there."

"Of course they do," said Mr. Friend. "The kid spends his spare time reading about aqueducts. And how are the folks?"

"Good. Mom's going to Teachers College uptown and helps out at Lump's school. Dad's been working with Dimitri's contractor. Carpentry, mostly. He seems to like it."

Mr. Friend nodded before gesturing at Maggie's tattoos and nose ring. "What does Mom say about the new look?"

"Nothing at all. I'm an adult. She's happy that I'm happy."

Susie returned with Mr. Friend's milkshake and set it on the table along with a straw and spoon. She was about to leave when she cocked her head and squinted at him. "Anyone ever tell you that you look like Paul Newman?"

And there was the smile. Its wattage could have powered a city. "You're the first."

She laughed. "I don't believe that for a minute. Mind if I take your picture? My wife adores Paul Newman."

The smile became somewhat fixed as Suzie deployed her phone. Maggie kept a straight face until her boss went back behind the counter.

Mr. Friend sighed and stirred his milkshake. "I guess I asked for that."

"Yep."

He pointed to her laptop. "You writing the Great American Novel?"

"College essays."

A soft whistle of surprise. "No shit. So what's it going to be—Harvard or Yale?"

"I'm not Lump."

"No," he replied. "You're Maggie Drakeford." There was a mischievous twinkle in Mr. Friend's eye.

Maggie shot him a nonplussed look. "Is that supposed to be funny?"

"Apparently not. Seriously, though—what do you have in mind?"

She fiddled with her jade ring before answering. "I'd like to stay here, in the city. NYU seems more my speed, maybe the New School, but Jason wants me to apply to Columbia."

Mr. Friend cocked his head. "Who's Jason?"

"You remember, that boy in Rome. The one at the train station."

Mr. Friend almost choked on his milkshake. "The *poet*? Jesus, Maggie . . ."

"He's *not* a poet. He's studying architecture."

"My ass. Everyone says they're studying architecture."

"Why would he make it up?"

"Because it's 'sexy.'"

Two could play at air quotes. "Oh yeah?" said Maggie. "Well, I can assure you he's not studying architecture to be 'sexy.'"

"Good. It's a losing cause. Please tell me you aren't—"

Before he could finish, Maggie shook her head. "We're just friends. After Zurich . . . I'm still not ready for that stuff."

Mr. Friend nodded and considered his milkshake. "Not bad," he remarked. "Well, if you need a letter of recommendation or anything, let me know. I can speak to 'exceptional courage in the face of supernatural adversity.'"

"You're hilarious," she said dryly.

"Oh, come on," he chided. "It's okay to smile, you know." When she did not reply, Mr. Friend watched out the window as a cab tried to squeeze past a delivery truck. He sounded mildly petulant. "Hell, I thought you'd be glad to see me. Aren't you happy to see that I'm alive?"

Leaning forward, Maggie hissed, "I *already knew* you were alive! It's the only reason I didn't faint when you walked in."

Laszlo looked indignant. "Who told you?"

"The Signora."

He clucked his tongue. "So she's been in touch."

"She was here for Fashion Week," said Maggie. "We went to lunch, and she asked how you were doing. Before I could tell her that you were *dead*, she mentioned seeing you in Rome. Apparently, you were delivering a truck containing five tons of magic-saturated obsidian."

Laszlo groaned. "The logistics were a nightmare. Almost as bad as sending weekly bouquets to the grave of Isabella de Castignole."

"Well, apparently you managed to smooth things over," said Maggie. "The Signora told me about the poem you commissioned. She was pleased—said it ran in every newspaper in Italy."

"Yeah, and do you have any idea what that cost?" said Laszlo. The demon shook his head and looked again at Maggie's neck. "Does the Signora mind that you sold it?"

"The necklace? Not in the least. The Signora's a practical woman."

"That she is. Which is why I'm willing to bet your lunch wasn't purely social. She called in her favor, didn't she?"

Maggie sipped her coffee. "Over dessert."

"Naturally. And may I ask what this favor entails?"

"No, sir, you may not."

"Fair enough," said Laszlo, and returned to gazing out the window. The two might have been back in the Alps taking in the scenery.

Maggie tapped on the table. "Hellooo . . . ?"

The demon raised his milkshake. "Hello yourself."

Maggie could no longer play it cool. "This has to be a joke," she muttered, and picked up the napkin dispenser. "Are there hidden cameras around here? There have to be."

Laszlo looked amused. "What are you talking about?"

Maggie checked if Susie was nearby, but her boss had left the counter for the back storeroom. "Laszlo, so help me, I'm going to fucking kill you! *Where have you been?* The last time I saw you, you were on your face in the grass, right before I—"

"Went nuclear?" he suggested.

"Whatever you want to call it! And don't interrupt! In fact, you are not to say a *goddamn word* unless you're answering my questions. Is that understood?"

He saluted. "Yes, ma'am."

"How the hell are you alive?" Maggie demanded. "There was no trace of you!"

Laszlo set down his milkshake. "May I give a demonstration, Officer?"

She folded her arms. "Go right ahead."

From his breast pocket, Laszlo produced a pack of Korean cigarettes. He handed it to Maggie and asked her to stand it up on the table. She played along and stared at the pack expectantly. Ten seconds went by.

"I was told there would be a demonstration," said Maggie. Laszlo flicked the cigarettes with a finger. The pack toppled over. Maggie rolled her eyes. "You might need to workshop this."

Ignoring her, the demon made three passes over the cigarettes with his hand, then snapped his fingers. "*Ta-da!*"

Maggie stared at the pack still lying on the table. "Don't take this act to Vegas."

Laszlo chuckled. "Tough crowd."

"Honest crowd."

"That's why it worked."

She stopped looking at the cigarettes and looked at him. "What are you talking about?"

The demon held up his hand. A pack of Korean cigarettes materialized between his thumb and forefinger.

Maggie blinked, then poked the pack on the table. The illusion vanished at her touch. "Jesus."

Laszlo smirked. "It works even better when there's a Lord of Hell to distract everyone."

He tossed her the cigarettes. Maggie caught them and turned the pack over in her hands. It was as solid as she was. "So when I broke the tube . . . you'd already taken off."

"Like Jesse Owens."

She slid the cigarettes back across the table. "Okay. But that doesn't explain why you've been MIA all this time." Maggie tried, and failed, to keep the emotion out of her voice. "Why didn't you get in touch?" she demanded. "Why couldn't you let me know you were alive?"

The demon shrugged. "I had to lay low to see how things shook out. Androvore's disappearance caused some ripples, and when word got out that the Monk was still kicking . . ." Laszlo whistled and shook his head.

Maggie felt a rush of joy. "So the Monk's alive! Your father didn't catch him."

"Nope," said Laszlo. "He's out there somewhere, probably rocking a brand-new body. You're lucky he didn't keep yours."

"He would never," said Maggie firmly. "The Monk was compassionate."

"Yeah, well, he's caused a shitload of trouble." Laszlo again shook his head. "Lucifer hit the roof when he found out. He convened the Council and demanded that my father cough up a bunch of land and titles."

Maggie raised her eyebrows. "Did he?"

A smile. "You don't become Baal Zebul by coughing up land and titles. Dad's a master at this game. Maybe the best. The other Lords don't like him much, but they like Lucifer even less. The longer you're on top, the more dangerous your seat gets."

Maggie hesitated. "Will there be a war?" she asked.

Laszlo raised an eyebrow. "Like with armies and battlefields? No. Not if the Lords can help it. Too expensive."

"So what'll happen?"

The demon shrugged. "Alliances. Assassinations. Lots of deals being made in secret. You may have observed that about my kind—anything and everything is up for negotiation."

"Yes, I've noticed."

"You say that like it's a bad thing. It has its upside." Laszlo reached into his jacket once more and this time removed an engraved silver tube some six inches long. He rolled it across the table to Maggie, who picked it up and unscrewed the cap. Inside was a scroll. "That baby's notarized. Try not to lose it."

An intrigued Maggie slid the scroll from the tube and unrolled it. Its contents were brief and to the point.

HIS FIENDISHNESS LORD BAAL ZEBUL HEREBY RENOUNCES ANY AND ALL VENDETTAS AGAINST MARGARET DRAKE-FORD AND ALL MEMBERS OF THE DRAKEFORD FAMILY AND THEIR DESCENDANTS. IN DOING SO, HIS FIENDISHNESS PLEDGES THAT HE WILL NOT COMMIT HARM OF ANY KIND—DIRECT OR INDIRECT, PERSONALLY OR VIA THIRD PARTY—AGAINST SAID BENEFICIARIES FROM THIS DAY UN-TIL THE END OF DAYS.

At the bottom were the Grand Duke's signature and seal, along with those of seven witnesses—Laszlo and his siblings.

Maggie whistled and read it again. "Does this mean what I hope it means?"

He nodded. "You can stop looking over your shoulder. I've been there, and it's no fun."

An invisible weight seemed to lift from Maggie. She couldn't pretend that Baal hadn't loomed large in her thoughts and nightmares for the past year. She reread the scroll. "What did it cost you?"

Laszlo sipped his milkshake and stared indifferently out the window. "Nothing I care about."

Maggie studied him. Even looking at his profile, she knew he was lying. "So what was the nothing?"

"Promotion." He shrugged. "Dad keeps his essence; I remain a Class III."

"Damn," she muttered, sagging a bit. "I know how much you wanted that."

He waved off any sympathy. "It's okay. I'd probably have gotten drunk and chosen a stupid name like Androvore did—'Douchey McSchvantz' or something like that."

"Well, I'm glad you didn't. I could never fit it on my arm."

The two exchanged a look, then started snickering. Once she started, Maggie couldn't stop. She laughed until the tears came. Until that moment, she'd been too angry to fully appreciate just how much she had missed him.

Laszlo drove her crazy, but he also kept life interesting.

Those were the best kind of friends. Human or otherwise.

Maggie wiped her eyes with a napkin. "So what now? Back to the Society?"

Again, he waved her off. "Hell no. I'm done with that place. Bunch of dinosaurs. In fact, I think it's time they had some competition."

"What are you talking about?"

The demon had clearly been waiting for this moment. With a magician's flourish, he produced a business card that he slid across the table. Maggie picked it up.

Laszlo & Company
Curse Consulfants

LASZLO ZEBUL, *Owner and Founder*

She cocked her head. "What's a 'consulfant'?"

"What?" Laszlo snatched the card back and examined it. "I got a deal online. Goddammit."

Taking out a pen, he hastily corrected the typo. "I figure the world's full of losers without the first clue how to break their curses. They need advice. They need encouragement. They need a seasoned pro who can provide expert guidance. For a handsome fee, of course."

"Of course."

Laszlo took a sip of his shake. "Clarence is on board. He'll be the intel."

"Not the muscle?"

"Very funny. So what do you think?"

The demon's eagerness was so palpable Maggie almost started laughing again.

"Well," she said, "as someone who knows all too well what it's like to live under a curse, I wish you and Clarence the best of luck."

"You sure as hell can't take a hint." Laszlo slid her a second card.

Maggie turned it over and studied it for several moments.

Maggie tsked. "There's another typo."

A groan. "You've got to be kidding. What is it?"

She ran her finger over the title. "You misspelled 'partner.'"

Laszlo held up a hand. "Now, hold on. A respectable firm can't have twenty-year-old partners. Clarence is practically a thousand, and he's fine with 'associate.'"

"Clarence would polish your shoes."

"Be reasonable. You've still got a lot to learn."

"That's okay," said Maggie. "The Signora says I'm a quick study."

Laszlo's milkshake shot across the table. Without taking her eyes from his face, Maggie caught it and proceeded to take a long, decadent sip. It was impossible to say which was more satisfying—the chocolate on her tongue, or the look on Laszlo's face.

Setting the glass down, Maggie quietly closed her laptop. The essay could wait.

A demon's offer was on the table, and negotiations were just beginning.

ACKNOWLEDGMENTS

I wrote *The Witchstone* during the pandemic, at a time when I was eager—even desperate—to tackle a story that could offset my sense of isolation and anxiety. At first glance, choosing to write about a curse might seem odd, but the experience was oddly therapeutic. Whenever I was tempted to complain or shake my fist at the world, Maggie's predicament kept things in perspective. If my mood grew bleak, I could always rely on Laszlo or Clarence for a laugh. As the story evolved, other members of the *Witchstone* cast came to supply their own distinct brands of comfort. They were a colorful bunch, and I'm deeply grateful for them.

But of course, they're fictional creations (at least I think so). No book comes about without the help of many talented and tireless individuals. To this end, I would like to thank my agent, Caitlin Mahony, and the team at William Morris Endeavor for finding *The Witchstone* a home; and Daniel Ehrenhaft and Blackstone Publishing for embracing the story and risking their reputation on a semilovable demon. The task of taming this monster of a manuscript fell to Sharyn November, whose seasoned instincts made a tremendous contribution. Copy edits were handled by Riam Griswold, whose remarkable eye for detail ferreted out more errors—big and small—than I'd ever care to admit.

Last but certainly not least, I would like to thank those who shared my pandemic bunker. To my wife, Danielle, and our spectacular boys, Charlie and James, I can never adequately express my gratitude. Your warmth and company, your humor and unconditional love, make all the difference. None of this happens without you.